W9-AAA-840

SQUARE MILE

6.52 a.m. Monday, 18 March: Jeremy Walker, a director of the City of London's most respected global investment bank, Steen Odenberg & Co, is discovered in his luxury Wapping penthouse, strangled with his own silk Hermès tie. Anthony Carlton, a young colleague, is reluctantly drawn into the subsequent police investigation, only to learn that his initial enquiries lead to EPIC, the mysterious multi-million dollar property fund recently launched by the bank. As Anthony follows the trail of mounting evidence to Europe and on to the Far East, he becomes enmeshed in an international scandal of intricate and horrifying proportions. As he attempts to unravel this finely-woven and ever-expanding web of greed and deceit, Anthony begins to fear for his career, his livelihood and the safety of those he cares about.

SQUARE MILE

Paul Kilduff

CHIVERS PRESS
BATH

First published 1999
by
Hodder and Stoughton
This Large Print edition published by
Chivers Press
by arrangement with
Hodder and Stoughton Ltd
2001

ISBN 0 7540 1601 3

British Library Cataloguing in Publication Data available

Printed and bound in Great Britain by
BOOKCRAFT, Midsomer Norton, Somerset

To my former colleagues in the City of London

PROLOGUE

6.52 A.M.: MONDAY 18 MARCH: WAPPING, LONDON E1

Three hundred thousand people gravitate every working day to the City of London. They move trillions around the globe. They trade billions with each other. The more fortunate amongst them take home millions in their annual pay packets. It is the epicentre of the financial world.

No more do bowler-hatted brolly-carrying starch-collared gentlemen work alongside the revered Old Lady of Threadneedle Street. The Young Turks are to be found at Bishopsgate, Moorgate, London Wall, Liverpool Street and Broadgate. Narrow streets are largely deserted at this ungodly hour but with some notable exceptions. Lone sleek Jaguar saloons and Mercedes E-series tanks from Belgravia and Kensington commanded by uniformed chauffeurs arrive. They take chief executives and directors past automatic entrance barriers and down into underground car-parks at discreet rear entrances of head-office buildings.

Derivatives rocket-scientists from Putney, equity salesmen from Hampstead, fixed income research analysts from Fulham, swap dealers from St John's Wood and corporate financiers from Chelsea alight from exhaust-pumping black cabs. The smiling cabbies delight at the overly generous tip from their last but lucrative fare of the lonely night-shift. Company mobile telephones hum into action and

1

electronic pagers pulse as real-time information flows to those who need to know.

Motorcyclists in sharp suits park throbbing red Yamahas and chrome Harleys in side-street bays. They remove pristine crash helmets to reveal compulsory City haircuts. Fast-stepping pedestrians emerge from Central Line tube stations with half-read copies of the *Financial Times* under their arms. No *FT*. No comment. They join the queue for polystyrene cups of serious coffee at Benjys take-away and buttered bagels at Birleys reassuringly expensive deli. No coffee. No work.

These players ease their way past departing office cleaners and twenty-four-hour security guards into cavernous dealing pits. They sit in rows of seats at market-making desks built on raised floors to accommodate the miles of buzzing cables that lie beneath. Dealing floors are illuminated by overhead electronic displays showing the latest prices and by banks of digital clocks for all the global time zones that matter. New York, Frankfurt, Honkers, Tokyo, Singers and Sydney. Facial expressions like shell-shocked artillery gunners until the first bid-offer prices from their competitors flash up on the SEAQ dealing screens.

Research analysts speak at the seven-thirty a.m. presentations to hundreds of receptive ears about the overnight activity in the Hang Seng, the Nikkei and the Dow. They dare to predict what will happen in the next vital twenty-four hours of financial cut and thrust. Salesmen digest the essential research briefing and regurgitate it to hungry institutional clients, desperate to know the day's likely star stocks. And, more important, how to stay clear of the dogs. Always money to be made and lost. Today is no different from any other in the awakening City. Yet.

London's recently revived Docklands awake in the east. The silver glare of Canary Wharf rises from the East India Docks on the Isle of Dogs. Red flashing beacon lights atop the benevolent central tower deter low-flying turboprops and high-flying market dealers. Neighbouring marble-clad miniatures huddle alongside for mutual protection. Buildings largely populated by those American investment banks that value lower costs per square foot of office space above City tradition and staff convenience. Workplaces only accessible by the Docklands Light Railway, otherwise known as the Toytown Train, as regular passengers entrust spotty youths to turn keys in computer-driven trains perched on precarious rails twenty-five feet above main roads.

Envious commuter eyes occasionally turn skywards as British Aerospace whisper-jets and KLM City Hoppers swoop down on London City Airport, searching for that elusive finger of runway in the midst of the Royal Docks. Their cargo of eager Euro-businessmen immediately scurries for black cabs and the thirty-minute journey through the rush-hour Limehouse Link traffic. Pierre from Orly, Marco from Linate and Dieter from Frankfurt-am-Main all head for their nine o'clock meeting with their London counterparts to discuss privatisation deals, mergers and acquisitions, emerging markets forecasts, Eurobond issues, insurance premiums and brokerage rates.

Derelict sites to the east blend seamlessly with the high-rise council developments of Tower Hamlets and Poplar. Massive construction work overwhelms prewar communities as A-roads break through back gardens, outhouses, communal allotments and lean-tos under council compulsory-purchase orders. Cranes demolish Dickensian brick masterpieces in favour of prestressed concrete office parks delivered by convoys of filthy juggernauts manned by stubbled *Sun* readers. Offices all with ample executive car-parking spaces for those who still love to drive and pollute simultaneously.

Twelve giant cocktail sticks protrude from the U-bend at Greenwich peninsula. Seven hundred and fifty million pounds to spend on a Dome from Dome. A part of London primarily populated by abseilers, builders, giro recipients and traffic cones, still enduring the pangs of a difficult birth but with the promise of a better future.

Then the truly historic areas of Docklands. Wapping, Shad Thames, St Katherine's Dock, Southwark, Rotherhithe, Surrey Docks. Riverside pubs with authentic names serving as reminders of the glorious maritime past. The Prospect of Whitby, the Five Bells, the Town of Ramsgate, the Waterman's Arms, Booty's, the Mayflower, the House They Left Behind. Great beer, low ceilings, musty warmth and a genuine landlord's welcome. Streets with character where an inhalation still brought back memories of imported spices, tobacco and sugar. All change now in East London.

Welcome to the twentieth century. Grade II listed warehouses with overhanging gantry cranes and exotic names in faded white paint now converted into sympathetic apartment developments. Riverside balconies, Thames views, sunken baths with gold taps, health clubs with lithe residents, twenty-four-hour porterage, video entryphones and maximum security. Corner shops run by the Conran empire dispense freshly baked ciabatta, extra-virgin Tuscan olive oil, cut flowers and New World wines to the nouveau riche of London E1. A perfect idyll for investment bankers to inhabit for five days a week, between regular weekend commutes to their Home Counties converted eighteenth-century cottage with a view of the old mill and an assorted selection of mallards in the adjacent pond. A London base that is convenient and growing in social acceptability among their ever-so-important peers.

Radio Four blares from a bedside clock radio in one such Wapping penthouse. Annoyingly loud: Could someone please hit the snooze button and kill the news headlines and sports roundup? The liquid crystal display shows 6.52 a.m. Much later than usual.

The clock radio powers up at precisely one minute to six o'clock each weekday. Just enough time for one affluent Docklands resident to awake to the breaking news, enjoy a walk-in power shower, a rushed caffeine-loaded breakfast and hail an insomniac cabbie on Wapping Highway to head westwards to his job in the leading City investment bank of Steen Odenberg & Co. The radio plays on today, that ear-piercing volume enough to wake the dead. Almost.

Jeremy Ernest Walker, 49, a director of Steen Odenberg, is in his opulent bedroom. A split-level room with expensive lacquered Chinese wall murals, collectable antiques, custom-built furniture and french windows opening on to a well-planted balcony overlooking Butlers Wharf. The ambient

5

bedroom lights remain switched on. Unnecessarily so. His hand-tailored suit and poplin shirt hang on the handle of the walk-in wardrobe that houses the sartorial evidence of his accumulated wealth. Such wealth indeed. If only they all knew.

Highly polished black Church's shoes from New Bond Street and silk socks lie carefully beside the hanging garments, an ivory shoehorn poised at the ready. A pair of gold cufflinks with subtle embossed motifs lie untouched on the bedside table, adjacent to the pair of Gucci metal-rimmed glasses. Each item carefully prepared for the day ahead in the City. Only the seventy-five pound Hermès tie is missing from Jeremy's daily ensemble, already in use. The animal-patterned tie always goes well with the electric-blue shirt.

The tie is knotted tightly around his discoloured neck. Too tightly. The breaking sunlight angles inwards past the partly drawn curtains to rest on his anaemic face. His greying hair is dishevelled. Jeremy Ernest Walker lies motionless on the deep-pile carpet. He will not be going to work in Steen Odenberg & Co. today.

CHAPTER ONE

8.35 A.M.: MONDAY 18 MARCH: BAKERLOO LINE, LONDON W9

Anthony was late. He blamed the past two weeks spent working in the office in Singers. Eighty-five degrees and constant high humidity. Seven hours' time difference ahead of the UK. Thirteen hours Club Class on the Singapore Airlines mega-top last Saturday. His body clock hadn't yet adjusted to Greenwich Mean Time. Bloodshot eyes. He was exhausted even after eight hours' sleep of sorts back in his home patch of W9.

He knew about the joys of commuting to work in London. The daily routine. Leave his spacious Maida Vale apartment after the Kiss 100 FM news headlines at eight o'clock, turn sharp left by the communal gardens, across busy Sutherland Avenue, walk briskly down tree-lined roads for six minutes to Warwick Avenue tube station, take the Bakerloo Line south to Oxford Circus and change to the Central Line for his final destination of Liverpool Street. But today he had time only for a rushed shower and a blunt shave, skipped breakfast and worst of all knew that his tie didn't really go with the fine-check shirt.

The Bakerloo Line carriage was a temporary home to hundreds of other commuters. Anthony stood by the door only to be pummelled by departing and arriving passengers. Briefcases thrust into his groin, unnecessary brollies stabbed into his thigh, elbows jabbed into his face, hostile stares

7

from total strangers, body odour and bad breath permeated this rocking tin can. Then some luck as he grabbed a vacant corner seat at Paddington and relaxed for the first time. He sat back somewhat overly conscious of his regulation-issue City uniform. Peer pressure demanded it and he had to conform to the accepted norms. If he wore a short-sleeved off-white shirt and a shiny blue suit no one on the second floor would take him seriously.

His double-breasted navy pinstripe suit was made in Hong Kong last year by Harry Wu, his tailor over on the Kowloon side of Victoria Harbour. Let's be honest. It sounds better than it is. Harry was a tailor to many, in fact to anyone who had a few thousand Honkie dollars in cash and forty-eight hours to spare for a suit. The jacket came with his own name discreetly hand-sewn in gold thread on the inside pocket lining. Specially Tailored for Anthony Carlton Esq by Harold Wu Gentlemen's Tailor. Anthony knew this was excessive, but Harry insisted on identifying all his suits in such an overtly flamboyant manner. Harry's suits were cheaper than an off-the-peg job in Regent Street and avoided the necessity of taking an inch or two off the trousers. Anthony could never find a 40 Regular in Austin Reed W1 to fit. It was one of the hazards of being five foot nine and not the more ideal movie-star height of six foot.

The Thomas Pink shirt was amazingly well ironed courtesy of Mrs Harris, the reliable retired widow on the Harrow Road. Despite several years of hugely enjoyable bachelor existence, Anthony had not mastered the subtle art of ironing. Mrs Harris was his saviour, doing five or more shirts and resurrecting his apartment with a Hoover and a mop every second Friday. The definition of an optimistic investment banker was one who had five work shirts ironed at the weekend. Anything could happen in a week in the City.

Anthony was right. The check shirt did clash with the Hermès tie, where the thin back portion hung loose so that the printed designer horse logo was visible to all. Colleagues told him that was the way Hermès ties were meant to be worn, at least down on the dealing floor anyway. Conspicuously. Anthony had just the one Hermès tie. It was grubby around the knotted area from excessive use on a Monday morning such as this. He could justify the purchase of one such extravagant tie in LHR duty free, but no more yet.

He had the West End salon haircut, where only the proffered frothy cappuccino and watching the exposed midriffs of pre-pubescent blondes in clinging black leather trousers were free. Thirty-five pounds for a haircut was a rip-off of truly City proportions. His classically dark hair was combed back with just a suspicion of gel. Any less and it would spike up. Any more and he would have been a wide boy. No sideburns of any description, not in the City. His jawline protruded, not necessarily because of any strong features, but because Anthony had just nicked himself while shaving and needed to limit the blood damage along his shirt collar. The suntan from the recent skiing holiday in Andorra was almost gone. He would have preferred Verbiers or Val d'Isère but that was just too expensive for even seven days' self-catering for two.

In accordance with the accepted rules of tube travel, the fellow Londoners diligently avoided eye

9

contact and continued to read their newspapers in total silence. Very civil servants with *The Guardian.* The suits with *The Times.* Free-thinking spirits with *The Independent.* Builders with the *Mirror* stuffed in back pockets of painted jeans. Anthony always preferred people-watching to thumbing through the morning newspaper. Schoolchildren with Nike backpacks. Secretaries from Saaaath London. Lone middle-aged passengers with suspicious Tesco plastic carrier bags. Fellow office workers with worn briefcases. Stunning Asian girls in dark Principles suits. Arabs chattering in a foreign lingo. All sorts in the most cosmopolitan city on earth. Feel the adrenaline in London.

Anthony never bought a morning newspaper from the old Scottish vendor at the station. Why? He would arrive at the office with black ink engrained on his hands. Ever spot the perfectly groomed middle-aged lady reading the social diary in *The Times* on the tube in hottest July wearing a pair of black leather gloves? Anthony knew her logic. Why buy a newspaper when you can clandestinely read the edited highlights of every newspaper over the shoulders of your fellow passengers, including even the *Sun* if you're desperate? And why buy a newspaper when a freebie *Financial Times* was waiting on his black ash desk in a fourth-floor corner office of investment bank Steen Odenberg & Co? Or Steens, as they all liked to call it.

*   *   *

Anthony was doing his damnedest to be an authentic investment banker but still had some way

10

to go. The job requirements were clear. Firstly, talk the talk. Know the industry language so you can converse fluently with your peers without the need for a financial dictionary. Know a call from a put, know a currency swap from an interest-rate swap, know the cable rate from the Swissy rate, know an over-the-counter warrant from a listed equity, know a floating-rate sovereign bond from a fixed-rate corporate bond, know a SIMEX future from a Chicago contract, know when you are long or short or just square, know when you are bullish or bearish. Anthony was feeling quietly bullish this morning. Tired but certainly bullish.

Secondly, look the look. Get a decent suit and tie, a good haircut, a clean shave, a pair of Church's shoes and a set of vaguely humorous motif cufflinks from Links near the Monument, while noting that matching dollar and pound sign cufflinks are just a bit too common. Anthony almost had the required gear but alas not yet in sufficient quantities. His expected bonus from Steens next month would help to extend his burgeoning wardrobe.

Thirdly, walk the walk. Project that air of confidence whether you are standing to make a presentation to the board of a major client company, striding around the dealing floor of Steens or just throwing convenience food items in your trolley on your reluctant weekly trip to Sainsbury's fine shopping emporium in Ladbroke Grove. Anthony was working on this too. He had mastered the Samsbury's bit; the rest would follow in time.

Investment banking was a great business. One where a group of people can work on a corporate deal for a few months and earn millions for Steens.

11

A business where a salesman can take an order for a one-million-pound line of shares, charge his standard thirty basis points sales commission to some institutional pension fund and earn three thousand pounds for Steens with just a one-minute telephone call and a six-word instruction to the UK equity dealer who sat opposite him. Buy a million quid at market. A business where a twenty-seven-year-old mathematically gifted graduate with a doctorate in statistical science can earn a quarter of a million pounds a year at Steens working out where the gilt yield was heading in the next twelve months. A business where an East End lad from Dagenham or Barking can purchase a new house in May with his annual bonus after a successful year trading Deutschmark contracts or Sterling futures on LIFFE in Cannon Street. The 1980s had been good. The 1990s weren't too bad either, all things considered.

It was all about money, trading it, managing it, earning it, keeping it, investing it, spending it, wasting it. The true stars at Steens earned a fortune, something Anthony could only dream about. These chosen few travelled the world in Club Class style, chauffeured company limos and five-star hotels. Every excess on their Amex platinum card was rechargeable to a corporate client who didn't care. They had the glamour of show business, the internationalism of jet-setting and the incestuousness of an exclusive gentleman's City club. It was a licence to print big money, and best of all it was wholly legal.

There was a downside, but they never talked about it. It was tempting fate, and they had to remain maximum bullish. They feared cyclicality, when the economy was in recession, when interest rates and inflation spiralled, when sterling wilted in the face of a strong dollar, when a bear market reared its ugly head, when Labour was occasionally in power. Anthony and his peers were die-hard Conservative voters, with all-too-recent memories of Wilsonite exchange controls, devaluations and winters of discontent. They only voted Conservative in vain because there was no other party further to the right of the political spectrum.

And even when disaster struck, when emerging markets in Asia and Russia collapsed, when bonds and treasuries plummeted daily in value, when the Dow and the FTSE were fucked, when lesser banks and brokers folded, when offshore hedge funds defaulted on their complex derivative portfolios, when market volatility reached all time highs, when credit spreads widened by five hundred basis points, they knew what to do. Lie low in the dealing trenches, keep their heads below the parapet, avoid the lead bullets engraved with their surname, ride out the eye of the storm, wait a few months until the tide of doubt turned, until the markets just looked too cheap to ignore any longer and the sheer weight of liquidity out there overcame the remaining doubters. Then they were back in business.

Anthony knew personally of the other drawbacks. Dealers and salesmen came to work before others in more normal jobs had even risen from their slumber. They worked long hours, sometimes worked entire weekends and had their annual holidays cancelled at short notice. They spent twelve hours a day staring into flickering out-of-focus screens at rows of numbers and percentage points, at charts of price trends, bar graphs and indices performance. Their eyeballs automatically travelled from left to right after years of reading corporate stories and press releases on the screen-based news tickers. They listened endlessly to advice from their research analysts, to other dealers and salesmen from lesser competitor banks, to an omnipresent squawk box from the floor of some far-distant futures exchange, and to those who could shout the loudest on Steens' own dealing floor.

Anthony's colleagues existed on disgusting coffee from clogged-up machines, ate unseen food ordered by telephone and delivered to their desks by bicycle, drank bottles of lime-infested Mexican beer and fizzy poo at the Flute wine bar, and snatched burgers and fries from Mac's before taking a cab home to catch a few hours' sleep before the next day's assault on the global markets. It was punishing and relentless work and there was fierce internal competition within Steens. Staff who lost money trading for the bank or didn't meet sales targets were summarily fired, their company sports car taken back and their desk contents boxed by Karen in personnel and delivered by the ever-reliable FedEx to their mortgaged home. Bill in reception extracted their security pass as they left Steens for the last time.

The tension was the worst part. Every day the dealers lived on the edge. A European corporate could issue a profits warning and Steens' dealing position of hundreds of thousands of shares could plummet in value. A bond issuer could default on some biannual coupon payment, or Standard & Poors could downgrade corporate or sovereign bonds. An emerging stock market could plunge overnight and all their exotic holdings would depreciate instantaneously. Some bureaucrat from the Bank of England or the Federal Reserve could spook the markets with some unexpected yet prudent fiscal comments. A new issue could be stalled at the starting gate by poor investor perception, unenthusiastic press comment or just a bad day in the market, and Steens would be going to the annual general meeting of their corporate client in the Royal Albert Hall as an unwilling minority shareholder.

But there were great days, too, when the dealers sat at their desks, watched the markets soar effortlessly and clients fought each other on the banks of telephone lines to place their lucrative orders before the market ticked up another fifty points without their involvement. Days like that made it all worth while for them. It might have been a great career for someone like Anthony.

*   *   *

You needed physical stamina for any sort of sustained existence in the trenches of the second floor. To be able to drink a magnum of poo single-handedly in the Flute while your boss lines up the second. To get in at 7 am. and sit in the same seat every day, two hundred and fifty days a year, looking at a VDU. To entertain corporates until three in the morning and still make it in for the 7 am. research briefing. To sweet-talk clients and tell them what they wanted to hear, no matter how far it was from the truth. To come back from Manhattan on the red-eye flight and go straight

15

into work from Heathrow. Not for Anthony the crazy hours, the peer pressure and the insecurity of life as a Steens dealer or salesman. No thanks.

Anthony had chosen well. He was happy to be manager of the Control Group, an elite team of professionals that worked on projects and investigations within Steens. It wasn't a conscious career decision, perhaps only in hindsight. One year he was finishing up comprehensive school in his home town in Surrey, or Surrey actually, as the locals were prone to say. The next he had the scholarship to Cambridge, found the business degree too easy and then the big investment banks came round to the colleges each January to hunt the best graduates.

They were looking for motivation, intelligence and aptitude and were left with the distinct impression that Anthony apparently possessed these qualities. Mitchell Leonberg Inc. were reputed to be the best payers, but Anthony flunked the interview. He got on well enough, communicated effortlessly, impressed the Yanks but made one fatal mistake. The recruitment consultant told him afterwards. The interviewer didn't like his shirt and tie. That was all there was to it. Anthony would never make the same mistake again. Then Steens made him an offer that would have glazed the eyes of any student with a bank loan like Anthony's. His assistant bank manager whom he knew so well always told him that his overdraft permission was a limit, not a target.

Steens were accommodating. Anthony took a year off to travel the world. That was where he caught the travel bug. Had medical science invented a cure yet? He arrived at Steens' door one

16

Monday morning in early September as a definite means to repay the accumulated credit card debts of a year of leisure. His first two years were spent on the desirable graduate programme, with three months each in sales, operations, credit, risk management and control. He liked the latter best of all. There followed four years of an apprenticeship of sorts in Control until his previous manager was head-hunted by one of the few remaining UK investment banks. Promotion came instantly for Anthony. Now at the age of thirty he had a staff of four, an annual budget of almost a million quid and a direct reporting line to a director of Steens. Scary spice or what?

His job required an enquiring mind, a fine eye for detail and a natural interest in the business, three more traits that Anthony had somehow miraculously inherited from his father, that recently retired assistant bank manager in the Surrey regional district. His very friendly bank manager. Anthony's job gave him the opportunity to learn so much, see so many aspects of Steens' business, meet top management and network. It did mean less money than a player on the second floor, but also considerably less grief and a lot more sleep. A job that was interesting and varied, one where he could help Steens safeguard their reputation and go on to greater success, one where it helped to know right from wrong and one where he personally could help the directors of Steens to run a better bank.

Anthony worked for Derek Masterson, a director of the bank for many years. Derek was demanding and had a right to be as one of the best-connected players in the City. Derek knew that pressure worked; it helped them all to perform better. Derek was prone to uttering at all-too-frequent intervals on corporate occasions that today's laurels would be tomorrow's compost. Anthony guessed that Derek was in his mid-fifties and wouldn't be there for ever in Steens. Promotion for Anthony? Dream on.

Anthony was proud to work for Steens. He wouldn't leave Steens unless someone like Mitchell Leonberg Inc. came along again and realised what a big mistake they had made the first time. They would approach him via a head-hunter and offer him an obscene amount of money. Everyone has his or her price. The amount of hard cash to buy you off. Now and again Anthony got that much-loved phone call from the head-hunter and was invited to the free mystery lunch in some discreet corner of a darkened restaurant with some intense pouting leggy consultant. They would discuss a suggested new position, work not carnal. Anthony would feign nominal interest until he heard the name of the prospective investment bank. Then he would switch off. Nothing had sufficiently impressed him yet. Nothing was as good as Steens.

*　　　*　　　*

Out of the scrum of the tube carriage and on to Liverpool Street Station platform. Anthony had no choice as he was swept along with the tide of office workers heading up incessant escalators. Past the wall-to-wall recruitment advertising on the way up. More jobs. Better jobs. Sexier jobs. Through the combative ticket machines. Across the polished marble floor. Past the East End barrow boys at

18

their fruit stalls. Cox's: five for a pound. Tangerines, my dear? Past the Indian cobblers. Flashing lights from the photo-booth. Past the lazy man's dry-cleaning outlet, the 1990s niche retailers and the bastions of the British high street. Past lost tourists from the incoming 9 a.m. Stansted Express trying to feed coins into uncooperative ticket machines. Past Essex man alighting from the 9.10 from Bishops Stortford and other exciting locales.

The mêlée was worse than usual. Must get up in time to avoid this unnecessary hassle in future. Damn Singers trip. Damn jet lag. Through the arcade of designer shops much favoured by wonderful Vanessa and out into emerging hazy sunlight.

Broadgate Circle was busier than normal. There was a small crowd gathered. Media people hovering, pushing microphones in the faces of passing staff. Must be something going on at one of the banks or brokers located around the plaza? Perhaps a new issue was under way, a mega-takeover, an unfolding public relations stunt or even a decent corporate scandal breaking?

Surely nothing to do with the venerable blue-blooded institution of Steen Odenberg & Co. ?

CHAPTER TWO

9.35 A.M.: MONDAY 18 MARCH: CITY OF LONDON EC2

Broadgate Circle was the most impressive of all the temples to Mammon in the City. The tinted glass and Italian marble multistoreyed office buildings were clustered around a central circular plaza. These buildings spoke volumes, volumes of money and financial muscle. The bulge-bracket American investment banks were here. So were the secretive Swiss, the aspirational French, the bankrupt Japanese, the methodical Germans and, of course, a few untouchable local British institutions like Steens. They were all household names in Anthony's world. This excessive property creation of the late 1980s had broken the property developers, but that didn't bother those who worked at Steens who didn't personally pay the annual rental of forty-five pounds per square foot. Only the best would do for Steens. Anthony had two hundred square foot of his own space.

In the summertime the communal area of the plaza filled at lunchtime with the beautiful people from the adjacent offices. Major players in the equity and fixed-income markets sat on wrought-iron seats at wind-buffeted tables and downed chilled Pouilly-Fumé, fresh prawns and tossed rocket salads in the open air. In contrast, secretaries and operations staff sitting on the tiered steps facing into the concentrated sunshine ate more humble fare from nearby delicatessens and enjoyed the lunchtime entertainment provided by the City of London Corporation. It was a free lunch of sorts. By early evening they gravitated to the top-floor canopied terraces of wine bars showing the market prices on overhanging Reuters screens. They imbibed chilled fruit-filled jugs of Pimm's and discussed the day's winners and losers.

In the wintertime the plaza became a customised ice rink where bankers played the lesser-known Canadian game of broomball in a pseudo-friendly inter-bank competition. Hot whiskies and mince pies were generously dispensed to the supporting partisan and vocal spectators. By late evening Broadgate Circle was always deserted as the transient inhabitants left for Liverpool Street Station and home.

Shit. Nine thirty-five already. Anthony was real late. He strode across the plaza, effortlessly and subconsciously dodging others who cut across his path. It was a skill that everyone acquired working in the crowded Square Mile. Only today it was worse. These media people loitered in the plaza. Why were they here at all? Anthony recognised a sultry girl from the local London TV news speaking to a camera under the glare of an unnecessary spotlight. Scruffy press photographers in Barbours took bland snaps of City suits walking by. Sole journalists stood looking for a scoop of some sort. One sparkly girl in a long flowing black coat looked particularly interesting to Anthony. If he were going to talk to any of them then she would have been the one. But this wasn't the time for chatting up an unknown hack.

'Can you spare a moment to talk?'

'What's your reaction to the news this morning?'

'Did you work with the deceased?'

Someone dead? Anthony brushed past in a deliberate yet anonymous fashion, avoiding any direct eye contact. Waste of time talking to them. Rather be talking to Steens staff inside.

'Morning, Bill. Any idea what's happening out there?'

Bill wore his smart black uniform, white peaked cap and red trim braid. All security guards in the City were ex-army and looked identical. There must be a production line in some barracks churning out these elderly guardians. Bill normally voluntarily acknowledged Anthony but not on this particular morning. Bill was too stressed out by the crowd outside and was not his usual relaxed self.

'No idea, sir. They just arrived in the last ten minutes. I'm inside here and they're stuck out there. Suits me fine.'

Anthony ran his security pass through the swipe card reader and walked past the large gold and blue Steens crest in reception. He didn't recognise any of his fellow employees in the lift. Three thousand people worked in their London head office. Most of the others got off at the lower floors. The glass lift rose higher through the building's atrium, and Anthony alighted on the fourth floor. Monday morning in the City. Let the games begin.

*   *   *

Vanessa sat outside Anthony's office. She was his secretary, or rather the secretary whom he shared with Derek Masterson. Anthony liked to think she was his alone, just like Harry Wu in Hong Kong.

Vanessa looked well, as usual. Her combed-back dark brown hair shone, wrapped in a velvet hair band. She wore a black and white hound's-tooth check jacket with shining gold buttons, a respectable length black pencil skirt and sheer tights, the uniform of many of her peers. Her height and good figure helped her to get noticed in Steens. Perfect poise too. Just about perfect all round, in fact, in Anthony's humble opinion.

'Morning, Tony.'

Just two words. Vanessa had an accent to die for, the sort of accent that if she had been behind the screen on Cilla's *Blind Date* TV programme with two other hopeful girls, the lucky guy would be clambering over the tacky partition to select her as soon as possible. After all, the entire programme was based on the seductiveness of people's accents: that was why the Irish contestants always won. Anthony couldn't yet geographically place her accent but it sure worked for him. Touch of class about it. What he expected really.

Vanessa Rayner preferred to call herself a personal assistant and worked at Steens merely as a quasi-hobby. Anthony had it from the best sources that her parents owned sizeable chunks of rural Scotland. Working at Steens helped to pass the days until her inheritance came through. She was only in her mid-twenties, so it could be a long wait for the family loot, but she never seemed to be short of cash in the meantime. Fortunate, considering her reputation as a serial shopper and devoted fashion-aholic.

'Vanessa. In before me again? Don't know how you do it.'

'Easy, Tony.' She smiled knowingly. She could

23

call him Tony any time.

'What's all that activity outside in the plaza? Something happening today?'

Vanessa ambled into his office and over to the sheer glass overlooking the plaza. Anthony followed her, enjoying the view that was before him. Great calves rising to that hemline. They stood together for another view, this time of the bustling scene outside. Too close.

'No idea, Tony. They weren't there thirty minutes ago when I put the *FT* on your desk. If I find out you'll be the first to know. As ever. The only rumour I heard so far on the grapevine this morning is that most of the directors are in town today. Some new deal is going down on the second floor. Big money and all that sort of stuff. You know what I mean.'

'Are all the directors here?'

'Well, when I took some telephone messages to Derek upstairs, I saw all the directors sitting in the boardroom except for Johan from Amsterdam and Jeremy Walker.'

Anthony didn't know about today's big deal but he would soon. Steens were renowned for maximum self-publicity when a deal went well. Anthony sat on his high-backed leather seat. This was a great view, the whole of the City stretched out below him. The office was tangible recognition of his managerial status. He would take his present location every time above a seat at the end of some crowded dealing desk on the second floor as he fought to keep screens and telephone sets from encroaching into his personal space and inhaled cigarette smoke from colleagues poised two feet away.

24

His expensive black office furniture was fully coordinated. An original oil-painting of St Paul's and the City at the turn of the century hung behind him. Sure, it was part of the bank's art collection, but right now as it hung on his wall it was temporarily Anthony's. His desk had a chrome anglepoise reading light and a matching chrome desk set bought by Anthony on his last trip a year ago to the Frankfurt office. Precision German engineering. Come to think of it, their cars were pretty good too. Anthony enjoyed a two-litre red Audi Cabriolet paid for by Steens. Standard issue for managers. Sex on wheels. Vorsprung durch technik. It was like having a three-series BMW Cabriolet, but without the attached social stigma.

His desk had the compulsory networked PC but most important he had his own Reuters terminal, Downstairs everyone had Reuters, Bloomberg, Telerate, Knight Ridder and a television to watch England getting regularly thrashed at cricket. The competition and joke pages were an essential part of the average dealer's day at any bank in the City. Anthony was an expert on using all these lesser-known pages on the dealing systems but needed to improve his knowledge of the pages that mattered. Having a Reuters terminal on the fourth was a minor coup. Derek Masterson signed the monthly bills. Derek had two screens. He didn't need two; he just wanted two for show. The bank didn't shell out ten grand a year for the line rental for just anyone. If you had one of these, you had arrived.

'Afternoon, Tony.'

OK. So it was almost ten o'clock. But this was ironic, coming from Gary.

'Something big is going down, Tony.'

Gary Benson had a top shirt button undone, a striped polyester tie only loosely knotted and a creased suit. Enough said. He didn't look like he had even had a shower this morning. His mop of dark hair was unkempt and was just a bit too long to be taken seriously in the City, particularly when combined with the dangerously protruding quasi-sideburns. Long enough to be different, which was what Gary wanted.

'What's going down, Gary?'

'Dunno, but the directors are upstairs behind closed doors.

'It's called a directors' meeting, Gary. They have them regularly. No reason to get excited.'

'It's more than that. Bill Fitzpatrick has flown in from the States. Alvin Leung from Hong Kong too. Some of the wonderful girls upstairs dropped me hints by the coffee machine. Something's happening—but apparently a few of the directors didn't make the meeting.'

Gary's sources were usually reliable. He knew the most attractive secretarial support on the seventh floor. The young ones. Most intimately. Not many people went nightclubbing in London on Sunday night, but Gary often did and looked as if he had been out on the tiles last night. Despite his lifestyle of excessive partying, late nights and alcohol consumption, Gary was fit and usually beat Anthony when they played two sets of sweaty squash at lunchtime.

Gary was nevertheless an able and competent colleague. He mightn't look wide awake on the exterior, but inside he was supremely confident, a fact that helped enormously when he worked for Anthony in the Control Group. It also attracted the opposite sex, a fact that Anthony had personally observed in the nightclubs of Manhattan's Greenwich Village to the wild bars of Patpong Two in Bangkok.

Gary stretched his arms in the air and yawned. He had indeed been out all night and revealed slightly bloodshot eyes as he went to examine that wonderful view. Gary made do with a desk in the general office area. Anthony followed his gaze down into Broadgate Circle.

'So what's the deal, then? Is this crowd down there involved or what?'

'Dunno, Tony, but in this business information is everything. And right now we haven't got it. So how did Singers go? Any serious tottie in Brannigans bar this time at all?'

Sometimes work was more important to Gary than after-hours pursuits, but not often.

'Singers went fine. The office is in good shape. So are the clientele of Brannigans bar.'

'Anything juicy to report?'

Was this a loaded comment about some Sarong Party Girl? Anthony took the work option.

'Usual stuff. Few dealing tickets not booked, tickets not time-stamped, some personal staff accounts not reviewed, errors on client commission rates, incorrect margin calculations, a few accounts without documentation, some dealing limit excesses. No showstoppers at all.'

'So the MAS won't close us down, then?'

Ever since the well-publicised SIMEX débâcle, the Monetary Authority of Singapore demanded that all investment banks and brokers undertook an annual review of their local operations. It was fine the first time around, but Anthony found three

27

trips in as many years just a bit repetitive. Gary could do the Singers review next year.

'We're safe with the MAS. Once I word my written report very carefully. I'll give you a look at it when I've done a draft for Derek this week.'

Vanessa suddenly interrupted their regular Monday morning banter.

'Sir James's secretary telephoned, Tony. The directors want to see you immediately.'

Gary spun around from his window view.

'See, I told you so, Tony. Something is afoot. Anyway, it's been nice working with you. Shall we box up your pics and flashy desk lights and stuff and FedEx them to you at home?'

*   *   *

Anthony ascended in the lift and exited on the seventh floor. The floor of the gods. His heartbeat raced. Steens didn't cut corners when it came to impressing clients. The interior fittings were opulent. Expensive furniture. Good art. Tinted glass. Coordinated colours. It spoke of a world of excess. He passed the extensive reminders of Steens' history which decorated the spotlit walls. They were there to impress the corporate clients who came to worship. Old ochre-coloured photographs of overseas offices, smartly dressed gentlemen standing by antique desks with quill pen in hand, original but expired bearer-bond certificates for South American railroad companies and Middle Eastern dams, and framed newspaper tombstone advertisements to evoke more recent memories of ground-breaking deals.

Steen Odenberg was founded in the middle of

the last century in London, not many miles from the current head office. Old man Steen was a Jewish banker who moved from Germany; Odenberg was a banker from Sweden. According to Steens' folklore, they met in a London alehouse and pooled their meagre resources into financing the origins of the bank. So many of the world's major investment banks could trace their roots back to prudent Jewish founders. They knew how to look after their own money and, perhaps more important, other people's money too.

Steens prospered with the growth in international trade. Offices were opened all over the world. Shanghai, Hong Kong, Sydney, Rio, Singapore. Never once did Steens get into the business of retail banking, banking for the man in the street. They had higher aspirations and were quite happy to leave that to the clearing banks. Instead they courted large corporate clients, raised tens of millions for multinationals and sovereigns, and financed property, trade and infrastructure. They trailblazed, created, innovated and led the competition. They remained true to their founders' aspirations. Steens' expertise was in marrying investors with funds to corporate clients requiring funds, and they thrived on this basic principle.

Steens had become more focused since the Big Bang in London in the late 1980s. One business unit was primary markets, where Steens arranged global equity and bond issues for corporates who wished to raise funds, bonds for banks secured on credit card receivables and for motor manufacturers secured on car lease payables, bonds for emerging Indonesian telecommunications companies, polluting Indian chemical companies, secretive

Swiss pharmaceuticals companies and green Scandinavian timber producers. They arranged billion-dollar global bond issues for sovereigns, from AAA-rated Canadian provinces and European nations to debt-ridden Latin American and African nations. Steens ranked top of the annual league tables of book-runners of international equity issues, with billions raised each year.

Steens advised corporates and governments on all facets of investment and finance, new issues, acquisitions and mergers, disposals and divestments, joint ventures and partnerships, and valuations of business. They earned enormous fees when their clients successfully acquired competitors in hostile takeovers, where Steens were equal to the every move of the target's own advisers. They took their fees like any other investment bank in percentage terms, on average one or two per cent of the deal consideration. A billion-dollar M&A deal brought in ten million bucks or more. It was the norm in the industry. They advised national governments all over the world on privatising telephones, water, oil, gas, electricity, post and any other service where the public would pay for something that they already owned.

Another business unit focused on sales and trading, their secondary market business, securities, bonds, warrants, futures and options already in issue and ready to be traded and dealt by Steens for a client agency commission or a principal dealing profit. The commission on their agency business kept flowing no matter what, whether the market was up or down, whether the clients were buying or selling. Perfect.

30

A stooping lady in her early forties wearing a loose cardigan and glasses came towards Anthony in the corridor. She was walking fast, too fast, heading towards the ladies' restroom by the lift. Anthony smiled at her, the sort of mutual acknowledgement that one gives an unknown colleague in Steens, particularly so when you are on the seventh floor. She could be important or well connected. She looked back briefly but without the merest hint of recognition. Anthony saw a single tear run down her cheek. She was flushed as she moved past without a word. Obviously distressed about something.

Anthony passed an open office door almost camouflaged by tall plants, no doubt one of the enormous offices occupied by one of the directors. A man in shirtsleeves exited into the corridor at speed and almost collided with Anthony. He nearly apologised, but he didn't need to. Anthony had just made a career move of the wrong sort, he realised, as he recognised the imposing face from the bank corporate videos and annual reports.

'Morning. It's Mr Fitzpatrick?

Bill Fitzpatrick, or more correctly William Joseph Fitzpatrick II, the head of Steens' New York office. Called Bill usually, but not right now, up so close face to face. Fitzpatrick was responsible for all of Steens' operations in the US and was the chairman's most likely successor. A tall, rangy American, and with a surname like his he just had to be half-Irish.

He was known to live the good life in downtown

31

Manhattan, commuting to his Wall Street office from his family spread in the refined stockbroker territory of upstate Westchester County. He was on the board of governors of the New York Metropolitan Museum, fanatically supported the Mets in Shea Stadium from Steens' private box and was once lucky enough to be Grand Marshal of the St Patrick's Day parade down Fifth Avenue walking alongside the mayor. That mayorship was probably the only other permanent job that Fitzpatrick currently aspired to outside of Steens.

Fitzpatrick had not yet elevated Steens in the US into the same league as Wall Street firms such as Mitchell Leonberg Inc., but he had cornered the market there in international bonds and equities. If some mega US fund wanted to buy IBM stock or US T-Bills they went to their usual US firm, but if they wanted a Japanese stock or a German Bund or a SIMEX currency future then they bought via Steens' New York office. Fitzpatrick had exploited the most significant weakness of the largest economic nation on earth, that severe insularity which left them uncomfortable whenever they left their hallowed protected shores. Fitzpatrick gave them the comfort that they needed. He acknowledged the near miss in the corridor.

'Yes, I am. And you are . . . ?'

Anthony had heard Fitzpatrick speak at company functions and on the annual corporate video. He was incredibly impressive, charismatic without being overbearing, confident without being arrogant, and totally dedicated to Steens. A role model for every aspiring young investment banker within Steens, including Anthony, only this time Fitzpatrick didn't look his usual composed self. His regulation Brooks Brothers white shirt with button-down collar was creased and stains of perspiration could be seen under his armpits. If Fitzpatrick himself had taken the trouble to jet over from JFK in the front cabin of the red-eye BA flight, something must genuinely be afoot. It was a matter of great personal regret that Fitzpatrick did not know Anthony. Yet.

'Anthony Carlton. Manager of the Control Group.'

There was a momentary pause, an awkward silence while each evaluated the situation. Here was the great man in the flesh who must surely earn hundreds of thousands of dollars plus each year and who wielded so much clout, just a foot away, but Anthony just dried up. His voice left him. The occasion overtook him. Fitzpatrick broke the silence.

'Derek suggested we call you up. This way, please.'

They entered the main boardroom, Anthony following at a polite distance. Opulence beyond belief. A full-length mahogany table with walnut inlay, big windows revealing St Paul's on Ludgate Hill in the distance, old pictures of hunting scenes and foxes gone to ground, silver decanters on small nests of antique rosewood tables. A sea of faces to take in. Anthony knew immediately who was the most important person in the room.

'Morning, Anthony. Come in.'

Amazing. Sir James Devonshire, the executive chairman of Steens, knew his name. Anthony must be doing all right. Sir James looked the part, immaculately dressed in the classic City uniform of dark suit and striped shirt with double cuffs protruding to the correct thumbnail extent. He was about fifty years old but had the energy of a much younger man, an excellent representative for Steens, the sort of person who led a corporate board meeting simply because the other attendees deigned to his mere presence. Well built without being overweight, groomed silver hair rather than grey, not an oiled hair out of place and a precision parting down the side of his cranial globe.

Sir James was one of the leading figures in the City, and he attended the premier functions, dining with the Prime Minister at number ten and sitting at the top table with the Chancellor and the Lord Mayor at the annual Mansion House black-tie bash. Sir James had contacts in almost every Footsie 100 blue-chip company and knew when to use them to Steens' financial benefit. Only a few individuals could influence the mood of the City, and here was one. When Sir James spoke, the City listened. What had Anthony done to deserve this reception? Either fame or infamy was about to come his way.

'Anthony, have you met Alvin Leung before?'

Of course not. How often does a middle-ranking manager meet someone rarely seen in this part of the world, the director for Asia Pacific based in Steens' office in Central District in Hong Kong? Leung's known social habitat was any financial capital in Asia, but allegedly he was most observed in the clubs of hilly Lan Kwai Fong or the go-go bars of Wandhai in Hong Kong.

Leung was in his early forties, unmarried and known as a serious womaniser who chased the opposite sex relentlessly. If he couldn't meet the right girl using his own initiative, he was known to weekend in Bangkok or Manila, where it proved far less effort, provided you were a wealthy investment banker with a corporate card. Leung rarely travelled the thirteen-hour flight westwards to the London head office from the city of his birth. When he did fly he always chose Cathay Pacific Airways, because the most beautiful girls from fourteen different Asian countries staffed the flights and met his every need. Anthony understood his logic. When he had been waiting in the lobby last week in the five-star Westin plaza he was lucky enough to be graced with the regal presence of a Cathay flight crew. It was like your very own private Miss World contest unfolding before your eyes. Gary would have killed just to be there with him. Just to share an elevator with one or two.

'Morning, Mr Leung.'

Anthony regretted that Leung didn't look like a typical Steens' director. Apart from being of definite Chinese extraction, he had an oily and shifty air about him. He was believed to wear a toupee, a view that gained widespread credence from Hong Kong's fame as the declared wig capital of the world. Brave staff in Steens' Hong Kong office were known to put up notices of sales in rug shops on the noticeboards anonymously, hoping Leung would see them. Anthony could almost see the joining up close.

Leung had one overriding quality that had ensured his success in Steens. He was political and knew how to impress all the right people, especially corporate clients. He helped Steens win the best mandates to do deals all over Asia, but Leung represented the wheeler-dealer mentality in investment banking, which might go down well with the speculative gambling-addicted Hong Kong Chinese but was not expected of a London-based investment banker. Leung was their own lion among the fallen tiger economies of Asia. His operations garnered vast profits for Steens in Asia and grew every year in line with the growth of the region. They all hoped it would continue.

Sir James held court. 'And you know Derek?'

Nervous laughter in the room. Short-lived too. Of course he knew him. Derek Masterson was the finance director, Anthony's direct boss and responsible for the support activities that were critical to any investment bank: finance, tax, treasury, credit, risk management and control. Derek was six foot two or three, and large too, maybe sixteen stone-plus. He carried the weight well for a person in his early fifties. Derek had been in Steens all his working life. Derek always had a tan on his imposing face, the result of either a recent holiday in the islands of the Caribbean or from one of those renowned freebie stopover weekends in Bermuda on the way home from business meetings in New York. Derek used to say that he could leave Wall Street just before 5 p.m. and still make it via JFK and American Airlines to Hamilton's terraced waterfront bars before closing time was called. Derek took his cue from Sir James.

'Anthony. It was my suggestion that we ask you here this morning. Let's sit down.'

Derek was originally Scottish but had managed to lose his former regional accent. Now he had a sort of mid-Atlantic twang somewhere in between a Manhattan drawl and the public school Queen's

36

English, the sort of accent that you picked up flying Virgin Upper Class to the States too often. When required to on any particular occasion, Derek could change accents effortlessly, depending on whether he was in London or New York, to blend in with the locals.

They sat around the boardroom table. Gary was correct: all the directors were here except for Verhoeven in Amsterdam and Walker. And of course Lord Herne was missing today, as ever. That ex-Tory MP who enjoyed his five-figure non-executive directors fees and a cosy quarterly board meeting in this very room, all apparently justified by his myriad of lucrative business connections about town. The only cloud on his horizon were his recently rumoured underwriting losses at Lloyds of London, which he vehemently denied. Anthony now noticed one other man who lurked at the end of the table. He had no idea who the visitor was but he didn't look like a Steens' person at all. Not in a million years. Sir James had forgotten to introduce the visitor. Almost.

'Anthony, this is Detective-Sergeant Bob Palmer from Bishopsgate Police Station.'

Anthony exchanged initial eye contact with the policeman, and then they stood for the compulsory handshake. First impressions were not good. Palmer had a featureless face, bad skin and a worse shave. He wore a cheap shiny suit, light blue shiny shirt and a striped two-tone tie. Loosely combed greying hair had left a few white flakes on his suit collar. He was a slight man and also somewhat overweight for his height, which was a polite way of putting it. Maybe in his forties, but looked in his fifties. Stress? Palmer greeted Anthony. Sweaty palms too. This was looking ominous. What were the police doing here? Had there been a complaint? Had one of Anthony's prior investigations come back to haunt him?

Sir James assumed his natural role at the head of the table. 'I don't suppose you've heard the news yet, Anthony?'

Anthony was in the dark. No idea what Sir James was talking about. He shook his head.

'Jeremy Walker was found dead early this morning in his Wapping apartment. We received the news from D-S Palmer just an hour ago. It's a great loss to the bank, and we are all deeply shocked.'

Their Jeremy Walker. A director of Steens. Everyone knew of Walker because he had been there since the dawn of civilisation or the dawn of Steens, whichever was earlier. Anthony knew him to see around the building, bookish looks, receding wiry grey hair, stylish glasses, always well dressed with an extravagant silk tie collection accumulated from years working in the Far East. They spoke now and again on the telephone but it was rare enough. Walker had been the king of the equities floor well before Anthony joined. Walker could sell anything. Ray-Bans to the blind, Gucci loafers to the crippled, Moët et Chandon to teetotallers, a double bed to the Pope.

Walker had worked in their Hong Kong office for years and returned to London more recently. After he had made enough money from his sales commissions and annual bonus he became the director of compliance of the bank. Walker had been responsible for ensuring Steens' compliance with the Bank of England and FSA regulations that govern modern-day investment banking in the City. It was an easy directorship before his eventual mutually agreed retirement date. Walker didn't need to work any more but the Steens' directorship nicely filled the time between administrative tasks, holidays and frequent overseas business trips.

Anthony remembered his last contact with Walker, two weeks ago at least, just before the Singers trip. Tuesday three weeks ago, to be precise. Anthony had mistakenly received a client letter of complaint in the bank's internal mail from Steens' Amsterdam office. Some client called Scholten had written to Johan Verhoeven, their director in Amsterdam. The letter amazed Anthony at the time. The client was really pissed off about the performance of the Dutch equities in his account, claimed to have had no reply to his recent enquiries and threatened to pass the matter on to a lawyer. The tone of the letter was strong, almost bitter in its accusations. It was one of the more serious client letters that Anthony had ever seen in Steens. He could still recall the contents vividly weeks later. Anthony thought Walker should know about it. It was the right thing to do, standard procedure. The late Walker had never responded to him about the forwarded mail. Anthony wondered why he had even bothered. Probably attributable more to office protocol than to anything else. It had been his last chance to deal with a man who would no longer be working within Steens. Anthony's natural curiosity got the better of him, even in such distinguished company.

'Sir James, can I ask, how did Jeremy Walker die? An accident of some sort?'

Sir James dodged the question, exhibiting all the

corporate finesse he had accumulated over the years. 'The police are investigating. We will give them every assistance possible. That's why the D-S is here today. Palmer wishes to get some background information on Jeremy. We have a busy day ahead of us so we would like you to act as the liaison point with D-S Palmer on his investigation. I know that it's not typical Control Group work, not exactly in your job description, but I am sure you can help us out this once, given the circumstances?'

Sir James had spoken. Anthony had no choice. The directors rose. Sir James explained: 'We have a prior appointment downstairs. A major new issue is under way and the issuers' management is waiting. Unfortunately on such a sad day as this, life goes on in the City.'

For some. A director of Steens was dead. Life would not be going on for Walker. Anthony had to work with this cop Palmer. Truly an awful start to the week.

CHAPTER THREE

10.20 A.M.: MONDAY 18 MARCH: CITY OF LONDON EC2

Palmer took out a packet of king-size cigarettes and lit one up. He was smoking in Steens.

'Staff are not permitted to smoke except in designated smoking areas,' explained Anthony.

'Then it's lucky that I'm not staff, isn't it?'

Anthony and Palmer were alone in the

boardroom. Anthony took the initiative.

'So what do you want to do first, Detective-Sergeant?'

Palmer was in no particular hurry, perhaps enjoying the luxurious surroundings within Steens. Surely an improvement on the interior of Bishopsgate Police Station? Palmer walked to the window and then swivelled around to reveal yellow tobacco-stained teeth. 'Nice view. Not bad at all from this height. It's better than the view from my office anyway. Nice boardroom too. I guess we're seeing how the real professionals work.'

'We don't all work in rooms like this. This is probably the best in the building. I don't want to seem rude, but I wonder can we get to the point? I've got a day's work ahead of me.'

As soon as he spoke, he knew it sounded rude. Unnecessary haste?

Palmer seemed to focus. 'You can tell me exactly what you do in the bank. It will be useful background for me. I'm not really an expert on this line of business at all.'

Anthony wasn't sure how relevant this was to the enquiries under way, but he obliged, never one to sell himself short, even to the police.

'I manage the Control Group at Steens. We do project work, regular reviews of the overseas offices, work on new systems in development and some work on any special investigations within the bank, if such occur. We work with the Compliance Department and the Legal Department on these matters. They don't have many staff, so we oblige. There's a lot of variety in our work and also overseas travel to Steens' offices. I'm just back from Singapore. And that's what I do.'

41

Palmer looked more puzzled than before and took another smoky inhalation. 'So what's the point of the Control Group?'

'Investment banking is a risk business. Every day we risk hundreds of millions of pounds of capital on our trading strategy and dealing positions. We deal with other investment banks, counterparties and with thousands of clients all over the world. There are different types of risks in this business, market risk, liquidity risk, credit risk, operational risk, suitability risk and financial risk. We help to minimise these risks by coordinating the bank's control efforts.'

This still wasn't registering with Palmer. Anthony could see it in his eyes. Time to put it all in context. Think about those newspaper headlines, Detective-Sergeant. Wake up.

'You've heard of the disasters that have befallen some major names in this business. Rogue futures traders in Singapore, copper traders in Tokyo gone mad, US bond traders in New York losing billions of dollars over years of trading, fund managers losing hundreds of millions of investors' money in offshore Luxembourg shell companies, London option traders with ninety-million-pound black holes, US hedge funds losing all their capital, major Japanese broker dealers going bust with billions of debts. We give the directors of this bank some comfort that Steens is being run in a sound manner, that there are no surprises out there waiting to strike us either in London or in any of our overseas offices. Experience elsewhere shows that very often when something goes wrong in this business, it's in a far-off place where you least expect it. Just look at the examples in other investment banks to date.'

Anthony had tried to avoid the City jargon that might confuse Palmer. It worked.

'I understand. And me? I'm based in Bishopsgate Police Station and run a small group keeping an eye on crime in the City. Bit like your job in a way? Only my crimes are different. Theft, pickpocketing, car accidents, muggings, assaults, the like. Haven't had a decent investigation like this in years. Hope it goes well. Last one like this was a stockbroker who killed himself in a market crash a few years ago. Young guy with a wife and three kids. Saddest case I've seen in twenty-three years in the job. That's how long I've been in the force. Six more years and I'll catch my old man. He did twenty-nine before he retired, but he never made D-I in all that time. Pity. I might yet.'

Like father, like son. Anthony too was following in his father's footsteps. Palmer got back to the case. 'So I gather you would have worked with Walker on some compliance matters.'

This was turning into a mini-inquisition. Not what Anthony had expected. He debated whether to mention the recent contact with Walker, that letter from Scholten regarding the Amsterdam office. No. The less the police knew about Steens' private affairs, the better. 'Walker was the director of compliance and ran an entirely different department from mine. I rarely spoke to him, and even then it was only work-related. I don't know much about him either, so I don't think I'll be able to help you.'

'Then let's get to work. Show me Jeremy Walker's office.'

*   *   *

Anthony was lost in the maze of offices before him on the seventh floor. He didn't know which belonged to the late Jeremy Walker. Embarrassing. He accosted a passing secretary.

'Where's Jeremy Walker's secretary?'

'She sits over there usually, but she's not here now. She's very distressed today. Bill Fitzpatrick wanted to send her home, but she wouldn't leave. Faithful to the end, I guess.'

The lady he passed in the corridor?

'Where was Walker's office?' Past tense. Poignant.

'Second on the left, back down the corridor.'

Anthony and Palmer followed her instructions. Anthony recognised those tall plants as he realised that he had been here recently. He stopped at the same office that Bill Fitzpatrick had exited from less than half an hour ago. The door was half-ajar.

Anthony paused perhaps out of respect for the dead. Palmer had no such qualms and brushed past him.

'Let's see what Walker was working on of late. Might give us some ideas.'

Anthony stood observing while Palmer unceremoniously trashed the spacious office. He couldn't pry into a director's office. But Palmer wasn't bothered as he opened every drawer of the black ash desk, pulled out every filing-cabinet drawer and opened every correspondence file. It didn't look promising. Just lever-arch files with Steens' memoranda and letters on official letterhead. All business stuff. Palmer was out of his depth, lost in a financial morass. He went for the

44

obvious.

'What about Walker's computer? What's on it? Can we access it and see his files?'

'It contains confidential bank matters. We would have to get someone from the Systems Department to come up and break in, circumventing Walker's log-on ID and passwords.'

Palmer was frustrated. He walked to the window, sighed, turned and looked around the office. His face lit up with the enhanced view of the room. 'Wow. Nearly missed that.'

Anyone could have missed it. Unless you stood right by the window. A briefcase lay on the floor hidden beside the desk. The embossed initials were a giveaway. JW. Good-quality black leather. Palmer lifted it up on the desk and tried to open it. No joy. Firmly locked. He took out a rusty penknife from the worn suit pocket, jammed it into the lock and shattered the locking mechanism. The briefcase opened to his touch but was empty except for one thin manila file. Anthony wondered about the contents. Palmer was excited.

'So what do we have here then? And why keep this particular file under lock and key?' Palmer was putting two and two together and getting fifty as he opened the file on the desk. 'These are letters addressed to some foreigner called Johan Verhoeven. Know him at all?'

'Johan Verhoeven is the head of our Amsterdam office and is our director for Europe.'

'Where is he today?'

'Amsterdam, I guess. At work.'

Anthony leaned forward. He recognised the first letter in the file. That letter from Scholten in Amsterdam from last week? Walker had locked it

45

away out of sight. Why had he done nothing about it? Surely his job as the director of compliance involved more than just storing it under lock and key and hoping the problem would go away in time? Anthony went to pick up the letter but Palmer stopped him.

'No. Don't touch it. We might check this for fingerprints later if we need to.'

Jesus. Don't do that. Anthony's grubby prints were all over that page. Should he declare immediately that he knew about this letter? He didn't have a chance to speak. There were more similar letters underneath. Palmer was simultaneously digesting the contents of each letter as he moved them over left to right, one by one with the chewed end of a cheap Bic biro, again produced from that bottomless suit pocket.

'These letters are all complaining about your Amsterdam office. People called Scholten, Smit, Mulder and Faber are losing money on shares. What does the Amsterdam office do? Is it a bit of a disaster?'

Time to defend Steens from an unwarranted attack. Sir James would have demanded it. 'No, it's not a disaster. Steen Odenberg NV deals mostly in Dutch equities. The clients are either large Dutch financial institutions or wealthy local private individuals. Every couple of years people from my Control Group visit the place to see what's happening there. The office is well managed and ticks along nicely. A director of the bank closely manages it so we expect it to be all right. It makes good money, too, every year—no problems at all, same as the rest of our bank.'

Palmer was exhibiting almost canine behaviour,

like a dog with a meaty bone. 'What's the procedure for handling client complaints like these?'

'Client complaints are forwarded to Jeremy Walker in the Compliance Department. Well, were forwarded, I guess now. Past tense. It was his job to decide if we investigate them further. If some on-site work is required, staff in my Control Group do the work. We have the resources to do it, Compliance don't. Walker only had one secretary working for him who seems to have been overcome by events this morning. There are four of us in the Control Group and we have less routine work to do.'

'I wonder why Walker kept all these letters? Are client complaints like these common?'

Anthony engaged in a damage-limitation exercise. Anything to stop Palmer getting excited. 'We are a big investment bank and we get occasional letters of complaint. There are always a few cranky private clients who complain about everything, from our investment banking practices to our commission charges to the directors' remuneration even to our recycling policy. There are people who love writing letters, but any serious private client complaint was always investigated independently by Walker.'

The answer was a model answer for any Steens' employee. Palmer stopped him in his tracks.

'Yeah, sure, except these ones? This last letter is from some company called the Nederland Investment Corporation. Ever heard of them?'

'Everyone in this business knows NedCorp. They're big Dutch investors.'

NedCorp was the Netherlands' biggest

institutional investor, handling billions of guilders of pension funds, insurance company moneys, mutual funds and investment trusts. They were the biggest client of Steens Amsterdam and a major investor in Dutch equities. If they were buying Dutch equities, the Amsterdam market rose. If they were dumping Dutch equities, the market plunged. They could unilaterally move the local stock market in Amsterdam with the sheer weight of the money they sloshed around the system. Palmer pushed the piece of NedCorp's nationalistic blue and red corporate stationery towards Anthony. The letter was dated 5 February last and was from the NedCorp head office off Dam Square and was addressed to Johan Verhoeven.

'Ever heard of EPIC then?'

The first line of the letter was in bold capitals, the name of a company, EPIC NV, a Dutch company. Anthony had never heard of it. Must be a crappy little company then? He began to wish that Palmer had never located the file. He pleaded the Fifth Amendment.

'This assumes some prior knowledge about what they are complaining about and I've never heard of EPIC. It can't be much, if I haven't heard of them.'

Palmer had come to a decision. 'This file of client letters must be investigated further. It might be important. I'd like to know what they were doing in London. They are all addressed to your Johan Verhoeven, yet Jeremy Walker seems to have been in possession of them. Someone should at least ask Verhoeven about them. Either your bank's internal mail is seriously screwed up, or someone out in Amsterdam is trying to tell you something.'

Anthony didn't like what he had read. The less the police knew, the better. Time to volunteer for work that was best done by a Steens' employee rather than by the authorities. 'I'll check it out.'

'How?'

'I'll take a day trip to Amsterdam. If things look all right, I can sort it out there and then. If not, then some of the staff from the Control Group will go back for a more detailed look.'

'A day trip to old Amsterdam—not too bad.'

'When you've done so many of these day trips, I can assure you that the interest wanes. You don't get to see much in one day apart from the inside of taxis, Heathrow or Gatwick, aeroplanes, a restaurant and a Steens' office.'

'When are you going?'

'Some time this week.'

'How about tomorrow? No time like the present.'

'I'll see if I can get a flight.'

'There are flights every day. I'm sure you'll have no problem. I'll leave these letters here for you. Scholten, NedCorp and the others. Good luck tomorrow.' Palmer gathered the file together in his nicotine-stained hands.

Anthony was puzzled. 'What about the fingerprints?'

'Relax. That was a joke. This isn't Murder One, you know. They're only a few letters.' Palmer handed the file and a small printed card to Anthony. 'This is my number at Bishopsgate Station. Give me a call when you get back. Do you have a business card? In case I need to call you.'

Anthony's business card was impressive, but Palmer just stuffed it into that bottomless trouser

49

pocket of his. 'I got a collection of these this morning. Let me know how you get on when you return.'

That was it. Or was it? Maybe Palmer could be of use. He could give Anthony some information because, as Gary had so recently confirmed, in the world of investment banking information was everything. Then Anthony could tell Gary and Vanessa, perhaps even impress Derek if he got the chance.

'What can you tell me about Walker's death?'

'Nothing.'

Palmer killed his question stone dead. Easily too. Anthony tried the friendly approach. 'I thought we were on the same side? Working together?'

'We are. It's just that I don't know any details about the death yet. It's early days. I'm waiting for the forensic guys to finish up in his Wapping apartment and then we'll do a post-mortem down at Guy's Hospital morgue.'

'So it's definitely not an accident?'

'Sure ain't. Talk to you again.'

'OK, Detective.'

'Detective-Sergeant, actually.'

The closing handshakes were as loose and unenthusiastic as those at the opening of their unscripted meeting. Anthony knew Palmer resented his City career and the associated material trappings of success, but most of all the detective resented what he represented. Anthony in turn resented the fact that Palmer was running the show. He liked to be in charge. They passed that tearful woman sitting at the secretary's desk outside. Walker's secretary had recovered

50

sufficiently to resume her station. She gave them a look of surprise, wondering who were the two intruders in her former boss's office.

'I'm Anthony Carlton from downstairs and this gentleman is from the police.'

The mere mention of the police triggered a reaction. She was about to burst into tears yet again. She composed herself and had the courage to direct a question at Anthony. 'What's that file you have?'

'It's some letters we found in Jeremy Walker's office.'

'Make sure you return them to me. Jeremy was always careful about his personal files.'

*   *   *

The word had spread already from the seventh floor. Gary and Vanessa burst into Anthony's office. Everyone in Steens knew by now that Anthony had spent thirty minutes with the law.

'Well, Tony, what's it all about? Walker's dead. Are you in big trouble with the police?'

'It's just routine, Vanessa. No need to worry about me.' Routine? It sure wasn't. He was beginning to sound like a policeman himself. Maybe he had already had too much exposure to the likes of Palmer.

'It's about Jeremy Walker's death, isn't it?' she persisted. 'How did he die? Tell us.'

'It's gotta be a murder,' opined Gary.

'Why, do you say that?'

'Look at all that press still down in the plaza. If Walker dropped off under his duvet or snuffed it in the Jacuzzi, they'd hardly still be hanging around.

51

They're looking for an angle on the death of one of the biggest names in the City. You didn't do it, did you, Tony? Where were you last night? Have you got an alibi?'

Anthony unfortunately had no alibi for last night. He exchanged a knowing glance with Vanessa. It was a matter of extreme mutual regret. 'No, I don't have an alibi, in the unlikely event that I needed one. I was jet lagged last night. I was shagged.' If only he had been. 'Do you have an alibi, Gary?'

'Yep. Last night, or more correctly this morning, I was on the dance floor at the Ministry of Sound at the Elephant and Castle. I have at least a thousand other clubbing eyewitnesses who saw me there between ten and two o'clock. So I am in the clear. Maybe that's why the police weren't looking for me? And what about you? Guilty, m'lud? Seriously, what do the police want you to do, Tony?'

Gary seemed to have some psychic powers, although they were rarely evident at work. Anthony believed Gary's nocturnal alibi. His present shattered physical condition was testament to a night of ecstasy—the experience, not the drug.

'Some copper, D-S Palmer, wants me to investigate some letters of complaint from clients that he found in Walker's briefcase, one of which is from NedCorp. Have you ever heard of EPIC, Gary? It's Dutch. People in Amsterdam are complaining about it.'

'Is it one of those porno channels which you can get on satellite television?'

'I think it's a Dutch company with a Stock Exchange listing in Amsterdam.'

'Is this connected with the Amsterdam office at

all, then?' interjected Vanessa.

'Might be. Looks like Johan Verhoeven is involved in this.'

'Really? Show me.'

Anthony produced the manila file. The complaints were worrying. Five against one office in a month was unprecedented in Anthony's experience. Two of the letters referred to previous letters that had not been acknowledged and to unreturned telephone calls and cancelled appointments with Verhoeven.

They got to the NedCorp letter. NedCorp had invested a substantial sum in new listed shares of this EPIC stock two years ago, but now claimed their investment had been unsatisfactory. They were unhappy about the manner in which the shares had been sold. Since this new public issue of shares was syndicated and arranged by Steen Odenberg, they wished formally to express their dissatisfaction. It was all written in legal speak. Jan Peters, who described himself as Chief Investment Manager, Nederland Investment Corporation NV, signed the letter. Peters rounded off by threatening that NedCorp would cease to give business to Steens. That would be a big loss to the Amsterdam office. This was serious. Gary had the first decent idea of the week so far.

'Well, Tony, there's one easy way to find out more about EPIC. Look it up on Reuters.'

Gary leaned over the keyboard on Anthony's desk. Anthony was a step ahead already.

'Do you actually know the Reuters' mnemonic stock code for EPIC, Gary?'

'No. I know the sports pages on Reuters. I thought you would know how to search for it.'

Anthony didn't know. He rarely checked out the company share prices on Reuters, except one. Steens itself was listed on the London Stock Exchange, currently capitalised at just over four billion pounds. Anthony had received thousands of Steens' shares under various management incentive schemes over the years and was also part of the management share-option scheme at an outrageously cheap price. It was all part of his lucrative compensation package. The only downside was that he was locked in, committed to wait five years before he could exercise any of the options, but the options were all well in the money.

Steens had him by the balls. A set of golden handcuffs of the best type.

He knew the Steens' stock code and could tell Gary exactly what the bid-offer was on the Steens' share price right now under STN.L, but there was no way he could do the same for some obscure EPIC stock listed on the Amsterdam Stock Exchange.

Vanessa had an alternative solution. 'Let's telephone the Amsterdam office. They'll know the stock mnemonic.'

'No telephone calls to Amsterdam. Not yet. EPIC is a new share issue which we arranged.'

'Try Dave on the syndicate desk downstairs. He sells new issues, so he must know about it.'

Anthony could telephone David Chilcott-Tomkinson on the second floor, but he did not know exactly whom he would speak to on the shared telephone lines of the syndicate desk. He was not keen on having his sudden enquiry recorded on the desk's telephone tapes. All the telephones of the second floor were recorded in case of a trader error, a salesman's order execution mistake or a subsequent client dispute.

In any event a walk down to the second floor would be a chance to experience the pulsing heart of Steens' flagship London office.

CHAPTER FOUR

11.19 A.M.: MONDAY 18 MARCH: CITY OF LONDON EC2

Anthony looked at the continuous digital display in the lift as he descended to the second floor. Nowhere in Steens' head office could you escape the fact that you were in the City. The FTSE 100 was down five points but had come back from its morning low at the opening. Anthony wondered if the FTSE index reacts to deaths of leading investment bank directors? Probably not.

The dealing and sales floor was euphemistically called the front office, in contrast to the back office where the operations and support staff toiled. Anthony was not in the front office mould, and never would be, but he wanted to blend in as much as possible on the second floor. He left the jacket of his Kowloon suit behind upstairs. Anyone wearing a jacket on the second floor would look out of place. He thought about loosening his tie and rolling up his shirtsleeves, but then he would look too much like a salesman. Perish the thought.

The lift door opened on to the second floor, and he could hear the noise of dealers and salesmen in action. About eight hundred people worked on the second floor, and he was using the word 'work' in the loosest possible sense. All eight hundred must be here today. Their business continued even if one of their directors had died not a mile from where they all sat. He knew where he was going to from experience as he walked down the centre of the brightly lit high-ceilinged cavern.

He passed various sales desks. The biggest desk sold UK equities to domestic and international investors. He went past the Far East desk staff, selling Hong Kong, Taiwanese, Korean, Singaporean, Indonesian, Thai and Malaysian equities. You name the exotic country, they could get the shares for you. They were coming to the end of their trading day, given the seven-hour time zone difference, and they were mentally and physically at ease. He went past the desk selling Jap equities and warrants. Winding down also. Now was the time for them to talk to clients on the telephone and fax out copious research notes and tomorrow's recommended buys and sells.

The sales desks looked as if they had been blitzed. A myriad of screens: Reuters, Telerate, Bloomberg, Datastream and Knight Ridder. PCs and Excel spreadsheets, Access databases and price charts. Total organised chaos. The latest research on every company, industry sector, economy, country and region piled like towers on the limited desk space, expounding on every initial public offering and rights issue, every origination and syndication, every takeover and merger, every vicious rumour, subtle innuendo and positive sentiment. Information was immediately past its best-by date once published; it was only worth something when you had it and no one else did.

56

Then the dealing desks where Steens traded million-pound positions in securities, bonds, futures, swaps, FRAs, FX and options, where the big hitters gambled Steens' money on a daily basis. Only it was better than mere gambling. They were so powerful that they won more often than any mere casino participant for the simple reason that they were not just merely part of the market—in many cases they *were* the market. If they were buying, then the City was buying. If they were selling, everyone started selling. It was a self-fulfilling prophecy of the best kind.

The money they gambled with was not theirs, it was Steens'. Someone had given these dealers in their twenties a rack of multi-million-pound Vegas-style gambling chips to play with and the green baize stretched all over the globe. They were a unique breed, these dealers. Hyperactive, crude, loud, tough, wealthy for sure. Anthony knew the difference between a bond and a bond dealer. A bond eventually matures.

Tension was in the air. All eyes focused on the syndicate desk. The new issue that Sir James had mentioned was under way. Monday was their favourite day to launch. Never risk it on a Thursday or Friday. If you were left with part of the issue, then you would likely be stuck with it for the weekend. You incurred the funding cost of financing the position for a minimum extra two days. And so much could happen over the weekend to spook the markets. World leaders could die. Governments overthrown in bloodless coups. Aggressive neighbours invade small unknown countries. Assassinations take place at political rallies. Bank of England governors or Federal

Reserve chairmen give policy-changing interviews or make unexpected after-dinner speeches. Sure, these happen any day of the week, but at the weekend Steens were powerless to sell stock with every global market closed for two entire days. Steens might have been happier if weekends were discontinued around the world.

Anthony looked up at the executive conference room. Yes. Full of suits. Those same Steens' suits he had met an hour ago with Palmer in significantly less celebratory circumstances. Sir James mingled. Fitzpatrick and Masterson and Leung hovered. Anthony did not recognise the five Chinese gentlemen who looked out in awe on to the second floor. He presumed that they were the management of the issuer client. Another emerging market issuer in Asia had been persuaded by Steens to come to the international capital markets. The Chinese clients were smiling. It could be that the new issue was selling well today. Amazing to see those same directors smiling, just hours after learning of the death of their esteemed colleague. Business always came first in Steens.

But the tension was still there. Something wrong? Wasn't the issue selling well? The syndicate desk was on a slightly raised platform and looked out over the sales and dealing desks. Its very physical presence confirmed its importance to Steens' success. The sale of all new equity and fixed income bond issues was coordinated here. Anthony knew David Chilcott-Tomkinson, the head of the syndicate desk, quite well. Anthony and Dave had joined Steens on the same Monday morning nearly five years ago. They thus found themselves in the same annual induction class and struck up a good rapport early on. Anthony stood obviously near Dave, but one of his colleagues at the desk spoke first. 'Dave's just wrapping up. He should be free in a few minutes.'

The salesmen were simultaneously working the telephones, their instrument, their lifeline. Without it, they were incommunicado. Desks piled high with telephone banks and switchboards and extensions. Direct lines immediately available to the major banks, clients and markets with flashing lights on the boards and lines ringing unanswered as incoming calls stacked up in queues. Anthony dodged the extended cables of the telephones that trailed dangerously to allow salesmen to stand away from their desks, hands in motion, handsets held awkwardly against their shoulder as they looked at rows of screens in front of them. That way they had instantaneous eye contact with Dave's syndicate desk.

Anthony did not need to ask about the new issue. He knew that the entire syndicate desk was living and breathing this new issue right now and probably had done so for several days and during all of the past weekend. If any syndicate staff had a moment to spare they would tell Anthony just how unbelievably good the issue was. The unknown colleague obliged.

'We're selling off another international blue chip today,' the syndicate desk guy smirked. 'South China Iron and Steel Company. SCISCO for short. Forty million GDSs at ten bucks each. Four hundred million dollars' worth of shares have just about gone out the door. Another satisfied issuer.'

Anthony tried to look impressed. Dave saw him. 'Oh, my God. The thought police have arrived!'

The locals were not keen to see staff from Anthony's Control Group down on the second floor, least of all Anthony himself. They wondered about the reason for the impromptu visit, whether there was a hidden agenda, but Anthony knew David Chilcott-Tomkinson too well for that. Despite the double-barrelled surname, Dave was as normal as you got on any syndicate desk.

A lanky, wiry sort with a shock of sandy hair and fashionable glasses to make him both see better and look more intelligent. Energetic and hyper at the best of times. Darting eyes. He dressed loud because he could afford to. Fine-check lilac shirts, bold stripes, occasional braces, yellow ties, heavy dangling cufflinks, double-breasted suits. Not all at the same time, of course. The two had a lot in common except for their appetite for risk. Dave was more entrepreneurial than Anthony. His natural home was on the second floor getting his daily fix selling all he could. Dave would not enjoy working in the Control Group, which required a different mind-set. He would miss the money too.

Dave had an *alter ego* of sorts. He could be a best-mate Dave with sleeves rolled up shouting at hassled salesmen as he shifted some more stock, or he could be a Mr David Chilcott-Tomkinson as he attended formal client presentations and took the syndicate roadshow around the world to meet potential investors. Anthony was sure that Dave's parents told their friends that their son was an investment banker in the City of London. That sure impressed the gentrified country folk of middle England. The truth was that their son Dave flogged paper to punters.

Dave continued in the same somewhat

60

predictable original vein. 'What have I done? Where are the handcuffs?'

'Relax. I've just come down here to shoot the wounded.'

'Well, feel free to start at the syndicate desk right now. We are not quite there yet. Pull up a chair. Gimme a minute and I'll be with you.'

Dave's eyes had hardly left the screens arrayed in front of him. Beads of perspiration were speckled on his forehead. There was indeed tension.

'This is the state of play. We've got three ninety million done and have just ten to go. We started with four hundred million bucks of equity to sell, and we just have this fucking ten million left. It's gotta go right now. We're not keeping any of this SCISCO paper ourselves. No bloody way. Not with the Footsie now down fifteen and still on a down tick and the Dow expected to open weaker over the water.'

The Footsie had lost ten points in as many minutes. Another few hundred million wiped off the market. Dave's language was never the best and was mixed with a tendency of his to become overly animated. Right now he was in the heat of battle, with adrenaline coursing through his veins. He swore, too, whenever he lost in two straight sets to Anthony in their regular tennis game in W9.

Dave stood up and faced the numerous salesmen at all the desks. 'Come on, guys. Ten million left to go. Who's it gonna be? Let's shift this paper.'

No takers on the floor. Every one of the salesmen was on the telephone, in some cases communicating on two or three phones simultaneously, evidently having no luck in persuading institutional investors

61

to buy up the remaining shares in South China Iron and Steel, whatever that company did apart from the obvious. An innocent-looking salesman stood up and shouted back at Dave to break the selling dilemma. 'Delta Global Fund Managers take a million bucks.'

'For fuck's sake, who's interested in a fucking million? We'll be here all day. I want ten or nothing. Now.'

Dave sat down, hidden behind the screens, and grinned out of sight of the frantic salesmen. 'Excuse the French, Tony, but it's the only language that these salesmen understand. I always find that saying please never really works as well with them.'

The tension rose as time passed. Dave fidgeted nervously. The ominous silence was broken. Someone shouted back from the sales floor, an older salesman, one of those with long service at Steens . . . well, with at least three years' service. 'Scottish Colonial takes the ten.'

'Thank God for that. Well done. Drinks are on you tonight in the Flute. All done.' Dave breathed a sigh of relief. 'You can't beat this sort of pressure. It's better than sex. Four hundred million dollars of this Chinky metal-bashing company gone. One hundred million pre-sold via our New York office before we even came in at 6 a.m. today. One hundred million sold in the Far East, in Hong Kong, Tokyo and Singapore at their close of day. Two hundred million sold in London and Europe and it's all gone now. At least, I think it is.'

Dave momentarily had doubts. He shouted to a young girl called Debs at the end of the syndicate desk to check the final allocations by client and make sure that it came to forty million shares. If it were more, Steens weren't bothered. They would scale back client allotments on a pro-rata basis and bring it down to four hundred million dead. Or else they could cut back a particularly pushy institutional client who had pissed them off in the past week and needed to be taken down a peg or two to show them who really ran the show.

It was more important that they were not under the forty million share total. Steens would take the unsold balance on to their own trading book and trade it out in due course. This would not be easy. Once the market learned that a lead manager like Steens were sitting on a rump of unsold stock, the overhang would depress the new issue share price and would guarantee losses. The lead manager underwrote the deal for a juicy underwriting fee. It was like insurance, only real expensive insurance. Steens were obligated to buy the unsold portion so that South China Iron and Steel Company got what they were due, or at least they got the issue proceeds less what Steens took out of the deal. Steens wanted the deal fees, not secondary market trading losses.

Anthony got a good look at Debs for the first time. Tall, thin-waisted, long dyed hair, dressed in a trendy black top with a short purple skirt and unnecessary stiletto heels. Anthony was beginning to think that perhaps after all he could handle a job working on the second floor. All the assistants, who worked with these salesmen and dealers on the second floor had one outstanding common feature, which was instantaneously recognisable. Then his illusion was shattered when she shouted back that her spreadsheet came to forty million shares exactly. In a broad Essex accent. Too much to listen to for too long.

'It's a miracle. Another share and we would be out. Gimme a printout soon, Debs.'

Dave leaned back in his chair, shoes up on the desk, looked up at the executive conference room from where the directors watched. He gave a thumbs-up sign. Sir James noticeably frowned at this somewhat vulgar display. The Chinese guests were happier.

'Those Chinese guys are delighted. Not because they have just floated off their company. Rather because we gave them a freebie trip over from China in business-class style, three nights in our regular Tower City Hotel and a few guided tours around London's sights and nightspots. It's a paid holiday but officially it's a marketing trip. Everyone does it. They love it.'

One acknowledged Dave with a wave, then looked embarrassed. Dave was unwinding.

'Not bad? We get a one per cent underwriting fee for carrying the issue risk and a one per cent selling fee for selling the entire issue to our institutional clients. It doesn't take much to work out that two per cent of four hundred million dollars is eight million dollars. That's five million sterling. Deduct, say, a round sum million sterling for our expenses, legal fees, marketing and travel. Say four million sterling net profit. Not bad for a day's work, and it's still only half-past eleven on a Monday morning. We could knock off for the rest of the week and it would still be a good week, but we won't. We're only as good as the last deal. We'll get on to the next one.'

In an instant Dave had mentally finished with

South China Iron and Steel. It was a done deal. His active mind moved to the next news topic immediately. One that mattered more. 'Jesus, Tony. Hear about Jeremy Walker?'

'Yes.'

'Big shock. Even though Walker is dead we didn't stop this issue today as a mark of respect. Old Jeremy would have wanted it this way. He wanted the deal to be done. He said as much last week. Besides, no one person is bigger than a deal like this. We've had tens of people working on this for months. No dead director is going to make us forgo four million in fees, even if the whole board was wiped out. This investment banking lark is a dangerous business to be in. One day you can be here working away and the next day you are stretched out stiff as a plank like Walker.'

Anthony was puzzled. 'I don't necessarily think that his death is work related.'

'Of course it is. That's what we all think down here, anyway. Did you know Walker as well as we did when he used to work with us here? He just worked and worked. Steens was his entire life. If he were murdered, then it's got to be work related.'

'In what way?'

'I dunno. If I knew everything, I wouldn't be on this desk. I'd be a bloody dealer over there, or I'd be picking winning numbers on the lottery each week. Maybe Walker wound someone up the wrong way or was up to no good somewhere and got burned. Maybe he was shagging someone's wife here. Or shagging some nineteen-year-old sales assistant and got a coronary in the process. Or maybe he was just unlucky, in the wrong place at the wrong time. He had no real life outside this

65

bank after his marriage with Sylvia ended.'

'I didn't know that he had split up with his wife.'

'They got divorced two years ago. It happened when he was working in our Hong Kong office. Irreconcilable differences and all that. Sylvia stayed on in Hong Kong and still lives in sin there with some flashy American lawyer. Walker came home to London to work with us. It affected him badly at the time, but he never spoke openly about the split at all.'

'You should talk to the police about Walker.'

'What?'

'I talked to a copper named Palmer today who's interested in Walker's compliance work.'

'That conversation didn't take long, I'd say. He did fuck all compliance work that I saw. It was all a veneer. Why did the police pick on you?'

'Derek and Sir James nominated me. I had no choice. Guess I was unlucky.'

'Not as unlucky as Walker.'

Anthony didn't want to say more. Discretion was an important part of work. Duty called. 'So tell me, is South China Iron and Steel a good company?'

Dave shrugged those square shoulders in apathy: 'Do I care? I don't decide what we sell here at this desk. The flashy corporate finance guys upstairs behind the Chinese Walls do that. They find these companies around the world and bring them here ultimately to my humble syndicate desk. Like in this issue, it was originated jointly by our Hong Kong office primary industries group and the emerging-markets sales desk here in London. Hence we are honoured with Alvin Leung's presence in the office today. I just flog the paper to the market, and I can sell whatever they decide to offer. Steens never

66

fails in that regard. We have the clout'

'But you do know a bit about South China Iron and Steel? In case the clients ask you?'

'First of all remember that it's SCISCO, not the long-winded full name. That's one of the key jobs of corporate finance upstairs, to get a good easy-to-use abbreviation for the issuer. I only know what I have been told by the research guys. It's like having a rake of lagers and a few hot Thai green curries afterwards. Your favourite meal? I can regurgitate it any time. The research guys give me piles of meaningless figures which I remember for a few days and then forget for good afterwards, like the fact that we just sold SCISCO on a price-earnings ratio of eight when most of the world's major steel companies are on a p/e of ten plus.'

'So SCISCO is basically a good investment?'

'It depends on your definition of the word "good", doesn't it? In a way all the new issues that we sell here are good investments. Otherwise they wouldn't make it this far to my syndicate desk. The clients know that and they trust Steens. A cynic might say that now and again Steens might sell shit, but at least we sell the best-quality shit in the City.'

Anthony sometimes found it difficult to tell when Dave was winding him up.

'Buying a new issue is a mug's game. The buyers of new issues get hooked because our sales and research guys do such a good propaganda job. Someone is selling and someone is buying, but who really makes the decision? The sellers sell when it suits them alone. It's like if I were selling you my second-hand car, but you've never even seen it; there's no chance of a test drive and I alone decide the price. If you offer me too little, then I don't sell.

67

If you offer me too much, then I take it and run. It's a win-win situation for the seller. We were once doing a new issue for a company that was trying to mine gold in Canada. The company directors pulled the issue at the last minute and we lost our deal fees. That hurt. The reason why? The company struck a massive ore deposit in Alberta and they were damned if anyone else was going to get their hands on their filthy lucre. QED.'

Dave joined his arched fingers behind his head and stretched his vertebrae to the maximum. 'The acid test is whether I myself would invest my own money in SCISCO. I might, or I might just put it on a fancied nag in the 2.30 at Kempton Park. Either way, it's a gamble. The fund managers who bought these shares today are not really buying a piece of SCISCO. They are buying a piece of the Chinese dream. China's economy will take off in the future, because, let's face it, it's starting from a pretty low base. When that happens all the primary utility and infrastructure companies will do well. If not, then the bet on SCISCO is a waste of time. It depends on what's hot. A few years ago South-East Asian issues were hot. Then the Berlin Wall fell and Eastern Europe became the place to invest because everything could be bought at half the price than in Western Europe. Lots of special funds to invest in Eastern Europe were floated off, buying property and bankrupt companies and ailing industries for next to nothing. Right now, China is hot. Investors will buy anything coming out of China. It's our very own takeaway.'

A pause for breath, then more wisdom from Dave: 'Geographical distance helps a lot too. If we sell a UK issue here in London then the clients know all about the company, the markets and the economy. They can second-guess us and make life difficult. However, if we sell an overseas issue, then we are in the driving seat and faraway hills always look greener and cheaper. That's why we like Chinese issuers so much at the moment. None of the clients knows much about them at all. The fund managers think they are buying something cheap compared with what's trading in the rest of the world, but you can always buy crap cheaply, or pay good money for quality. The choice is yours.'

'So what happens if you can't sell the issue. What if the clients won't buy the shares?'

'I'm sorry, run that by me again. You lost me near the start.'

'Are there bad issues?'

Dave lowered his voice, realising that he was on delicate ground, perhaps even hallowed. 'Well, no issues that anyone outside of Steens would ever hear about. It's unthinkable for Steens to be behind a bad issue. It would ruin our premier reputation. There is always a lot of pressure from the directors to get the issue away successfully. Not overt pressure, but I know that if I were left with stock here at the syndicate desk, it would be a big negative in my bonus calculation at the year-end. Sir James and Derek would be pissed off. I would not wish to be sitting here with ten million dollars of SCISCO paper today. Other banks have problems that we hear about. One of the German investment banks launched an Emerging Markets Fund that invested in South America bonds just before the markets collapsed there on local currency fears. Now we call it the Submerging Markets Fund. It's all about confidence. People have confidence in Steens. They buy what we sell.'

'Ever heard of EPIC?' Anthony did not know why he, too, had instinctively lowered his voice as he uttered the question. Force of habit.

Dave immediately recoiled. 'Jesus. That stock is a dog. Have you got some?'

'No, I don't, but just tell me about it'

'Hold on. Where are you coming from on this? Is this an official enquiry or just a chat.'

'Which do you want it to be?'

'Just a chat. A favour from me to you. But not here. Let's go for an early lunch in the Flute. At twelve?'

Anthony was puzzled by the cloak-and-dagger approach. Surely an overreaction on Dave's pant? What more could there be to EPIC than just another Steens' deal?

CHAPTER FIVE

12.08 P.M.: MONDAY 18 MARCH: CITY OF LONDON EC2

Anthony and Dave sat at a corner table in the Flute. They were early, and the wine bar staff outnumbered the assembled diners. Dave looked around for familiar faces since it was the local haunt of most of the second floor. He seemed satisfied that they could not be overheard. The background muzak muffled their conversation. They started on two of the world's most expensive bowls of pasta con funghi and frosted bottles of designer lager. Glasses must be extra. Dave was never one to waste time.

'EPIC is a fucking disaster, and it could blow up right in our faces. I was wondering when someone else apart from me would realise that. The most worrying aspect is that the people most involved in it are Walker, Verhoeven and Fitzpatrick. All directors. That's why we are having this conversation off-site.'

Anthony leaned forward, eager to learn more and taste the aromatic lunch before him. 'Tell me more.'

'EPIC is one of those Eastern European new issues sold by my desk two years ago. EPIC is another abbreviation dreamed up by the corporate finance guys. Epic disaster more like. The full legal name is the European Property Investment Corporation. I was never happy about it. Never. It was set up to invest in property in Eastern and Central Europe just as the Berlin Wall came down and Westerners supposedly poured east to do business. Everyone thought property prices there would soar because of the future demand and that rental yields would go through the roof, no pun intended, all that sort of sexy stuff. God. In hindsight it sounds too good to be true, doesn't it? That's one of the oldest lessons in this business. If an investment sounds too good to be true, then it usually is. Steer clear of it.'

'So what went wrong with EPIC then?'

'Nothing went wrong. Nothing went right. In fact, just about nothing happened at all. Absolutely zero progress has been made in developing property in Eastern Europe.'

'How much did they raise?'

Dave paused to digest the assorted pasta shapes,

71

then recovered his ability to speak.

'Fifty million dollars, say thirty million sterling. Shares were ten bucks each. It was a small issue by our standards. We got deal fees of a million bucks. I always remember the fees.'

'How has the EPIC share price performed?'

'Badly, in a word. The issue was mostly sold to a small group of sophisticated investors, large institutional investors in the US and Europe. The company has not delivered, so they are now keen to offload the stock, but there are no buyers, according to the salesmen here. The stock is listed in Amsterdam. I checked the price before I came here. Four dollars and ten cents. Less than half of the issue price. The Reuters' screen showed that four bucks ten is the high price for the year to date.'

'Is there much volume in the stock?'

Dave was grimacing. Something about EPIC? No. It was something far more important than any mere fund. 'This needs more Parmesan. Waitress, Parmesan over here, please. No one would touch this company now. It's strapped for cash because it has bought so much crap property. It's not an issue that Steens would be proud to be associated with, but then again the Amsterdam office drove it all, so we are in the clear here in London. Johan Verhoeven in Amsterdam was a big mover in the EPIC issue, and when a director like him is behind it nothing can stop it. He is some pushy individual. The Dutch punters thought they were on to a sure thing right in their own back yard. They thought they were buying in cheap, and they were, only they could buy in a lot cheaper today! More beer, Tony?'

They were all supposed to be one big happy family, including the overseas offices like Amsterdam, but Steens was competitive, and the inter-office rivalry was acknowledged by all who worked there. It made them all perform just that bit better. Get those beers in.

'Sure. You say EPIC is priced in dollars? Why not in guilders if it's listed in Amsterdam?'

'Two more beers over here when you're ready too. Our investors like dollar issues. It improves the marketability of the issue and takes away a lot of the currency risk for the investors. Take the SCISCO issue today as an example. We could have issued local Chinese shares in Chinese currency, whatever it is, but who would touch them then? Their currency is a joke currency, sort of like the Indonesian rupiah or the Greek drachma. The foreign exchange rate can collapse overnight. Instead we have issued US dollar denominated Global Depository Shares. GDSs. We stick the shares in a depository bank in Wall Street and they issue certificates which represent, say, ten shares and which are settled through Euroclear. If in doubt, you go for a dollar issue. In a word, it's sexier. And sex sells.'

'Can you remember how the issue of EPIC went on the day? Was it as easy as SCISCO?'

Dave wiped his lips with a napkin, apparently still gastronomically unfulfilled. 'Jeez, that was a small helping. We'll go somewhere else next time, Tony. Hey, none of these issues is easy. There are just degrees of difficulty, and from what I recall EPIC was a bitch to sell even then. Bill Fitzpatrick in New York originally thought that US investors would like to invest in an emerging part of Europe, but when push came to shove the Yanks kept their wallets closed. London clients were not that keen either. We ended up with Verhoeven selling most of it via the Amsterdam office. It wasn't the way we planned to sell it, but we shifted it all, as usual. I don't know how the hell he sold hundreds of thousands of those shares, but he did and that's all that counts.'

'So if I were an investor who was still holding these EPIC shares now, what could I do?'

'Fuck all. You could sell them and take a big loss, but no one does that really. Investors are eternal optimists. They always think that the stock price will come around and they will make back their money and more. Hell, I bet even some of the EPIC investors might be buyers of more EPIC shares at this price. They can average down their cost of acquisition and that way their loss doesn't look that great, but it would take balls of steel to buy more EPIC, so they rarely buy.'

He threw down a crushed napkin. Fork in the bowl. Bottles empty. Finished in every sense.

'They could complain. They could claim that Steens were negligent and misrepresented the merits of the investment in EPIC to them. At the end of the day that would depend on what was said in the prospectus that was given to the potential investors. The EPIC prospectus will be full of legal disclaimers, making it clear that it was a high-risk venture. Once that disclosure is made, we are covered. Unless there is some seriously misleading information in the prospectus, which is highly unlikely. We have lawyers who crawl over every word to make sure that it's watertight and won't come back to haunt us. They cost us a fortune but

74

they are our insurance policy against some pushy investor.'

'So basically, as an investor I'm screwed?' Anthony asked.

'Yes. There are only two breakeven ways out of EPIC if you are an investor. First, Steens might take a view that the issue which was syndicated by us has been unsatisfactorily managed, and might decide to repay the original subscription moneys to the investors, even with interest included. We would just take the loss on our own books.'

'Is that likely?'

'It's very rare. I don't think it has ever happened in Steens, but it has been done in other, lesser City banks. They get all the clients to sign legally binding confidentiality letters so that no one can talk about it officially. It might happen if the investors in question were big punters who gave us a lot of business, and we didn't want to sour our relationship with them. We could make our loss back in extra commission income from them over time, if we kept them as clients.'

'And the second way?'

'Clients might threaten legal action against us. We wouldn't want a big court case and all the adverse publicity, so we might do a compromise deal out of court before it hits the press. In this business, our reputation is everything. Steens has an excellent reputation in looking after the best interest of the clients and we want to keep it that way.'

Dave considered the next line carefully. 'Ah. Third choice. You could go out and kill a director of the bank who sold you the deal. You wouldn't get your money back, but you might feel a damn sight happier afterwards.'

Not funny, Dave. Keep this conversation serious.

'Who is behind EPIC? It's not really a company, is it? More like an investment fund.'

'Correct. It's different from most of our issues. Like, say, SCISCO is a company producing steel in China, with a workforce, a factory, customers, stocks and the rest, but EPIC is a closed-end fund. It just raises money and the appointed directors of EPIC decide where to invest the money, with the advice of some specialist property advisers. The directors just convert cash into property and then sit back and wait for the market to develop. The investor relies a lot on the fund directors doing a good job.'

'So where is the fund operated from?'

'It's run from our Frankfurt office. That's our biggest Steens office nearest to Eastern Europe, so it made sense to base it there. All the paperwork is kept there too. Some boring bean-counter called Wilhelm Gausselmann does all the admin work. Every detail you need to know will be in the issue prospectus. And I got a copy of it for you.'

Dave handed over the prospectus. It looked impressive, gold lettering on the front, quality thick paper inside, flash typeface and colour pictures of capital cities overlaid on a map of Eastern Europe. More impressive than the laminated lunch menu at the Flute.

'That's another lesson you should learn,' advised Dave. 'The more impressive the prospectus, the more cautious you should be. Read it and come back to me if you want.'

Dave caught the eye of a passing waitress and gave the internationally recognised mime. Open

76

left hand poised and imitation writing with the right hand. He needed the bill.

'It's been a real education, Dave.'

Dave put two twenties under the empty pasta bowl. It was too much, but did he care? They smiled at their Aussie waitress by the door. Dave made an unwarranted discreet comment about how she filled her pair of black 501s. Anthony agreed but didn't say much more. He had other love interests. They walked back across Broadgate Circle, towards the familiarity and sanctity of Steens' offices. Two model citizens of the City earning half a million pounds between them. Only Dave earned ninety per cent of it. Pity.

'Tony, any more word from the cops on Walker's death?'

'No. Palmer left our office hours ago.'

'If the police tell you who killed Walker, then let me know immediately.'

'Why are you so interested in all this?'

'There's big money at stake.'

Was that all? Another joke? A broad grin from the head of the syndicate desk.

'I'm running a book here for the most likely suspects. I have to know first so I can rip off the others. My money's on someone in Steens. The other guys think that a client probably did him after Walker took all that commission from them over the years, or someone in another City bank. Someone asked whether Walker had any enemies, and then others asked whether he had any friends even? One salesman wants a bet on his ex, Sylvia, in Hong Kong, who will surely get part of his massive inheritance and must hate his guts anyway. I'll put you down as a hundred-to-one shot seeing as you are now involved. No, on second thoughts, I'll make you fifty to one. Meeting the old bill on day one must shorten your odds considerably.'

'I'm honoured even to be considered, Dave.'

'No problem. I gotta get back to checking the paperwork and fees today for SCISCO. In ten days' time we have to receive four hundred million dollars from our clients and pay over three ninety-two mill to SCISCO. If this money actually gets throughout the archaic Chinese banking system on-time and to the correct bank accounts, it'll be a miracle, but it must. Otherwise my enormous year-end bonus may not be so enormous!'

He wasn't joking. Dave would be on close to a two-hundred-thousand-pound salary with a bonus of maybe another one hundred per cent, if he were there at the end of April on bonus day. It was only a matter of weeks to go to bonus payday. The prospect of an extra two hundred grand in your April payslip. Nice. There was no reason why he would not be here, not unless some major disaster happened in Steens between now and that golden day. Unlikely in an investment bank with the pedigree, history and financial clout of Steens.

*   *   *

The City of London visibly salivated about bonuses between 1 January and 31 December. The serious business was done between January and March. In the second quarter they suffered from fatigue. The third quarter was holiday time, when the markets were too quiet to make a killing. The fourth quarter was the wind-down period. With the year end in December, paying the bonus as late as possible meant that no one left Steens in the first quarter of the year, not unless they were seriously mentally challenged.

This year was going to be a good year at Steens. They all knew that. Equity and bond markets had risen significantly so their traders and market makers must have made a shed full of money. Secondary market volumes had been at record levels all year so their agency commissions would be high. Buoyant markets had led to a stream of primary-market issues, which brought in sizeable fees, just as EPIC and SCISCO had.

When the times were good, they were very good. It was a case of another day, another City millionaire. It was difficult to have a drink in the Flute wine bar across from the office without hearing about someone who was about to receive a typed piece of bank memorandum paper from their boss with several glorious noughts written on it.

Now it was fast approaching the moment of truth, where the fortunate were told exactly how much they would receive at the next month end. Some investment banks paid out in March, but Steens paid out on the last Friday of April, a day that was indelibly engraved in the minds of every single employee. When the City bonuses were announced there was the usual biased diatribe in the press as sensational stories of top packages were selectively leaked to the media, and were then comprehensively denied by every managing director and head of human resources.

Paying the biggest bonuses in the City was not the most important factor. It was more important that everyone in the City *thought* that you paid the biggest bonuses. That attracted the talent from the competitors. There were those prudential moral guardians who said that paying half a million pounds to a trader in his mid-twenties was not right. People in Steens just thought that it was not wrong. Subtle difference.

Steens and other comparable City institutions were not well-managed companies. Money was the only form of measurement that they knew. At Steens you either made money or you lost money or you broke even. If you made money you were God. If you lost money you were toast. If you broke even you were on probation. Sir James and the directors of Steens didn't know how to reward staff in any way except by monetary gratification, and so they paid them better every year. And they all knew that no matter what happened, the bonus would always be more than the previous year. That was the benchmark. If they paid less, then the talent walked. No one ever dared to lower the delicately poised bar.

More money could be earned by annually blackmailing the banks. If they didn't get enough loot then the dealers exited one evening and joined a German or Japanese or American investment bank across the road next day for even more loot. It was a magic roundabout, and they loved getting on and off. Job security was never an issue. Every time they moved they received golden hellos and signing-on fees that would have been the envy of any Premiership star striker. They were as mobile as their GSM telephones.

Salaries and bonuses were also rising throughout the City due to the increased inter-bank rivalry. Large foreign banks were desperate to grow their investment banking business, where the historic return on capital was treble the return on their existing commercial and retail banking business. It would take them years to grow organically so instead they went out and poached staff *en masse* from competitors, sometimes hiring whole teams of salesmen or traders. The record was a Latin American sales and research team of seventy-eight poached from rival US bank Mitchell Leonberg Inc. by an aspiring regional German bank.

The banks were fighting for a place in the future of investment banking. It was the end game of the industry where a small number of players were consolidating their global positions. Steens would be there without a doubt. So would Mitchell Leonberg, and so would a few of the European banks. The rest had no future in the major league, and in the intervening period relied on gazumping other remuneration packages to maintain some mediocre market share and stave off their ultimate demise. In the meantime the finite number of experts who worked in the City had never had it so good as their skills were bid up on a daily basis by the banks with bottomless pockets.

These excesses of remuneration led to excesses of expenditure in turn. Dealers and salesmen didn't have just one home, they had an apartment in Central London, a weekend retreat on the South Coast and a summertime villa somewhere adjacent to the Mediterranean. Their homes had everything they needed, Jacuzzis and saunas, designer kitchens, manicured gardens and, most important of all, staff. They didn't have just one holiday per year, they had a week's skiing in the Alps, two weeks' tropical sunshine in the Seychelles or Nassau, romantic weekends in timeless Paris or bohemian Prague, shopping trips to Fifth Avenue or Milan, and countless English country weekends to join shooting parties, county hunts, hot-air balloonists or gourmet culinary experiences. They didn't have just one car, they had a sporty German coupé, a four-wheel drive off-roader and a spacious family saloon, with at least one set of personalised registration plates courtesy of the civil servants in the DVLA in Swansea.

The beneficial monetary effects of their wonderful industry were not confined just to the City. There was a trickle-down effect to the rest of London, even to the rest of South-East England. Turnover at the Flute rocketed at this time of the year, and they were regularly sold out of Moët & Chandon, Laurent-Perrier, Dom Perignon, Taittinger, Krug, Bollinger, Lanson and Pommery. In times of such emergency the players from Steens were even known to drink poo from Veuve Clicquot and Louis Roederer and other allegedly lesser names.

The designer fashion shops around Broadgate Circle enjoyed the boom. Vanessa did her own little bit to help them out on her addictive lunchtime shopping trips. Ultimately the effect reached the prime London property market as bulge-bracket bonus-bloated big-shot bankers went looking for houses in Hampstead, Chelsea and Holland Park. Then it tackled on to the residential stockbroker belts of Surrey and Hertfordshire and then on to the country houses and estates. These City buyers didn't need to worry about a mortgage. They were cash buyers up to seven-figure amounts. Sold.

There were few dealers and salesmen over forty years old still working in Steens. There was no need to work after years of annual corporate generosity. They didn't need the money any more, and, more important, they didn't need the pressure and the long hours. No one could work at that pace until their official retirement at sixty years of age. They got out with their sanity intact and their bank balances swelled out of all proportion to reality.

They bought residential property and lived off the rental income. They watched their wisely accumulated equity investments pay them dividends many times over. They drank wine from the carefully selected stocks laid down over the years in rented cellars. They collected classic cars and raced them at Silverstone and Brands Hatch. The more adventurous did what they always wanted to do: bought thoroughbred racehorses and stud farms, moved to live in picturesque cottages in Normandy or Tuscany, sailed fifty-footers around the Caribbean or the Great Barrier Reef. Such wealth. Something that Anthony could as yet only dream about.

*   *   *

Wealth mattered more so when you never had any. Anthony blamed Austin Thomas, a banker thirty-one years his elder, someone whom he had never even met. A man who was a close personal friend and a trusted work colleague of his father, Ted Carlton, that unrewarded and recently retired assistant bank manager of the Northwold branch in deepest rural Surrey. It all had been so unfair.

The financially secure world of the young Carlton family began to crumble when a widowed pensioner arrived in the Northwold branch one

Monday morning. She asked to withdraw five thousand pounds in cash from her deposit account to present to her brickie grandson who was about to step on to a long-haul Quantas flight and a new emigrant life in Sydney. She specifically asked for her regular contact at the branch, that very nice polite man she always spoke to, one Austin Thomas.

Then total surprise, because Austin wasn't at work that morning. But he was always there, without fail, she insisted. The bank investigators discovered later that Austin had succumbed to a bout of severe gastroenteritis and hadn't the energy to crawl from his sickbed, let alone make it down the high street to his regular place of work behind the bullet-proof cashiers' window in the branch. It was one of the very few unplanned absences that he had experienced in his nine years of service in the Northwold branch.

The alternative junior cashier, in her first month of real work with the bank, was puzzled. The pensioner in front of her had a deposit book written up over the past six years by Austin Thomas. It proved that she had twenty-six thousand pounds on deposit. Yet the ever-reliable head office mainframe computer showed a balance enquiry screen with only four hundred and twenty pounds in the account. The pensioner was adamant. Then more vocal. She wanted her money now. Austin Thomas never queried her like this. She wanted someone in charge. Call the manager. Call Ted Carlton.

Anthony's father knew as soon as he saw the paperwork. It was a recipe for disaster. One bank employee with sole control over an account owned by an aged customer who couldn't read the small print of the annual computer-generated statements that arrived in the post, and so left them unopened on her mantlepiece. She preferred the personal touch from Austin Thomas and his verbal assurances that all her savings were safe with him. Personally. Only no one knew now where her alleged funds were.

Ted Carlton telephoned Austin Thomas at home. It was a mistake. Austin would explain all tomorrow. Only he never did so. A courting couple spotted his Ford estate parked in a lay-by that same evening. The grey smoke inside the car puzzled them both. The policeman identified the lead oxide in the air immediately. He didn't need to see the coiled vacuum hose on the exhaust pipe that ran into the closed rear window of the car. Austin Thomas never did return to work in Northwold.

The auditors from regional head office uncovered the appalling facts. Twenty-two accounts defrauded by Austin Thomas, over two hundred thousand pounds embezzled in five years. Mostly from retired folk with cash savings, all now puzzled at the discrepancy in their accounts. Word spread in Northwold. Queues of worried OAPs lined up before the nine o'clock opening time each morning. There was never a scandal like this ever before in the sleepy village. The *Northwold Bugle* ran the story every day for a month.

Then there were the customer loans, all authorised by Austin Thomas in his capacity as junior lending officer with a delegated lending limit of thirty thousand pounds from Ted Carlton. Car loans to young professionals, university tuition loans to students, furniture loans to first-time house buyers, working capital loans to start-up businesses. But there was no paperwork, no agreements, no files and no one willing to repay the fictitious loans, including the deceased ex-employee in the rear seat of the poisoned Ford estate.

Where did all the money go? Austin Thomas's wife and his three young children never knew. He successfully hid his gambling addiction from them for years, stopping off in out-of-town bookies on weekdays to play the sport of kings, taking trips to London to visit Victoria's seedy casinos, even playing poker with East End criminals in after-hours dens in Dagenham and Rainham at a grand a hand. Austin just lost too often.

It was never the same in the Carlton household after the incident. That's what they still called it in the family. An incident. Understatement of the year. Anthony's father never wanted to talk about how their friend committed suicide, how a trusted colleague betrayed them all, how the bank blamed Ted Carlton for allowing the fraud to happen, how he was demoted to assistant manager, how he never got another promotion in sixteen further years of loyal service, how the bank took back their company car, how there was never enough cash to enjoy a fuller life. All because of one black mark on the debit side of life's ledger.

It was difficult, too, for a twelve-year-old such as Anthony. Hard to explain to distraught Mark Thomas, just one year behind Anthony in the local comprehensive, how his father was not responsible for the death in the Ford estate. But Anthony had learned a lesson. Never to take people at face value, even when they are trusted colleagues.

Always independently check out the warning signs, however apparently insignificant they might seem. Never to suffer those same adverse consequences as Ted Carlton.

*   *   *

Anthony saw that the Footsie had regained ten points of the morning's loss. Another few hundred million of market capitalisation had been recovered. It was a volatile business. He looked at the glossy EPIC prospectus in his office. Photographs of office buildings, hotels and leisure complexes were superimposed on a map of Eastern and Central Europe. The name of the company was written in gold lettering, with the enticing slogan about an opportunity to avail of outstanding property investment opportunities. Steens' logo was on the bottom of the cover. The prospectus looked good all round. It was very impressive. If Dave's rule of thumb was anything to go by, this in itself should be a warning sign to any potential investor.

The first page after the contents page was a short history lesson about the collapse of Communism in East Germany, Poland, the Czech Republic, Slovakia, Hungary, Romania and other countries. The piece went on about the economic growth that was forecast for the years ahead, and how the economies were ravaged under years of misrule and bureaucracy. It continued about the opportunities that this gave to Western investors. Property could be bought at realistic prices.

Anthony took this to mean that it was cheap, really cheap. It forecast good demand for

87

commercial premises as Western firms moved into the East to exploit the markets after years of bureaucratic exclusion. It forecast rising rentals and property prices and growing tourism in the area, but stated that there were an insufficient number of hotels and leisure facilities. Property was always a safe investment. Too good to be true, thought Anthony, so it probably was. Dave's second rule of thumb. EPIC was a big issue. Fifty million dollars was a lot of money to invest and a lot of money to lose.

As he paged through the text again, his eyes came to rest on the inside front cover. He focused on a name that he recognised. He hadn't noticed it before. There was an alphabetical list of the directors and advisers of the EPIC fund. The company secretary was named as Jeremy Walker, a director of investment bank Steen Odenberg & Co.

What was Walker's involvement in all this? Whatever Walker may have been up to, Anthony was determined to ensure that it did not affect the reputation of Steens, their most priceless asset in the world of investment banking. Time for action. A telephone call to Derek Masterson.

'Derek, I'm going to the Amsterdam office tomorrow.'

'Why?'

'D-S Palmer wants me to. Walker had some letters in his office.'

'What sort of letters?'

There was no easy way to break the news to a director. Well, tactfully at least. 'Client letters of complaint.'

'Who from?'

No need to mention NedCorp yet. 'Some private

clients.'

Derek saw the light. 'Cranky private clients, no doubt. Wasting our time. Sure. Go over there. Let Johan know first, though. And what about your Singapore trip? What's the outcome of your review of the office there?'

'It's OK. Clean bill of health all round.'

'Really? Excellent. We don't want any trouble with the regulators out there ever. Don't mess with the MAS. That's what they say. Give me your draft report on the office by the end of the week. No later.'

He hung up and walked outside. Anthony leaned dangerously close to Vanessa at her desk. That perfume did wonders for him. 'Can you book me on the first BA flight to Amsterdam tomorrow morning, coming back at, say, six or seven p.m.? Can you get me a few hundred guilders in cash for the trip and send a fax to Johan Verhoeven there? Let him know I'll be there for the day.'

'Certainly, Tony. Lucky you. Nice trip on the company.' She glanced around the office. No sign of Gary or anyone else. 'Anything else I can do for you? Like, say, this evening?'

She had an insatiable appetite. Anthony's missed alibi was keen to visit Maida Vale.

*　　　*　　　*

Anthony stood again in a crowded tube carriage heading northwards. On this occasion he threw thirty pence at a vendor for an *Evening Standard*. They knew how to write a bestselling headline. Usually they went for a guaranteed commuter story like MORTGAGE RATES HIKE FEARED or

BALLOT CALLED FOR TUBE STRIKE or BILLIONS WIPED OFF SHARE PRICES. Today's headline was different but still attention-grabbing. QUEEN'S MONEY MAN MURDERED.

Some hack at the *Standard* had dug out a royal connection that was actually true. Steens' asset management division managed a few billion of the Queen's enormous liquid wealth. She was the most private of all their private clients. So Jeremy Walker was loosely connected to the Queen as a director of Steens. Big deal. Everyone in the City managed some of the Queen's wealth. God knows, there was enough of it to go around.

Anthony read the front-page story, conscious of the others in the carriage who took the opportunity for a free read. He tried to look uninterested in case they deduced that he worked at this great institution currently plastered on the front page of every newspaper.

'City of London police are investigating the suspicious death of a leading banker in his Docklands home. Jeremy Walker, 49, was found early this morning at his Wapping apartment after local residents contacted the police. A spokesman would not disclose the cause of death while they awaited the results of a post-mortem but did not rule out murder. Mr Walker was director of compliance at leading City investment bank, Steen Odenberg & Co., where he was believed to earn in excess of £200,000 per annum.'

A journalist called Jennifer Sharpe had penned the piece. Never heard of her. Yet.

CHAPTER SIX

6.00 A.M.: TUESDAY 19 MARCH: MAIDA VALE, LONDON W9, TO AMSTERDAM

Anthony rolled over in his king-size bed and admired Vanessa's form as she slept facing him. Her auburn hair lay across the pillow, a natural smile played on her full lips and up close her complexion was unblemished. Tanned bare shoulders protruded over the edge of the white cotton sheets. Anthony enjoyed it when she stayed over and this was Tuesday morning. It wasn't even the weekend.

Since they had discovered each other at the Steens' black-tie Christmas party in the Savoy Hotel just three months ago, Anthony had been unable to get Vanessa out of his mind. As time passed he thought that he would discover too much about her, which in turn would lessen that initial attraction. Anthony was a critical person by nature—it was his job—but he was beginning to think that Vanessa was just about faultless. The only difficulty was waiting until the right moment to tell their colleagues in Steens. Gary would love to know. Until then it was their mutual secret.

Vanessa was amazing. He was so lucky to know her. He could have spent years looking for someone as special, someone to spoil rotten and to take care of. There could have been wasted years of eyeing up girls walking across Broadgate Circle, drinking champers in the Flute, window-shopping on Regent Street, clubbing in the West End, playing tennis in Paddington Sports Club, pressing against him in overcrowded tube trains. Yet he would never have discovered someone like Vanessa. She had been sitting just ten feet away from his desk in Steens. Amazing good fortune.

The alarm on the bedside clock radio had not disturbed her. Anthony had hit the snooze button just in time, then slid out of bed and subconsciously walked to the bathroom with a fresh bath towel. He had D-S Palmer to thank for the necessity of rising at this antisocial hour and the resultant missed opportunity to spend an extra hour lying flesh to flesh with his tactile colleague. Pity Vanessa hadn't been round on Sunday evening. She would have been a good alibi for Walker's death, if in fact he ever actually needed one for D-S Palmer.

The hot water revived him immediately, and he let it pour down for several minutes as he faced the polished chrome showerhead. A power-shower was the only way to wake up. He went directly to the kitchen. It was ten-past six already and he was on a tight schedule. He keyed in the telephone number that he knew too well. The reply was instant.

'Maida Vale Cabs.'

'A car for Heathrow please. Six-thirty. Pick up at 77 Clyde Mansions.'

'That's for Mr Carlton, isn't it?'

Anthony was using this mini-cab firm too frequently, the result of too many trips to Heathrow on Steens' business. He had a bowl of cereal for the carbohydrates, a glass of fresh orange juice for the vitamin C, a banana for the slowly measured release of energy and vanilla yoghurt to finally cleanse the palate. No time for making decent coffee. He never understood people who skipped breakfast.

He'd bought this apartment only a few years ago when the previous unfortunate resident defaulted on his mortgage payments and the mortgage company repossessed it. It was a sign of living in London in the late 1990s. Some thought that buying a repossessed home was morally wrong, but Anthony just wanted one that wasn't possessed by anyone, except by himself. He was mortgaged to the hilt but still had the apartment completely renovated, replumbed, rewired and recarpeted by a little man engaged full-time on the work in hand and also on claiming his social security benefit. Anthony paid cash, but not much and reluctantly.

The apartment was too big for just one person to live in, but he liked the space. A bright airy kitchen, large lounge, bathroom and three bedrooms. One bedroom was for friends and family visitors. One was his study, with books, a PC, hi-fi and walls covered with photographs from his travels to the capitals of the world. And Giza, the Taj Mahal, Bermuda, Sydney Harbour. And one bedroom was for the king-size bed and someone like Vanessa. No. Definitely for Vanessa. No one else came close.

The door of the bedroom wardrobe creaked as he closed it. Vanessa stirred and opened her eyes slowly and raised her head in his direction. 'God. That was good, Tony Carlton. That was better than that night after the Savoy Hotel. Our first time. And that night of après-ski in the snow. I'm absolutely wasted.'

'Well, isn't that what you wanted, Vanessa?'

'Isn't that what we both wanted?'

It had been some night. Starting off with a

lingering soak for two in the oversized bath, Vanessa lying behind Anthony as she ran long fingers and warm soapy water down his chest. Then straight to the king-size where he lay face-down as she voluntarily massaged his back muscles with aromatic oils bought in Singapore. Then she rolled him over, face up on the bed and sat astride him. She eased downward in the climactic communion of two aroused bodies and arched backwards until they collapsed in mutual exhaustion. If the apartment walls weren't so well built, the neighbours would have surely complained about the noise.

Vanessa stretched out her slender arms and yawned, sat up fully in the bed, her breasts rising over the edge of the crisp sheets.

'You're not decent, Vanessa.'

'I know. I never am. That's why you like me. Isn't it?'

Six twenty-five am. He checked the essentials. PMT. Passport, money, ticket. He took a tie from the wardrobe, the same Hermès tie from yesterday, his favourite. No one today would know that he had worn it for two consecutive days. It was intertwined with some of Vanessa's many fashion accessories, belts and scarves and wraps. She was leaving more in his flat than ever before. Definitely a good sign for their future but still confusing all the same. 'Vanessa, you've got a lot of stuff in here,' he said, pointing to the bottom drawers in the wardrobe.

'I know. I'm losing things. That Gucci scarf with the foxhunting scenes. I was looking for it yesterday. It's not here and not in my flat. It's expensive. I must have left it somewhere and now it's gone for good.'

More shopping gone AWOL. Anthony knew the scarf she was talking about, so politically incorrect in the current climate. He leaned over to kiss Vanessa. She pulled him closer. Curiosity got the better of her. 'What's up in Amsterdam?'

'I can't talk shop at this hour of the morning, Vanessa.'

'Go on. Why are you going over?'

'Just some loose ends to tidy up.'

'Is it to do with Walker's death? Is that why you're going over at such short notice?'

'It's sort of related to Walker. But don't worry about it. Go back to sleep.'

The communal downstairs doorbell rang.

'I've got to go, Vanessa. I think I love you.'

'And I might too. Have a good trip. Bring me back some tulips.'

He stood in the door of the bedroom for a lingering look. The doorbell sounded again.

'Tony, do you feel that I'm using you for sex?'

'Vanessa, I hope so.'

*   *   *

An F-registration Ford Sierra was parked outside with the giveaway sign of a mini-cab, that second aerial fixed to the boot. There was no conversation as they headed down Edgware Road and into Park Lane, past the wealth of London residing to the left, in Mayfair, Belgravia and Grosvenor Square. Park Lane symbolised the ultimate lifestyle to which they all aspired. Car showrooms dazzled with gleaming BMWs, Lexus, Daimlers and Jaguars.

They passed the Dorchester, the Hilton and the

95

InterContinental, never frequented by Londoners, just for visiting businessmen on expense accounts and wealthy American tourists with more dollars than sense. On the other side of Park Lane, Anthony saw a sole horserider in Hyde Park cantering around the earthy bridle path. He imagined the luxury of owning a horse in Central London.

They travelled west along Cromwell Road and finally on to the M4. The traffic was solid coming the other way towards the heart of Central London. There was a newspaper on the back seat of the car. Anthony ignored it. He never read while in a car. He suffered from carsickness, something the Americans quaintly called motion discomfort. He just looked at the world outside, on the all-too-familiar route to LHR.

They passed the giant model of Concorde guarding the tunnel approach to the terminals. Some day he would get to travel on this speedbird. There were deal-hungry corporate financiers at Steens who flew Concorde, but not many. Most abused the privilege; they would delay booking their usual flight and then just have to book Concorde at short notice to get to that Wall Street meeting on time. Some were known to fly over and back on the same day just for a two-hour face-to-face meeting with some head honcho of a NYSE listed company. The outrageous three-thousand-pound fare was passed on to a corporate client, so Steens didn't care about the British Airways extortion, and it melted into insignificance compared with a multimillion-pound deal fee.

All British Airways flights to Amsterdam left from Terminal 4. Anthony had heard of the poor foreigner who just assumed all BA flights to Europe go from Terminal 1. Not so, and not something you want to find out when you are standing bewildered in the concourse of Terminal 1 with thirty minutes to go for your Amsterdam flight. Perhaps BA was keen to keep it a secret from the unsuspecting public? It was ten-past seven now and the flight was in thirty-five minutes. Good timing. Anthony disliked missing flights, but he equally disliked killing time.

It wasn't worth going to the Executive Club Lounge with so little time before boarding. Harrods wasn't open yet. If you travelled once a year, the duty-free shops were an opportunity for some cheap shopping. If you travelled as often as Anthony did, you lost interest in duty-free. In any case, Anthony didn't smoke, didn't drink spirits and there was only so much Fahrenheit aftershave that he could get through in a year. He would buy something really special for Vanessa at Schiphol on the way back, and maybe even those tulips as well. He sat at the terminal window looking outside at the planes on the apron, still too early and grey outside. At times like this, the pseudo-glamorous life of the international jet-setting businessman wasn't all that it was supposed to be.

There was a crowd waiting to board BA174. Anthony could identify the Dutch immediately, those passengers with manicured hands and long groomed hair, dressed in carefully coordinated pastel-coloured jackets. And that was just the men. There were also the excessively earnest business passengers trying to carry on four pieces of oversized hand baggage. Eventually the BA stewardess would put three pieces of luggage down the airside chute for storage in the plane's hold, and would sour the relationship between the passenger and allegedly the world's favourite airline.

Anthony was fortuitously seated in Club Class. Steens' people just didn't do economy class. They knew it by other names: cannelloni class or steerage. Initially he declined the offer of a complimentary newspaper. Then he thought about the recent death at Steens and asked for *The Times*. He was looking for only one item on the front page, but surprisingly there was no immediate mention of the late Jeremy Walker. He leafed through the paper quickly and found what he was looking for in a column on page seven, under the headline POLICE CONFIRM MURDER OF CITY BANKER.

'City of London police have confirmed that Steen Odenberg banker Jeremy Walker was murdered late on Sunday night. Police received the results of the post-mortem and also confirmed that they were following several definite lines of enquiry, but they have yet to establish a motive for the murder. Local sources in Wapping, where Mr Walker lived, said that there were no signs of a break-in at his apartment. Yesterday former bank colleagues expressed their regret at his death. The chairman of Steens, Sir James Devonshire, said that Mr Walker had worked at the bank for twenty-four years and had made an invaluable contribution in that time to the growth in global equities business at Steen Odenberg.' Not much new information to be had today in *The Times*. It was a relief of sorts. One seismic shock per week was enough for anyone.

Anthony declined the proffered pseudo-breakfast. He didn't need a second breakfast today. He watched the man in 3B beside him carefully remove the foil of his hot breakfast as if it might explode as he uncovered a sausage, bacon, tomato and mushrooms. Anthony got the impression that 3B was expecting more. 3B was a middle-aged guy in a dull three-piece suit. He wore thick glasses when boarding the plane, and had peered at the boarding card. Anthony guessed that now the glasses were off he couldn't possibly read what Anthony was about to read again. Steens' business was always confidential and should not be unnecessarily disclosed to anyone, including 3B.

Anthony took out the thin file with the five letters that Palmer had given him. He read the NedCorp letter first, the one that worried him the most. Anthony needed to find out more about their complaint about the European Property Investment Corporation. He glanced through the EPIC prospectus again. He had read the entire document yesterday, and at least he now knew of Walker's role as the company secretary of EPIC. Anthony wondered what Walker's duties had been.

He looked at the other four letters. Scholten's letter he knew well from weeks ago. He wondered how come he had received it in the internal mail in London. Faber's letter was similar, complaining about bad shares in his portfolio. Dr Smit's letter was very detailed but unfortunately quite factually uninformative. He must be retired if he had the time to write long letters like this. Mrs Mulder's letter was vaguely moving. She was a widowed pensioner and expected more from her investments made through Steens. None of these four clients mentioned any specific shares they bought. Only NedCorp had done so. Anthony wondered if any of the private clients were also investors in EPIC. He hoped not.

*   *   *

Anthony sensed the plane begin to descend, and like any experienced flyer he yawned deliberately to clear his ears. The Amsterdam suburbs below looked as uninviting as the Heathrow he had left behind for twelve hours. Soon he was inside Schiphol, which all things considered was a damned good airport. Boring, but efficient. He had no luggage for his day trip and walked straight through to the taxi rank, getting into a large Mercedes.

'130 Herengracht,' he requested of the surly driver.

The automatic purred along the motorway but was still unnerving. Anthony never got used to being driven on the wrong side of the road. Soon they neared the centre of Amsterdam, and the driver took a sharp turn down a narrow cobbled one-way street that ran parallel to one of the main canals. The best addresses were along three historical canals in Amsterdam, the Kaisergracht, the Prinsengracht and the Herengracht.

The narrow, badly cobbled street was lined with cars parked right alongside the canal. Cars often had to be recovered from the watery depths. The taxi driver dodged the badly parked vehicles and courteously facilitated some slow cyclists ahead. They pulled up by a highly polished brass plate outside an impressive office that confirmed to all visitors that this was Steen Odenberg NV. It was important for every investment bank to have a good office location, to send the right message of reassuring affluence to clients.

'I'm Anthony Carlton from the London Control Group. Mr Verhoeven is expecting me.'

The receptionist asked him to take a seat for a moment. She was somewhat unfriendly. Maybe she deduced that Anthony was here to check up on the office? She knew what the Control Group did.

'Mr Verhoeven will see you immediately.'

Now was the time to call on all of Anthony's experience. Verhoeven had been managing director of the Amsterdam office for more than ten years. He was a big player among players. A native of this city, Verhoeven joined Steens in London as a graduate trainee and rose up the ranks at the European sales desk in London. When the top job in the Amsterdam office became available, he returned home to take it. Verhoeven knew everyone in the Amsterdam business world, and since his arrival the office had prospered. He had attracted new institutional clients like NedCorp, and lots of wealthy private individuals. More recently he had been elevated to the board of Steens and became the director for Europe, an immensely powerful position.

Verhoeven also had a negative side. Anthony had met him only briefly once before, but he knew his reputation much better. Verhoeven was smooth, a good talker, polished, confident, a persuasive salesman and an even better investment banker, but with a reputation for turning aggressive if the occasion so warranted. This might be one such occasion. Interrogating a director could be a career-limiting move if he went too far. A subtle conversation was a better alternative.

Verboeven was sitting casually in his shirtsleeves behind a modern light wood desk He looked relaxed, at ease in his own domain, and made steady eye contact with Anthony. A picture of confidence and apparent geniality. Crisp cotton shirt and pastel tie. More Dutch than City. Sallow skin. Sharp features. He ran a hand through his combed-back blondish hair. Then immediately stood up to reveal six foot of an athlete's body with a leanness that belied his age and excessive lifestyle. A natural smile. Salesman's mode.

'Good to see you again, Anthony.'

A surprisingly enthusiastic greeting. Verhoeven must have a good memory of their one prior meeting. He spoke good English, but there was an underlying guttural Dutch accent.

'Likewise,' Anthony acknowledged with a firm handshake.

Verhoeven seized the initiative like any good investment banker. 'The news about Jeremy's death at the weekend was terrible. I heard yesterday morning when Sir James telephoned me from London.'

'It was terrible indeed. Quite a shock to us all.'

Verhoeven was on first-name terms with Walker, but then they had been fellow directors for a long time. Anthony didn't know how to address his chief suspect. Johan was too informal, and he didn't feel like addressing him as Mr Verhoeven or sir. He skipped the salutation. 'You must have known Jeremy well?'

As soon as Anthony asked this question, he wished that he hadn't bothered. It was just the sort of question that D-S Palmer would innocently ask.

'We worked together a lot over the years, including some of the same deals.'

EPIC was surely one such deal, but he hadn't the courage to mention that just yet. Events of the prior day went through Anthony's mind.

'I gather that most of the directors were in London yesterday for a big new issue launch. I thought that you might have been there.'

Verhoeven reacted at the mention of the South China issue. 'I heard that SCISCO went well, but there wasn't much interest here from clients in Amsterdam so I didn't think it was worth the day trip to London. In any case, I was out at an important meeting with a major client first thing yesterday morning.'

Verhoeven didn't mention the name of the client. But who could be more major than NedCorp? Verhoeven continued: 'I was a bit surprised when I heard that you were coming over here. I thought the sad events in London would take precedence over any of your work. Your visit is connected to Walker's death? It's also very short notice to give us here.'

Verhoeven's imagination was running riot, but was somewhat accurate none the less. Verhoeven was scoring points early on.

Anthony countered. 'That's the nature of working in the Control Group. I often never know what's coming up until a day beforehand.'

No need to alarm Verhoeven too much in the first few minutes. He had to play Verhoeven like you played a fish on the end of a line. Verhoeven poured two small coffees and gave one to Anthony. He just assumed that he wanted coffee. It was typically strong Dutch coffee, and it was lethal.

'So what can I do for you today? It is just today, isn't it?' Verhoeven looked anxious.

'Yes, I've got a flight back this evening. We've been looking in London at some new issues that Steens has done over the past few years. One of them was partly sold by the Amsterdam office. It's called EPIC. Do you recall it?'

'I do. It's not one of Steens' greatest issues.'

Anthony said nothing but waited for Verhoeven. The art of a good interviewing technique was to wait, let the silence take over and let Verhoeven dig a hole for himself. Anthony had presented him with a large shovel, and he didn't see how Verhoeven could improve an issue like EPIC, but the Dutchman gave it a damn good try.

'It's a simply brilliant company.' There was only one way to go from an opening statement like that. Downwards. 'They have a wonderful commercial property plan for Eastern Europe, but the property development is taking longer than expected.'

'I know a bit about the current status of EPIC.'

'Like what?'

'Like the recent share price performance.'

'Oh, that's temporary. All the investors know that. This was never meant to be a quick easy buck for them. They have to be there for the longer term. If they want to sell out now, they will have to get a bit less for their shares than they originally paid for them.'

'Like four dollars ten for a ten-dollar investment per share.'

Verhoeven frowned for the first time that morning. His fist was clenched as he rested it on the side of the chair. The other hand was stroking his jaw, partially covering his face. A bad sign.

Guilt? A single pointed finger emerged from the clenched fist. In the definite direction of Anthony. Time to go on the offensive.

'We bring investors lots of great investment ideas and they make a pile of money from them. There is always going to be the odd under-performer in the short term, but some of these people can't even take one loss, and then they start bitching about it.' Verhoeven was beginning to show his true colours. 'In any case, it's not as if it's their own money. These big institutions just handle pension-fund and investment-trust moneys for clients. The ultimate loser is the average man in the street who might lose a few bucks. It's so small at that level that it doesn't matter to anyone.'

'So all the investors in EPIC are large institutional investors, no private clients?'

'It wouldn't be an appropriate investment for private clients.'

'Are NedCorp a big shareholder in EPIC?'

Verhoeven gave him a knowing look, as if he knew Anthony had the answer himself. 'Yes, they are the single biggest investor, with one million shares.'

Jesus, thought Anthony. NedCorp had twenty per cent of the entire issue. At ten bucks each, they had ten million dollars riding on property development in the far-flung corners of Eastern Europe. They had taken a bath. Just like Anthony and Vanessa had last night, but so much more expensive. They were down at least six million dollars. Anthony didn't wish to push Verhoeven too hard on EPIC yet, not at least until he had more to go on, and that would come later. He wanted to keep Verhoeven guessing. 'I want to review the files of some private clients here.'

'What do you want to do that for?'

'It's just routine.'

It was another standard police response. Thanks, Palmer.

'Well, it's not routine as far as I am concerned. Private clients want to keep their affairs private. They don't want people investigating their dealings.'

Verhoeven was getting difficult. Time to up the ante. 'You might be aware that clients complained in writing about their accounts here.'

Verhoeven scowled back. This was becoming ugly. 'Which clients? What's their problem?'

'They are complaining about poor investment performance.'

'That's just typical. Some of these people are never happy. I'll sort it out for you.'

'That's not the way the bank handles written complaints.'

Verhoeven looked resigned. He had been at Steens long enough to know the protocol. 'I know the procedure. If we get a complaint, then we send it to Compliance in London. We would send it to—' He paused and reflected—'Well, we would have sent it to Jeremy Walker, but not any more, I guess. What do you want to do?'

'I want to look at the contract notes, statements and any correspondence.'

'I'll get the files for you. Tell me who they are.'

Verhoeven was making a play for the other client names. Anthony was not falling for it. If he gave him the names, Verhoeven could collect their files and could be gone for a while. Anything interesting could be removed from the files.

'I'd prefer to get the files myself.'

'This is way over the top for a few shitty complaints.'

Verhoeven's English was so good that he even knew the required swearwords. The two men sat in silence as Anthony wondered if he had gone too far or if Verhoeven would yield. His request was standard bank practice. The rules applied to everyone, including the directors. Verhoeven knew it too.

'OK. Look at any bloody client file you want.'

Verhoeven buzzed the intercom and a smart secretary in a white silk blouse and well-tailored black culottes entered. An air of efficiency accompanied her presence in the room.

'Anne, take Mr Carlton to the filing-room, and get him an office somewhere nearby.'

She acknowledged Anthony. Nice face too. Hair tied back in a neat ponytail and perfectly applied make-up without overdoing it. He recognised her. Yes. Anne somebody. She had been here last time he visited.

'When will you be finished?' asked Verhoeven.

'Early this afternoon, I expect.'

'Unfortunately, I have a lunch engagement at 12.30. Otherwise we could have had lunch.'

Anthony thought this was a hollow invitation that he was glad not to accept 'I'll go out for something to eat instead.'

'I'll get something ordered in for you,' offered Verhoeven.

Anthony thought he should test it for poison first. 'That'll be fine.'

'I'll be out for the afternoon so, if I don't see you later, have a good flight home.'

107

Anthony got the impression that Verhoeven was hoping for a fatal airline crash somewhere over the North Sea.

*　　　*　　　*

Anthony and Anne Somebody went upstairs to a windowless room full of metal fireproof filing-cabinets. She unlocked each row of cabinets methodically.

'We've met before. Last time you were here. I'm Anne van Halle.'

That was her name. They got on well last time. Anne was organised, and it showed.

'The files are here in alphabetical order, A to Z this way, but there are no Zs.'

Anne was friendlier when Verhoeven wasn't around. If there were some sort of banking gold medal awarded for tolerance under enemy fire, she would have won it easily.

'And there is a spare office,' she said, pointing to a bright room along the corridor.

She left him in the filing-room, and he set about his task alphabetically. First Faber, then Mulder, Scholten and Smit. The NedCorp file was enormous, not surprisingly given the volume of business they did at Steens. He took the five buff files to his recently acquired office.

Anthony thumbed through the pink copies of contract notes. Every time a client of Steens anywhere in the world bought or sold securities, they got a contract note in the post next day. It told them exactly what security they had bought or sold, how many, the price and, most important for Steens, the commission charged on the transaction.

108

The contract notes also told Anthony in what capacity Steens had acted, either as an agent or principal, a crucial distinction in the securities business. As an agent, Steens had a duty to obtain the best price for the client and pass on exactly that same price to the client, nothing more and nothing less. These agency deals are always done with other brokers. Buy from the broker and sell to the client, or buy from the client and sell to the broker. Either way, Steens never owned the securities. They were just the agents in between the client and the market. Agency business was risk-free.

Anthony did not want to see a large number of contract notes. Private clients should not be in the market buying and selling every day. That was an abuse they called churning the client, a favourite trick of many salesmen in investment banks of a lesser standing as they turned over the client account just to make more commission. If a client sold shares and immediately bought other shares, then Steens made commission on both deals, but Steens only advised this when the market conditions dictated the need, or when a suitable opportunity arose for the transaction.

Anthony did not want to see private clients speculating in the short term. Steens' brokers in Amsterdam should be advising clients to hold securities for the longer term, buy blue chips and take the reliable dividend income and steady capital appreciation over time. That would suit these private clients, especially if they were investing their savings for later in life.

Most important was the monthly statement that all Steens' clients received, which showed their investments, how much they were worth and how they had performed in the period since their purchase. Faber's month-end statement showed he had about forty different securities, all Dutch. Faber had just under two million guilders in securities, a nice nest egg. Then he saw the EPIC shares. Faber owned two thousand of them. It wasn't what Anthony expected after his conversation with Verhoeven. There was no correspondence from Faber to Steens, or vice versa. Verhoeven would likely approve. If someone complained in writing direct to him, maybe he was not keen to put it in a file for all in the office to see.

Next, Anthony read the Scholten file, the client who wrote the original letter that he had seen in London. The month-end statement revealed just over three million guilders in about fifty securities, again all Dutch. Scholten had shares in banking, retailing, pharmaceuticals, property and leisure. A good mix. Then he saw the EPIC shares under the property classification. A pattern was developing. There was no sign of any letters from Scholten in the file, including the one that Anthony had received. He wondered again how it had been sent to him and what had happened to Verhoeven's copy?

Anthony was immersed in the files and had forgotten what time it was. There was a knock on the door and Anne obliged with the lunch she had ordered. Thanks for remembering.

'You all right?' she asked.

'Fine.'

A long awkward silence. Anne seemed as if she wanted to say more, but held back. She left him alone. Anthony read Smit's file as he ate his crusty baguette with Edam, spilling warm crumbs over the pages. Smit's file was similar. He had three thousand EPIC shares. There was no unusual correspondence, in fact no correspondence at all. Verhoeven was careful. The last file was Mulder's. More of the same.

He took the most recent statements of all four clients and photocopied them on the machine outside the office. They showed how their investments had performed since the start of the year. They were all down money, between ten and thirty per cent each. The Dutch market was down about ten per cent overall. The clients hadn't done too badly. Steens couldn't do much if the entire market was down.

He opened the NedCorp file. They must be doing several hundred deals per week. The file was enormous. Anthony didn't mind the volume of trades for an institutional client. You couldn't churn an institutional client. These clients were too smart, especially one like NedCorp. He saw the million EPIC shares on their statement They were valued at four dollars and fifteen cents each, less than half of their purchase price of two years ago.

He photocopied the NedCorp statement, all twenty-seven pages of it. All two billion guilders of it It wasn't all their Dutch securities. They utilised many other investment banks to buy and sell, to keep the investment banks guessing and to keep the commission charges down through competition for their lucrative business.

Anthony was puzzled. The last NedCorp contract note was dated 28 February and there wasn't one single trade in March. Maybe their recent contract notes had not been filed yet? No. The private client files contained March contract

111

notes. Puzzling. It was unlikely that NedCorp hadn't done a single trade via Steens in the past three weeks. They were the biggest clients of the Amsterdam office.

By four o'clock he had seen enough. He met Anne outside. She seemed disappointed.

'Oh, you are going? Mr Verhoeven is not back yet.'

'I've got a plane to catch. Thanks for all your help.'

It was just himself and Anne alone in the corridor, and he had nothing to lose by asking the question he had been debating all afternoon while he read the five client files. Could he trust her? There was a good chance that Anne would be naive enough to answer. 'Do you ever see letters of complaints from clients?'

He expected her to recoil, based on standing instructions from Verhoeven. She didn't. 'Yes, I do see some.'

God bless naivety.

'And what happens to them?'

'I give them to Mr Verhoeven.'

'Are these letters kept somewhere?'

'No. We shred them.' This was the answer that Anthony didn't want to hear. 'Mr Verhoeven gives them all to me after he has read them, and I shred them in this machine here.' She pointed to a small white shredder that looked well used. The black plastic bag lodged underneath was bulging with the irrecoverable evidence.

'You said all. How many letters do you get?'

'About five to ten letters, I'd say.'

'Each month?'

'No. Each week.'

112

So much information could be got from a few minutes' conversation with the managing director's secretary, rather than twenty fruitless minutes with a lying managing director himself, or hours spent reading incomplete client files. But it had to be done informally on the spur of the moment. It had to look impromptu and unscripted, and it had to be done one to one. Anthony could learn more from Anne about Verhoeven's business practices. Almost.

'So what's going on here. You two having a chat? Anything interesting?'

Verhoeven had arrived and was not pleased. Anne lied before Anthony could even get a line out 'Anthony was just asking me to order a taxi for him.'

A good lie. She did well. But why had she lied? Anthony was shepherded by Verhoeven to reception, turning only to express his appreciation for Anne's assistance. 'You've been very helpful,' he said. She had. Pity Venhoeven had disturbed them.

*   *   *

The taxi driver was pissed off. Anthony gave him the address as they left the Herengracht. His destination was in the centre of town. Anne had probably mentioned Anthony was going to the airport, and the cabbie was hoping for a good fare all the way there. Instead, all he was getting was ten guilders for a trip down the canals. It was exactly four-thirty, the time that Anthony had agreed with Jan Peters yesterday during a brief telephone call from London. No one else from Steens knew that

Anthony was having a rendezvous with this major institutional client. Once Anthony had mentioned EPIC, Peters had made time in his diary immediately.

He was ushered upstairs to NedCorp's investment department and into a large, brightly lit office. He expected to meet an older investment manager, but Jan Peters was a youngster, probably about the same age as Anthony. He was a weakish-looking man with prematurely receding hair and a face pasty from too much time spent indoors staring at computer screens. He looked intellectual, with stylish designer glasses, and wore an olive shirt and a pair of bottle-green trousers, not something that could be worn in the City but acceptable here in relaxed Amsterdam. They exchanged business cards.

'I was surprised to get your telephone call yesterday. I wrote our letter of complaint about EPIC directly to Johan Verhoeven.'

'We got a copy of your letter in London so I thought that I would follow it up.'

'I spoke once by telephone about EPIC with Jeremy Walker in your Compliance Department but he was of no help at all. Do you know that Walker is a director of EPIC? I find it unsatisfactory that when I want to complain about EPIC, I have to talk to someone in Steens who is also a director of the fund. It's hardly fair. Why isn't Walker here helping you out and doing his compliance job now?'

Peters didn't know of Walker's demise. Walker wasn't front-page news on the Continent.

'Unfortunately, Jeremy Walker died at the weekend.'

'Really? I'm sorry. I didn't know. And he was still quite young. What was the cause?'

'The cause of death is not exactly known yet.'

'Is it suspicious?'

'Possibly. Do you want to tell me more about the EPIC issue?'

'Not particularly. There's nothing more to say, is there? EPIC is a disaster. That investment company will never do anything. It was, and still is, grossly mismanaged. We are down almost six million dollars at current prices, Mr Carlton. We at NedCorp are not happy about this issue at all.'

'Well, if you want to tell me more, maybe I can help.'

'What's the point? We have done as much as we can.'

'Surely you could take matter further if you feel that you have a case against Steens?'

Peters shifted uneasily in his seat. Unhappy at Anthony's mention of possible cause.

'Mr Carlton, we do indeed have a case. I think that you might be a little out of touch with what's happening here in Amsterdam. We have stopped using Steens as one of our brokers since the start of this month. I am damned if we are going to pay commission to Verhoeven's people when his office got us into this issue in the first place. He will miss the commission greatly. It's quite amazing the reaction that this has produced in Johan Verhoeven. He has been on the telephone to me nearly every day promising all sorts of things to accommodate us. He was round in this very office first thing yesterday morning for hours trying to resume our business. You didn't know that?'

Verhoeven had not volunteered this information.

Anthony knew now why Verhoeven hadn't made it to the SCISCO issue launch in London.

'What happened in the meeting?'

'It was worse than I imagined. Verhoeven offered me an inducement to resume business. He promised some better deals in the future, to give us better prices at which we can buy and sell Dutch securities. I don't know how he can be in a position to do that, unless he can somehow forecast the performance of the equity markets.'

'Hardly. If so, then we'd all be millionaires. So do you intend to sue us to get back your ten-million-dollar investment in EPIC?'

'You are being somewhat innocent, Mr Carlton. I have been in this business for enough years to know that now and again an investment is lost. No legal action will ever come to court. What do you think the publicity would do to the image of NedCorp here in the Netherlands? We would be a laughing stock, and what would our clients think? They would panic and leave us in their thousands. People trust us to put their money into good investments. Steens have let us down.'

'What do you want us to do?'

'In an ideal world I would like NedCorp's money back, but this is business reality. We have stopped business with Steens to make a point, but we are not going to sue Steens and end up going to court. Such is life.'

Peters stood up. He was finished. It hadn't exactly been the useful information-gathering exercise that Anthony had hoped for. It had been more bad news, but he had to acknowledge Peters' willingness to meet him. It hadn't been a discussion: rather a lecture. Peters stood by the door. 'What are you really doing here in Amsterdam? You didn't fly over here just to spend twenty minutes with me. Did you? What else are you doing?'

'Nothing much else. There's no hidden agenda.'

'Maybe there should be? Why don't you look at what's going on at the Herengracht.'

'Is there anything specific you have in mind?'

'I don't know specifics. It's a gut feeling. It comes with years of experience in this business.'

Peters returned to look at some local market screens on his desk. In all his years in Steens Anthony had never heard a major client talk so dismissively about his employers. Worrying.

*   *   *

Anthony was dazed as he sat in the back of the black cab from Heathrow. The driver wanted to talk about politics, but Anthony wasn't interested. He broke the habit of a lifetime and opened his briefcase to read the various scribbled notes that he'd made during the depressing day in Amsterdam. He began to feel nauseous. He didn't know if it was caused by the speeding of the sulking taxi driver along the M4 or by the evidence before him.

Verhoeven had lied his way through their meeting. Anne knew more, but she wouldn't dare talk openly. The Amsterdam office was receiving too many complaints from clients and had just lost their single biggest institutional client. Peters had subjected him to twenty minutes of verbal ear-bashing as if Anthony were in some way personally responsible for Steens' failings. Peters was unhappy about Verhoeven. The EPIC issue was a disaster and the late Jeremy Walker was connected as a director of the fund. There were too many unanswered questions.

It was past nine o'clock when Anthony arrived home. He hadn't the energy to do anything, least of all to call Vanessa and try to get her to visit W9 for the night. He tossed and turned in the king-size but not in the exact way he would have preferred.

He had been so addled that he had forgotten to buy those tulips at Schiphol.

CHAPTER SEVEN

8.49 A.M.: WEDNESDAY 20 MARCH: CITY OF LONDON EC2

'We'll have to investigate what's happening in the Amsterdam office immediately. I'll brief you and Steve at ten o'clock.'

Gary nodded in agreement. Anthony couldn't ignore the mounting evidence but first needed the approval of his boss to undertake the investigation. Derek Masterson was available in his office, lounging in a comfortable leather chair.

'How was your Amsterdam trip, Anthony?'

'I couldn't do a lot in just one day, but we should send Gary and Steve over.'

'Why do you want to go back? Is it really necessary?'

'Those client complaints are more widespread than I thought. Palmer asked me to investigate so I think we should oblige. It's what Sir James requested.'

'Is there enough to warrant a second visit? After all, the office is managed by a director of the bank.'

Anthony was tempted to say that might be part of the problem but dared not.

'It shouldn't matter whether a director is involved. The principle is the same.'

Only of course it did matter. Derek still looked unenthused at the prospect.

'If you think it's really necessary, then go ahead. I can't imagine that you'll find much there. It will be a waste of time. Do the standard pro forma letter and I'll sign it before we fax it over to Johan. How's my Singapore report coming along?'

'It isn't, yet. Give me a few more days.'

'Until the end of the week, then.'

Time for a change of topic. 'Is there any word yet on why Jeremy Walker was killed?'

'No news yet, Anthony. No progress in identifying a suspect or a motive for the murder. And in the meantime the media have just rehashed our own press releases as they dig around for details about Jeremy's time at Steens. They're just looking for dirt on Jeremy. But there isn't any. I told Karen in personnel not to field any more telephone calls from these journalists. Some of them are really pushy.'

Anthony paused by Vanessa's desk.

'Where are my tulips?' she enquired.

There was no one else within earshot.

'Apologies. My mistake. My first? Gary and Steve will be off to Amsterdam, so can you get them tickets for a flight early this afternoon. The sooner they start over there, the better. Grab the usual guilders too. And can you do me a politely

119

worded memo with the usual pro forma stuff about a routine visit to the office as part of the bank's scheduled programme of reviews of overseas offices. Make it sound official. Then get Derek to sign it and fax it to Johan Verhoeven before lunchtime. And get me a few copies of these letters and client account statements.'

Vanessa jotted a few notes down as Anthony spoke. She took the letters and the account statements. Anthony wanted to make progress elsewhere. 'I'll be down on the second floor for ten minutes.'

*   *   *

The lift display showed the Footsie down forty-eight points. He walked towards the syndicate desk. Dave was in his usual place. A good dealer never left his desk during peak morning trading hours. Anything could happen. He might lose a deal. 'Tony, can we be quick?' he said.

'Isn't this a good time?'

'Yes and no. Yes, because we are not selling any new issues today. No, because the markets are down everywhere. We had a bad day in London yesterday. Footsie was down sixty points. Then New York was hit as well. Dow lost about ninety points overnight. Tokyo closed down a few hundred points on the Nikkei also. The Hang Seng is fucked too. This morning has opened weaker. Confidence is not good at the moment, but let's look on the bright side. At least we got the South China Iron and Steel issue away just in time on Monday. I wouldn't fancy trying to sell it today in this market.'

Anthony could see the SEAQ screen at Dave's desk. Red screens meant prices going down. Blue screens meant prices going up. There were only a few blue prices in the hundred FTSE index stocks. Despite the choppy conditions the salesmen were still busy first thing in the morning. Most of their sales activity was done immediately after they held their morning meeting at seven-thirty, when selected research analysts would speak on the PA to the second floor. Not a place for those with stage fright.

'Heard you were in Amsterdam yesterday.'

'How do you know that?'

'One of the guys on the sales desk over there said you were looking at client files. Verhoeven was mouthing off about your presence to the desk staff.' Word spreads fast in Steens. Too fast. 'You get one question. Time starts now.'

'Jeremy Walker was the company secretary of EPIC. Did you know that when you sold it?'

'Yeah, I knew that. It's in the prospectus. It's no secret.'

'Isn't it unusual? I've never seen that before in other issues that we've originated. Steens' directors don't often end up on the boards of client companies do they?'

'No, they don't, but it does happen. It adds prestige to the company, looks good to the investors. EPIC was real tough to sell, so his directorship was arranged as a confidence-building measure. In any event, any outside directorship has to be approved by our board.'

'What does a company secretary do in a listed fund?'

'Helps out with board meetings and annual

121

general meetings. Liaises with the banks and legal advisers and investors and auditors and any third parties. Organises some of the administration of the fund and makes payments if they are also an authorised signatory.'

'Payments?'

'Yes, he signs cheques and bank transfers for expenses, salaries and asset purchases.'

Anthony needed to find out if indeed Walker had been an authorised signatory. The power to write blank cheques from a fifty-million-dollar fund had to be in the right hands. Someone shouted over from a nearby sales desk.

'Mitchells are holding on two. A new issue is on the way. They want to sell us some. Poor bastards. Let's do some business, Dave.'

'I gotta go, Tony. Is this EPIC fund connected to Walker's murder?'

'Dunno yet.'

'Maybe I should shorten some of these odds I'm quoting on his death? Link the odds to the EPIC share price, if some connection exists? Anyway, see you this evening as usual?'

'Wouldn't miss it for the world.'

* * *

Vanessa caught Anthony's attention as he returned to the fourth floor. 'The fax to Verhoeven has gone. The tickets can be collected at the BA desk at the airport later. The money is on the way. Here are the photocopies. Happy?'

'Ecstatic.'

'Is now OK?'

Anthony looked up. Gary was on time.

'Sure. Ten o'clock on the dot. Is this a conversion, Gary?'

'No. I just set my own watch five minutes ahead, so I'm nearly on the same time as everyone else. Steve's ready too.'

Steve Massey was a mere twenty-five years old, the veritable junior of the department. His work ethic had already impressed Anthony in a short space of time. He was a young man in a hurry, but at the same time he had formed good working relationships with all those he had encountered in the bank. He had a slight build that would surely develop over time on a solid diet of stodgy late-night overseas restaurant meals, excessive alcohol consumption in the Flute and total lack of any sort of physical exercise.

He was a pensive sort with a low speaking voice that revealed a somewhat unfashionable South London accent, but his demeanour would change in time and he would develop the pseudo-arrogant streak that they all needed in order to survive. Steve was someone you could throw in at the deep end and know that he would survive. And right now he was about to go off at the deep end in Amsterdam, where there was at least one local shark circling with intent.

Steve had joined the year before on that much-loved graduate recruitment programme. The brightest graduates were given a hard time in their first year, with long hours, management pressure, unattainable work targets and short-notice overseas assignments. Those who didn't make the grade were asked politely to leave. They usually obliged, and with Steens' name on their curriculum vitae they had no trouble joining another bank of lesser standing. Anthony had survived the gruelling induction. So had Dave. And now Steve.

Steve looked good for a career within Steens. Maybe he was too good. Some other bank might come looking for him. Head-hunters were always after their best staff for the big American banks. They would wet themselves over his CV. Steve could be a target soon.

Anthony had interviewed him twice but had failed to spot his one significant failing. Steve was a chain smoker. Although he couldn't smoke within their building, he disappeared from his desk regularly to have a covert cigarette. Steve needed a cigarette before big meetings and immediately after them. Right now Anthony could sense that pervasive nicotine odour, just like when Palmer had lit up two days ago. They sat in Anthony's room.

'We have to look at these letters of complaint from Amsterdam's private clients. The bank's practice is that these are to be passed to the Compliance Department to follow up, but that hasn't been happening in Amsterdam. I was over there yesterday, and Anne, Verhoeven's secretary, told me that they get about five to ten letters per week, which she shreds. There are no copies kept anywhere.'

Anthony let the words sink in.

'The level of complaints is unprecedented within Steens in my experience, and we need to find out exactly why they are being received. I was sent a copy of one, and the late Jeremy Walker was sent copies of four others. We need to find out who sent them from the Amsterdam office. That might make our job considerably easier. There may be a mole

124

in the office whom we can use to our advantage.'

Steve took notes, given his inexperience. Anthony handed around the documents. 'These are copies of the five client complaints that we have. Read them. Unfortunately, they are not very specific. And here are the clients' account statements, some light reading before you get stuck in. Jesus, that's interesting. I didn't see that before.'

Gary woke up and looked at the assembled papers. 'What?'

'These four private client accounts, Gary. Do you see the common denominator?'

'What do you mean?'

'The client account numbers.'

The client account numbers were at the top right-hand side of the statement. Every Steens client had his or her own unique account number, just like a regular bank account number.

'The accounts have a D after the number. They are discretionary accounts.'

The alarm bells rang immediately. Discretionary accounts were always more prone to abuse than any other type of client account. Most accounts at Steens were advisory accounts where the client and salesman spoke to each other, and, based on the salesman's advice or the client's own ideas, the client bought or sold equities or bonds. But discretionary accounts were a different matter, since the client gave Steens' salesmen full discretion to buy and sell equities for the client's account. The client never knew what equity was bought or sold until he got his contract note or a monthly statement in the post.

There was nothing wrong with these accounts in principle. Every investment bank had them.

Discretionary accounts suited clients who travelled overseas a lot, suited retired people who didn't stay in touch with the market, and suited clients who felt that Steens' salesmen would do a better job at equity selection and strategy than they would themselves. This was generally true in Steens, but maybe not in the Amsterdam office.

'And the four account numbers are also flagged with an H.'

Serious too. H stood for hold mail. Another warning sign. Many wealthy private clients did not want to receive mail in glossy Steens envelopes showing they had hundreds of thousands of guilders in equities. They were afraid their neighbour or the taxman might find out about their lucrative investments or, worse still, that their wife might find out about their unknown wealth. These clients asked Steens to hold their mail in the office and they would visit the office in person, sign for their mail and take it with them in a discreet briefcase.

The clients always signed a standard indemnity to protect Steens, but there were always a few lazy clients who never visited the office to collect contract notes and statements. They knew what was in their account only when they telephoned their salesman in Steens or got handwritten account statements faxed to them. They put their trust in Steens' employees.

No one said it aloud, but all three of them understood the obvious. If a salesman wanted to abuse a client account, change buys or sells, park equities or whatever, then he would use a discretionary account. If it were a hold mail account, then all the better. No one in the office

126

would question the trades, and the client would never be the wiser until it was too late. It made the pending Amsterdam visit all the more important.

'These four accounts need some closer review, and any others like them. That's item one. The second matter is to have a look at EPIC NV, which I mentioned to you on Monday, Gary. The European Property Investment Corporation. We sold part of the issue out of the Amsterdam office, and NedCorp are bitching about it. The share price has gone through the floor. Everyone hates the stock, even Dave downstairs, and he sold the issue. This is EPIC,' said Anthony, handing over copies of the prospectus. 'Have a good read of it, both of you. Johan Verhoeven somehow sold a lot of it to Amsterdam clients. See who owns the shares over there. On no account should you talk to any clients, especially NedCorp, without clearing it with me first. Jeremy Walker was the company secretary of EPIC, so look out for any involvement by him. Any other questions?'

Gary didn't offer any immediate revelations about EPIC, but he was thinking laterally. 'Walker's death is the common denominator, isn't it? I mean, the complaint letters were sent to Walker and he is involved in EPIC?'

'I don't know if there is a connection, but if so then the police might get too interested. Walker had the complaints in his briefcase. D-S Palmer knows about them. EPIC has lost a lot of money, and when there are millions of dollars involved I guess that anything can happen. So start today and see what you can get done by the weekend. I've booked some flights for you early this afternoon. Go home after this. Pack a few things. With any luck you'll get half a day's work done today in Amsterdam.'

Gary and Steve organised some files and were gone in a cab within ten minutes.

*   *   *

Vanessa brought the news to Anthony. She sat on the edge of his desk and provocatively placed knee over knee, knowing that the close-fitting skirt was just too short for such a dangerous manoeuvre. God. Anthony would love to take her right there and then. Right now, toss all the papers on the floor, lay her across the empty black ash with the chrome desk light. Unbutton those shining gold buttons on the blouse and peel back the layers of silk. Run his hands through her hair and then all over her. If only they were alone instead of being in a glass office with dozens of voyeuristic passers-by outside.

This subterfuge in the office, no one knowing how much they cared for each other, was slowly driving him mad. Gary would guess soon. Vanessa had blown him out on day one. Not her type, she said. Too many rough edges. Anthony would have to tell someone soon, someone in authority like Derek. Then the sparks would fly. They all knew the company policy. No relationships between staff who work together. End of story. Derek would move Vanessa to another job, maybe even to another floor. Anthony would not be able to stare out at her in awe from his office. His quality of life would be significantly diminished. Best to postpone the event.

Vanessa proffered the newspaper. Anthony's

128

attention was miles away until he saw that Steens featured as the front-page story in the *Evening Standard*. Today it didn't feel so good to be an employee of Steens.

'Today the police released the results of a post-mortem conducted by a pathologist at Guy's Hospital morgue, which confirmed that Jeremy Walker died from asphyxiation when a silk tie was knotted tightly around his neck. Fellow directors from investment bank Steen Odenberg & Co. later formally identified the body of the dead director. No further details of the circumstances of his death were disclosed, but D-S Palmer of the City of London Police said they are following certain lines of enquiry.'

*   *   *

Anthony was a set up, five-three up in the second and was about to serve for the match. One of the reasons for buying his apartment was that it backed on to Paddington Sports Club. This was the easiest game of tennis he had played against Dave for a long time. Either Dave had his mind on other things or the two Maida Vale babes in white shorts playing a shrill singles match on the next savannah court had ruined his concentration. The service game was won decisively to love. Anthony and Dave downed a badly needed isotonic drink inside the clubhouse on this perfect still evening for tennis. Dave was looking out at one of the two girls, who was leaning into a fully extended serve. 'Jesus, look at that. The way she moves when she serves. That's some awesome sight.'

'And that's exactly the reason why you played

crap this evening. I can't remember the last time I hammered you this easily. I must get those two girls to play beside us more often.'

Dave took his gaze off the girls, who were changing ends. 'You're right, in a sort of a way. My mind was not on this game of tennis at all.'

'What was it on?'

'Work, actually.'

'You sad bastard, Dave. Give it a break. We're not at Steens now. Unwind.'

'If only it were that easy, but it isn't. Between you and me, there may be some trouble brewing over this South China Iron and Steel Company issue, the one we did on Monday when you were down with us on the floor?'

'It was fine when I was there. You sold it all. What's wrong with it? Is the price falling?'

'No, the price held up very well in the after-market. Some of the Asian markets have come back a bit in the past few days, but SCISCO has fared well. It's still at a nice premium above the issue price, enough to keep the investors happy but not too much to make the Chinese think that we gave it away too cheaply. Something else about that issue doesn't look right.'

Dave looked around to ensure that no other recuperating players were sitting nearby in the small clubhouse bar.

'There's a lot of competition between investment banks to get new issue mandates in Asia. Everyone wants a slice of the action and to stake their claim for any future business. China should be the most lucrative market of them all in the years to come. GDP there is growing at eight per cent per annum; here it's just one per cent. We were fucking delighted when Steens won the mandate to do the SCISCO issue because we beat lots of other big players, including those pushy Yanks in Mitchells. Since Monday, though, I got a few telephone calls from my peers at other syndicate desks in the City claiming that we won the SCISCO mandate unfairly, which initially I put down to sour grapes on their part.'

'So what's changed that view?'

'Today I had more of that bloody expensive pasta in the Flute with a syndicate guy from a Jap investment bank. The local Communist Party officials in Guangdong ran SCISCO before we sold it off. He heard that there's talk that a bribe was offered by Steens to the government officials in Guangdong. The figure being mentioned in the market was a round-sum million dollars—US, not Hong Kong dollars. I just ignored his comments until this afternoon, when I got some other evidence.'

This was beginning to sound like something that Anthony should be investigating.

'What evidence?'

'After each issue we work out the profit Steens have made. We include our fees and commissions and our trading revenue in the grey market, and then we deduct any sub-underwriting fees and salesmen commissions, deal expenses, legal fees, travel, public relations and marketing costs and we get the bottom-line net profit for Steens'

'So?'

'I normally just get to see the bottom-line profit. One of the directors approves all the details, but now we are short a director. Sir James and your boss Derek were in meetings all afternoon. I was the next most senior person on the second floor who was available. So one of the accounting guys from finance came down with the final numbers on the SCISCO issue. I had a look at the detailed items because the bottom-line profit was a bit lower than the number I expected us to earn.'

'Why?'

'There was an item that I wasn't expecting, simply called introductory commissions, and it came exactly to a million US dollars. That was when I remembered the comments from the competition. It was too much of a coincidence, so I questioned this accounting guy. He looked at his files and showed me this memo which one of the directors wrote a few weeks ago saying that there would be an introductory commission to some Chinese advisers in respect of the deal. I asked for the payment details and he showed me a list of five Chinese advisers who will each get two hundred thousand dollars.'

'Well, it could be for legitimate business advice on the issue. China is a complicated market. Local knowledge and contacts could be important.'

Dave reacted in disgust, shaking his head. Some others looked in their direction. 'Bullshit. I recognised those five names. They are all directors of SCISCO. One is the chairman, one is the finance director, one is the production director and the other two are local Communist Party officials. They are the same guys we saw up in the goldfish bowl from the dealing floor last Monday morning. We have slipped these guys a load of hard currency in order to get the SCISCO mandate. Shit. Anyone with two hundred thousand bucks in China is a multimillionaire. There's no other word for it. It's a

132

bribe. If word of it gets out it will ruin us in that part of Asia. We'll never get another Chinese government mandate. New issues will dry up. It will really screw up my year-end bonus for starters.'

'You said that one of the directors wrote the memo regarding the commission? Who was it?'

A wry grin from Dave. Eyes raised skywards. Resignation to the inevitable. 'Guess who?'

Easy, really. Man of the moment. 'Jeremy Walker?'

'Correct in one.'

'And who is the director who usually reviews the final profit on new issues?'

'Walker reviews them. Sir James is always busy at corporate functions. Derek Masterson doesn't get involved in front office matters much. The other directors are always overseas. I would never even have seen the final deal numbers except that Walker is dead and there was no one else to review them. And then I would have just forgotten about those rumours from the other syndicate guys in the City.'

'If you hear any more about this, let me know.'

'Will do. Listen, I've gotta go. I've an eight o'clock to make.'

'Hot date?'

'Yeah. Wouldn't you love to know? See you in the office or else next week here on court one. Same time, different result.'

Anthony was looking for an angle. Steens launch a new issue on a Monday morning where a director has agreed to pay an illegal bribe to win a deal mandate but on the eve of the issue that same director dies in his apartment Anthony couldn't see any angle yet. Game, set and match to Dave in reality.

133

*   *   *

Alone at home in Maida Vale, there was only one course of action. Call Vanessa. Her home number was stored in his telephone memory. Number one. She was number one in every sense. Her number was engaged. Good. She was home. Kill some time. Anthony flicked through twenty channels of dire cable television, tried the choice on Kiss FM, and then opted for a favourite soul CD from his extensive collection.

Ten minutes later he hit the redial button. Still engaged. Come on, Vanessa. Get off the phone. Smooth R&B music emanated from the state-of-the-art stereo system. Great music to play lying beside Vanessa in the king-size. Good driving music, too, if he ever got the chance in between work to use the Audi.

He hit redial again. It rang this time. Excellent. It still rang. Come on. Pick up. She must be there. She was there ten minutes ago. Then her voice. In luck. No. Just the wonderful sound of her voice on the answering machine that he knew so well. He rang the number again just to hear the message for the second time. Total frustration. Where had she gone?

'Vanessa. It's Tony. It's nine o'clock. Give me a call, please.'

Every evening without her was time wasted. There was so much more to learn about Vanessa. She was an enigma of sorts. Anthony had been to her apartment only twice, a newly built spacious two-bedroomed pad in Notting Hill Gate that cost an extortionate amount in rent each month. Lucky her. Anthony could never afford anything like that, to rent or buy. All thanks to her munificent father who showered her with cash to finance a lifestyle of luxury. Vanessa preferred to visit Anthony in W9 than vice versa.

He still knew little about her background, her childhood, her family. She never talked about her early years, her education, her first job. Anthony had to delve deeper to find out what made Vanessa the wonderful person she was. He didn't even know about her previous relationships, if indeed any existed. She rarely talked about her parents, so much so that Anthony was wondering if he would ever get to meet them. His future in-laws? This relationship was getting real serious.

He slouched on the sofa, resting his aching bones from the exertions at the tennis club and looked out at the leafless trees beyond the window. He read the *Standard* again and he thought about Walker, EPIC, SCISCO, Verhoeven, Anne, bribes and what Gary and Steve might find in Amsterdam. Most of all he thought about Vanessa and where she was.

CHAPTER EIGHT

12.21 P.M.. FRIDAY 22 MARCH:
CITY OF LONDON EC2

Anthony sat with his feet up on the edge of the desk, looking at the ceaseless news ticker on his Reuters screen, half-wondering would a headline about EPIC, NedCorp or the SCISCO issue ever pop up? It was difficult to concentrate on mere work when more pressing matters occupied the minds of everyone at Steens. Why had someone decided to kill Walker on a Sunday evening in his own apartment? It was so much more intriguing than writing his report on a trouble-free visit to the Singapore office.

It was quiet in Steens without Gary's and Steve's presence. Anthony was almost grateful for the hunger pangs that reminded him that lunchtime had arrived. Time for a change of scenery. He strolled outside into Broadgate Circle and over to the Italian delicatessen on the corner to order a prawn and avocado on wholewheat brown with Thousand Island dressing and extra freshly milled black pepper.

The sandwiches here were good. You didn't go in and order a ham and cheese or a beef with salad. This was the City. You ordered dressed crab, curried turkey, dolphin-friendly tuna with mixed peppers, chicken and sweetcorn mayonnaise, BLTs. Anything except the mundane. The sandwiches cost more than a British Airways share, wouldn't last as long, but were entirely satisfying in the short term.

Anthony read a borrowed *Standard*. Waste of time, in fact, because the first edition at midday always had zero news in it. He simultaneously digested the apparent lack of news and the prawns. But Vanessa had mentioned that there was an article about Walker's death in the paper. That's all she said. Even when Anthony had pushed her on her whereabouts two nights ago she was vague. Too vague. She was out for a while, she said. Forgot. Didn't check her answering machine on her return.

136

Was she losing interest? He hoped not.

The article was an obituary flanked by a flattering photograph of Walker taken several years ago and making him out to be much younger than his forty-nine years. His educational achievements at Oxford University were chronicled, then his wonderful sales and trading skills, his time in the Far East, his market knowledge and intelligence, his City contacts. The obituary was surprisingly thin on what he did outside work, if anything. He had spent all his working life at Steens. There was no mention at all of the ex-wife. It read like City propaganda pushed out by Karen in Steens' personnel department, but it would sit well among Steens' City competitors and clients. That same journalist again. Jennifer Sharpe.

Vanessa distracted him from gathering up those few remaining prawns. 'D-S Palmer rang. I told him you'd ring him back. He says that you have his card.'

Anthony paged through his Rolodex of business cards on his desk with sticky Thousand Island fingers. It was crammed with Steens' cards from bank executives throughout the world, cards of his peers in the financial world, cards from great restaurants and bars and cards of tennis partners, W9 residents, old girlfriends and other enemies. If the size of your Rolodex were truly a measure of the quality of your life, then Anthony was enjoying a full and diverse existence.

He was looking for just one card, that of the only detective-sergeant whom he knew. He had previously felt the urge to use the shredder beside Vanessa's desk and watch Palmer disappear in tiny white pieces into the bin. But the more responsible and organised part of him had made sure he kept the card.

It must be under P, he thought. P for Palmer or police. No luck. Then he found it under B. Bishopsgate Police Station. Obvious once he remembered. He dialled 9 for an outside line, then the number and leaned back again in his seat, one eye observing the City at lunch outside his window and the other eye still on the Reuters screen. Steens' share price STN.L was down twelve pence. Anthony couldn't see any particular reason for the fall. Weak market sentiment. The telephone annoyingly rang five or six times.

'Bishopsgate Police,' answered an anonymous switchboard voice.

Obviously police resources did not extend to direct telephone lines, as in the City.

'D-S Palmer, please,' asked Anthony.

The line went quiet. A minute passed. No response. Anthony grew impatient. He was about to put the telephone down when the voice returned. 'D-S Palmer is out.'

'Tell him Mr Anthony Carlton of Steen Odenberg returned his call.'

'What's that name again? Steen what?'

One of the few mortals who had never heard of Steens.

'Odenberg. It's an investment bank in the City.' Anthony spelt it for him. Palmer would probably get a message that an Anthony Odenberg from Steen Carlton called.

'Hold on a minute. The D-S left a message for you. You are to meet him at an apartment in Wapping owned by Jeremy Walker. He's down there now. Quick as you can, he said.'

Quick as you can? Get real. Anthony had a job to do in the City. The Singapore report hadn't even been started yet. Derek was giving him grief about it already. Yet Palmer just summons him like a hired hand. Quick as he can? Anthony didn't want to head down to Wapping, but maybe there was something in this for him? This was an opportunity that rarely presented itself. A chance to see inside the home of a dead Steens' director, to see how the other half lived. Perhaps even a chance to learn more about Walker's lifestyle or those client letters or about EPIC. Worth the effort, at least.

The *Standard* article had said that Walker lived in somewhere called Anchor Yard in Wapping, only Anthony didn't know the exact address. He went to Vanessa's desk. She wasn't there. Probably gone shopping again in Liverpool Street Station arcade to replace that missing scarf. He took the Central London phone book from her chaotic shelves and thumbed through the W section. He went down the list quickly. No sign of any Jeremy Ernest Walker.

Walker must have been ex-directory. Everyone agreed that he had been a private person, or else he was just too wealthy to be included in the telephone book with the mere mortals. Directory enquiries confirmed that Walker was indeed ex-directory. Anthony had another option. He dialled Steens' personnel department. A well-spoken girl answered politely and promptly. 'Personnel. Karen speaking.'

Anthony recognised the voice of someone he had not spoken to for a while, not at least since he had met Vanessa at the Savoy party. 'Karen. It's Tony here. How are you?'

'Hi, Tony. I'm fine. What are you up to these

days?'

'Top secret, but I'll do you a trade. Something for something. Are you interested?'

'I'm always interested. What's the deal?'

'Dinner for two at my favourite Thai restaurant by the canal in Little Venice.'

Vanessa would not approve, but it was only idle banter about a dinner. It should be enough to get what he wanted.

'And what do you want from me, I wonder?'

'I'm looking for the address of Jeremy Walker's pad in Wapping.'

'I can't give out the home address of a director. It's private. It could be a security risk.'

'It's important. Please. In any case it's hardly a security risk if the man is already dead.'

A pause, then she fell for it. 'I'll just get Walker's file.'

Sound of shuffling of papers and files near the telephone handset lying on her desk.

'It's number thirty, Anchor Yard, Wapping, E1,' she said.

'Thanks, Karen. I'll be in touch about that dinner.'

'Will you? I wonder.'

* * *

No one would miss him from the office for an hour. No sign of Derek. Anthony could walk to Wapping, if he felt like it. Just go down Houndsditch towards Tower Hill, and he would be there, ten minutes maximum. But he had no idea where Anchor Yard was. He chose the easier alternative and looked for a black cab outside Broadgate. Instead he got into a pink cab, one with the *FT* logo emblazoned on the side. The cabbie turned around looking for the destination.

'Anchor Yard,' requested Anthony.

'Hey, isn't that where that banker was murdered at the weekend? Somebody strangled him? I saw it in the Sun on Monday. Do you live near the dead guy? Know him at all?'

'Just take me there please.'

'Where exactly is Anchor Yard, then, guv?'

'Wapping.'

'Whereabouts in Wapping?'

'I thought you knew every street in London? You have the Knowledge, don't you?'

'Yes, I do, but these new places in Wapping are springing up every day. Converted warehouses, penthouses, apartment complexes, and they're all called something bloody nautical. Quays and wharves. Docks and harbours. Don't you know what street it's off?'

Anthony had never got a name of any nearby street from Karen.

'Just drive down to Wapping and we'll ask some locals when we get there.'

'OK, guv. You're paying.'

In less than ten minutes' battling against London traffic, they encountered the cobbled streets of Wapping, and the taxi lurched up and down until the cabbie slowed out of necessity. Anthony peered out of the window looking for this Anchor Yard place. No sign of it anywhere. More worryingly, there was no sign of any locals to ask either.

Wapping during the day was quiet, while the residents made their living in the City before returning home to swim in their indoor pools, use their communal gymnasium or sit on their riverside balconies watching the sun set over the Thames with a glass of Pinot Grigio. At least that was the dream they were sold when they bought their properties in Docklands in the late 1980s. Many of those same residents were now in the negative equity trap, owing more to their building society than the value of their apartment or town house.

Suddenly Anthony saw a police car parked down a side road. A white Rover saloon with the characteristic City of London Police crest on the door.

'Stop here.'

Looking past the police car he saw a large advertising hoarding. More apartments for sale at Anchor Yard. Success. He gave the cabbie a fiver, enough to include a tip. Anthony buttoned his jacket as he walked sideways into the fresh wind coming from the direction of the Thames. Anchor Yard looked great from the outside, brand new but tasteful. Subtle red and orange brickwork rose to five storeys high. Large wrought-iron balconies protruded from the apartments, with green plants flowing over the edges. Tall arched windows were recessed into the walls, and the roof was turret-shaped in places. There were three different blocks of apartments, which were located around a central courtyard with numbered car-parking spaces and a small Japanese-style water-garden. The only problem was getting inside. Anthony had no wish to alert Palmer of his arrival just yet. He needed to see the inside of the apartment.

The entrance gate for cars was eight foot high and was firmly shut. A side gate for pedestrians was set into the wall in front of him. Access was by a combination code keyed into a number pad. There was no other way into the complex. Anthony wondered how a murderer would gain access here. He didn't see how it would be possible. Letterboxes with doorbells were built into the wall. Anthony looked closely. Number thirty was there. Walker's name was written beside it. Anthony even recognised Walker's cultured handwriting on the white card inside the Perspex slot. He needn't have called Karen after all.

A car horn startled him. He turned around to see a white Ford Transit van close to the main gate. On the side of the van was written East End Contract Cleaners Ltd. Disgusting rock music blared from inside the van as the young male driver with a shaven head, earrings and cheap sunglasses honked impatiently. The gates began to open electronically. The van drove inside. The gates began to close again, but without a moment's hesitation Anthony walked inside.

As he approached the three apartment blocks, he saw a small lodge on his right. A security guard inside in a peaked cap looked closely at him from behind green-tinted glass. Anthony walked confidently onwards, using the latter of the three requirements to be an authentic investment banker. The guard returned to reading his newspaper. Maybe he thought that thieves don't go around in good City suits and ties. Well, not unless they work as equities salesmen in an investment bank.

Number thirty was in the middle of the three blocks. The cleaning van had stopped outside this block too. Anthony could just buzz the intercom to number thirty, but he feared that Palmer would simply come downstairs to talk to him. He wanted to see Walker's pad. The odds were three to one that the cleaner was working in the block that Anthony wanted. The odds looked good. Anthony slowed his walk. The cleaner got out and walked towards the entrance door of the middle block. He held a single key on a piece of string. Anthony reached the door just in time, nodded knowingly to the cleaner and walked into the hallway after him. The door closed behind them both. Perfect timing.

A wall sign confirmed that number thirty was on the top floor. He pushed for the lift, hoping that Palmer wouldn't simultaneously be coming down in the same lift. The top floor was where the best apartments and penthouses would be. In a way he was surprised that Walker had bought high. The secret of his success on the sales floor in Steens for so many years was to buy low and to sell high. The solid-wood door to number thirty was partly ajar. Palmer must be inside. Anthony pushed the door open and was inside Walker's apartment at last. It was his first visit to a murder scene.

'Anyone there?' he called.

'Who's that?'

Anthony recognised Palmer's voice immediately.

'Me,' said Anthony unnecessarily, as he made eye contact with Palmer.

Palmer stood by a doorway in the hall. Beside him was a burly uniformed policeman who seemed speechless. Palmer was in his casual gear. Of sorts. A fake shiny leather jacket with well-worn elbows and cuffs. Underneath, he wore an open-neck long-collared shirt crowned by a V-neck sweater with yellow and grey diamond patterns. Val Doonican on Tour 1978 perhaps.

Anthony's first impression was that the hall was enormous, bigger than most of the rooms in Anthony's own modest apartment. This was expensively furnished too. Anthony's attention was drawn to the original oil-paintings on the wall and the Chinese vases carefully placed on period furniture. Many obvious reminders of Walker's years with Steens in their Hong Kong office. An explanation was required.

'I phoned you at the station, and they told me to come down here.'

'I wanted to know how your Amsterdam trip went.'

Anthony had to be careful about what to disclose of Steens' ills, if they in fact existed at all. The purpose of this visit was not to educate Palmer. The less he knew the better. 'We are still investigating the letters of complaint, but there's nothing concrete to report yet.'

A lull in the conversation. Anthony looked past Palmer and the policeman into the large lounge that he could partly see. Too obvious. Palmer took a step back to improve the view.

'The real reason you've come down here is to see Walker's apartment, isn't it? Well, what are you waiting for? Have a look around, then.'

'Isn't this a crime scene? Isn't there evidence around here?'

'Not any more. We've had the forensic guys in here for the past three days doing their dusting and examinations. They've been through this flat from the hall door to the back balcony, and everything in between. I can assure you they missed nothing, but it was unfortunately not a very productive exercise. Do you want a guided tour?'

145

Palmer was unnecessarily accommodating as he took Anthony into a room off the hallway.

'First off, this is the main living-room. Three full-length windows overlooking the Thames. Bloody incredible views. I was here last evening, and the view of the sunset was something else. One sliding patio door to the spacious balcony. Just in case you're wondering, the patio door was locked from the inside when we came here on the morning after the murder. No signs of forced entry anywhere, including the hall door, as you no doubt saw on your way in here. Pine floors with some flash oriental rugs. Expensive antiques. Harrods comfy sofa and chairs. Bang & Olufsen TV and music system. Stand-alone drinks cabinet. Nice?'

Anthony indicated his agreement Palmer. walked to a door leading off the main room.

'The kitchen. Mega equipment too. Everything looks brand new. Rarely used, though, I'd say. Only the microwave was in regular use. Walker wasn't a cook, I guess. We found the remains of a last Chinese meal in the bin. Sweet-and-sour crap, fried rice and the like.'

They went back towards the hall.

'Over here is the master bedroom. One enormous double bed with layers of bed linen. Walk-in wardrobes full of City suits and shirts and ties and loads of shoes. Mostly the sort that you wear, actually. Ties called Herpes or something like that. No, I'm wrong, Hermès. Sort of a City uniform, I guess? *En suite* bathroom with a Jacuzzi, shower and steam room in the back. And there are two other bedrooms off the hall, but they are unused. No beds or anything. Just some boxes and household bits and pieces in storage.' Palmer could

146

see the envy on Anthony's face. 'And we all think that we live in quite nice places, too, until you see a place like this.'

Compared with Anthony's apartment, this was indeed a palace. He didn't like to speculate on Palmer's natural habitat. Anthony now realised the real reason for his visit. He hadn't come just to view the interior of Walker's apartment. He had come to see the crime scene, to see the exact spot where Walker died.

'Can I ask you where Walker died?'

'How about I just show you?' Palmer pointed to the floor beside the bed. 'That's where we found him. Lying there.'

Anthony had expected to see a pool of blood on the subtly patterned carpet.

'There's little evidence left after a strangulation. Just some saliva and hair on the carpet that we swabbed up for DNA tests. The DNA was Walker's. No one else's hair was found here. No blood at all.'

'What happened exactly?'

Palmer looked uneasy, mentally evaluating the request.

'I'll be honest with you. You're helping me with those bloody letters of complaint, so I'll help you out a bit. Quid pro quo and all that. I presume you can keep a confidence, in the same way that I will if anything horrendous transpires about your bank?'

'Yes,' Anthony lied.

'We haven't disclosed the exact circumstances of the death yet to the media. We don't want to alarm too many people around here. We found Walker lying naked on the floor with a silk tie around his neck, and his hands and ankles tied behind his back

147

with ties also. We know they came from his walk-in wardrobe—same designer names. He was also gagged with one that fatally impaired his breathing. It wasn't a pleasant sight. Whoever did this did a professional job. The post-mortem yesterday didn't tell us much. No bruising at all to the body except where the restraints were.'

Anthony winced. It was a painful way to go. He subconsciously loosened his own silk tie around his neck. It was now a little too tight for comfort. Palmer was getting into his stride.

'You will have noticed when you looked around this apartment that everything here is tidy. There was no violence in this death. No one messed up the flat, no fight, no broken locks or smashed glasses. Walker even had his wallet, with two hundred quid in cash, and credit cards and ATM card still on him. That was a disappointment to us because sometimes these cards are used afterwards and we can trace them. And that Chinese food in the kitchen that I mentioned? There are two pairs of used chopsticks in the bin. Whoever was here must have had a meal with him before he died. Weird or what?'

Anthony was thinking in his inherent investigator mode. A hazard of his chosen vocation. 'What about fingerprints on the chopsticks?'

'We got a set of dabs off the chopsticks. One set is Walker's. The other set belongs to someone else and currently they are not on the files of any police force in the UK. We ran them by Interpol, too, but no joy. We drew a total blank on them.'

'What about the Chinese food? Where was it bought and by whom?'

'Good question. You're not bad at this lark at all,' acknowledged Palmer. 'The food was bought from an East End place around the corner. The receipt in the bag shows the sale was made at 9.27 p.m. The owner has identified the customer as Walker. He came into the shop alone and his car was parked outside while he ordered. Owner can't recall if there was anyone else in the car at the time. No leads at all there. Next question?'

'Doesn't anyone else live here? *I* know Walker was divorced and that his ex, Sylvia, lives in the Far East now. But what about their kids? Where were they?'

'They never had any kids. Almost twenty years of marriage and nothing to show for it, really. Except a divorce and an acrimonious court settlement.'

'Are there witnesses in the apartment block on the night of the murder?' Anthony asked.

'No one heard anything on Sunday night. I guess being strangled is a quiet way to go.'

'Who did Walker socialise with?'

'That's been a dead end too. Very few people seemed to know him. Many of his friends who knew him and Sylvia as a loving couple deserted him when they split up. The people who knew him best all worked at Steens or other banks in the City, but they never met him outside work. He was a private man who rarely talked about anything other than work. He seems to have been a bit of a loner of late. Walker worked seven until seven, day in, day out. No one got close to him in the Compliance Department. Not even his blubbering secretary.'

'Didn't the residents here know him?'

'Only for nodding to on the stairs or letting each

149

other in at the main gate. That sort of thing.'

'Who found the body?'

'A yuppie couple next door called the station first thing last Monday morning. Some guy was going to work, noticed Walker's door ajar and the clock radio blaring from inside. He said it was unusual, so he went inside and threw up in the bathroom when he found the body.'

'The *Standard* said that you are following some lines of enquiry. What are they?'

'There are no lines of enquiry. That's just crap put out at the request of our press boys. We're hardly going to issue a press release saying that we haven't got a bloody clue as to why he was murdered. And it might scare the shit out of whoever killed Walker. I hope so.'

Anthony was rapidly running out of good questions. But he had one left. A classic. 'What about motive, then? Did anyone have a reason to kill him?'

'You're still asking all the right questions, but we've looked at that too. Think about the usual motives for a murder. Greed, lust, envy, hate, fear, blackmail. They could all be motives, only right now I can't see an angle on any of them. Can you?'

'No, I can't, maybe except greed. Walker must have been well off.'

'Well off? Walker must be absolutely loaded.'

Anthony already knew Walker was very wealthy. All the directors of Steens would be rich enough. He wasn't impressed if Palmer was evaluating wealth on the basis of what a City of London Police detective earned—probably only in the low five figures?

'It wouldn't surprise me if he was a millionaire

when he died.'

'You're joking. He must have been a millionaire several times over. Steens must pay well,' countered Palmer.

Surely not. A director of Steens earned hundreds of thousands per annum, but Walker couldn't have earned millions at Steens. Palmer saw his look of incredulity and took him into a study room.

'We went through Walker's post. This is his current account statement. Last month the pay credited to his bank account from Steens was seven thousand quid. And look at the current account balance. It's eighty thousand quid. Imagine having that amount of cash in your current account. There are also blank lodgement forms here for offshore bank accounts, so he must have more cash stashed away there. Funny thing is, though, we couldn't find any more evidence of this. There are no statements from prior months anywhere in the apartment. They must be stored somewhere else or were trashed by Walker. And think about the value of this apartment. Must be almost half a million. He bought it for cash. No mortgage at all. And the two cars outside? A Merc and a Range Rover. One person. Two cars. What a luxury.'

Anthony gazed at the bank statement, still puzzled by the massive numbers he was hearing, yet the facts were clear before his eyes. Walker was filthy rich. Greed could indeed be the motive for his death. Not those crappy client letters or anything about EPIC or SCISCO. 'So who gets all the money? Is it his ex-wife? That's a motive, isn't it?' asked Anthony.

'It could have been a motive. Walker's will was

151

read this morning. It might have given us a lead if Walker had left all his loot to someone unexpected or unknown to us, but he didn't. He left the whole lot to his aged parents in Suffolk. I guess they're wondering what they are going to do with it. And I think we can rule them out as suspects since they are both almost eighty years old and were at a dinner party with other old fogeys last Sunday night.'

Palmer paced the room in apparent frustration, hands clasped behind his back. 'We're waiting for a break in this murder investigation, and I've no idea where it's going to come from. That's the real reason for my coming down here again. My fifth visit in as many days. I just hope that something will become obvious to me here, but it hasn't yet I could say that the only hope we have now are those letters which we found in his desk at your bank. It's a sorry state of affairs if we are hoping for a lead from them. Is there any?'

Palmer had been open. It was time for Anthony to be more honest. Sort of. 'Maybe. Maybe not. The visit to Amsterdam this week wasn't that productive. There are a lot more letters like the ones we found in Walker's office. I spoke with Johan Verhoeven, the managing director in Amsterdam, about them.'

'And what did he say about them?'

'Verhoeven says the client complaints are unfounded.'

'Well, he would say that, wouldn't he? We have to follow up every lead in a murder investigation like this. Is there anything else in the Amsterdam office that might be connected to Walker?'

'No. Nothing else has come to light,' Anthony

replied.

'Do you know if Walker had been over to Amsterdam recently?'

Anthony hadn't answered this question yet. He shook his head. 'Dunno.'

Palmer persevered. 'So what's the next step?'

'I sent two of my staff over there to do some further investigating. I'll make sure to advise you of the outcome of their work.'

'Just keep on investigating as best you can. I'm relying on you.' Palmer had the apartment keys in his hand. 'Seen enough? Then let's go.'

They walked towards the main entrance gate overlooked by a closed-circuit television camera. The mute uniformed policeman followed them. Anthony was waiting to see how Palmer would open the gate. The gates opened automatically. Palmer saw Anthony's surprise. 'There's a sensor in the wall there. As you approach the gate from the inside it opens automatically. Anyone can get out once they get in. Not great for keeping in murder suspects, is it?'

Anthony started to look for a cab, never easy to find in these quiet side streets of Wapping, away from the Highway and the traffic flow. Palmer obliged. 'We're going to Bishopsgate Station. It's near your office. Wanna lift?'

Anthony took the opportunity for his first ride in a police car as the uniformed driver took them back towards the City. At Tower Hill the traffic was snarled up with a tailback along Lower Thames Street. Anthony blamed the road closures in the City since the terrorist outrages. The Wall of Plastic Cones, as they called it. He was still thinking about the exit from Walker's apartment complex.

153

'Doesn't that CCTV camera record everyone who enters the building? Have you looked at the footage for last Sunday night?'

'It shows Walker's Merc entering at 9.37 p.m., but the camera is positioned too high for a clear view. You can see the car, but you can't see the occupants in the car. We also looked at the tape for all of Sunday evening, and every single car is accounted for because they all belong to other residents. Mostly returning from weekend country breaks.'

'Did anyone leave later in a car or on foot?'

'The cars that left later that night all belong to residents. The camera doesn't cover the side gate for pedestrians. That works by a sensor too. Anyone could have left the place undetected. Nice try, though.' Palmer looked at the jam and leaned forward in exasperation. 'Fucking traffic. Put the lights on.'

The driver flicked a switch below the dashboard. A siren started up and Anthony could see the reflection of blue lights on the double-decker open-top tourist bus beside them. Japanese tourists magically appeared over the edge of the top deck, gleaming Nikons and Canons in hand, wondering if they should record this moment for posterity.

The traffic ahead parted and they sped towards their destination. In five minutes Anthony alighted outside Steens. The police car moved off smoothly. Vanessa was returning from her very late lunch, carrying several shopping bags, spending her inheritance already. She looked surprised as she watched the police car head up towards Bishopsgate.

'Between that chat with the police on Monday

morning and now a trip in that car, people will think you're involved in Walker's death in some way. Tell me what that was all about.'

'Vanessa, as they say, I'm just helping the police with their enquiries.'

They encountered a group of macho dealers leaving for an even later lunch, probably substantially liquid in nature. They, too, had seen Anthony's celebrated arrival from the inside of Steens' reception lobby. Dave was among them and was the first to speak.

'Wow, Tony, dropped off by the police at Steens? I'm going to slash those odds on Walker's killer. You're now officially suspect number one. Guys, Tony Carlton is now five-to-one odds-on favourite as the Wapping Strangler. Game on?'

A beery colleague pulled out his leather wallet and showed a bundle of notes to Dave. 'I'll have a monkey on that.'

CHAPTER NINE

10.20 A.M.: MONDAY 25 MARCH: AMSTERDAM

Anthony had just stepped off the first morning flight from London. He hadn't expected to be back among the bustling canals quite so soon, exactly eight days after someone had tightly knotted a tie around the neck of Jeremy Walker.

'This place is a fucking disaster.'

He had never before heard a comment like that about any part of Steens. Gary had telephoned him

155

at home on Sunday afternoon. 'Everything we look at here is being manipulated by Johan Verhoeven. I've never seen anything like it in Steens in all my years here.'

Gary was taking liberties, having been at Steens for only three years. Gary and Steve looked physically and mentally drained. They had worked through the weekend on site in the Amsterdam office. So much had been uncovered that they simply couldn't leave. Anthony needed to see the evidence for himself. This was rapidly becoming the most serious investigation that his Control Group had ever undertaken.

The tangible evidence of the work to date was obvious as the three of them sat in the main conference room, impressive and large enough to seat twenty people around the dark boardroom table. Bulky computer printouts, files, deal tickets, pads of A4 paper, lever-arch binders and photocopies of client account statements were laid out. The remainder had overflowed to the floor. Pizza boxes and McDonald's bags discarded in the corner. The one token waste bin was overflowing with empty Coke and Sprite cans. No sign of any Amstel or Heineken beer cans. Gary was taking this job seriously.

Gary had delegated the task of writing the draft report. Steve committed the edited highlights to the hard drive of the laptop computer as he sat keying evidence and statistics into the pro forma report template. Verhoeven had ignored their work apart from a non-committal opening meeting. Whenever he had seen Gary or Steve in the office he simply gave them a distant stare. Maybe Verhoeven was confident that they would find nothing, just like those visits to Amsterdam in prior years? Maybe Verhoeven felt immune as a director of Steens? Maybe Verhoeven just wasn't interested? Anthony certainly was.

'Just tell me what you've found here, Gary.'

'First, you can tell us something, seeing that we're cut off in this backwater here. What's the latest news on Jeremy Walker?'

'Walker was murdered, but the police have no suspects and no motive. He was seriously loaded when he died. Lots of cash and his penthouse is mega. It looks as if being a director of Steens pays well. It's a good incentive for the rest of us.'

'Tony, isn't it scary when a guy who works in your office gets murdered and no one knows why? It makes you wonder what might be going on in Steens.'

'Let's not speculate. Leave that to the dealers. Let's discuss Amsterdam instead.'

Gary arched his intertwined hands behind his head. It was the classic power play, the body language they had all learned to use in Steens.

'I thought the best starting-point would be to get a printout here from the trade system of those who hold EPIC shares. Just stick in the ISIN stock code of EPIC and get a list of the account numbers of the clients who hold shares. The list from the computer system had about two hundred client accounts on it. The clients are not what you'd expect.'

Gary produced from one of the lever-arch files a computer list covered in annotations and with several client accounts circled in red ink or fluorescent yellow marker. 'Don't worry about the scribbling. It's my manic writing. Just look at the account types.'

Anthony looked down the list, which was ranked in order of the number of shares. At the top of the list was NedCorp with just under a million EPIC shares. Strange. Anthony thought they had an exact round million. Must have sold some recently? The rest of the list showed small shareholdings in EPIC. The accounts were all private clients, lots of unpronounceable Dutch names. Anthony didn't recognise any of the names, but he was worried. EPIC was not the ideal investment for a private client.

'See the names? They're all private punters. Look at the account codes. They are the same as last week at the briefing. They are all discretionary accounts, and some hold mail accounts too. We've looked at some of these client accounts in detail. Here are their account statements showing all their buys and sells in the last two years since EPIC was floated off.' Gary produced some Steens statements.

'Here's the NedCorp statements first. They managed to sell thousands of EPIC shares in the past week. What's unusual about that? Nothing, except look at the prices they got. It's exactly the same price that they paid originally, ten bucks each. They broke even. Unbelievable.'

Anthony gave Gary a withering look, one of severe doubt. 'But NedCorp can't have sold them at ten bucks. The price has been less than five bucks for months. Dave told me as much. How did NedCorp get such a good price?'

'The shares weren't sold to the market. Some clients inside the office here bought them.'

'Which clients would be stupid enough to buy

EPIC shares now at ten bucks?'

'The discretionary clients. Only they never knew they had bought them until much later. I think NedCorp must have been pissed off at the way the share price was going. Verhoeven must have been under pressure, so he bought them back from NedCorp and sold them to these poor discretionary punters who had no say in the matter. It's a terrible abuse.'

'Why didn't NedCorp sell all their shares at ten bucks?'

'Given time, maybe they will. But I guess that there's only so much crap you can put into private clients' accounts before they start to complain. It was a start for NedCorp.'

Anthony needed to find a culprit fast. 'Who booked these deals between NedCorp and the private clients?'

'One guilty suspect. I've seen the original trade tickets for the deals. They are all in Johan Verhoeven's handwriting, and he even initialled the trade tickets. The staff in Operations here confirmed to me that Verhoeven originated the deals. They were keen not to be associated with the bookings themselves. They say that they just book the trades they're given. It's more than their job's worth to query trade bookings from a director of Steens.'

Gary was delivering a litany of bad news. Verhoeven had sold the shares to NedCorp two years ago in April. They had all watched the EPIC share price go down, and then NedCorp complained. Verhoeven effectively reversed their purchase, NedCorp got the full price back for some of their shares, and then he got the discretionary private client accounts to buy into EPIC at the original price of ten bucks. It was a sure thing for the institutions, but a sure loser for the private clients who trusted Steens. Gary saw Anthony's disbelief.

'There's more. See this account here on the client list?' Gary said, pointing to a name circled in red. 'It's some Dutch word, but it translates as warehousing. It's a bloody warehousing account.'

Many of Steens' offices used warehousing accounts for intraday business. No one could buy a hundred thousand shares in one fell swoop without alerting the market to a big buyer on the prowl, and then the price would rise before the buy could be made and the client would be pissed off and would go elsewhere for his next trade. So they used the warehousing account.

It was easy. Buy, say, twenty thousand first thing in the morning. Then another twenty thousand in mid-morning. Another thirty thousand just before lunch. The balance early in the afternoon after the market opens and the brokers are still sated by a heavy lunch. Then you had your total hundred thousand by stealth. The market never knew that a Steens' client was getting into the stock big time. Book the buys to the warehousing account and at the end of the day book the entire hundred thousand out to the client. Then the warehousing account had nil shares. Case closed.

Only the warehousing account here still had EPIC shares. No client legally owned shares in any warehousing account, and if the clients didn't own them then by cruel default they belonged to Steen Odenberg NV. Steens still owned some of this damn EPIC issue. It should have been all sold.

160

Dave back in London would not appreciate that Steens were left holding a rump of this magnitude. One hundred thousand shares that were down five bucks each was half a million dollars down the pan. That was half of the deal fees that Dave had earned in London.

Gary wasn't stopping now. 'The next logical step for us was to get the account statements for the warehousing account to see how the EPIC shares were acquired.'

He opened a bulging folder of statements, hundreds of pages of computer listing. 'This is just one year's activity, and I have never seen a warehousing account like this before. There are more trades going through this account each day than there are going through other entire Steens' offices in a week.'

The transaction volume was enormous. Several hundred entries in and out of the account each day. It was far too many. No one needed to put this many entries through a warehousing account.

'And what do you think of the prices? Pick any page.'

Anthony scanned the prices, expecting to see the same prices on the buy side and the sell side, to see that the in and out account moneys balanced out to nil and to see that no profits or losses were made in the account. But all the entries were at different prices, and each day there was a profit or loss on the account. Steens were making a profit or loss out of this risk-free service they provided to clients.

Gary couldn't be stopped. 'We looked at some of the prices of the trades. We got some price histories from the London research analysts using statistics from the Reuters screens. We got them for the major Dutch stocks, Phillips, KLM, Royal Dutch Shell and Polygram. The prices at which these trades go through the warehouse account are different from the quoted share price in the market on the day. Sometimes they are way off. It's classic off-market pricing.'

Steens couldn't do this either. Securities deals had to be executed at the market price. If you did an agency deal via a local stockbroker in the market, then the price reflected the current market price, but Steens were booking deals between clients internally, which bore no reflection to the reality on the floor of the Amsterdam Stock Exchange. One client account made a killing; the other client was hung out to dry. Anthony realised that the numbers in the warehousing account looked seriously big.

'Is this warehouse account in the black or the red?'

'In the red, big time. Year to date it has lost five million guilders. Another three million or so in the preceding twelve months. It's a black hole, and it's getting worse, not better. The recent fall in the Dutch stock market has taken its toll. And the losses haven't been reported to London yet. I checked with our finance people there. The losses are held in limbo in this account in the meantime.'

This wasn't a warehousing account. It was a principal dealing account. It was for punting in the market. It was the exact sort of principal dealing that was prohibited by London in the Amsterdam office.

Gary had found another angle on the unrealised losses in the account. 'You know that the office here is required to make a monthly return of its

162

liquidity surplus and capital solvency ratios to the Dutch Central Bank. The monthly returns are incorrect, and Verhoeven personally signed all the returns in the past year. An intentional breach of reporting requirements to the banks' principal regulator in the Netherlands is a serious matter, and Verhoeven is personally responsible.' He rose and pointed out another account on the list of EPIC holders, one with a red circle around it. The account owned just a few thousand EPIC shares. He grinned. Strange. Not much to laugh at here.

'Look at this account with EPIC shares. It's called Hoop. I just thought it was some Dutch company. I asked some of the reception staff in our hotel for a translation. The account name just means Hope. The name puzzled me. So I got the client file out, but there's nothing in it except an account-opening form. I hassled a clerk in the Operations Department here. He wasn't keen to tell me about it, but I leaned on him. It's a staff slush fund. He says they buy and sell a few shares in it most days and try to make money in it. Then every now and again the cash profits are used to pay for a staff party, drinks out, a trip or just a cash bonus for all the staff. They love it because it's all tax-free for them. It's a bribe to keep them loyal, I guess, but loyalty only goes so far. You can see the cash payments on the statement. Ten or twenty thousand guilders at a time.'

'Who actually operates this account?'

'Verhoeven signed the account-opening documentation two years ago, and I've got a copy so he can't do anything about it now. And he has signed for all the cash withdrawals. He knows what's going on. The guy in Operations here confirmed it. Here's another account. It's called Leopold. I thought, That's a strange name, either someone's surname or first name. I asked who was the person behind the account, and the guy just kept on laughing. Then he says, It's not a person, it's a horse.'

'A horse?'

'Yeah, a bloody horse. Leopold is a three-year-old flat-racing nag that races in the UK. It even wins now and again. The account was opened when the horse had its first decent win, and the rest of the syndicate gave the money to Verhoeven to invest it in whatever shares he saw fit. The account buys and sells shares and takes the profits out in cash every few months. Guess who owns the horse? A syndicate owned by Verhoeven and a few of his local cronies. The account is bloody profitable too. This horse is a genius when it comes to picking shares. It should become a City fund manager and give up racing. I mean, how can Steens here have an account in the name of a horse? It's ridiculous.'

Steve was smiling too. He had obviously learned a lot here in the past few days, about events that should not happen in any investment bank, especially one with the reputation of Steens.

Gary was growing more animated with each passing revelation. 'We reviewed the discretionary client accounts. Some of these clients are in the most risky types of investment that even you and I wouldn't touch. They have lost so much money that a high-risk strategy is the only one that will possibly recoup their losses. They have been investing in call options that become worthless when the share price falls. They are also buying warrants on some Dutch stocks, only they, too, have expired

164

worthless. It's not just a partial loss on their investment, it's a total loss.'

Anthony's professional opinion of Gary was growing by the minute.

'Most of the accounts have broken the basic rule of investment. Diversification. They have all their funds in just one share so that their entire return is based just on the vagaries of that one share. Pick a good one and you're laughing; pick a dud and you're fucked entirely. And in a falling market, Verhoeven has not been good at picking winners. His accounts are under-performing the ASE market index. Some of his clients are buying and selling the same shares on the same day for a quick buck, instead of investing in the longer term as they should. Nice bit of textbook churning for extra commission. Others are buying speculative unknown shares that are just not worth investing in at all.'

Gary cheered up momentarily. 'There is a funny side, too, at times here.'

'Like what?'

'One other account on the EPIC list here is a numbered account. Top secret. The client had been described to us as Verhoeven's girlfriend, but really she's just a bit on the side. The guy in Operations just had to tell me. He couldn't stop himself at that stage.'

'So what about the account?'

'More important, what about the girl? The guy in Operations says he saw her in the office several times, mid-twenties, more than twenty years younger than Verhoeven, short black skirts, serious bod, great set of pins. God, I'd love to meet her. We must interview her as part of this investigation.

I don't think theirs was a platonic friendship—purely physical, more likely. I'm told Verhoeven's wife knows nothing about her.'

'There's no law against having a girlfriend on the side with an account in the office. Is there, Gary? Jealousy will get you nowhere.'

'Correct. But there is a law against sticking profitable backdated trades into her account, at the expense of some other client. Here's how the account works. Verhoeven goes out with her in the evening on the town and has a damned good shag. Comes into the office next morning with a big smile on his face, but is totally knackered. Verhoeven moves a good trade of a few days ago from some poor sucker's discretionary account into the girlfriend's account on one ticket and then sells it out of her account to some other poor sucker, leaving a cash profit in this girl's account. Mostly it was just, say, a thousand guilders' profit per trade. Not a bad return for a youngster like her, and a nice reward for putting up with someone like Verhoeven. Her statements in the past few months show that there isn't a single unprofitable trade in her account. It's classic manipulation. There's a cash payment of about fifty thousand guilders a few months ago. More or less cleaned out her account. What a service this office provides, as long as you are a friend of Verhoeven's.'

Gary was concluding. 'Tony, you'll see all these facts in our draft report, but there's so much here that it will make Verhoeven's position as a director untenable. Verhoeven has shafted the private clients here in every way possible. Think about what happened with those EPIC shares with NedCorp. And those clients buying and selling shares from the warehousing account and making big losses, too, dealing at off-market prices, and the trades that are backdated to get the maximum advantage. That's probably the worst part. Imagine being able to buy a share today but at the price that it traded at, say, last week. It takes the whole gamble out of shares. You simply can't lose: you don't buy unless the price has gone up in the past week.'

Anthony tried a different angle on the worsening scenario. 'We're all sitting here thinking that Verhoeven is behind this activity. But is there enough proof? Do we have enough on him personally?'

'That's what we wondered at the end of last week, so we asked people here about some of the deals. The guys who work in Operations who process all these trades all swear that Verhoeven directs the bookings that we've found. We have the trade tickets. They say that Verhoeven himself made all the bookings to the warehousing account, and to the Hoop account and to the girlfriend's account. He's as guilty as hell.'

'Maybe Verhoeven can explain things?'

'It would have to be one hell of an explanation.'

'What's his motivation? What has he actually gained personally?'

'Lots. Firstly, consider EPIC. If you've sold some crappy new issue to your best institutional client then you're in trouble from day one. If they are unhappy, then you lose their future business and the office commission revenue plummets. So Verhoeven accommodates them, takes some shares off them and allocates them to the not-so-poor but innocent private clients. So he has reduced his

EPIC problem. But the best bit I've saved until last. Nearly everyone who works for Steens anywhere in the world has their own personal account. Verhoeven has a staff account here where he buys and sells shares in his own name. It's a bit ironic, but even he had a few thousand EPIC shares himself. Probably bought them when he ran out of private clients to shaft. We had a look at his statements for the past year and he's made a fortune in his account. Some of his trades match up with trades in the warehousing account or with trades in the other client accounts. While they made the losses and complained, he made the profits personally. It just looks like sheer greed. Again, he has practically no loss-making trades in the year.'

'But aren't copies of his account statements sent to the London compliance department?'

Everyone in Steens who had a personal account had it automatically copied to the compliance department so that they could independently review the account activity. It had been part of Jeremy Walker's department's responsibilities.

'Nope. Verhoeven had the copy statement suppressed on the computer system. One of the girls in the Operations Department said that he instructed her to delete the copy to London Compliance when the account was opened years ago. No one independently saw the activity in his personal account.'

Anthony thought about the impact of the evidence before him. Verhoeven was a director of the bank. The result of this investigation would be a report that would be a damning indictment of one of the most powerful people in Steens' worldwide. It could be a major coup for Anthony and his team, or it could be a career-limiting decision of epic proportions. 'What's the status of the draft report?' he asked.

'Steve has a draft. It's thirty pages long. We'll follow normal procedure and discuss the draft with Verhoeven before we leave, so that he can reply to it as soon as possible.'

Anthony wasn't sure he would follow normal procedure. This was no longer a normal investigation.

*　　　*　　　*

Anthony left the boardroom to get a drink in the office canteen. It was devoid of people, quiet and fortuitously well stocked. He raided the fridge for a chilled diet Coke. It was there for the taking, and the caffeine was a good stimulant in times like these. As he left the kitchen he was pleasantly surprised. Again.

'Anne.'

'Anthony.'

They spent slightly too many moments looking at each other, searching for the next conversation piece. She spoke first in a slightly hushed voice. 'I am glad to see you here again, Anthony. Can I talk to you some time?'

Anthony wasn't expecting the conversation to go in this particular direction. He wondered whether it was about work or about something else.

'I want to talk to you about what's going on here in this office.'

Work. This was neither the time nor the place to ask her what she meant by that comment. 'Sure.

169

When?'

'The sooner the better. Meet me at one o'clock in the bar on the other side of the canal, the one with the big red canopy outside.'

Anne left the kitchen as suddenly as she had appeared. She hadn't even got what she came in for. Her sensation of hunger or thirst had passed. Her mind was on something else.

Within the hour, Anthony sat at a table for two. He didn't choose a table outside by the still canal and the gaze of the passing public. He sensed that Steens' staff should not observe them talking together and went inside. This was an authentic Amsterdam bar, what the locals called brown bars. A chiselled mahogany bar ran the entire length of the dim establishment. The dark wood-panelled interior had nicotine-stained walls and ceilings from the smokers over the years, decorated with memorabilia of Amsterdam's colonial and nautical past. The bar hadn't changed in over a century, just the way it was supposed to look. A range of beer taps was arrayed along the counter of the bar, but Anthony as a rule didn't drink at lunchtime, particularly if he had to confront Verhoeven later that afternoon.

Anne was punctual. She moved her chair so that she faced the entrance door a few steps above. Anthony felt that it was an instinctive move on her part. She could see all entrants from that position.

'I hope you don't think that this is too weird, my asking you to meet up here.'

'I never turn down an invitation to lunch.'

'Let's order in a minute. I am so wound up. God, I just had to get away from the office. When I saw you I thought that maybe you can help me. Why are you here in Amsterdam?'

'I can't tell you that right now.'

'It's about those client letters, isn't it?'

Anthony didn't acknowledge her well-informed question. He waited for Anne to go on to see if she knew what she was talking about. The thought suddenly crossed his mind that Verhoeven had sent her on an intelligence-gathering mission. He feigned ignorance. She persevered.

'The letters of complaint that we keep getting from clients? God, I am so sick of them. I am in the front line. I open Verhoeven's post every morning, and there are so many complaints coming in to us. It's terrible. And there's the telephone calls. The clients ring in and ask to speak to Mr Verhoeven. He won't take their calls, and they just take it out on me over the telephone. The worst part is when they visit the office in person. I have instructions not to let them near his office. Some of the older clients are in tears when they leave. They all seem to be losing lots of money, and they hate Verhoeven and they hate Steens. I think they even hate me now. I don't know what's going to happen.'

She was taking this opportunity to exorcise her frustration. She was genuinely concerned. It wasn't an act. A waiter hovered beside their table. It wasn't the right time to order, but Anne stopped talking. The waiter instinctively looked at Anthony and spoke in Dutch. Anthony was lost. Anne ordered without a glance at the menu. The waiter left.

'I've ordered something quick and Dutch. You'll like it. Did you get the Scholten letter?'

She knew about the Scholten letter. He was speaking to the anonymous source of the internal

171

mail sent to London.

'Yes, I did. What made you send it to me?'

'Anthony, I thought that no one would listen to me. I am just a secretary. If I did anything, Verhoeven would fire me and I need this job. He would make it difficult for me to get another job. He might not give me a reference. So I decided to send some of the client letters anonymously to London. The truth would come out. I thought the best recipient would be the Head of Compliance, the director called Jeremy Walker. Do you know him? I sent him about ten letters over several months, but he did nothing at all. Then we received the letter from NedCorp, so I sent that to London, because I thought that a big institutional name would grab Walker's attention. Nothing happened. It was a great disappointment to me. I remembered you from your short visit here last year and that you sometimes worked on the same assignments as Walker. I sent that one letter to you. And now you are here. I am so glad. I hope that you are investigating the letters.'

'Yes, I am.'

'And there's a team of you here?'

'There are three of us here.'

'Good. I was worried. When I heard last week that Jeremy Walker had died at home, I thought that no one else would investigate these letters. Pity he died so young too.'

Anthony had just appreciated what Anne didn't know. Walker had died violently on a Sunday evening in London's Docklands. Management in the Amsterdam office had not bothered yet to tell her of the exact circumstances of Walker's demise. The local press would not have picked up the

172

London story. Anthony had to tell her, but in the gentlest possible manner. Again, the waiter appeared with the worst possible sense of timing. He placed some substantial soup, crusty buttered bread and green salad before them. Anthony couldn't start to eat until he told Anne the full story. 'The police believe that Walker was murdered.'

She dropped the metal soup spoon on the table. The clatter distracted nearby diners.

'My God. Who would want to murder him?'

The police don't know.'

'Is this to do with the client letters I sent him?'

'I don't know. There are probably other lines of enquiry for the police.'

'Like what?'

Palmer had no other decent lines of enquiry. Anthony couldn't offer Anne any comfort 'I can't think of any immediately.'

'Because maybe there aren't any. God I sent him those letters, and now he is dead.'

Anthony was speculating too. Anything could happen with a bunch of angry clients and an investor like NedCorp who had lost six million dollars to date on EPIC.

'God. I am scared. So alone.' She paused for dramatic effect. 'I don't want to be alone. Do you want to meet up this evening? I can cook at my place. I will feel safer.'

Temptation personified. A loaded question. But Anthony was already spoken for.

*   *   *

Anthony, Gary and Steve went for a traditional

173

Dutch evening meal, specifically for an Indonesian feast off the Leidesttaat. It was almost the national dish for the locals. The rijsttafel was famous, literally a rice-table. Over twenty different dishes arrived—pork in spicy satay sauce, roast meats in coconut sauce, spicy pimento and fish paste and much more—all complemented by varieties of rice and soups, mixed fruits in syrup and locally brewed Grolsch. They talked shop during most of the meal. It was a hazard of the job.

Afterwards they walked down by the canals. Anything for a change from that boardroom. Gary and Steve headed towards the Oudezijds Voorburgwal off Dam Square to see one of Amsterdam's most famous tourist attractions, the red-light area of Zeedijk. Tiny narrow streets with huddled men in winter coats, hands in pockets, eyes wide open, strolling by the young pseudo-models in the open doorways and brightly lit windows, cigarettes in hand, in one-piece curve-hugging lace lingerie and pancake make-up.

Anthony had seen it all before, and once was enough. He left the voyeurs. It was a strange form of relaxation, but it was all Gary and Steve were going to get before tomorrow morning's difficult closing meeting with Verhoeven. Anthony arrived back at the Grande Hotel on Dam Square. The duty manager confirmed that a suite was booked in his name.

'I see that you, too, are booked in at the special Steen Odenberg corporate rate?' enquired the lonely guardian of the reception desk at the unsociable hour of almost midnight. Steens never paid full rates anywhere. Why should they, with the amount of business they gave to the members of the Leading Hotels of the World? 'We get many visitors from your bank here. It is good for our business.'

Presumably he was referring to the salesmen and research analysts and corporate finance experts who visited all the overseas offices. Anthony said nothing to encourage this futile conversation, but the manager needed to break the monotony that lay ahead of him into the small hours of a Tuesday morning. There was an open drawer behind the reception. Anthony was noticed staring at the contents. Another opportunity for some conversation.

'It's lost property, sir. We get so much here. People leave the strangest things behind. I go through it now and again to see if I can get rid of the items after a few months. It's a very popular task among the hotel staff. Some good items sometimes for us to keep.'

Anthony was looking at one item, a scarf with a fox-hunting scene emblazoned across the silk folds. He knew that scarf. He had seen it worn in London by a very close friend. 'That hunting scarf there? Is that a Gucci scarf?'

The manager examined the label. 'Yes, it is, sir. The label says so. Do you recognise it?'

'I'm not sure.'

Anthony was one hundred per cent sure. Vanessa's missing scarf. But it should be lying in his W9 apartment or in her Notting Hill Gate pad, not in a lost property drawer in Amsterdam.

CHAPTER TEN

9.04 A.M.: TUESDAY 26 MARCH: AMSTERDAM

Anthony blamed his lack of sleep on the noisy canalside Grande Hotel, the anxiety of the confrontation to come with a director of Steens and the risk of doing serious damage to his career. Was he mad? Should he just pack up and return to London and forget all about this? Was it worth the risk of falling foul of someone like Verhoeven? Would Derek back him up in London or leave him to the wolves?

The closing meeting had been arranged via Anne for nine o'clock in Verhoeven's office. The early start meant there would be enough time to discuss all the issues. They sat at Verhoeven's imperious desk. Verhoeven had changed since Anthony's fast visit last week. Gone was the smiling oily veneer. He was annoyed at their presence and was hostility personified even before Gary gave him a copy of the draft report. It was now thirty-six pages long, and the inside contents page read like a litany of abuses. Steve had done a good job on the draft. He would indeed be hard to keep if other predatory banks moved to poach him. Anthony made his usual introductory speech.

'This is a draft report which summarises the results of our review. The report will be finalised after you've had time to read it and have supplied us with a written response.'

Verhoeven cut in immediately as he turned the

first page and saw the contents page. 'Jesus Christ. What are these items here? What's the point in dragging all this up?'

'These alleged matters concern some private client activities, the warehousing account, other house and staff accounts, and also the EPIC share issue.'

'You can't be serious. This has nothing to do with you.'

Verhoeven had not yet denied the facts. His first reaction had implicitly agreed the findings of their work. Verhoeven paged through the executive summary and the detailed commentary, visibly unhappy with the textual matter that he digested instantaneously.

'There's no way in hell that this report is going futther than this office. No bloody way at all. Let's agree right here and now that this report has got to be canned. You work for Derek Masterson, don't you? I'll talk to Derek. I will talk to Sir James. This report is out of order. The best thing that you can do is leave right now before I say something I will regret. In any case, I have another meeting in ten minutes.'

Anthony didn't want to further infuriate a director of Steens. Verhoeven rose from his desk. It was a definite sign to them to leave. There were no goodbyes. They didn't shake hands, and before long they found themselves in the corridor outside Verhoeven's closed door. Gary and Steve hadn't even uttered a single word in the abortive meeting.

Anthony slumped in a boardroom chair. Gary and Steve packed a couple of banker's boxes and put the copies of files and printouts inside, any original documents being left behind as was their usual practice. The Amsterdam office could express-courier the boxes back to the London head office, but on this occasion Anthony was taking no chances. They would take the files as baggage to Schiphol and put them in the plane's hold. This was the evidence for the prosecution, if such was required.

Their original flight departure time of mid-afternoon had been slightly optimistic in hindsight. Anne changed their flights to mid-morning and booked a taxi. Anthony and the team were carrying their boxed files down the steps of the office when Verhoeven reappeared.

'Hold on, Mr Carlton.'

Verhoeven must have read the report by now, and he would be seething. Surely he wasn't going to discuss it on the office steps. They would have to start the meeting all over again. Verhoeven descended and stood very close to Anthony, pointing at the boot of the taxi. 'What the hell is going on here? You can't take files with you. They belong to this office.'

'These are photocopies and duplicate printouts. All the originals are still in your office.'

'You have no fucking right to do this.'

'With respect, we do. The board of Steens empowered the Control Group to take copies of whatever information we need on our visits to any Steens offices.'

The tension was broken when the impatient taxi driver decisively slammed the boot shut. Verhoeven swore and climbed back up the steps without another word. The taxi pulled away. Round one to Anthony, but the bout was only beginning. And Verhoeven had more experience and contacts in his corner than Anthony would ever possess.

*　　　*　　　*

The trio flew in a turboprop Fokker F-50 plane from Schiphol direct to London City Airport. They shared a black cab on the twenty-minute trip westwards, past Jeremy Walker's penthouse apartment off Wapping Highway, and finally into the familiar City. Anthony was back on the fourth floor just before lunchtime once he wound his watch back by an hour. There was a pleasant sense of security and continuity working from base, rather than existing in some borrowed office or shared conference room.

He first had to insure himself against the backlash that was sure to come from Amsterdam. His boss was the best insurance policy. Derek saw him first and came directly over.

'What the hell happened in Amsterdam, Tony? I just had Johan on the phone. He's really pissed off. He called Sir James too. This is getting serious. He asked that we scrap your investigation immediately. Can you do that?'

'It's not that easy.' Anthony ran off a copy of the report on the laser printer in his office. He handed the warm pages to Derek. 'Have a read of it and then we can talk about it.'

Anthony made for a delicatessen downstairs as Derek returned to his office, report in hand. He waited in the queue, got a turkey salad with port and cranberry stuffing on a granary bap with extra mayo, walked back across Broadgate with one eye on the variety of talent ahead of him and took the lift back to the fourth floor just as Derek returned

179

to his office.

'Jesus. All this can't be true?'

Anthony spoke through a mouthful of turkey breast and radicchio leaves. 'Yes, I'm sure it's true. We have the evidence,' he said, pointing to the recently arrived banker's boxes of files set out on the floor in the corner of his office.

'We've enough to worry about here at the moment with Jeremy's death. We can do without this. What does Johan say about it all?'

'He refused to give the report any credibility. Our closing meeting was five minutes long, and he just attacked our work. It's as if he believes he is immune because he is a director.'

'Who knows about the contents of this report?'

'You and I do, and so do Gary and Steve and Verhoeven. That's all.'

'That's probably too many people already. Who has a copy of this draft report?'

'There are only two copies in existence. Verhoeven has one and you have the other.'

'Good. We must find out if there's any substance to these allegations. I'm going up to the seventh floor to talk to Sir James before this all gets out of hand. This could be very damaging to the reputation of Steens if word leaks out anywhere.'

Derek returned from the executive floor in less than ten minutes. 'We just had a conference call. Johan didn't want to talk about it over the telephone, but he read the report this morning. He wants to put everything in context and says that what you have written is biased and factually incorrect in places.'

'So what happens now?'

'Sir James has called a meeting upstairs for ten

180

o'clock tomorrow morning. You, Sir James, Johan and me. That gives Johan enough time to get over here tomorrow morning. Then we can resolve this matter once and for all. You'd better be prepared for a tough meeting. We don't want to waste Sir James's time. Do we?'

*　　*　　*

Anthony planned a quiet evening because he needed to prepare before he presented the facts to Sir James the next day. Then he wondered if he should instead invite Vanessa over to Maida Vale this evening. She would be a pleasant distraction from other pressing matters. Sex was just about better than investment banking. They could go for a meal where Anthony was always given the best table overlooking Little Venice and the multicoloured barges moored along the Regent's Canal. The staff there liked big tippers from the City who carelessly handed over the Amex corporate card when the bill arrived.

Then they could go home and enjoy each other in the king-sized bed. Maybe he could find out subtly when she was last in Amsterdam and why? That Gucci scarf still puzzled him. Maybe it belonged to someone else?

Vanessa returned from her lunch and Anthony cornered her immediately by the coffee machine. Worth a try now at least. 'How are you, Vanessa?'

'All the better for seeing you.' She kissed him briefly yet meaningfully. 'How was Amsterdam again? Find anything exciting over there at all?'

'All I can say is that it was an experience.' He pushed his luck and steered the conversation

181

subtly. 'I like Amsterdam. We should go there some time. Ever been there yourself?'

'Yeah, sure. Lots of times.'

'Been there recently at all?'

She shifted uneasily, almost spilling the piping-hot plastic mug of stagnant brown gunge. Coffee they called it.

'Depends what you mean by recently, doesn't it?'

Was she denying that she had just been to Amsterdam? Could he push her? She still hadn't answered his last direct question. He didn't dare mention that scarf in the hotel lobby drawer. There was no point in having an argument now. Leave it until later that evening.

'Fancy coming round later this evening?'

'Sure.'

'Say at eight? We can talk about our break in Amsterdam and get something to eat.'

'Tony, I already know what you want to eat.'

She ended the conversation abruptly by taking the decaff no-milk back to her desk.

*   *   *

Anthony watched Vanessa in the late afternoon through the glass window of his office. She was speaking on the telephone and her side profile was perfect, a gracious face, elegant fingers wrapped around the handset. He wanted her tonight. Badly. She began to frown, then she noticed him and turned. She called to him from outside his office. 'There's a telephone call for you, Tony.'

'Who is it?'

'Johan Verhoeven.'

Anthony had no option but to take the call.

'Hello, Anthony.'

Verhoeven was trying for the warm personal touch. Anthony had difficulty making him out clearly due to the background traffic noise. Johan explained. 'I'm on the mobile on the way in from Heathrow. I want to talk to you before our meeting tomorrow morning. Can we meet up this evening?'

Verhoeven sounded almost sociable. Anthony couldn't find an immediate reason not to meet him. Perhaps it would make their meeting tomorrow morning less confrontational and less of an ordeal for all concerned? He agreed. Verhoeven was pleased.

'I am staying in the Tower City Hotel near Tower Bridge. I'll be there as soon as this M4 traffic jam clears. Let's meet in the hotel lobby at seven o'clock.'

Time to go. Anthony tidied up his desk and passed Vanessa.

'What did Johan Verhoeven want?'

'Just business. Nothing to worry about.'

Anthony left for a meeting with a Steens director, for which he had no agenda whatsoever.

*   *   *

The Tower City Hotel was a short cab ride. On the way Anthony used his mobile to book a table at the Little Venice place for eight-thirty. This meeting with Verhoeven couldn't take more than thirty minutes. The cab fought against the juggernaut traffic coming from the News Corporation fortress printing works near Tower Bridge where *The Times* and the *Sun* were produced by the million every evening. He was driven past Walker's apartment for the second time that day. Here was another square mile of London, so different to his own beloved Square Mile. This area contained the most historical of London's bridges, Verhoeven's Tower City Hotel and Walker's vacant apartment.

He alighted at the covered lobby entrance of the Tower City Hotel just before seven o'clock. Perfect timing again from Anthony. At least, that's what Vanessa always claimed. Anthony loitered in the anonymous lobby for a few minutes, looking for Verhoeven. Then, as if on cue, his subject appeared from the bank of lifts. He shook hands warmly for some reason. 'Hello, Anthony. Thanks for coming along at short notice. Have you eaten?'

'Not yet.' Anthony was about to mention that he had a hot date at half-past eight but missed the opportunity to speak before Verhoeven decided for both of them.

'Let's get something here in the hotel. All I got on the plane over here was rabbit food.'

Verhoeven had not invited him here just to share a meal. There had to be an ulterior motive. There always was with Verhoeven. They went into the adjacent brasserie and took a table near the entrance. Anthony subconsciously sat in the better seat with his back to the wall, facing towards the rest of the brasserie. He could engage in his favourite hobby of people-watching. Vanessa or Gary or whoever always accused him of grabbing the best seats in restaurants. Why not?

Verhoeven looked tired. Sitting up close at the table, Anthony could see that his eyes were slightly bloodshot. His pupils rolled as accuser kept steady eye contact with accused. His shirt was badly creased, probably from sitting in a cramped

184

aeroplane seat for too long. He hadn't showered when he had reached the hotel, and his top shirt button was undone. His tie was at a slight angle. Tousled hair. For the first time, Verhoeven didn't look like a director of Steens. He looked addled.

They ordered quickly from a standard menu that had been solely created for homesick carnivorous American tourists. Enormous blue steaks, deep-fried chicken, varieties of pasta, deep-pan pizza, and pasty French fries with everything. Verhoeven ordered a bottle of a substantial red and went for a sirloin steak with fries, onion rings and the works. Not a health-conscious person. Anthony took a side salad. Verhoeven looked unimpressed, but he didn't know that Anthony had to eat later on. Verhoeven got down to business as he took a satisfying taste of the decanted wine. Then a large gulp. Down in one. Quick drinker.

'You know why I asked you to meet me here?'

'It's about my report?'

'You're right, but first of all I want to apologise for my reaction today and for swearing at you as you left the office. I spoke out of turn. Apology accepted?'

Verhoeven was too accommodating. Anthony was beginning to see where the conversation was going. This was the softly softly approach by Verhoeven. He could try it, but it wouldn't work with Anthony.

Verhoeven continued, taking Anthony's silence as acceptance of his dilatory contrition. 'I have since reread your draft report. Sure, some of it is true, but most of it is not, or else the facts have been distorted by your team—by Gary and Steve, I stress, not by you.'

Just too civil.

'I don't want us to have a disagreement tomorrow morning in front of Sir James and Derek. There must be a better way of dealing with this. It does none of us any good to fight among ourselves within Steens. We are all part of the same bank.'

'What do you suggest?'

'I suggest that we reconsider this report. Think about what you really want to say, but cut out any references to the private clients and drop everything you have said about EPIC. Just tell Sir James that you wish to reconsider the contents. You and I will sit down and we will agree a revised report that's a proper reflection of the facts. Can we compromise on that?'

There wouldn't be much left to write about. It would be a climbdown. 'I don't think we can, actually.'

Verhoeven sighed, topped up his glass and took another long drink. He ominously fingered the rim of the almost-empty glass on the table and looked pensively at Anthony.

'Let me spell it out for you. I am a player in the world of finance in Amsterdam. I am head of the biggest investment bank in the Netherlands. I have spent years building up the reputation of our office, and if any of the items in your report get into the public domain then I will be finished in Amsterdam. I have enough problems with Jan Peters and NedCorp at the moment, trying to keep them sweet. I will be an outcast in my own home city, and I am not going to let that happen. I would never work in this business again. And it will all be your fault. Can you live with that?'

Verhoeven was shaking. Actually shaking. As he held another full glass, Anthony could see the meniscus of the red move steadily. Those eyes were still strange. Glazed? Wandering around? Anthony countered what was becoming an increasingly desperate plea. 'So the NedCorp facts in the report are true?'

'Forget about those. Just put an end to this report.'

'That's not within my power. I'm simply reporting the facts as they exist.'

'Let me put it another way for you. I am a director of Steens. Sir James is a good friend of mine and has been for many years. He asked me to this meeting tomorrow morning and that's why I am here in London tonight, not because of you or any of your team. Sir James is not going to side with you against someone whom he has trusted for years to run the European operations so successfully. He's going to stand by me, and then you will be left totally exposed. Are you ready for that? Are you ready for a hard time tomorrow morning? Are you ready to be unemployed? P45 time?'

Anthony wasn't ready for the latter scenario but bluffed a response. 'I am prepared to debate the facts tomorrow. I have the full support of my boss, Derek.'

'Him? Derek has spent all his time in finance and administration and all the other support activities in Steens. He's just one big cost centre. He has never brought a single cent of income into this bank. Not like me and Sir James and Jeremy Walker and the other directors in the States and the Far East. We keep this bank going, not people like you and Derek. You are just getting in our way with your petty attitudes. Don't mess me about, Carlton. If you stand by this report tomorrow morning, I'll see to it personally that you have the shortest career in this bank. And that's a promise, not a threat.'

He had reverted to surnames. The tone was mean and personal. Verhoeven had a fist clenched tightly and put it down on the table hard, shaking the wine glass and the china plates on the crisp linen tablecloth. Some red spilled over and immediately spread into a large noticeable stain. An embarrassed couple sitting at the table next to them looked over to see who was creating the unpleasantness. Their waiter glanced over. Verhoeven was coming close to the end of the bottle of red. Anthony had had enough of this tirade.

'I came here to meet you in good faith tonight, but I don't have to sit here and take this sort of abuse. I'm just doing my job, and the real decision lies with Sir James and the other directors. Then I'll move on to the next investigation.'

'Why don't you do that right now? Just forget about Amsterdam and do something else?'

Anthony had decided in the past twenty-four hours on his next assignment

'My next trip will be a visit to our Frankfurt office, where I understand the EPIC fund is administered. That entire deal needs to be looked at.'

'What? EPIC? You can't look at that. No way. That's the issue that I saved at the last minute. There's nothing wrong with that. I will make sure with Sir James tomorrow morning that you go nowhere near the EPIC deal, let alone our Frankfurt office. This time you will be stopped in your tracks before you even begin.'

Anthony had had enough. He dropped his napkin on the table. 'I'm going. Thanks for the meal.'

Anthony had eaten nothing at all. Verhoeven stood up also. Wobbled slightly.

'You are just going to fuck off home and leave me here? You dig up all this shit about my office and then EPIC. You just have no idea what this will do to me. Do you? Where's your fucking sympathy?'

Anthony was already heading towards the exit as Verhoeven vented his audible anger at him. He didn't answer the last rhetorical question. He had never encountered anyone in Steens who possessed that elusive emotion called sympathy, not even in the wider investment banking world for that matter. Sympathy meant weakness and compromise. Sympathy was something that traders with million-pound losses or salesmen with falling commission revenue hoped for but never got until they were politely asked to leave Steens.

Anthony saw the waiter staring. Obviously, this sort of hostile encounter didn't frequently happen in the hallowed environs of the brasserie of the Tower City Hotel.

*   *   *

Anthony thought about Verhoeven's state of mind while he sat in his cab on the way home to Maida Vale. The guy was screwed up inside. He could do anything. As they travelled along the Embankment

189

before heading northwards through the West End, Anthony looked forward to a more appealing meal with Vanessa within the next hour.

By twenty to nine he was totally exasperated as he sat alone in his apartment flicking through the relevant pink business pages of the *Evening Standard* for the third time. There was no sign of Vanessa. He'd telephoned her twice, but there was no answer from her apartment. Just that damned answering machine again. Then his mobile telephone rang. It must be her. No. It was the restaurant in Little Venice. Where was the Carlton party of two booked for half-past eight? Anthony lied with a decent excuse and cancelled the unnecessary booking.

At nine o'clock he nuked some unrecognisable plastic food from the freezer in the microwave and ate solo in the kitchen, looked out at the red-bricked mansion apartments across the communal gardens and contemplated Vanessa's unexplained last-minute absence. Again.

CHAPTER ELEVEN

8.55 A.M.: WEDNESDAY 27 MARCH: CITY OF LONDON EC2

Anthony wasn't often nervous, but today was different. He was about to meet Sir James Devonshire, Derek Masterson and Johan Verhoeven in the boardroom on the seventh floor. This was a chance to impress the right people. If all went well, Anthony's career prospects in Steens would be significantly enhanced. If, however, the Amsterdam report were rubbished and Verhoeven went on the offensive with the support of Sir James and Derek, then his career in Steens could be short and sweet. Anthony knew the entire Amsterdam report verbatim by now and was lost in deciphering Gary's scribbled file notes when Vanessa appeared and stood in the doorway, posing provocatively against the wall.

'Sorry about missing last night.'

'What happened?'

She leaned on the desk, her body scent arousing his senses. Tresses of hair tumbled downwards. He was more disposed to an apology than he was last night.

'I had to see a girlfriend who was ill. She asked me to call at short notice. Am I forgiven?'

Her smile meant that he had no choice.

'Sure, but next time a telephone call would be a good idea. How about tonight instead?'

'I'll let you know later.'

She was playing hard to get today. Anthony's attention focused back to his work. He wished he hadn't come in so early. Derek appeared just before ten.

'Ready?'

'Ready as I'll ever be, Derek.'

Anthony wore his suit jacket, compulsory attire on the seventh floor. They rode the lift together and stepped out on to the thick-pile carpet. Derek led the way through the hallowed environs and the maze of private offices. Suddenly Anthony saw Sir James alone in the main boardroom. He sat at the head of the long polished mahogany table, looking as if he always sat at the head of every conference table. It was his right. It was only five minutes to ten, but Sir James had made it to the boardroom first. Not a good start. Sir James was immediately sociable towards Anthony. It was a promising sign. Nevertheless he didn't make small talk.

'You have done some detailed work out in Amsterdam,' he said, looking at an open Amsterdam report on the table. He had made a copy of Derek's from yesterday.

Sir James sat back, folding his arms in a subconsciously defensive manner. More Steens' body language that Anthony had learned to read. A bad sign.

'This report makes surprising reading. There are always two sides to every story, so I hope that Johan will be able to put these items in context this morning. Then we can find out if indeed they are correct. Derek, how many copies of this report are now in circulation?'

Maybe Sir James wanted to can the report or was Anthony reading too much into his words?

'There are now four copies in existence. You, I, Anthony and Johan have one each.'

'It's best to keep this to a minimum circulation until we know exactly what has happened in Amsterdam. That piece about a horse having an account there. That can't be true, surely?'

'I believe it is true.'

It wasn't the time to mention that Gary was convinced that the account-opening form for that particular account should have had a hoof print. They sat without conversation for a few minutes until the wall clock showed five minutes past ten. Sir James broke the silence. 'Where is Johan?'

Neither Derek nor Anthony could offer an

192

immediate answer. Sir James took a decision.

'If Johan isn't here in the next five minutes, I'll get Carole outside to call Amsterdam and find out what flight he is on or find out if he was staying overnight in a hotel here. I've got an eleven o'clock with some of the dealers after this. I can't wait around here too long.'

Of course, Anthony knew where Verhoeven had been staying last night. The Tower City Hotel was only ten minutes from the office. Johan couldn't be stuck in traffic. Maybe he had overslept? No. Investment bankers don't oversleep. They are too hyperactive, and missed meetings meant missed deals, missed fees and missed bonuses. He was about to offer his opinion when there was a firm knock on the door. Verhoeven at last. A secretary opened the door and spoke to them all collectively, but she was looking only at Sir James.

'Excuse me for interrupting you, but there is someone here to see you.'

'That will be Johan from the Amsterdam office. You know him, don't you, Carole?'

'Yes. I know Johan. But it's not him. It's a policeman. D-S Palmer.'

Sir James did not look pleased. 'We are about to hold a meeting. Tell him to wait outside until we are finished.'

'He says he must speak to you now. It's very important.'

At that moment Palmer brushed past Carole and entered the boardroom. He was wearing that shiny blue suit again. It must be the only one he possessed. He looked excited. 'Excuse me, gentlemen.' Then he saw Sir James staring at him. 'Hello, Sir James.'

193

Sir James gave him a hard look. Palmer didn't waver. He had the nerve to sit down at the end of the table directly opposite the chairman.

'I take it that you are all senior management so I can speak freely. I want to tell you . . .'

Sir James cut in, his demeanour growing more agitated by the minute. 'Can you keep this short? We are expecting the director of our Amsterdam office here at any moment for an important meeting.'

'I'm afraid he will not be coming. We had a call at seven o'clock this morning from the Tower City Hotel. They reported that a guest had been found dead. He was Dutch, and his passport is in the name of Johan Verhoeven.'

The three Steens people were stunned. Sir James spoke first.

'You can't be serious. There must be some mistake? How can he be dead?'

Palmer relaxed, knowing now that he had the undivided attention of the Steens trio.

'I've just returned from the hotel. We believe that it is Johan Verhoeven. The face of the deceased matches the passport photograph. Man in his late forties. Blondish hair. Lanky. Glasses. I knew that he was a Steens person the minute I entered his room. A copy of that same report that you have here on the table was on the desk in the room. I recognised the bank's logo on the front immediately.'

Sir James asked the obvious question no one else dared to ask. 'But how did Johan die?'

'He was found lying face down on the concrete roof over the main lobby entrance of the hotel. It seems that he fell from the balcony in his room;

194

he'd consumed a lot of alcohol before he died. The post-mortem will tell us more later.'

Only Sir James had the strong constitution to think logically.

'Is there anything that we can do to help?'

'First we need someone to formally identify the body. I gather you all knew Verhoeven, so I thought one of you could oblige.'

Sir James was not keen. Derek nodded reluctantly. Anthony prayed it wouldn't be him. Sir James expounded their collective view. 'I'm not going to that morgue again. One visit last week to identify Jeremy Walker's body was enough for a lifetime. And I guess that goes for Derek too.'

All eyes turned to Anthony, who was not enamoured by the prospect of looking at a corpse. Verhoeven had been bad enough when he had been alive. But he had little choice from the way Sir James was looking at him. Time to volunteer. 'I'll do it.'

'Is there anything else you need?'

'We want to find out more about Verhoeven's last movements in London. The hotel staff say he checked in at half-past six last night. We want to find out whether he went out last night, met people or anything useful like that.'

Time to volunteer again. However reluctantly. Better now than later. 'I met Johan yesterday evening.'

Sir James and Derek both looked at Anthony with surprise.

'Verhoeven telephoned me at about six o'clock from a cab on the M4 and said that he wanted to talk about the Amsterdam report. I met him last night in his hotel. He insisted.'

'What time did you meet him?'

'Seven o'clock.'

Recognition dawned on Palmer's face. He took out a notebook and flipped the pages. 'Did you have a meal with Verhoeven in the hotel brasserie?'

'Yes, I did. Why?'

'The hotel staff saw Verhoeven having an argument with someone who fits your description around that time.'

'It wasn't an argument. It was just a discussion, but Verhoeven got carried away.'

'What do you mean?'

Anthony thought back to yesterday's fraught conversation. He was beginning to wish that he had never visited the Tower City Hotel. He was rapidly becoming the prime suspect. 'Johan was reasonable at first, but he got confrontational. We talked about the Amsterdam report and the EPIC fund.'

'And when did you leave?'

'Half-past seven.'

'Short meal!'

'It was unpleasant. He threatened me about my future career in Steens.'

'What mood was Verhoeven in when you left? Angry, depressed, agitated?'

'I'd say all three.'

'Do you think he might have been suicidal?'

'I don't honestly know how a suicidal person behaves.'

'Did he drink much?'

'Yes. He downed a bottle of red wine in ten minutes. It was a good vintage, too.'

Sir James cut in. 'This discussion can be held at some other time. I need to contact the other directors, the remaining directors that is. Anthony, you should go and identify the body as soon as possible.' Sir James motioned for them to leave.

Palmer spoke directly to Anthony. 'Let's go and do the formal identification of Mr Verhoeven.'

*   *   *

Anthony got into the marked police car parked outside Steens, his second trip in this car in as many weeks. Fortunately, Dave did not see him sitting inside or his odds in Dave's murder book would have been even shorter. Bill the security guard looked uneasy as he viewed the scene in the knowledge that a police car did not convey the right impression to Steens' corporate clients who passed by on their way into the sumptuous lobby to attend meetings about friendly mergers, hostile acquisitions and finely priced new issues. Perhaps they would think that the police were here to drag away some Steens' employee in handcuffs who had been caught cheating clients. Unlikely in Steens. More likely in lesser banks.

Ten minutes of lunatic driving later, they had crossed the river, entered Guy's Hospital and pulled up outside a low nondescript building. A sign indicated that this was the hospital morgue. They parked on a double-yellow line directly outside, one of the perks of driving a police car around Central London. Damn the parking regulations.

Inside, there was an overpowering disgusting odour of sickly disinfectant. Anthony immediately felt uncomfortable in this 1970s NHS environment, preferring the modern air-conditioned environs where he was an expert and people respected him

197

for his knowledge. Here, in this unfamiliar sterile building, he was a nobody in a hand-tailored suit. Palmer knew where to go, and they turned into a room off the main corridor. A man in a grubby white coat with protruding assorted coloured pens in a top pocket acknowledged their arrival.

'You're here for the Dutchman?'

The morgue attendant led them into another room. He evidently knew Palmer well.

'Second body in as many weeks, D-S. This is getting to be a bit of a habit.'

Palmer shook his head. He didn't want to discuss Walker right now. 'This gentleman here is from the bank where the deceased worked.'

The room was cold, like stepping into an open refrigerator. Three walls of the morgue were tiled in gleaming white; the fourth had a row of metal doors. In front of an open door was a steel trolley. The outline of a body under a dark green surgical sheet was clear. For a moment Anthony wondered if perhaps the dead man wasn't Verhoeven. Perhaps it was all a mistake, and after this they could all go back to Steens and just carry on with normal work and the Amsterdam report and life in general as if nothing had happened. If only.

Anthony was transfixed by a line of ten toes which protruded from the end of the sheet. They were jaundiced and stiff. On one hung a plastic tag with a computer label and a bar code. The deceased was just a number. Anthony felt early pangs of nausea as he wished there was something he could steady himself against. That clinical smell was overpowering.

The mortuary attendant looked at Anthony to ensure that he was ready to view the body. Worse nausea. There was no going back now. Anthony conveyed his readiness. The sheet was slowly rolled down to reveal a man's face. Anthony looked hard at the face and recognised the sandy hair immediately. It was definitely Johan Verhoeven. Palmer waited for Anthony to confirm verbally Verhoeven's identity. He didn't. He needed to be prompted.

'Can you identify the body? Is this Johan Verhoeven from your Amsterdam office?'

'Yes, it is.' He almost threw up as he said the words. He needed to leave the room as quickly as possible and strode out of the morgue to control escalating nausea. Palmer followed him, four or five paces behind. Anthony wanted to get back inside Steens as soon as possible. He was sick of Palmer intruding into his normal working day. Palmer interrupted his train of thought.

'Take one of these. Polo mints are a wonderful cure for looking at dead bodies. They take away the smell of this place and get your mind on something else quick. It's an old trick. Works every time with the few people I bring down here.'

Anthony ignored Palmer as he stood in the fresh air taking in big gulps. He was recovering. Time to get back to normality in the City. Palmer had other ideas.

'Would you like to come with me in the car?'

Anthony had had enough of the alleged thrill of a trip in a police car. 'No. I'll get a cab instead.'

Palmer stood before him. 'I'll rephrase that question. I'd like you to come with me, Mr Carlton. I'd like to talk to you down at the police station.'

'What? Why?'

'I want to talk to you about the deaths of Walker

and Verhoeven.'

Anthony had had enough of Palmer. 'No way. What do I know about them? Anyway, you can't make me go to the station.'

'You are, strictly speaking, correct. But there is a hard way and an easy way to do this. I could make you go to the station if I wanted to. Neither of us wants to do that, do we? Coming along voluntarily is the best option for all concerned. It's a lot less hassle than getting a warrant, or even arresting you.'

Anthony had no choice. Reluctantly, he got into the car for the second time that morning and crunched a Polo mint. It was better than saying something he might regret later.

*   *   *

The interview room at Bishopsgate Police Station was awful. Nasty fake wooden tables, harsh fluorescent lighting, a total absence of windows, and uncomfortable black plastic chairs that seemed to have four legs of differing lengths. Anthony was getting a headache by merely being in this room. He could now see why Palmer had been so impressed with Steens' offices on the seventh floor. Palmer and some uniformed sidekick sat opposite across the narrow table. There were three white plastic cups on the table containing the worst coffee Anthony had ever tasted. It seemed to be compulsory. The sidekick hadn't said a word yet, but instead was poised with a notepad and pen. Anthony was livid.

'This is outrageous. I came into work as usual this morning, then you drag me down to the morgue to identify a dead body, and then you force me to come here to talk to you.'

'I am sorry that we have inconvenienced you, Mr Carlton, but this is a necessary part of our enquiries.'

Palmer had resorted to calling him Mr Carlton. Too formal. Palmer produced two tapes and placed them in an ancient taperecording machine by the table. Anthony was surprised.

'Hold on a minute. What's with the tapes?'

'It's normal procedure. You can take one with you afterwards. It's for your benefit too.'

That was trite and they all knew it. Anthony didn't like what he saw.

'Don't I have some rights here? Should I get a solicitor?'

Anthony was desperately trying to think of the name of a suitable solicitor. He knew many ex-Cambridge types who had become solicitors, but they all worked in the City. They were experts on company law, Eurobond issues, prospectus-drafting, tax-avoidance measures, special-purpose vehicles and offshore company formation, but they wouldn't know what to say to a man in a police interview room who was about to be questioned about the deaths of two directors of a leading investment bank.

'Mr Carlton, relax. You are not under arrest Remember that you have come here voluntarily. Do you really want a solicitor? Do you think that you might need a solicitor?'

Palmer phrased the last question in a precise manner. It was an insult. Anthony was going to bluff him instead. An honours graduate of Cambridge could outwit a couple of policemen, even on their own home turf. If only they were all in Anthony's office. He would feel more secure there. Palmer hit the play button on the tape and there was no going back.

'Interview with Mr Anthony Carlton of Steen Odenberg. Time is half-past eleven on Wednesday the twenty-seventh of March. Present are D-S Palmer and PC Wilson. Mr Carlton has come here voluntarily. Isn't that correct, Mr Carlton?'

Anthony nodded but said nothing.

'For the tape, please.'

'Yes.'

'We wish to discuss the recent events in Steens with you, concerning the deaths of Mr Walker and Mr Verhoeven. Firstly, can you describe your job in Steens.'

Anthony stated the obvious for both of them.

'And did you know both gentlemen who died?'

A loaded question, a curved ball. Palmer was enjoying this. Anthony did his best to field it 'Yes, I knew both of them, but not very well. You could say that all three thousand people who work for Steens in London knew them since they were both well-known figures within the bank.'

'Just answer the question if you can, please. Where were you on the night that Walker was murdered?'

Jesus. Palmer was asking him if he had an alibi. This got worse. Shit. If only Walker had died a week earlier. Anthony would have been six thousand miles away in Harry's Bar on Boat Quay having a pitcher of San Miguel with a few of the Singapore office staff. Perfect alibi. Damn.

'On that Sunday night I was at home. I was tired because I had just arrived back from a two-week

202

business trip to our Singapore office on the Saturday morning and I was still jet lagged. So I had an early night after watching some television.'

'Alone?'

'Yes, alone.'

'When Mr Walker died, you agreed to investigate some letters of complaint which had been received from Amsterdam clients just before his death.'

'Correct.'

'Can you tell us about the results of that investigation?'

'I investigated the complaints and found that there was some substance to them.' Anthony wasn't going to disclose any more to Palmer voluntarily. There was no benefit to be gained by hanging out dirty washing in the full view of the police. But Palmer wanted more.

'What sort of substance?'

'Some of the clients may have a valid complaint about the conduct of their dealing accounts in the office. Prices of share transactions may have been adjusted, and certain connected or house accounts may have been favoured to the detriment of other client accounts.'

The sidekick wrote this jargon down in his notepad but said nothing. He wouldn't understand it at all. Perfect. Palmer, though, seemed to have taken it on board.

'So the clients have lost some money?'

'Possibly.'

'Much?'

'Hard to tell yet. Depends on what your definition of "much" is, doesn't it?'

'Much' to Anthony was a few hundred thousand.

'Much' to Palmer was probably closer to a fiver, the amount of money he spent on a soiled polyester tie. Palmer reached a dead end. Anthony wouldn't say any more. This was Steens' business. Palmer changed tack.

'Let's turn to Mr Verhoeven. You met him last night?'

'Yes.'

'What happened?'

'He wanted me to abandon my report on the Amsterdam office. He was pleasant enough at first, but then he made a bit of a scene. He threatened me. That's when I left.'

The waiter believes that you threatened Verhoeven also.'

'No. That's ridiculous.'

'You were the last person to speak to Verhoeven?'

'Is that a statement or a question?'

'It's a question.'

'No, I can't possibly be. Surely he spoke to the hotel staff after I left?'

'No, he charged the restaurant bill to his room and left the brasserie. The receipt shows that was at seven thirty-eight. We've shown his photograph to the lobby staff. No one saw him in the public areas of the hotel. The doorman didn't call him a cab or anything like that. We know Verhoeven didn't leave his room again. The room doors in the hotel are all activated by a credit card-type key— just slide it in and out of the lock. The magnetic strip records all activity, and we had it interrogated by staff in the reception area. The last time the card was swiped through the lock was at seven forty-two. That's four minutes in the lifts to get to his room. Nothing after that at all on the card.'

Anthony decided to say as little as possible.

'Did you go directly home after the meal with Verhoeven?'

'Yes, I did. I was at home all yesterday evening too. I just read the paper, ate a bit and watched television for a few hours.'

'Alone?'

Anthony had been waiting for Vanessa to arrive last night, but she had never turned up. He wished now that she had. Not for the fantastic carnal sex that he had forgone in the king-size, but for the perfect alibi she would have provided for him. Anthony had just happened to be alone in his apartment on the two nights that the directors had died. Big pity. 'Yes, alone.'

'Finally, Mr Carlton, do you have any opinion on the deaths of two of the directors of your bank in such a short space of time?'

'Only that I don't like what is happening in Steens. I guess the deaths must be connected.'

'Connected? How?'

'Connected since they both worked for my investment bank, albeit in different countries. I suppose to lose one director in a week is unusual, but to lose two is too much of a coincidence.'

'Do you think someone out there has a grudge against the bank and maybe they are taking it out one by one on the directors?'

Anthony wondered if Steens was going progressively to lose all its directors over the next few weeks and if there would be more vacancies on the board as a result. It nught even be good news for him from a career point of view. He answered politically. 'I can't comment on that.'

'Thank you, Mr Carlton. That's all we wanted to ask you. Thanks for coming in.'

The sidekick stopped the recorder and took out one of the tapes. He handed it to Anthony. 'This is your copy.'

'I don't really want it, to be honest.'

'You have to take it, it's the procedure.'

Anthony took the tape and put it in the pocket of his Kowloon suit. He was still livid. He rose to leave. Palmer was a total bastard, and he wouldn't speak to him again unless Palmer had a court warrant in one hand and a pair of handcuffs in the other. Palmer stood up, blocked his exit and firmly motioned for him to stay.

*   *   *

Palmer relaxed and pulled back his short-legged chair from the table. He changed his demeanour almost instantly. Anthony didn't know if this was the softly softly approach.

'I think I owe you a sort of apology.'

Anthony also thought Palmer did but waited for his adversary to expand.

'There is a story going around our police station. Some of the other guys on this case were asking me who you are, and what you do. Their imagination is running wild. They insisted that I pull you in and talk to you about Walker's and Verhoeven's deaths. They all know that you knew Walker, corresponded with him, and that you've just spent time with Verhoeven in Amsterdam and now that you met him last night. So I had to bring you in and interview you. Procedure demanded it. The PC will get our taped conversation typed up and that will

206

keep the others happy for a while. Friends?'

Anthony wished that Palmer had mentioned this earlier in the conversation. Protocol had prevented it. Maybe Palmer wasn't that bad. Better to have him on your side than against you.

'Now that the formality is over, can we talk off the record about Walker? We might have a lead in his murder enquiry, and I need your help.'

'You have a suspect?'

'When you and I were travelling back from his apartment, you asked me about the surveillance cameras in the apartment complex. I did some lateral thinking. We know that our suspect wasn't there when the neighbours called us. All the cars parked overnight are accounted for, so our suspect must have left on foot and walked around in Wapping.'

Anthony was with him so far. Palmer was on a roll.

'So how did our suspect get home? He could get a bus, but there are few buses in Wapping at that time of the night or morning. It's bad enough during the daytime. So that's not very likely. He could have got a cab, but that's unlikely too. Cabbies don't cruise around Wapping looking for business at that hour. It's too far out of the way for them. So what's the alternative? Wapping tube station is just around the corner from Walker's apartment and it's open until midnight on Sundays. If I were the murderer, that's how I would get home.'

Anthony nodded in agreement. It's quicker by tube, as they say.

'There is a surveillance camera as you walk into Wapping tube station. No one can avoid it. We got the transport police to lend us the tape for that night, and we went through it for the few hours before the station closed at midnight on Sunday. It looks promising.'

'You've got the murderer?'

'Not exactly, but there were only about ten people who entered the station during those few hours. God knows why they keep the place open for that number of people, but they do. These are the mugshots of the people who came in. Any familiar faces?'

Palmer produced a collection of large, glossy photographs from a buff file and placed them on the table. Jesus. Palmer was asking him to identify a suspect, even a murderer. Maybe one of these photographs would be of a Steens employee, someone whom Anthony knew. A dealer or a salesman or an operations clerk? Anthony looked at each photo carefully. An old couple. Two guys in suits. Two girls. Old dears. A few kids and their parents. A young guy. No one he recognised. Anthony was almost relieved to be able to report a nil return. 'I don't recognise anyone.'

Palmer deliberated. 'Me neither, but then I made some deductions.'

'Like what?'

'Do it by a process of elimination. Eliminate the old couple and the old dears. It's very rare that you find someone in their seventies with the strength to strangle a man in his late forties. Eliminate the parents with the kids. People don't bring their entire family when they are going on a murder trip. Then consider the two girls and the two guys in suits. People don't murder in groups. Murderers are solitary animals, in my experience. In any case

208

the station staff recognised the two guys in suits. They run a wine bar in Wapping and close up every night after eleven o'clock. They always catch the tube at that time.'

'So we are left with this young guy?'

Palmer put the black and white computer-enhanced picture of the youth in front of Anthony. He was in his early twenties, looked Asian or Chinese, possibly of mixed race, wearing a baseball cap with some indistinguishable red logo, the peak pulled down over his eyes. He was clean shaven with an earring in his left ear, and wore a dark bomber jacket with his hands in his pockets in a somewhat furtive manner.

'I was hoping you might pick out this guy. Perhaps he is an employee of Steens?'

Anthony looked closely at the picture. If it were someone from Steens, then they would have an impossible job justifying their presence at Wapping tube station near Walker's flat that evening. But Anthony was certain of his earlier judgement. Steens was full of white Anglo-Saxons, few others, but there was one obvious giveaway.

'He doesn't work with us. Who the hell would get a job in Steens with an earring?'

Palmer hadn't thought of that. The two of them looked at the photograph. They were both of the same mind. Palmer spoke. 'He is our best hope for a suspect.'

Anthony agreed. Palmer gathered up the photographs. Anthony was still troubled by his visit to the police station. Still pissed off that Palmer had dragged him there.

'Am I a suspect in the eyes of your colleagues because I knew both directors and I have no alibi for either night and was the last person to see Verhoeven alive?'

'Of course not. I told my colleagues that you are a City gent, and City gents don't murder other City gents. Do they now?'

CHAPTER TWELVE

12.44 P.M.: WEDNESDAY 27 MARCH: CITY OF LONDON EC2

Anthony was grateful for a deserted office at lunchtime after the appalling morning. Gary was out for a drink at the Flute. Derek was booked at a long-arranged flashy lunch with clients on the seventh floor which he couldn't get out of, even on the day of the death of another director. Vanessa was out picking up trinkets in the designer shops of Broadgate Arcade, where only the wealthy dared to tread.

He hunted down an early edition of the *Evening Standard* to see if there were any more articles about deaths in Steens. The paper was lying on the photocopier, obviously left there by someone who had copied the crossword. Dossers. Probably Gary. No news today. Verhoeven's death had been uncovered too late in the morning to make the first edition. The photocopier was beside the fax machine. Anthony noticed an incoming fax on the machine, still unread. The header on the page caught his attention. Tower City Hotel— tranquillity in the City of London. He wasn't sure if Verhoeven would wholly agree with the bland sentiment.

The fax was addressed to a David Masterson of the Accounts Payable Department. The hotel had got both Derek's first name and his job title wrong. There was a big difference between working in the Accounts Payable Department and being Steens' finance director, specifically a six-figure salary difference. The fax referred to a guest who was an employee of Steen Odenberg & Co., one Johan Verhoeven, and in the circumstances the hotel requested the London office to settle his account. The guy was only dead less than twelve hours yet they wanted his account settled. For one lousy night. They must be tight.

The bill for room 812 was two hundred and thirty-five pounds and was fully itemised. One hundred and sixty pounds for the room. A bit steep when Verhoeven hadn't even used it for most of the night, preferring for some reason to lie outside on the concrete roof of the hotel lobby. Thirty-five pounds for that abortive meal in the brasserie, where the confrontation was included in the price. Forty pounds for room service. Verhoeven must have been very hungry. Attached to the bill were receipts for the latter two items. If nothing else, this hotel was efficient. Anthony screened the receipts out of natural curiosity. The brasserie receipt was timed at 7.38 p.m. The room service receipt was a surprise.

Anthony expected the usual room service fare. A triple-decker club sandwich or a plate of sticky pasta with a lukewarm beer, the typical investment banker-snatched meal after a deal-consuming day. There was only one item on the receipt, however. A bottle of Moët & Chandon champagne at forty pounds. Cheap enough. It was a strange order for Verhoeven, given his state when Anthony had left him. What was he celebrating? And the delivery time was a surprise too. The receipt showed that the order was placed at 10.14 p.m. and delivered at 10.21 p.m. by a waitress named Maria. Verhoeven had been up late drinking in his room.

Anthony recalled his own experiences. If he were on a business trip somewhere, when would he order a bottle of champagne at that hour? There was only one occasion, when he had the company of a female in his hotel room and he wanted to impress the hell out of her easily. That was in the old days, when he played the field with airline stewardesses from Singapore Airlines and MAS, secretaries from corporate finance departments, and lithe floor-dancers from Manhattan nightclubs. Heady days but bad days. Now he had Vanessa and that was where his future lay.

Verhoeven was like Anthony in the old days. Someone else had met Verhoeven later that night. Hopefully. Good news for Anthony, who did not wish to remain as the last known person to have met Verhoeven. Someone else should be in the frame instead, someone else who did not have an alibi around the time of the events that took place in room 812 in the Tower City Hotel.

That would be one for D-S Palmer to figure out. He returned to his office and dialled. 'D-S Palmer, please.'

He was there this time.

'Palmer speaking.'

Anthony wondered just how technologically advanced the Bishopsgate police were.

'Me again. Have you got a fax machine down at

212

the station?'

'Yes, we do.'

'Then stand by it. I'm sending you Verhoeven's hotel bill from last night. It shows that he ordered champagne at 10.14 p.m. Check it out with the waitress who delivered it to the room. Her name is Maria. Find out if someone else was in the room with Verhoeven at the time it was delivered.'

Anthony faxed the evidence. It was up to Palmer to investigate this further. He held the successful fax transmission report in his hand, as if it were his own royal pardon. God. It felt good to give Palmer some instructions for a change. What Anthony had deduced just proved to himself that Palmer knew absolutely nothing about investigating a suspicious death. Would he ever find Walker's murderer? Or the real cause of Verhoeven's death?

*   *   *

Derek entered Anthony's office. He didn't knock. He didn't need to.

'I heard the body was confirmed as Johan Verhoeven's.'

'Yes, it was.'

'That's bloody awful. Sir James gave me his instructions about the draft Amsterdam report. He says to put everything on hold until we find out more about how Verhoeven died. We can't run with a report which is a damning indictment of a man who never had a chance to defend himself.'

Anthony agreed.

'Sir James wants the four copies of the report shredded. He has shredded his own copy. I binned mine. Do the same to your copy now. I don't want

213

anyone outside this bank getting wind of what might have gone on in Amsterdam under Verhoeven's tenure.'

Derek personally supervised Anthony as he fetched his copy of the report, ripped off the plastic ring binding and fed the pages in bundles into the ravenous shredding machine in the stationery room. Gradually the report disappeared, much to Derek's satisfaction. 'Now wipe the report file off the network. Trash those boxes from Amsterdam too.'

Anthony brought up the file on his PC screen, dragged the mouse over to the delete button and binned the file. It disappeared from the file directory. Gone for good. Mission nearly accomplished, but there was one problem that Anthony had identified.

'Where is Verhoeven's copy of the report?'

Derek realised the awful truth. 'That cop Palmer said he saw it in the hotel room. It's still in Johan's hotel room. Get down immediately to the Tower City Hotel and bring it back here. And then shred it.'

'How can I do that?'

Just do it. This is important.'

*   *   *

Anthony took his second black cab from Steens to the Tower City Hotel in as many days and went directly up to the now-infamous room 812. Who'd want to stay in that room ever again? The door was guarded by a uniformed policeman and was closed off with regulation-issue blue and white chequered police tape. No entry. This was going to be impossible. Shit. Then the uniform spoke.

'Can I help you, Mr Carlton?'

The policeman knew him? Anthony looked again. The same burly cop who had driven Palmer's car. The one who had sat with Palmer across the interview table. The one who didn't talk much. PC Wilson. Thank you, God.

'I'm here to retrieve a copy of a confidential report that belongs to my bank.'

The policeman was not impressed. The scene could not be disturbed. Forensic people were still inside behind the closed door. Nothing could be removed until they had finished.

Anthony hadn't got the time to wait around all day. He could not return to face Derek without the report. He was desperate. 'Your boss, D-S Palmer, said it was all right to take the report back. It's business-related, and Palmer says he has no interest in that at all.'

The policeman acknowledged the name. It worked. He opened the door and showed Anthony inside. The room was chaotic, with broken glass on the floor and scattered bedclothes, pillows and duvets. Two plain-clothes policemen were out on the balcony dusting the top of the metal balcony railings with white powder. They looked uninterestedly at Anthony. Hc was fascinated by the scene. Eyes darted around looking for the report. But first he noticed a full ashtray and three cigarette butts. Strange. Verhoeven didn't smoke. Pieces of greenish tobacco in a plastic pouch beside it. One of the men on the balcony came into the room.

'Who are you?'

Anthony lied to minimise the complications of

215

the current situation. 'I work with D-S Palmer.' Sort of true in a way. Loosely, anyhow.

'See those butts? The guy who died was into pot. Smoked a few joints last night, and it sure ain't tobacco. Strong stuff too. Best we've seen for a while in London. Guess it's easy to get hold of it over in Amsterdam.'

'What effect does it have?'

'Makes you real heady, hyper too. Dilates the pupils. Insulates you against the world. Sometimes you feel you can almost fly.'

Looks like Verhoeven may have even lit one up before last night's meal. No lipstick on the charred remains either, thought Anthony. Verhoeven smoked alone. Then success as he saw his blue-crested report lying on the bedside table. He didn't need a second invitation and left the room as quickly as he could, report in hand. It had been easier than he had thought.

In the office he showed the report to Derek, as if proof were required Derek was satisfied. 'Shred it immediately.'

Anthony took his redundant report to the shredder and switched it on. This time the machine didn't respond. It was jammed with paper. Fuck. He had neither the time nor the inclination to delve into the sharp jaws to rectify the problem and lose a silk tie in the oily process. He would leave the report with Vanessa to shred. No. She wasn't there—still out? This was too confidential to leave on her desk in her absence. He took the report back to his office, put it in his filing-cabinet and locked the drawer. He would shred it later. Derek cornered him again.

'What are you working on at the moment? The

216

Singapore report, I presume?'

Anthony hadn't touched that yet. He was too preoccupied with other matters. He dodged. 'That's in hand, all right. I was planning to look at the EPIC fund.'

Derek signalled his evident disapproval. 'Are you sure? That's connected to Verhoeven and Amsterdam?'

'It's got more to do with the Frankfurt office. They administer the fund. A guy called Wilhelm Gausselmann does the paperwork there, according to Dave downstairs.'

'So what exactly do you plan to do on EPIC?'

'Go to Frankfurt and review the deal files for the issue. See how it was handled at the time. But I'll need your agreement before I go ahead.'

'Just don't do any more work if it leads to Amsterdam. Tie up the loose ends. You know Sir James's wishes. Slow down too. Don't kill yourself.'

Anthony knew Sir James's wishes all right, but he couldn't sit back and wait. He had an inherent interest in the business, and his curiosity about EPIC had been aroused in the past two weeks. It just seemed the right thing to do, even if he didn't yet know what the consequences might be.

*   *   *

By six o'clock Anthony needed some alcohol. The Flute was the best option. Gary might be there. Or Steve. Or Derek. And then home to Vanessa. No doubt this time. He finished his preparatory work on EPIC and the Frankfurt office, gathered his flight ticket and Deutschmarks for next week and left for some rest and relaxation.

The Flute was always full of fashionable locals celebrating their success of a week in the recently bullish equity and bond markets. But tonight it seemed different, perhaps emptier? Some Steens' faces were there, but there was less laughter than usual. Perhaps the events of the past two weeks had taken their toll.

No sign of anyone from his Control Group. Worse still, no sign of Vanessa. He had seen so little of her this week. In fact, there was no one that he could talk to immediately. Worth waiting though. Anthony took a stool by the window and ordered a bottle of chilled Pouilly-Fumé and one glass. Sad. The solitary drinker alone in the City. Alcoholism, here we come.

He people-watched around the bar in the vain hope of a sign of recognition from colleagues or otherwise. None was forthcoming. He was close to the midpoint of the bottle when the swing doors spun and a typical City creature entered. Tall, confident-looking, she wore an expensive, flowing coat that stopped just short of her high heels and slim ankles. She looked to be in her mid-twenties and carried the late-edition *Evening Standard* and a mobile phone in her left hand as she glanced around the wine bar, running her right hand through her hair nervously, perhaps looking for her hunky date for the evening.

They made eye contact for a moment. Was there some recognition? She was unsuccessful in her search for that loaded dealer or corporate financier with a wallet as big as his ego. She was momentarily alone. She walked towards Anthony, sat on a stool two away from him and waited. Dangerously close to Anthony. He risked a glance. She was even

218

better up close, jet-black hair, perfect skin, full lips, fragrant, elegant fingers too. Vanessa would never know. And what's the harm in talking? None. No law against it. There was absolutely nothing to lose as Anthony fingered the now-warm wine bottle.

'Want a glass while you're waiting?'

'Sure.'

Anthony couldn't place the accent. Maybe south of the river, but worked on. He had consumed sufficient wine to overcome any initial nerves. Conversation was easy for him. The second glass arrived.

'Good week, or bad week?'

'Dunno yet. It isn't over yet.'

Anthony poured her a glass as they sat by the window. She threw her coat over a nearby stool to reveal a well-tailored dark suit with a crisp white silk blouse beneath. They at least had something in common: good City dress sense.

'Nice suit.'

'Yours is good too. Hand tailored, I'd guess. Expensive?'

He shrugged. A mutual compliment. She had a good eye. She responded to Anthony's easy manner. She moved over to the stool right beside him. Promising.

'What about you? Good week?' the gorgeous creature asked.

'Shit week. Worst fucking week I've had in a long time.'

'What's the problem?'

Anthony was always careful in his work. He debated his next line carefully. The wine was beginning to work on his usual inhibitions. She used the temporary silence to place her newspaper

219

on the marble top. The front-page headline was solid bold text. It screamed out at Anthony. SECOND CITY BANK DIRECTOR DIES. Verhoeven was now officially news. Everyone knew.

'I work at Steens. We lost two directors in as many weeks, and the police are all over us.'

She acknowledged the mention of Steens. She knew of their reputation and their clout.

'I read about that. Walker and Verhoeven, isn't it? Are you involved?'

Obviously from another bank in the Square Mile. He shouldn't talk about it outside work, but she was keen. She opened the paper fully and her hand brushed against his. Just for a moment, but it was enough. Warm flesh on warm flesh. She was hot. If he didn't talk she might just get up and leave, and he would be a solitary drinker again.

'I'm actually helping the police with their enquiries into the deaths.'

'That sounds ominous. You must be important in Steens.'

She was saying all the right things. She was really interested. She was flirting. Definitely. She flashed those eyelids and raised her eyebrows. Next stop Flirt City. All aboard.

'What are you helping the police with?'

If Anthony weren't yet drunk, he was well on the slippery slope to a garrulous state.

'I'm investigating our office in Amsterdam. Some clients complained about irregularities there to Walker, who was dealing with them when he died.'

'Complaints about what?'

'I can't be more specific. It's confidential to

Steens.'

She used her City knowledge and eased even nearer to him.

'It would have to be about the client accounts, wouldn't it? It must be.'

She was intuitive. Anthony reacted facially, but ever so slightly. She noticed it.

'I am right? Are they serious complaints? Could they be enough to kill someone? How much money is involved? Who do you think killed Walker?'

'I have no idea.'

'And Verhoeven? Did he jump or did someone just make it look that way?'

She was indeed well informed

'No idea.'

'C'mon. I need to know. It's fate.'

'What do you mean, it's fate?'

'I was one of the first people to hear of Walker's death. I was going to work early a week last Monday morning and a guy said that there was a commotion down in Anchor Yard, and that some wealthy banker was dead. I went down there on a hunch, I guess. I know that Anchor Yard is a flashy place. Some of the penthouses there cost close to a million pounds each. I guessed that this dead banker might just be someone important. When I got there I couldn't believe my luck when I found that it was a director of Steens who had died.'

She was up early because of her job? Perhaps a fixed income trader or an equity derivatives saleswoman or a research analyst? She paused and looked guilty.

'I didn't mean that to sound the way it came out. I am sorry Walker died, but we all have a job to do. I spoke to a few policemen and residents there and

221

then dug out some of Steens' annual reports in our business library to learn more of Walker's role.'

Anthony was worried. What did she do in the City? Why this morbid interest in the deaths? She stretched towards her glass, and the sleeve of her blouse moved to reveal more about her. Not a precision Swiss watch. Rather a knotted brown leather wristband Never worn by a citizen of the City. Worrying. Time to find out.

'We haven't been introduced Anthony Carlton of Steens. My friends call me Tony.'

'Jennifer Sharpe. Mine call me Jenny.'

That name rang a bell. She solved the puzzle in Anthony's hazy mind.

'I'm a journalist. I work for the *Evening Standard.* I wrote this front-page piece today.'

Jesus. That's who she was. What had Anthony said about the deaths, about clients, about Amsterdam? He wished he could retract it all. Jenny swung around on the stool.

'You were down at Guy's morgue today, weren't you?'

How the hell could she know that? She enlightened Anthony. 'I was at Guy's this afternoon, and their records show that an Anthony Carlton from Steen Odenberg identified today's body from the Tower City Hotel. I asked the morgue attendant for a description of you before I came to Broadgate this evening. He was right about your dress sense. I was planning to drop into your office and then fate smiled. I was waiting in reception with Bill contemplating my next move and then you walked out for the Flute. I had to wait a while before joining you here. Anything immediate would have been too obvious.'

222

Anthony had been trapped and grilled by a journalist, and he never knew until it was too late. A smile revealed her perfect white teeth.

'You're not a suspect are you, Tony?'

This was the second time he had been asked that question by someone he lusted after.

'No.'

'I've been following this story from the start. I'm keen to see how it develops, so can you tell me in detail what you've found?'

'I can't divulge bank business to the press.'

'Make an exception for me.'

'Why should I?'

Anthony could see her enthusiasm.

'I'm really desperate. At the moment I write stock market commentaries for my prehistoric boss who's been at the *Standard* since the dawn of the printing press and he's a right shit to work for. I'm only a temp there, and I want a permanent job because it's a great paper. But my boss and I don't get on. He wants to let me go, says that most of the stock market commentary is coming in electronically now and there's no need for a journalist to write up that copy any more. My job will cease to exist if he has his way. God knows I need the money too. I've got to pay my rent tomorrow.'

Anthony thought that for a temp journo on a low salary she looked remarkably well.

'Then this Steens story comes up. I wrote a piece on Walker's death on the first Monday. My boss tells me to bin it. I go to the main editor and show him. He likes it and says to run it. My boss is pissed off that I went over his head. Once this Steens story disappears, then so do I. I was born to be a

223

journalist This is my big chance. I may not get another.'

He deliberated. She was keen. She poured another glass for each of them and crossed her sheer legs comfortably on the stool, contemplating her first visit to Broadgate just over a week ago.

'I was outside Steens' office on the day after Walker's death at seven o'clock looking for some staff to talk to, but no one would talk to us then. It was a wasted morning. I should have stayed in bed. It's just the same now. No one will talk except you. C'mon.'

Anthony remembered where he had first seen that coat and the gorgeous girl wearing it. He had seen her there on the Monday morning. Lust at first sight. Was it reciprocated? Maybe, but right now anger was uppermost in his mind.

'I haven't talked.'

'You have. You've said plenty. There's something going on in Steens that has resulted in the death of two directors. Jesus, this story could be bigger than I thought. I'm off. I've got my copy to write. Exclusive copy, too, for a change. That'll show my boss.'

She got up, put on that black coat and was gone. Anthony felt used as he sat in the tube carriage on his way home. Deception hurt, and it hurt all the more from someone as alluring as Jennifer Sharpe. He had been used.

* * *

Something was missing. It just wasn't the same. They lay naked side by side, sweat still glistening on warm bodies, just a foot or two between them,

224

but it felt like miles apart. Tired eyes stared up at the ceiling of the bedroom examining the creeping hairline cracks and the fluted cornices of the slowly subsiding hundred-year-old mansion flat. There was no mutual eye contact. Anthony made the effort and turned to Vanessa. 'You all right?'

'Yeah. Sure.'

Anthony knew she wasn't. She was different. What had happened? Perhaps it was obvious? 'Are you upset by the deaths in the bank? Walker and now Verhoeven?'

She smiled as if he had given her the easy way out, the quick answer. 'Yeah. It's scary. I need someone like you to take care of me, Tony.'

He rolled nearer and cradled her. He would care for her. Wouldn't he? His attention was drifting. The horizon clouded by a woman perched on a bar stool in the Flute. Not his Vanessa. A certain Jennifer Sharpe. Guilt overcame him. Got to get her out of his mind.

'Tony, why don't we go away for the weekend? Just you and me. Get out of London.'

No. She wasn't going to mention Amsterdam, surely. Not there, please. Memories of that Gucci scarf in the hotel lost-property drawer flooded back. Never got a direct answer. Now was not the time to try either.

'I'd like to go to the West Country, Tony.' Phew. 'I'd like to spend a couple of days away from all this. Drive down in the Audi on Friday evening, stay in an old cottage with a log fire, walk the hills and come back as late as possible on Sunday night.'

Great idea. If only. Work prevailed. As ever.

'I'd love to, Vanessa, but I've got to go to Frankfurt on Sunday.'

CHAPTER THIRTEEN

3.50 P.M.: SUNDAY 31 MARCH: HEATHROW TO FRANKFURT-AM-MAIN

Another wasted Sunday afternoon. More traffic jams on the A40, the M4, the Hayes bypass and the Heathrow spur road. More queues at the check-in counters, even in Club Class. More people who couldn't find their tickets or their passports or their lonely brain cells. Pushy security staff frisking innocent passengers as if they got some perverse enjoyment out of it. Airline staff asking the usual inane questions for security reasons. 'Just the one bag, sir?'

'No. There are two imaginary bags beside the one you can see.'

'And is this your bag, sir?'

'No. I just found it lying around.'

'Has it been with you all the time today?'

'No. I left it in Central London for a few hours earlier today.'

'Did you pack it yourself?'

'No. I employ a full-time professional luggage packer.'

'Are there any prohibited items in the bag? Fireworks? Flammable items?'

'Sure. I never go anywhere without them.'

'Have you read this security notice?'

'No. I'm illiterate.'

If only. It was easier to acquiesce. Be a yes man. Past the same old airport shops selling Italian names at designer prices to fashion victims. A

226

glance at the overhead screens. More departure delays due to technical problems or late incoming flights from somewhere else in Europe. What was the destination this time? Frankfurt. Did it matter? German cities were never the most entertaining, and Frankfurt didn't have the fashion and style of Dusseldorf, the sights and fresh seafood of Hamburg or the well-stocked bierkellers of Munich.

Anthony defended himself against a *Sunday Times* thrust towards him by the stern trouser-clad Lufthansa stewardess. Just think of all that tactile black ink. He saw an *Evening Standard*, then realised that the *Standard* didn't print on a Sunday. It was Friday's. Two days late. How untypical of Lufthansa. Anthony grazed the business headlines about takeovers, profit warnings, rights issues, share tips, fat cats, golden hellos, sacked chief executives.

Suddenly he noticed Steens' crest in the top right-hand corner of a page. There was a picture of Steens' Broadgate head office, with inset black and white photographs of the late Jeremy Walker and Johan Verhoeven. There was a large bold headline. WHAT IS REALLY GOING ON AT STEENS? Jennifer Sharpe had penned the story. His worst nightmare.

The facts were all there. The stellar careers of Walker and Verhoeven and the mega salaries they earned. Two suspicious deaths in as many weeks. Jennifer was looking for a link between them but couldn't find one. She regurgitated old news from the week's *FT*. Anthony was relieved. No scoops today. Towards the end of the article she started to speculate. Always dangerous in the City, unless it's

227

with someone else's money. An unnamed source within Steens had spoken to her. Serious irregularities and client complaints in the Amsterdam office were under investigation. Jesus, she had written exactly what Anthony had told her. He was the source. She confirmed that the bank's own internal expert was leading the investigation. No names mentioned, though. Anthony might get away with it. But Derek wouldn't like it at all.

Everyone in the office would read this and wonder if there was a mole in Steens. He hoped that no one had seen him sitting in the Flute with that well-dressed girl who just happened to be a journalist, that most hated of human species in times of corporate crisis. Why the hell had he sat with her at the table by the window? Should have gone elsewhere, somewhere more discreet. Why had he even spoken to her? Because she flirted, of course. It had worked. If he ever had the misfortune to meet her again, he would give her a damned good seeing to. In his dreams.

*   *   *

It made economic and geographic sense to base the administration of a fund such as EPIC in Germany, being much more developed than some of the backwaters of Eastern Europe. The locals knew how to handle Deutschmarks in size. Frankfurt was Steens' biggest office in Germany, but the location also made Anthony uncomfortable. It was always easier to hide something untoward in a distant financial outpost where head-office management like Anthony rarely ever visited. There had been too many recent financial disasters in this great industry, where ignominious overseas branches had brought the sudden downfall of a much larger head office.

Frankfurt loomed out of the low cloud with the river Main snaking through the grey city centre, home to seven hundred thousand locals. The cityscape was instantly recognisable with its recent rash of anonymous skyscrapers as each major German bank tried to build a taller head office, only to be usurped by the next building of some domestic competitor. It wasn't called Bankfurt for nothing. A walking tour of Frankfurt takes the visitor around the tallest ten office buildings, which essentially is a tour for particularly sad bastards.

Anthony had done the sights of Frankfurt on his first visit to the city years before. He had set out at ten o'clock in the morning. He was finished by midday. And he was a slow walker. What's the main tourist draw? An oversized bronze bull outside the DAX, the German Stock Exchange? The largest railway station in Europe? The two tallest buildings on mainland Europe? The site of the European Central Bank? Yawn. Enough said.

Another standard hotel room with droning air-conditioning and unlimited toiletries that Anthony had long since tired of stealing. A television set with fourteen channels of viewing pleasure but nothing worth watching. Lying comatose on the bed fingering the remote control and summoning the energy to do something, just anything. Another room-service menu with the same regulation dishes as Hong Kong or Toronto or Paris, where they charged you to deliver the food, to eat a bread roll, to have a glass of insipid tap-water, almost to open your room door to the surly waiter who was scrounging for a decent tip for three minutes' delivery work. Sharing the lift with other suits who didn't voluntarily start social conversations with total strangers. Especially in Germany. Having a silent breakfast while hiding behind the protection and anonymity of a *Financial Times*. The joys of international travel.

*   *   *

Sometimes you can tell what a person is like merely by the sound of their name, and the chief accountant of Steens' Frankfurt office was one such person. Wilhelm Gausselmann was a small man with an unkempt, greying beard and a sleeveless pullover that mercifully hid his shirt and tie. Anthony's immediate impression was that Gausselmann looked worried and rightly so, given the reason for Anthony's visit.

'I'm here to look at the EPIC deal.'

Gausselmann spoke deliberately and clearly in good English. 'I see. You know that Jeremy Walker was the company secretary? He came over from London to us to work on EPIC. Are you replacing him in this role?'

'Yes,' Anthony lied. It seemed a plausible explanation, for which he was grateful.

Gausselmann stroked his beard. Anxiety personified. 'I am worried. I am involved in administering the EPIC fund. Some people in the office here joke that I should be very careful. Maybe I might be the next person to die? My wife is scared. She jumps when the doorbell rings at home and calls me even if I am delayed by only ten minutes when I go home in the evening. What is happening at Steens?'

'I know only that the police are still investigating the deaths. Let's start with the original EPIC deal files for the issue of the shares. Then I want to see everything on the property purchases that have been made by EPIC.'

Within ten minutes Anthony was reading the first of the deal files. This was the logical start, so that he could see how EPIC came into being. The first few pages on the early days of the planned issue were ominous, with memoranda from bankers on file confirming that the issue had become difficult to sell, suggestions of downsizing the offer to a smaller dollar amount and file notes about extending the duration of the marketing and selling period in order to attract money from more investors. There were notes about going for an issue of only thirty or even twenty million dollars, but the files concluded that this was not an option. Steens just didn't scale back new issues. It was a matter of corporate pride.

Anthony read about external experts who had been retained to work with the EPIC fund, a firm of German civil engineers, a landscape company, a firm of Frankfurt architects and an exclusive French interior design company. They were going to be paid several hundred thousand dollars each in retainer fees to work for EPIC, but reality had transpired differently. The money from early investors was passed on immediately to these advisers with the proviso that the advisers reinvest their advance fees back into buying EPIC shares. The advisers hardly even saw their money, but they didn't mind. It was still an advance fee for no work whatsoever. They thought they were on to a winner. Anthony calculated that this ruse helped to sell another three million dollars of EPIC shares. Worrying.

Then he glanced through some papers from the Amsterdam office dated the day before the issue closed. Johan Verhoeven confirmed in a memorandum that he had sold twelve million dollars of shares in the fund to his clients, and he wanted some recognition of his efforts. Attached was a list of the investors. Anthony recognised some of the Dutch surnames, those same discretionary private clients specified in his Amsterdam report. They were not the institutional client types who should be buying into a high-risk venture like this. Verhoeven had indeed saved the EPIC issue with twenty-four hours to go by stuffing his private clients with this rubbish, just as Gary and Steve had suspected.

There followed some rough notes about how many shares had been bought by investors, but the drafts indicated that Steens were still slightly short of their target of fifty million dollars. It was clear that the issue was not going to be fully subscribed. Steens simply couldn't have a failure; they had a reputation for success. Then Anthony saw that Verhoeven took the balance for some familiar-sounding accounts in Amsterdam. Accounts in the name of that girlfriend, perhaps, Leopold the horse again and the Hoop staff slush account. That warehousing account took a large line of EPIC stock. It was a small price to pay for the reputation of the world's greatest investment bank as a successful lead manager.

Steens always wanted a profit, and this deal was no different. If they had saved the issue they were going to get as much back as they could from EPIC in as short a period of time as possible. EPIC was loaded with additional fees. The biggest such fee guaranteed Steens an annual one per cent of the value of the fund for the provision of macro-economic and statistical research on European property trends. It was a wonderfully vague and meaningless service, but it meant that Steens got half a million dollars every year for doing nothing apart from the provision of their existing research papers from their London-based property sector analysts to EPIC. Easy money.

Steens found another lucrative fee. The EPIC investors were buying shares denominated in US dollars, but EPIC planned to buy property that was mostly denominated in Deutschmarks. Businessmen in Eastern Europe love the Deutschmark. So much better than the Czech crown or Hungarian forint. Steens already had listed foreign currency funds that allowed investors to speculate in exchange-rate movements or else hedge their currency exposure. EPIC chose the latter, or rather it was chosen for them. EPIC put millions of dollars into the currency fund and arranged to take it back out in Deutschmarks at various future dates. The currency fund charged front-end fees based on a percentage of the value of the funds invested. This was another five hundred thousand dollars for Steens. They were well on the way to recouping their investment of three million dollars. And EPIC hadn't even bought a single property yet.

Near the end of the last file was a proofed copy of the tombstone, that gloating advertisement that every lead manager places in the bottom right-hand corner of the inside section of the *FT* after a successful issue. It featured Steens' name and crest prominently and was dated in April two years ago. There was a thick red pen line through the entire advertisement and one simple word: pull. Someone closely involved in the deal obviously didn't want to draw too much attention to this particular new issue. Anthony knew the handwriting. The same as on the entrance to number thirty Anchor Yard in Wapping. Jeremy Walker's personal involvement in this deal was clear to see.

Anthony had seen enough in his first day in Frankfurt. EPIC was doomed from the very start. He needed some more recent information, rather than two-year-old deal files. He grilled Gausselmann in his office.

'Where are the year-end accounts for EPIC? Since their year-end is 31 December, we should have their results by now. Is it in profit?'

'We don't know the current financial state of EPIC. It might be technically insolvent.'

'Impossible. It had fifty million dollars. Where did the money go?'

Gausselmann shrugged his shoulders. Anthony went to the heart of the matter. 'What property does EPIC actually own now?'

Gausselmann put a single page in front of Anthony. A short list indeed. Too short.

'EPIC owns five properties. The biggest single investment is a hotel with ample development land near the university town of Heidelberg, to the south of Frankfurt. It's not even in Eastern Europe, but it's close. The EPIC management felt at the time that the area would benefit from any wider economic boom. It's going to be called the

234

Heidelberg Golf & Country Club when we have finished. We paid just over twenty-five million dollars for it.'

Anthony picked up on all the nuances. 'Why do you say when you have it finished? Isn't it in business?'

'Not yet.'

'Why? What's wrong?'

'We had some local difficulties. Development delays.'

Too vague. This looked bad. There was no diversification. If you had fifty million dollars to buy property, it made much more sense to buy ten properties at five million each, rather than go out and buy one place for twenty-five million. Surely the future of EPIC didn't rest on one single property? 'What else did EPIC buy?'

'Four other small hotels in various places. One in Prague. One in Budapest. Two others elsewhere. They are doing well, but we paid only a few million Deutschmarks for each.'

'Excellent. If EPIC raised fifty million dollars, then even with these fees and payments and hotel purchases, they must have several million left.'

'Not exactly. In fact, we are overdrawn at our Frankfurt bank. They want security for our overdraft. It's rather ironic, but they want to take a charge over the hotel and land in Heidelberg. We are short of cash.'

'But where could the money have gone?'

'We had many expenses here. The money just seemed to flow out.'

'What do the investors think?'

'These big institutional investors aren't stupid. People like NedCorp in Amsterdam know what's going on here. I heard they were very vocal. Some guy called Jan Peters works there, and he was the worst. Walker used to mention him when he came out here to see how the fund was doing. The investors know that a lot of the money has been wasted, and that's why the share price is stuck at four dollars each.'

'And what about the smaller investors, the ones who can't afford to lose money?'

'That's not my problem. Verhoeven took care of them.'

It was a disaster. Millions of dollars had been wasted, but Anthony didn't yet know where it had all gone. He would have to take a day away from the office and see the evidence for himself.

*   *   *

The choice of hire cars was typical, the standard fare of Escorts, Corsas, Fiestas, Polos and Puntos. Even if it were for only one day, Anthony didn't want one of these runabouts primarily designed for corner-shopping and school runs. He probed the sales staff for something more appealing. They had a new Porsche Boxster, just delivered, but it was expensive to hire for one day. Five hundred Deutschmarks. Petty cash, especially when Steens were paying on the corporate card. He pulled out of the Avis showroom at speed with the soft top down, stereo up and shades on. Smooth soul radio music enhanced his driving enjoyment. He had to see exactly what EPIC had bought for twenty-five million bucks.

Anthony had some rudimentary directions from the hotel concierge but still needed a city map to get out of Frankfurt to head south. Soon he was on the autobahn to Heidelberg and the abortive Golf & Country Club, doing a hundred miles an hour as locals in BMW 7-series Panzer tanks effortlessly overtook him in the outside lane. The drive took him less than an hour on the autobahn, limitless in their extent and speed. Thanks, Adolf. The town of Heidelberg nestled along the Rhine, but Anthony didn't need to enter the town centre. Instead he found a modest roadsign at a junction which indicated that the Golf & Country Club was a kilometre away down a badly maintained gravel road.

He was greeted by their prime investment, a crumbling three-storey near-ruin of what once looked like a hotel. A car-park overgrown with weeds, peeling cream paint on the walls, boarded-up windows and wandering stray farm animals possibly looking to check in for the night. Jesus. How had EPIC forked out twenty-five million for this place? Whoever sold them this heap was laughing all the way to the casino. So, in fact, would be the local real estate company who facilitated the sale. Worth checking out?

A drab hoarding at the locked metal gates mentioned a real estate company: Richter Properties of Heidelberg. Time for some independent property advice. Anthony drove back into town to see what he could learn from someone other than a biased Steens' employee. Richter Properties was no earth-shattering experience, with its small, sparsely populated office. He was noticed immediately. Maybe the staff recognised his well-cut suit and expensive coat? Anthony knew from experience that the senior people in real estate offices sit further to the back. He made for the oldest gentleman in the office, a man in a navy blazer, oiled-back hair and a strong jawline topped by stern metal glasses.

'Speak English?'

The man was looking both at Anthony and past him at the Porsche conspicuously parked on the kerb outside. Probably a capital offence in Germany. He was obviously distracted by the tangible demonstration of apparent wealth. If only.

'Yes, I do. I am Albert Richter, the proprietor.'

'Excellent. I act for some overseas investors. I am looking for some decent investment property in this area. Perhaps you can tell me what you have in the million-dollar-plus range?'

The estate agent stood up, believing that Christmas had arrived several months early. He reached for a bundle of leaflets, but before he commenced the standard sales patter Anthony threw him a curved ball. 'I noticed a hotel nearby which is vacant, a Golf & Country Club. Is that still available?'

'I am sorry, sir, but we sold that just over a year ago. It's not on the market at present. But we do have some other similar places that I could tell you about. We have here . . .'

'But that hotel is empty. Why is nothing happening?'

'It's not that simple, sir. The buyer is a big Dutch property fund, but they didn't get proper legal advice before they bought the hotel. They made an expensive mistake.'

'What did they miss?'

'They bought the hotel and the surrounding land for a major golf club and leisure development But

238

they never checked for full planning permission beforehand. Now the local council will not give them planning permission.'

'Why not? Isn't the council keen on new business in this area?'

'Yes, it is, but sometimes federal government priorities take precedence.'

'Like what?'

'A new autobahn extension is being built very near the hotel. The route will cut across the planned golf course and the leisure facilities. There is no way the buyers will get planning permission, no matter what they do.'

Anthony sensed an implicit message. 'What do you mean exactly?'

'Rumour has it locally that the owners have offered cash to our city councillors to change their decision and to reroute the autobahn away from their planned development. There are stories of large brown envelopes of Deutschmarks being passed around in Heidelberg's finest Michelin-starred restaurants.'

*   *   *

Follow the money. That was the adage in the Control Group. If you needed an answer, then see who got how much and when and why and where. On his next day back in the Frankfurt office, Anthony summoned Gausselmann.

'I want to see the records of all payments made by EPIC.'

'Why do you want to see them?'

'Standard procedure.'

Gausselmann obliged. Anthony looked through

the EPIC payments files. There were payments to accountants, legal advisers, property advisers and design consultants. He even found the payment to Steens for the services in originating and selling the issue, exactly one million dollars, as Dave had recalled.

'What's this all about? Why was this changed?'

He had found an invoice for Steens' expenses on the issue. There was a narrative about legal expenses, marketing, travel and research, and the invoice totalled a round-sum amount of three hundred and fifty thousand dollars. A few pages further on Anthony found a draft of the same invoice. This one was for two hundred thousand dollars but had been crossed out in pen. Steens had found a way just to add one hundred and fifty thousand dollars to the fee. Amazing. Gaussehnann pleaded the Fifth Amendment.

'I don't know why that change was made.'

'Who made the change? Whose writing is this?'

He knew the answer before he asked the question. He tested Gausselmann. He was truthful.

'It's Jeremy Walker's writing. He made the change.'

More evidence of Walker's role. Anthony found an invoice from the Inter-Continental Hotel in Prague. It was for just over sixty thousand dollars and mentioned Verhoeven's and Walker's names on the face of the invoice, along with some others including Gausselmann. The latter individual was embarrassed.

'That trip was a mistake in hindsight, but we did it at a very difficult time for EPIC because some of the large shareholders and retained advisers were unhappy at the lack of progress. We had to placate them somehow. Walker suggested that we hold a shareholder presentation in Prague just to show that, in fact, things were going very well. He invited a few of the larger shareholders and the directors there, and EPIC footed the bill for first-class flights, limousine, accommodation at a five-star hotel and threw in a few dinners and entertainment in the evening. It was a confidence-building measure, but the effect was short-lived.'

Anthony spotted another familiar name on the hotel invoice.

'This guy Jan Peters? Is he the same guy from NedCorp?'

'Yes, he is. Do you know him?'

Even Jan Peters could stoop low enough to accept a freeloading boondoggle trip to Prague. So much for his high and mighty attitude back in Amsterdam. Anthony thought back to his trip yesterday to examine the now-infamous country club.

'Have we paid any money to local councillors in Heidelberg at all?'

Gaussehnann was rocked by the question. Visibly so. It struck a chord. 'Who told you that? How do you know that?'

'Never mind. So what happened?'

'We had a major problem with the planning permission for the country club and the golf course. The local council wants a new autobahn through most of the proposed back nine holes. Walker was incensed. He threatened them at first, but that only made matters worse. Then he decided to try to buy the council. He told me to draw out hundreds of thousands of Deutschmarks in cash from the bank here, and I gave it to him in sealed envelopes. He had them delivered to many of the councillors to sway their opinion. But nothing happened. We are still waiting for a decision, and the money is gone.'

'So how much exactly was handed over?'

'I didn't keep records of that. Walker asked me not to. I could find out how much was paid out by going back through the bank account, but that would take me a long time.'

'Ballpark numbers?'

'Millions of Deutschmarks.'

More money down the drain. Anthony asked the critical question. 'So did any other people benefit personally at any stage from EPIC?'

'Like who?'

'Like the directors of Steens.'

It was a bluff, but Gausselmann didn't know that. He was still wondering how Anthony knew about the bribes to the councillors. 'Walker and Verhoeven did.'

'In what way?'

Gausselmann sighed deeply, the sigh of a guilty man before he comes clean. EPIC paid them a cash commission on the side, for the work that they had done personally to save the issue when it was launched. They felt they deserved a reward so they withdrew funds from EPIC. As time went on they began to think of EPIC as their personal fiefdom, that they themselves owned the fund. It was like someone giving them fifty million dollars and just asking them to spend it. So they spent some on themselves.'

'How much? Millions of dollars?'

'Verhoeven got half a million dollars for saving the issue from Amsterdam. Walker got another half a million for his work on the fund in Frankfurt when he visited here.'

'But who made these payments to them? How can that happen?'

'Walker was the company secretary of EPIC, and he was a sole authorised signatory on all the bank accounts. He just wrote a cheque to himself and signed on the dotted line. I think he had some bank account in the Channel Islands, because that's where he mailed the cheque to from here. I posted it myself from our mailroom.'

Just as Dave had suggested on day one. Company secretaries with chequebooks. Dangerous.

'Didn't you think that all this was wrong?'

'When a director of Steens asks you to jump, you ask how high. I need my job here. I didn't dare question the wishes of Verhoeven or Walker.'

*   *   *

Anthony told Gausselmann that he was taking the next BA evening flight back to London.

'You can't go home yet. You haven't even seen anything of our beautiful city. You must stay one more night here. Go back to London tomorrow morning. We will go out tonight and have a good time. I guarantee that. I will meet you at seven in your hotel lobby.'

Civility won Anthony over. They started off in an Irish bar in Sachenhausen on the southern side of the Main, where the chilled Guinness was at least better than the tepid Guinness in London, which wouldn't be difficult. Then they went to a nearby restaurant, where the maître d' seemed to know Gausselmann, and they enjoyed traditional fare of offcuts from various unknown farm animals that probably died from natural causes: pigs' knuckles, beef liver, veal steaks and more. All came with anaemic chips, watery cabbage and undercooked broccoli stalks. The food was lukewarm. Rounded off with slices of Frankfurter Kranz cake. A typical German meal all round. His German colleague was much happier.

'I am glad that everything about EPIC will be out in the open. When Walker died I wondered how I would carry on with my work. Now you will be able to get some help for me in London. Please remember that I only followed the instructions of my superiors.'

That line didn't work at Nuremberg, and it probably wouldn't work in Steens either.

'What will happen to EPIC?'

Anthony took a grateful break from the gastronomic feast.

'Steens' board in London will decide in conjunction with EPIC. At the very least I expect that we'll get the shares suspended from the Amsterdam Stock Exchange as soon as possible. The investors who are buying and selling shares at the moment are trading in a false market. Then maybe Steens can pump some money in to the fund so that it's a success. Or else Steens will have to unwind the fund and repay the investors' money. Either way, I'd say it is going to cost Steens about twenty million dollars-plus to make good this fund.'

They went on to a traditional bierkeller. Instead of trying the local pilsner, Gausselmann insisted they had elbwein, an apple juice with a high alcoholic content, more like potent cider, in truth. It was sweet and insipid and Anthony drank too many of the small glasses. Then they went towards the main railway station. Where on earth was Gausselmann going? Were they taking a train somewhere? No. They entered narrow side streets. Large three- and four-storeyed buildings with red bulbs glowing in the windows and, inside, a warren of well-lit corridors and metal stairways that led to separate hallways, each with open or shut doors. The red-light district. Not again, thought Anthony.

Shut doors meant that there was some wholly legal Deutschmark business going down inside. Open doors were temptation personified, as young girls dressed in lingerie or PVC lay on double beds bathed in fluorescent spotlights and idly applied even more make-up or slowly teased their dyed blonde hair suggestively to the rhythm of the jungle music that blared from the rooms. Pairs of policemen climbed the steps with the punters, dressed in regulation green jackets and white peaked caps, revolvers hanging from their waists.

Despite the blatant security, Anthony felt uncomfortable in this seedy atmosphere. It was merely a voyeuristic experience for too many single businessmen and potentially unfaithful husbands. It just wasn't the type of thing that investment bankers did. Vanessa would not be proud of him. It was all becoming rather predictable and sad. Gausselmann's ulterior motives were becoming apparent.

'You have had a good time tonight? Good beer, good food, good entertainment? You will report back to London favourably on my role here?'

In truth, the evening was a bribe to ensure Gausselmann's survival.

'I will report the facts. That's my job. The
245

directors will decide. Sir James and the others.'

'I badly need this job. I have a wife and four young children to support. I am well paid by Steens. It would be very hard to find another job here that pays as well.'

Anthony gave no guarantees. Gausselmann was the wrong man in charge of EPIC at the wrong time, and events could soon spiral out of Anthony's control. The past few weeks in London and Amsterdam had hardened him just a little bit. It was going to be survival of the fittest soon, and nothing could be done for Gausselmann despite his best intentions.

EPIC was their very own game of musical chairs. Walker and Verhoeven were no longer participants. When the music stopped, as it shortly would, Gausselmann might find that he had no chair. Anthony didn't know how he personally would fare either.

CHAPTER FOURTEEN

8.40 A.M.: MONDAY 8 APRIL: CITY OF LONDON EC2

Derek was the first person whom Anthony met on his return to the office. He was seething.

'Tony. What the fuck is going on with this Amsterdam investigation? I thought we'd canned it, and then I open the *Standard* and see a two-page spread saying there are clients complaining about us. Who talked to that bloody journalist Sharpe?'

This wasn't the time for honesty. Anthony

preferred diplomacy. 'I don't know what her source is. Maybe she's just trying it on, looking for an angle?'

'She'd better be. If I find out who leaked that information to her, they needn't bother coming in to work for us again. They are finished in Steens. If you hear anyone in the bank talking about this, then let me know immediately. Right? What happened in Frankfurt? Anything I should know about?'

There was indeed. Cash payments to Walker and Verhoeven. Bribes to local government officials. Millions wasted on useless property. But this was neither the time nor the place to further annoy Derek. In any event, Anthony's job was only half-finished. Best to hedge. 'I'll do you a memo with the facts later. Then we can discuss it.'

A memo can always kill an enquiry stone-dead. An unwelcome visitor interrupted them.

'Morning, gentlemen.'

D-S Palmer hovered. Derek looked uneasy, unhappy to see Palmer's return to Steens' environs.

'I trust you want to talk to Anthony? I'll leave you two alone.'

Thanks a lot, Derek. Thanks for nothing. That blue suit again. The glare was overpowering.

'What can I do for you this time?' enquired Anthony in a somewhat uncivil manner.

'Let's talk in your office,' said Palmer.

Vanessa appeared suddenly, passed by them and sat at her desk. Palmer was looking out through the smoked glass, eyeing the serious talent from inside the office. Dream on, thought Anthony. She's mine, only I can't tell you that yet. I can't tell anyone, in fact. Soon, though. Palmer eventually

247

obliged with some relevant conversation.

'I made some progress while you were away with that fax you sent of Verhoeven's hotel bill. Thanks for telling me about that. But I'm sure that I would have located it myself in due course.'

Anthony wasn't so sure. Palmer needed all the help he could get. Anthony would do what he could to save himself. His alibi for the night was in sight.

'Turns out that this Maria person who delivered the champagne to Verhoeven was a temporary contract worker filling in for some permanent staff. We finally tracked her down through the fly-by-night catering agency that employs her. Maria is from Brazil and is an illegal immigrant in Britain. We had to do a deal with her and the Home Office to make her legal here for six months, before she even spoke to us. And then she speaks to us in Portuguese, little or no English at all. She's your average foreign hotel worker in London, I guess. You were right, there was someone else in Verhoeven's room that night. Maria gave us a decent description of the person. A really good-looking girl, she says.'

Good old Verhoeven. True to form. Palmer took out an old curled notebook from his pocket, Ripped through a few scrappy pages and finally read what he was looking for. 'She was about five nine, Maria thinks. Well dressed. About twenty-five years old. With a nice perfumed smell. It's not a bad description. My first hunch was that she was a hooker.'

Verhoeven must have ordered a bit more than mere room service. Typical of Verhoeven.

'But I'm not so sure now. Verhoeven made only one telephone call while in London on his mobile phone and that was to your bank's switchboard at about six o'clock.'

Anthony remembered that call. 'That's when he called me on his way in from the airport.'

'No calls were made from his hotel room, so how did he actually summon this girl? I dunno. He had only four minutes after he left you to pick her up. I don't think anyone can move that fast. He was hardly psychic. And this Maria in the hotel is convinced that the girl wasn't a hooker. Says the two of them in the room knew each other too well. The girl was too classy to be a pro. Very tastefully dressed. Cultured, even. Well spoken. I don't know who she is, but we need to find her soon. She's someone who knew him and maybe even met him in Amsterdam, too, and wants to keep it quiet? Someone who doesn't want to talk to the police? Maybe even someone from Steens. Know anyone like that at all?'

The mention of that city. Who went to Amsterdam and never talked about it? Reality dawned. Anthony looked out at his personal assistant who had returned to sit at her desk. Vanessa was twenty-six, tall, well spoken and always well dressed. That lost Gucci scarf discovered in an Amsterdam hotel drawer. And she missed that date in Little Venice on the night Verhoeven died. But surely it couldn't be his Vanessa? Palmer saw the recognition on his face.

'Do you know who she is?'

Time to cut to the chase, finally to question Vanessa on that Amsterdam trip, but there was no need for Palmer to be present. Anthony could be making a very big presumption, and he had no wish to harm Vanessa, that subtly perfumed beauty

249

sitting less than ten feet away. She was the one in Verhoeven's hotel room? Surely not?

'No, I don't. I was just thinking that the description sounds like a few hundred thousand girls living in London. Good luck.'

*   *   *

Anthony invited Vanessa in to his office. Palmer had gone. She brought a notepad and pen and sat poised to take a memorandum or some other instructions. Not so. Time to test the water for a reaction.

'Vanessa, let's forget about work for the moment. That policeman Palmer was asking me more questions about Verhoeven's death. The police think that a girl was in his room on the night he died. She's their only suspect at this moment, and her description sounds like you. It's a long shot but can I ask you where you were on the night that Johan Verhoeven died?'

For the first time in his life Anthony saw Vanessa lose her composure. Instantly. Her face reddened and she lost some of that self-confidence. She spoke hesitatingly. 'I can't remember exactly. I'm not sure. It's a while ago. I need to think.'

Her words faltered. She couldn't remember her own alibi. Anthony assisted.

'Weren't you visiting that girlfriend who was ill, like you told me at the time.'

'Yes, that's right.'

'Who is she? What's her name?'

'Why? Why do you want to know?'

She was hiding something. Vanessa looked down at the carpet and stared. Then Anthony saw a

250

single tear run down the side of her perfect mascara and drop on to her black patent-leather shoe. Vanessa was definitely in trouble.

'Take it easy. Just tell me anything that's relevant about that night. What did you do?'

Vanessa was trying to get the words out, and finally she did. 'I didn't visit a girlfriend. I was elsewhere in London. I met Johan Verhoeven.'

Surely not. A mistake?

'Why, Vanessa?'

'Anthony, isn't it obvious? I was seeing Johan. These things happen.'

Anthony suddenly felt as if he had never known the girl sitting before him. 'Jesus, Vanessa. I just can't believe that you'd see someone like Verhoeven. What on earth attracted you to an old married bastard like that?'

She rose to the jibe, eyes flashing, long fingers wiping away the tears. 'For the kicks, for the laughs, for the thrills. He was fun to be with, for God's sake. He burned the candle at both ends, in Amsterdam and in London. He didn't worry about getting up at six-thirty a.m. every day to be at his desk by eight. He didn't sell himself to Steens. He didn't just live for the bank; he made it work for him. And Johan was bloody generous too. I'm sorry, Tony. I just enjoyed being with him.'

She kept calling him Johan. It was too personal, and it hurt. Generous? Anthony had a fair idea by now how Verhoeven had had so much cash to spend, and it wasn't all wholly legal.

'Vanessa, you don't need his filthy money. You're loaded.'

She shook her head and ran her hands through her now-tangled hair. 'I'm not. That's just

251

something you have deduced all on your own. What's my salary here at Steens? You know well because you pay it every month. Twenty lousy K. Have you ever tried to live in London on twenty K? It's about a grand a month after tax. It isn't much. Wasn't it obvious to you? How can a secretary afford a fancy Notting Hill Gate pad, new clothes, a car, that health club subscription. Didn't you ever wonder how I was paying my bills? Some investigator you are.'

'I did wonder. But your folks are loaded. You told me as much months ago.'

'That was my easy way out. Tony, they're not wealthy. They're just normal people struggling to get by, like me. My folks live in Billericay in a small semi. My dad is a panel-beater in a garage and gets enough to live on doing nixers on the side for cash. My mother is a school dinner lady in a comprehensive. They don't have much. That's my allegedly privileged background.'

'Then where did you get all that cash to go shopping and buy those clothes?'

'Tony, Johan was good to me. Very good, in fact.'

'You mean Verhoeven paid you for sex, Vanessa? Jesus Christ.' He threw a clenched fist down on the ash desk. It hurt.

'No, Tony. It never felt like that. When we first met he took me out when he was in London. We'd go for great meals in the West End and on to clubs afterwards for a show or to a casino to gamble. And we'd go back to his suite in some hotel and have a night together. It never felt sordid or anything like that. It just evolved, and a girl loves being spoiled. You know that. Then it got complicated. Johan told

252

me that he had opened a securities account for me in our Amsterdam office. He told me that he would buy and sell shares on my behalf. He said that he knew the market so well that I would make lots of money. I begged him not to do it because I can't afford to gamble on shares. But he insisted.'

Anthony's own secretary had been one of Verhoeven's favoured clients, gaining personally as other innocents were ripped off. He tried to recall if Gary had examined the full account listing of clients in Amsterdam. He wasn't sure. Was Vanessa on the list?

'I thought I would make a little money in the account, but it was unbelievable. Every month I got a statement, and the account made money every month. Some months I made ten thousand guilders or so, and then I would get a cheque in sterling which I just lodged to my own Midland bank account. I thought it would bounce, but it didn't. And the money just kept coming. Month after month. So I spent it. Why wouldn't I?'

Anthony thought back to the trip to Amsterdam and Gary's observations. 'When you were in Amsterdam, did you ever go to our office there?'

'Yes. I went there a few times. So what?'

'Staff there saw you and Verhoeven together. They knew you were his girlfriend.'

'There's no law against it, Tony. It's called having fun.'

'Vanessa. Get your coat.'

'Are you firing me?'

'No. You and I are going down to meet D-S Palmer. You are going to give him a statement about your last night with Verhoeven in the Tower City Hotel. And we want the truth.'

'Jesus. Tony, believe me. I didn't kill Johan. What's my motive? None. He was good to me. It's more likely that you killed him.'

'That's a fucking stupid thing to say, Vanessa.'

'I'm serious. You were all over him in his last few days. He told me so many times. You were investigating his office, and you were determined to ruin his career. You were stirring up all kinds of shit. Why couldn't you leave us alone? Johan was all right until you came along and started making waves.'

*   *   *

It was Anthony's second visit to that disgusting interview room in Bishopsgate Police Station. The tapes were rolling. Vanessa gave her name and occupation for the record. Anthony had given Palmer the background details when he had called from the cab. Palmer kicked off.

'Miss Rayner. You have come down here with Mr Carlton voluntarily to give us a statement regarding the death of Johan Verhoeven? Correct?'

Vanessa was not enjoying the moment but couldn't leave. 'Yes.'

'I wish to ask you about the night of Tuesday 26 March last, when Johan Verhoeven died in the Tower City Hotel. Can you tell us about that night?'

Vanessa wiped her face. Her mascara was ruined. She wasn't the Vanessa Anthony knew.

'Johan called for Anthony at the office. I answered his telephone and Johan and I talked. He said that he was in town for one night, and he wanted to see me later. I said that I had other plans, but he insisted.'

'Go on.'

'I have been seeing Johan for a while.'

Anthony cut in. 'For how long exactly?'

Palmer didn't like it. 'I'll ask the questions. Vanessa, tell us when your relationship with Verhoeven started.'

'I met him at Steens' Christmas party for the first time about a year and a half ago.' She was making a habit of scoring at their annual party. A relationship of more than a year was serious. 'Johan visited London a lot, and I went over for some weekends in Amsterdam.'

Anthony knew conclusively that the scarf in the Amsterdam hotel was hers indeed.

'So what happened on the night of Verhoeven's death?'

'I went to the hotel as he asked. I didn't want to go there because I was growing tired of the relationship. I was growing much fonder of someone else. Someone more my own age.'

Please, God, don't ask her about her other relationship, Palmer. He obliged.

'Tell me more about that night in the hotel.'

'I arrived after nine and Johan was in a bad mood. He was all over me and wanted to have sex there and then. I refused, and he got a bit violent He pushed me around the room. He had drunk too much. He had a joint or two and tried to get me to smoke as well. I refused, and he didn't like it. He ordered some champagne, but I didn't drink any of it. He drank it all himself. Then some shorts from the mini-bar. Neat. He just scared me.'

'How, exactly?'

Vanessa waited to find the right words, knowing

255

that the tape was recording. 'I just sensed that he was going to do something stupid. He opened the patio glass door to the balcony. He wanted to look at the views of the Thames at night and the City and the silhouette of St Paul's. It was a nice view. But he was looking down from the balcony too and dropping empty bottles over the edge. I told him that I wanted to end the relationship, that I had found someone else who meant much more to me. Then he just seemed to crack. He lunged at me on the balcony and tore at my blouse. Tore the sleeve off it and just held me really tight. I was terrified. He was so drunk. He smelt of Jack Daniel's. He basically tried to rape me on the bed, but he was too drunk to do it. I told him that it was over. I fled out of the hotel room in tears.'

'So when you left the room, Verhoeven was still alive?'

'Of course he was. You don't think I did anything to him? I didn't push him or do anything like that.'

'What time did you leave?'

'About eleven.'

'We'll get this interview typed up and then you can sign it. It will take only a few minutes and then you can be on your way. Please wait here.'

Vanessa read the statement. Anthony went outside to make a telephone call on his mobile to Karen in personnel at the office. When he returned, Palmer used the momentary lull to converse with Anthony about the unsolved deaths.

'Verhoeven's death is looking more like a drunken accident, don't you think?'

Anthony would like to think so. Less ominous than another murder. Palmer tried his best.

'Consider the facts. A middle-aged guy dating an

256

attractive thing half his age. Showers her with cash and gifts. Bottle of red with you in the brasserie. Then she blows him out one night when he has already had enough to drink. High on wacky backy too. Cocktails of shorts. Add in the pressure of work, being a director of a big bank like yours, and that investigation that your team were undertaking in his office. Finally there's an open eighth-floor balcony door and an entire bottle of champagne. It's a lethal combination.'

One death solved? Perhaps. But still one to go. Palmer knew it too.

'On the other hand, Walker's death is a very difficult investigation. In many murder cases we go back to the oldest axiom of all. Find out how the victim lived, and then you might find out how he died. We have tried every avenue with no luck whatsoever. We've interviewed anyone who knew him at Steens. He didn't have any friends outside work. His ex has lived in Hong Kong for years. He has no children. His parents only saw him every few weekends at their country house in Suffolk. They've offered a reward for information leading to the arrest of his murderer. God knows they can now afford it with that huge inheritance. But all we've got in return is the usual telephone calls from cranks. Walker's investigation has reached a stalemate. It's so bad that we're going to go with the only option left in investigations like this. We're going to put Jeremy Walker on Crimewatch. It's on BBC1 this week after the nine o'clock news. Don't miss it.'

Vanessa rose unsteadily, signed statement in hand. Palmer motioned for them both to leave. Anthony stood with Vanessa on Bishopsgate

257

waiting for a cab to extricate them from this impossible situation. He had been utterly betrayed by someone he had once loved deeply. Worse still, he could talk to no one about it. If he did, then their relationship would be out in the open and he would feel like a total prat. Gary would get no end of one-liners and double entendres out of the news.

Vanessa had been about to ditch Verhoeven in favour of himself, so she claimed, but he didn't know whether to believe her. She had led a life of deception for months, and Anthony was now feeling the pain of rejection. The revelations about the money from the illicit securities account were worse. Anthony could never trust Vanessa again. Conversation was impossible for him. A cab arrived.

'I suppose you're going to sack me now, Tony?'

Anthony walked away alone, forgetting about the cab. He wanted nothing further to do with Vanessa. He took one last look as he negotiated the traffic. She stood alone. Mascara still running. lipstick smeared. Face reddened with tears. Who was she, really?

She didn't know it yet, but when she alighted at Steens she would find Karen from personnel and a stocky security guard waiting to help clean out her desk, retrieve her magnetic security card and show her the main exit door in the reception lobby. There was no place in Steens for someone like Vanessa. He didn't want to see her again at work.

There was no place in his life for someone like that either. He felt sick. Sick that he had wasted three months of his life on a cheat. Sick that he had wined and dined her. Sick that he had believed her easy lies. Sick that he had never guessed the truth.

258

Sick most of all that he would now once again have to begin that ultimate search for the perfect life partner.

*　　*　　*

Anthony returned late in the day. No sign of Vanessa. The evil deed was done. He called Gary into his office. Gary had seen them both leave earlier with Palmer.

'Where were you and Vanessa?'

'At the police station. Vanessa gave them a statement. She was with Verhoeven on the night he died.'

'Jesus. That's bad news for her. It seems that everyone in the department has been down to that police station to give them a statement. Maybe I should drop down there voluntarily before they ask me down anyway. Where's Vanessa? Why hasn't she returned with you?'

'She's gone. She won't be back, either.'

'Where's she gone?'

'Don't ask. Let's just say right now, it was for unethical behaviour.'

'What, exactly? C'mon, Tony. We work together. You can tell me.'

No. Best to make it look less personal. Stick to the facts.

'Believe it or not she has a securities account in the Amsterdam office. Verhoeven put good trades into her account and gave her a few thousand pounds a month out of it.'

'Jesus. Pity we missed that at the time.'

'We can still check it out. Get out that client account list and see if she's on it.'

259

Gary disappeared and returned in about ten minutes looking exasperated. 'I think you're wrong. There's no account in the name of Vanessa Rayner.'

Anthony looked at the list while thinking on his feet. 'If I were Verhoeven, then I wouldn't use her proper name since she was a Steens employee. You told me he had a girlfriend who had a numbered account there. He knows that we check employee accounts. She got a statement by post every month, so let's forget about names and just look through the home address fields. Vanessa lives in Sussex Close in Notting Hill Gate.'

Big mistake. Gary latched on to it immediately.

'You know her home address? How come?'

'I just do.'

'You've been to Vanessa's home? Haven't you? You've seen her outside work hours? It's just what me and Steve thought. You're having a relationship with her?'

Gary was almost right. Present tense no longer applied. Past tense was more appropriate.

'Yes, I was. Just look for her address. I don't want to talk about it.'

They scanned the printout looking for any London addresses. Gary pointed. 'There it is. Sussex Close. Number twelve. Verhoeven named the account 696969. Big joke? Thirty grands' worth of profits per this statement in a year.'

Vanessa had told the truth at least on one occasion. But Gary wouldn't let the matter lie. 'Unbelievable. The two of you going at it hammer and tongs. Wow. Does Derek know? What's she like between the sheets?'

'None of your business. Let's leave it there.'

'OK, but it must have been awful for you. Hiding the truth from all of us for months. Not able to tell anyone. Sort of like that Claudia Schiffer story?'

What on earth was Gary on about?

'Guy on a cruise is stranded on a desert island when his ship sinks. All alone on the island for weeks, and he's about to go mad. Then he finds footprints on the beach. Follows them to the other side of the island. Finds this amazing blonde who was on the ship too. Turns out to be Claudia Schiffer in person. Guy can't believe his good fortune. They get on great. Weeks of unbelievably great sex. Then the guy gets depressed, Claudia notices and asks if she can do anything to help. Guy asks if she would draw a dark moustache on her face with charcoal. Why? Don't ask, he says. She obliges with a thick moustache. Then he asks if he can call her Bob. Why? Don't ask, he says. She says it's OK by her. Then he turns to her, big smile and says, "Bob, you'll never guess who I'm shagging." Get it? That's the worst part. Not being able to tell anyone.'

*　　　*　　　*

Karen from personnel visited Anthony in the early afternoon. The minute he saw her, Anthony thought back to years ago when they first went out together. He was making a habit of failed office romances. She'd ditched him for someone more powerful and wealthier, she said. Pity. Karen still looked good. Short, fashionably cropped hair, expensive yet tasteful jewellery, no engagement ring yet. Approaching the psychologically damaging threshold of thirty years old but still trim from City gym visits, bottled Evian and lo-cal Lean Cuisine. Still a distant possibility, perhaps? She was always helpful and efficient.

'Everything go all right with Vanessa's departure?'

'Yes. Thanks for what you did this morning.'

'It's my job. Do you want to go to Jeremy Walker's funeral this Friday?'

'Not particularly. I feel morbid enough already. A funeral might tip me over the edge.'

'Let me rephrase the question. You're going to Walker's funeral, aren't you?'

'Says who?'

'Says Sir James. He asked me to ring around some of the more senior people.'

'Where is it? East London somewhere?'

'No, it's in Suffolk. It's in the village where his parents live. Some place called Farningham.'

'That's too far to go for a funeral. I'll give it a miss. I'm busy here.'

Karen's steady gaze held his attention. She wasn't giving up.

'I'll just clarify matters. Sir James has given me a list of Steens' people that he wants to see at the funeral. I don't think there's the option of not going.'

This wasn't a funeral. It was an official corporate outing. Anthony had no choice.

'You still owe me that meal out in return for Walker's home address.'

'That wasn't for me. That was for Derek.'

'Oh, sure it was. Well, now it's big payback time. Walker's secretary cleaned out his office this week. Such a worried busybody. I don't know how he stuck her at all. Secretary from hell, more likely.

262

Anyway, she retrieved a box of his personal stuff from our offsite storage facility in Hailey's Wharf. She gave me this banker's box to give to his parents. I wanted to tell her to do it herself, but she just left the box in my office, so now it's my problem. Well, actually it's about to be yours. I need to deliver it to Jeremy's parents because they're his only relatives. I don't want just to courier the box; it's too impersonal. I'd prefer to have someone from Steens deliver it tactfully. I can hardly ask Sir James or a director to deliver it. Will you oblige when you go up to Suffolk on Friday?'

'As long as there isn't too much to deliver.'

'I'll drop it round to you this evening. Then we can go for that meal afterwards.'

Vanessa was history. A date with Karen would be excellent. Game on.

'Serious?'

'Yes. Book a table for seven o'clock.'

* * *

Gary walked in to Anthony's office unannounced.

'Minor crisis, Tony. Steve's just walked. He's with Karen in personnel now signing off.'

Anthony knew the vernacular. The danger had always been there, and they both knew it. Steve had just resigned from Steens. A wind-up. You take someone in from college and just as they get to know the job, someone flashes a bigger bundle of notes in their face and they roll over. Once it happened, the member of staff had to leave Steens immediately. They didn't need disgruntled staff hanging around near the second floor.

'Where's he going?'

'Where else? He's going to Mitchell Leonberg.'

He had joined their biggest competitor. Those Americans with all those dollars.

'Why?'

'For the money, of course. He told me that Mitchells offered him a big package. Twenty grand more than here, big annual bonus, a vice president title, and they threw in the usual temptations too. Lots of world travel was mentioned.'

This was a sucker punch. Lots of youngsters wanted to travel the world. They hadn't backpacked around Europe and Asia after college because they didn't fancy sleeping rough in freezing Italian railway stations and existing on a few pounds a day in a Berlin hovel. Now they wanted to kill their travel bug in Club Class style, staying in the best five-star hotels and having it all paid for by a benevolent City employer. Anthony and Gary were experienced enough to know that travel was not all that it was supposed to be. After twenty trips to Manhattan or Paris, you never wanted to go there again. But travel opportunities glazed the eyes of the ever-impressionable youth.

'Mitchells wanted him badly. Apparently they're keen to improve their internal controls.'

Who wasn't? Steens were keen right now. There were enough control problems.

'They even used the BMW Cabriolet trick.'

This always worked. If you wanted a youngster badly, you just talked about the company cars that were on offer. You mentioned the favoured three-floored speedster from Bavaria, with the two-litre injection engine, the leather upholstery, the metallic paint, the eight-speaker CD player, the alloy wheels and the rear spoiler. And if in doubt you just threw in the soft top, very handy for cruising down the King's Road on a Saturday afternoon in July with your girlfriend in the passenger seat. Mitchells had made sure that Steve couldn't resist the temptation. Anthony was concerned. Gary noticed.

'Hey, don't worry. He's not that indispensable. We can hire again. Better still, we could get them back and poach one of their Control Group. Even out the score.'

And people wondered why City salaries and bonuses were so high?

Derek interrupted them. 'Guess you've heard about that shit Steve leaving us? I threw him out of here immediately. How much did he know about what you've all been working on of late here?'

Anthony noticed Derek's immediate concern and needed to allay his fears.

'He was involved in the Amsterdam investigation, so he knows about our problems there. He knows a bit about EPIC too, and about Frankfurt's involvement It's enough, but don't worry. He won't talk about it to anyone. He signed a confidentiality undertaking with us when he joined. It's in his contract of employment.'

'Yeah, the same contract that he's tearing up with Karen in personnel right now.'

'Yes, but what he knows is unsubstantiated. There is no documentation to prove anything. The reports are gone, files wiped. There's nothing he could show to anyone in Mitchells.'

Anthony had the guilt of knowing that the final copy of the Amsterdam report was still locked in his desk drawer. Somehow he'd not yet brought himself to shred it. It represented work he had undertaken, and it was all he had to show for a week of overseas toil. He placed the report in his briefcase. It would be safer back at home. They didn't need word of the current investigation reaching anyone outside Steens, least of all those who worked in their most feared and hated competitor investment bank.

There were more pressing matters. Anthony would have to do some recruiting. He had lost two members of his staff in one day. And a girlfriend too. Careless or what?

CHAPTER FIFTEEN

6.51 P.M.: MONDAY 8 APRIL: MAIDA VALE, LONDON W9

Karen arrived by black cab punctually just before seven o'clock and appeared at the hall door soon afterwards with one banker's box in hand. It was sad to see after Walker's long service at Steens that his personal effects finally came down to this single secure cardboard box. They walked together to the nearby Thai restaurant where Anthony had reserved his usual table.

They sat by the main windows looking out over Regent's Canal. Brightly painted barges and small rowing-boats were moored along the length of the canal on both sides, giving it a vaguely Continental appearance. Couples walked along the canal path hand in hand, with small terriers and spaniels gambolling ahead of them. That used to be Anthony and Vanessa.

Some end-of-day dappled sunshine broke through the trees that lined the side of the canal. It was hard to believe they were in the midst of a city of eight million inhabitants, but it was a romantic setting, just what Anthony wanted for this occasion. Vanessa was history. Time to regroup.

They talked about work initially, and then it got more interesting. Karen spoke, perhaps thinking about the delivery she'd just made. 'I still have no idea who murdered Walker, or what exactly happened to Verhoeven. Is there something going on that I don't know about? Is someone out to get the directors? Are Sir James and Derek Masterson and Alvin Leung and Bill Fitzpatrick all in danger?'

Anthony pointed out the obvious benefits of working in personnel. 'Karen, if someone like you in personnel doesn't know the answers, then how can the rest of us know? Personnel know all the best office gossip. I only agreed to come along here tonight so that I could interrogate you and find out what you know about the deaths.'

'Silly me. I know nothing. And I just thought you enjoyed my company.'

They finished eating, Anthony settled the bill generously and they walked back along the canal, heading in the direction of Anthony's apartment. This looked promising.

'Will you come back for a coffee or a Bailey's, Karen?'

'I'd love to . . .'

Very promising.

'But I can't tonight.'

Not so promising. 'Pity. Why not?'

'I've got to meet my boyfriend.'

A killer blow right to his solar plexus. Anthony

had hoped that she had lost that serious boyfriend. What a waste of a meal. He made light of it to disguise his disappointment. 'Who's the lucky guy? Anybody I know, by any chance?'

She smiled mischievously. Did he know the unknown man? There was one likely scenario, given their occupation.

'Is it someone who works at Steens?'

'Good guess.'

'Who? Give me a clue.'

She wouldn't oblige. There were thousands of head-office staff to choose from. He needed a clue. He thought about that day's revelations about Vanessa and Verhoeven. Was there a parallel? 'Is it someone quite senior in the bank?'

She looked surprised, as if he had inadvertently stumbled on some grain of truth. It couldn't be a director, could it? There were fewer and fewer of those as the weeks passed. Karen wasn't staying to dodge any more of Anthony's questions. She gave him a polite peck on the cheek, thanked him for dinner and then hailed a cab on Warrington Crescent. She was gone from Maida Vale as quickly as she had arrived less than two hours previously, and all Anthony had to keep him company in his apartment overnight was Jeremy Walker's personal effects. He would have preferred Karen.

*   *   *

The banker's box sat prominently in the hallway so that Anthony wouldn't forget to take it with him to Walker's funeral. But the longer the evening went on, the greater the overpowering presence this simple box assumed. Anthony was frustrated that

Karen had rejected him and needed something else to occupy his active mind. Every time he walked to the kitchen or the bathroom or the living-room he passed that box. Annoying.

He began to fantasise about the contents. What would be in it? What would Walker have stored away? Maybe bills and receipts and standard personal documents about pensions and tax advice? Or maybe more interesting things about money and investments and shares and bonds? He bent down to examine the box. Karen had taped the lid down with three strands of wide sellotape. He couldn't even open the lid.

By late evening there was simply no choice. He just had to see the contents. He knew it was wrong, but no one would ever know. He deftly slit the tape with scissors and took out the assembled contents carefully. He saw Walker's personal bank statements first. They were from all over the world. There was a bank statement in Walker's name from an offshore bank in Jersey with a balance of just over a million pounds. Then a statement from a stockbroker in New York with Dow Jones Index blue-chip shares worth another two million dollars. Next was a statement from a US mutual fund company showing units in various Far East and emerging market funds worth another million dollars, and a bank statement from a Swiss private bank in Geneva with exactly another million sterling. There was a depository certificate from a custodian bank in Luxembourg showing nearly three thousand ounces of gold held in safekeeping. Another million-plus. And a building society statement from an Isle of Man branch with nearly a million sterling also. If anything, Walker was well diversified. Anthony wondered just how much a director at Steens officially earned each year. Palmer had been correct. Walker was loaded.

Anthony marvelled at the amounts of money that were floating around. With his keen eye for financial detail, he got through the paperwork quickly. He remembered the Frankfurt trip. He wanted to see if that five-hundred-thousand-dollar payment to Walker had indeed been made by EPIC. Gausselmann said that it had gone to an account in Jersey, and there was one bundle of Jersey bank account statements. He knew the cash was paid about a year ago. The pile of statements were in careful date order, held together with green treasury tags. Walker had been tidy.

The statement of a year ago showed a lodgement of three hundred and thirty thousand sterling. The narrative said that there was a foreign exchange conversion of half a million dollars to sterling. The money was received from a domestic bank in Frankfurt, exactly where Gausselmann had said EPIC banked. It was conclusive proof. Walker had siphoned off half a million bucks from EPIC.

Curiosity led Anthony to continue looking at the details of the bank account in Jersey. There was a definite pattern to the account. Money came in regularly, and money went out very soon afterwards, leaving more or less a constant balance of just over a million pounds. It was as if Walker wanted to keep that sort of spare petty cash just lying around for a rainy day. More interesting was the narrative on the funds coming in to the account. It was always the same, whether it was for half a million or six fifty thousand or more.

The statements just said there was a funds

transfer from Steen Odenberg Asia Ltd. The money was coming from Steens' Hong Kong office. Anthony had been there a few times, and he knew the operations there well, but he had never seen payments like these being made to a director of Steens. He couldn't think of any legitimate reason for such payments. Walker was based in London and hadn't worked in the Hong Kong office for years.

Then he found a clue. On one of these regular payments was a slightly different narrative, and it revealed more than the others did. It mentioned the words Asian pricing account. Anthony didn't know what this meant. But he knew that he needed to find out what this Asian pricing account was and how it produced such wonderful amounts of money for Walker's own personal benefit. Anyhow, it was time for a new hand-tailored suit from Harry Wu in Kowloon. Time to fly? Perhaps. If Derek or Alvin Leung let him go.

He felt the instinctive need to keep a copy of the evidence, but he didn't have such facilities at home. Or did he? The corner shop had a photocopier. Anthony took a handful of Walker's bank statements, walked down the road and copied them immediately. As he paid he was sure that the shopkeeper must have thought it strange for anyone to be doing late-night photocopying. Didn't these City types ever stop work?

Anthony thought fast as he walked past Paddington Sports Club, his regular tennis haunt He decided to err on the side of caution. What he had in his possession was potentially serious, and he didn't want it lying around his flat where anyone might see it. What if Karen called round

271

unexpectedly? Dream on. Or Dave after a game of tennis? What if Vanessa came back to pick up her few possessions in the wardrobe? Hope not. Best to avoid any potential problems now.

He strode into the clubhouse and down to the men's changing-room. There was one person whom he did not want to meet tonight. Dave. No sign of him. Anthony went to his personally numbered locker. His key turned the fragile lock and the stench of stale sports gear almost overpowered his senses. Got to get Mrs Harris on the Harrow Road on the case soon. He placed the warm photocopies and that unshredded copy of the Amsterdam report in the bottom of the locker and covered them with a spare towel. They would be safe there, at least until he decided what to do with them.

What he had found was beginning to worry him. The sort of anxiety he last experienced when his father had returned from meeting the police to tell him that a bank employee had taken his own life when his fraudulent activities were uncovered. Bad times. Never again.

*　　*　　*

It wasn't often that Steens featured on prime-time BBC television. The opening credits of *Crimewatch* rolled, and the two glossy presenters ran through the contents of the programme. The usual clichés about police needing your help, that it was a live programme and that police-officers were standing by to take calls from viewers.

In the background, several self-conscious officers with sensible haircuts manned desks while trying to hide behind the presenters. One or two of the officers were on the telephone. Anthony wondered who they were talking to if the programme hadn't even started yet. Were they ringing their wives at home and saying, 'Hi, that's me in the top left-hand corner of your screen, dear'? The presenters mentioned a vicious armed robbery of a security van in the East End and a schoolgirl who had disappeared up north before Christmas.

'First we ask your help in solving the murder of a prominent City investment banker in Wapping just a few weeks ago. Police are anxious to see if viewers can identify a man seen in the area shortly afterwards. Our reconstruction starts on Friday 15 March in Steen Odenberg's offices in the City of London.'

Cut to Steens' offices in Broadgate. God, they looked good. There were clever camera shots taken from obtuse angles. Anthony hoped that his tennis club friends were watching this.

'Mr Walker left work at twenty minutes past six. This was the time on the closed-circuit camera in the lobby of his offices and the time he was last seen by his bank colleagues.'

Cut to footage from Steens' in-house CCTV cameras. It was poor quality, in black and white, but Anthony could make out Walker's face and figure as he exited the lift and went out of the main door. Anthony recognised Bill the security guard, who nodded to Walker. Walker had left alone. This was unusual of Steens' employees in general. Most left in groups after a hard week's toil and retired to the Flute to unwind and spend money.

'Mr Walker was also seen twice over the weekend in his local shop, where he bought

273

newspapers and foodstuffs on both Saturday afternoon and Sunday morning.'

Cut to another shot from a closed-circuit television camera inside a dingy shop. Jesus, the whole world must be on closed-circuit television. Was nowhere safe? Walker was buying the essentials. Bread, milk, fruit, a few tins and papers. *FT*, of course. Even on a Saturday. Then a shot of the outside of the shop which Anthony even recognised. He had passed it on his one visit to Walker's apartment.

'In the early morning of Monday 18 March, residents of Mr Walker's apartment block in Wapping reported an incident. When police arrived at his apartment, they found Mr Walker dead in the main bedroom. He had been strangled.'

Cut to footage of Anchor Yard and the exterior of the apartment. The other residents would not be pleased to see their valuable properties aired nationally as a murder location.

'Police have not established a motive for the murder. There were no signs of a disturbance in the apartment, and the murderer took no items of value. There were also no signs of a forced entry into the apartment. Police are keen to talk to anyone who has information on Mr Walker's death.'

Cut to a photograph of Walker, the photo from Steens' annual report last year.

'Police are keen to talk to a young man seen entering Wapping tube station at half-past eleven to catch the last train.'

Cut to a blurred camera still of the ticket machines in the tube station. Another staccato filmed sequence. Everything had been caught on

274

film except for the actual murder itself. Walker should have had a camera installed in the ceiling of his bedroom. The camera zoomed in on the one man who turned around after buying a ticket from a machine. It was the same slightly blurred still photograph that Anthony had been shown by Palmer last week. An oriental guy in a baseball cap. But who was he? An idea was beginning to germinate in Anthony's mind. This guy was oriental. Walker was getting cash from Steens in Hong Kong. Was there a Far East connection to this?

Cut back to the presenter. She was sitting in the studio with a man on her left. Anthony looked closely. The man looked like Palmer. Jesus. It *was* Palmer, and he looked impeccable. He wore a dark suit, a blue shirt and a discreet tie, given the sombre occasion. His hair had been carefully combed and blow-dried. Immaculate. What had happened to the shiny blue suit?

'With us is D-S Bob Palmer. Can you run through the description of the man you wish to question for us?' she asked.

Cut to the camera still again.

'He's about twenty years old, slim build, clean-shaven with pock-marked skin, short haircut. Believed to be of mixed race, possibly Chinese or Asian. And he was wearing a dark-coloured bomber jacket, black trainers with a distinctive flash and blue denim jeans. He had on a baseball cap with a small red logo. I should stress that we simply wish to eliminate this man from our enquiries. He may not be connected to the incident at all.'

The police were great. No matter how heinous

275

the crime, it was always described as a mere incident. Anthony liked what he saw before him. Palmer was brilliant on television. He came across as a rock of solidity in an ocean of gangland crime and motiveless murders. He spoke clearly and eloquently and was never once fazed by the bright lights and the stress of talking live to ten million people all over the UK.

For the first time since the start of the investigation, Anthony was glad to know and trust at least one policeman. Palmer had been friendlier since Anthony had brought Vanessa to the station, the mystery person in Verhoeven's hotel room. The two men had little in common but at least Palmer was someone he could turn to if Anthony were ever in need. Anthony thought about the evidence that was piling up in a locker not a million miles from his home. He had told no one, not even Gary or Dave or Karen. It would be good to talk to someone like Palmer if the need ever arose.

'And I understand that Mr Walker's family have put up a reward for information.'

The statement implied that Walker had left a family of wife plus children. Good for the sympathy vote among the viewers. There was no mention of the divorce from Sylvia two years ago, and the fact that there had never been any children. The interviewer concluded with the freephone number. Then they switched to the armed robbery in the East End that made much better television with actual footage of the robbery taking place.

Palmer had done well, but Anthony wondered if anyone would telephone in about the mystery youth. It was a long shot. Maybe they should show the broadcast in Hong Kong?

There were only two occasions when a denizen of the City could wear a white shirt and get away with it without impairing his credibility. One was on the first day back at your dealing desk when the brilliant Ariel-cum-Daz colour merely served to accentuate the deep tan earned during two weeks on a holiday in the Caribbean. The second occasion was when you attended the funeral of an ex-colleague, although Anthony never expected to be attending Jeremy Walker's funeral this soon. Wearing a white shirt on any other workday was like running up the white flag of surrender. Totally unacceptable.

Friday morning was gorgeous for an April day, with clear blue skies and bright sunshine. A perfectly crisp day for a country drive in the Audi Cabriolet with the hood down. Anthony left around half-past ten so that he would arrive at midday. He never drove in London during the week because it was impossible among fuming cabbies, monster double-deck red buses, suited salesmen in Vauxhall Vectras, courier motorcyclists and aggressive delivery trucks. Today he was glad to be heading out of London. He put the box containing Walker's personal effects out of sight in the car boot. He had replaced the contents meticulously and retaped the box. No one would ever deduce that he had been through the contents.

He drove towards Finchley Road. Karen had given a map to everyone who was going to the funeral. She was so efficient. Then on to the Ml and northwards before turning off at the A12 and

277

going east towards Suffolk and Jeremy Walker's parents' village of Farningham. The car was purring along.

He flicked through the ten CD multi-play system and found a good soul album to play loud. When Steens got him this company car, they asked him if he wanted either a security immobiliser or a top-of-the-range compact disc player. Anthony took the latter option. It didn't matter if the car was stolen. Steens would just get him another car. Good music mattered more. And it was his own CD collection, not the bank's.

Anthony drove fast, wishing that British speed limits were as lenient as Frankfurt's. As he drew close to Farningham he pulled in for unleaded petrol, put the hood of the car up and killed the loud music. It didn't seem like the right way to arrive at a funeral. He found the village easily. It was so small that the name signs were almost back to back on the road. He pulled up outside the archetypal country church at ten minutes to twelve. Perfect timing. Steens' people were there already. The tree-lined road was packed with Mercedes, BMWs, Range Rovers, Jags and one polished black Rolls with the distinctive numberplate of JAD 1. Sir James was here too.

Inside, the church was surprisingly small and empty. Anthony sat midway up on the left, not one to sit on the front row but at the same time never keen on the back row either. A bit like life in general, really. He recognised faces from the second floor at Steens but couldn't put names to them. Dave sat across the aisle from him. He had been press-ganged too. He nodded. He saw the directors at the top of the church. It was an

278

impressive sight. Even Alvin Leung and Bill Fitzpatrick had flown in from overseas to be there. Interesting. Alvin was over from Honkers. Away from his office. Anthony was formulating an idea.

It was a quick and impeccable service conducted by a vicar with perfect diction, notable only for the fact that Walker's aged mother in the front row broke down a couple of times. She did so again by the graveside around the back of the church. Anthony guessed that she never thought that she'd be at her son's funeral and expected the circumstances to be the other way around. Anthony couldn't see many family friends. In particular he could not identify any middle-aged woman who might be Sylvia Walker, the ex-wife who must surely have made the trip back to London from her new home in Hong Kong.

Derek Masterson approached Anthony outside the church gate. Anthony got the first word

'Good turnout from all the directors. Are they here for long?'

'Alvin and Bill are over for all of next week. We will meet to consider appointing some new directors.'

So Alvin would not be in Honkers next week. Speaking of Hong Kong and inherent curiosity. 'Which one is Walker's ex-wife?'

'She's not here. Couldn't make it back, apparently. Or else couldn't be bothered. Pity, really. By the way, you're invited back to the Walker home. It's down the road on the left, about half a mile. Follow the cars.'

Anthony went back to his car and immediately made a mobile telephone call to his temporary secretary in the office. She sounded very different from Vanessa. Pity. She understood his instructions perfectly. He was still thinking about Walker's ex-wife and was about to get into his car when he heard a familiar voice behind him.

'Hello, Tony.'

He knew that accent.

'Jenny, how are you doing?'

'Fine. Sombre affair?'

'Yes.'

They both knew that their first meeting had been a deception. Jenny made the required admission of guilt. 'Have you forgiven me yet?'

Anthony was still livid, but this was neither the time nor the place to have a stand-up row, not with the board and Walker's family looking on. He toned down his response. 'No, but I'm thinking about it.'

'Well, could you oblige me with a lift back to London? I came here on the train, and the service was so screwed up that I only got here just in time. I don't really fancy going home the same way, and you're the only person that I know here.'

Anthony was about to enjoy some modicum of pleasure in ruining her intended travel plans. 'I'm not going back yet. I'm going to the Walker family home. I'm invited.'

'OK. Then I'll go along too. I don't mind waiting.'

Before he could dissuade her, Jenny opened the passenger door and curled her long legs under the dash. Reluctantly, Anthony drove down the road following the cars in front, still wondering if he had actually invited her to the family home. The last thing Walker's parents needed was an *Evening Standard* journalist sharing a cup of tea and

280

crustless cucumber sandwiches in their lounge while simultaneously engaging in some investigative research. Jenny was keen— unstoppable, in fact.

'Did you see *Crimewatch* last night?'

'I think the entire staff of Steens saw it.'

'I thought of you while I was watching it.'

'Really?'

'I want to apologise. I was out of order after we met in the Flute, but I just had to write that piece for the paper. I was under serious pressure to write something. Otherwise my boss would have had his wicked way and I was off the story, and maybe even off the paper for good. That's what he wanted, the old dinosaur. It was a matter of practicalities. I had my rent due that Friday and that middle-page exclusive probably saved my job, my lifestyle and the roof over my head. The editor loved the copy. I'm his blue-eyed girl now. And I have you to thank for it. But I probably said too much in hindsight in the paper?'

'You did.'

'Apology accepted?'

At least Jenny knew when she was wrong and admitted so. Unlike Vanessa. And Jenny had just been doing her job, after all. As Anthony had of late. There was something about her that interested Anthony greatly, but he didn't know exactly what it was. Maybe they were on the same wavelength, that naturally inquisitive mind-set, the same spirit looking for personal advancement in life, but not wholly ruthless in their quest. Or maybe Anthony was being a fool, about to be suckered for the second time by an alluring journalist who would do anything to get that exclusive scoop. Time would tell which was the case.

The socialising inside Walker's parents house dragged interminably. Anthony had no time to meet Walker's parents as he continuously watched Jenny's manoeuvring and eavesdropping. She was a liability. The others from Steens wondered who she was. Did they think that Anthony had brought a new girlfriend along, and if so, wasn't it a strange place to go on a first date? Derek approached them both.

'Hello, Anthony. Who's this with you today?'

Anthony was going to lie. Jenny beat him to a response, proffering a gloved hand to Derek.

'I'm Jennifer Sharpe. Pleased to meet you.'

Derek immediately recognised the name, just as Anthony had days ago in the Flute.

'Jennifer Sharpe? The journalist with the *Standard*?'

'Yes, indeed. That's me.'

There was no handshake. Derek gave Anthony a hard look and walked away. Jenny examined the Walker family photographs on the mantelpiece. Jeremy Walker was in one or two of them. Anthony was afraid that Jenny would scoop one up and secrete it in her handbag, to produce later on the inside page of the *Standard*. Sir James came over to Anthony. His instructions were clear, and his language was not appropriate for the sombre occasion.

'Get that fucking journalist out of here immediately. We don't want her sort here. Are you mad bringing her here today?'

Anthony wanted to explain exactly what had happened, but there wasn't time. Sir James was gone. Jenny was upset by the overheard diatribe. The language had been loud and hostile. Anthony took Jenny by the arm and led her out of the main drawing-room.

'Where are we going?'

'Home.'

'Oh, Anthony, I never knew you were so keen. I haven't finished talking to half the people here.'

Anthony placed Jenny firmly in the front seat and drove off down the stony drive. That was an unfortunate scene, but Sir James had handled it badly. There was a right way and a wrong way to ask a lady to leave, and Sir James had let them all down. Jenny wasn't that bad at all. She was upset, but that made her all the more real to Anthony.

He was half-way down the drive when he remembered his secret mission. He reversed back erratically to outside the hall door, scattering gravel in a cloud. He opened the boot, took out the banker's box and left it inside in the hall. Jenny's curiosity was a hazard of the job.

'What's in the box?'

Anthony waited until he was out on the road heading back towards the A12. 'It's Walker's personal effects. His financial details and stuff like that.'

He thought that Jenny might be half-thinking of hopping out of the car at sixty miles an hour and going back to the Walker home. But she thought better of it.

'Tell me more, Tony. I'll do anything to find out what was in that box.'

'You and I are not going to utter a word about Steens or anyone employed in Steens, dead or alive, in the next ninety minutes until I drop you off at home. Wherever that is.'

'I live in a turn-of-the-century apartment just one minute's walk from the canal.'

The canal? Anthony only knew one canal. His own canal at Little Venice. 'Which canal is that, then?'

'Regent's Canal, near Little Venice. I love it there. It's central yet so quiet for unwinding.'

Unbelievable. In a city of eight million people and a million-plus homes, Jenny lives down the road. They did have something in common. She saw his smile of recognition.

'And where do you live? Is that classified information too?'

'I live near enough. You'll be outside your front door in no time.'

A lull in the conversation. Jenny admired the car, something close to Anthony's heart.

'This is a great motor, but get the hood down at least. What's the point of an Audi Cabrio if we don't get it down on a spring day like this? Pull over. Let's roll down the soft top.'

He obliged. Then Jenny went for the quadraphonic stereo. 'We need some good driving music. Some smooth sounds. I love soul.'

'Anything but Capital FM. They play the same twenty chart songs back to back all day.'

'I couldn't agree more. How about Kiss 100 FM? They play the best.'

Anthony's favourite station. Only the reception wasn't good this far out of town. Jenny dived into the cluttered CD collection underneath the glovebox.

'Wow, great CDs. Sisters with Voices, Sade, Jade, Toni Braxton. Better than Kiss FM.'

She looked at her right leg and winced. A long ladder in her black tights had appeared beside the sports gearstick. Snagged no doubt in the escape. Anthony gave it a look too. Nice view. She ran her hand up along her thigh in annoyance. Anthony almost rear-ended a juggernaut cruising in the slow lane. She had a ladder. She was real. Human. Normal. Alive.

She slid a CD into the stereo and flicked forwards to a chosen song. 'It's About Time' by SWV. And it was too. Four minutes and thirty-seven seconds of raw sexual energy on a CD. Jenny did her best in the bucket sports seat to sway to the music. She moved well. Arms gliding from side to side, occasionally rubbing shoulders with Anthony. Distracting.

Anthony didn't know where the next ninety minutes went, but they talked nonstop until suddenly they were back home in W9. By the time they got to Little Venice, Anthony felt that he had known Jenny for years. He fancied her like mad. They drove past Anthony's Thai restaurant, just filling up with early diners. Jenny pointed out of the open car.

'My favourite restaurant in the whole of London.'

Anthony had taken an executive decision. 'How about a meal there now?'

'Sure.'

'But first I gotta get out of this funeral suit. I feel like an undertaker on a lunch break.' He pulled in to the residents' parking spaces outside his home and killed the Audi.

'OK if I come up too? Just for a look?' asked Jenny.

Anthony changed while Jenny ambled through the apartment, apparently wholly satisfied with her inspection. Five minutes crouched on the floor examining the remainder of the CD collection, five minutes perusing the modest paperback collection and the rest looking at the art from around the world. That was all she needed to see. When Anthony reappeared he could smell something cooking. Olive oil, he thought. His olive oil? Jenny was standing in the kitchen, her jacket off and thrown on a chair. The hot wok was starting to smoke.

'What's the point of going out, Tony? Your fridge is packed. Prawns, bean sprouts, carrots, mange touts, mushrooms, lemon grass, ginger, red chillies. We've got everything we need for a stir-fry for two. How hot do you like it?'

*　　　*　　　*

Saturday morning was gorgeous in leafy Maida Vale. Anthony strolled to the local deli for fresh chocolate croissants and orange juice and made breakfast while Jenny lay on in the king-size until midday. It had been a great night. The sex was excellent. Great the first time and even better the second time around. Better than Vanessa, better than anyone else before her. Had Anthony stumbled on the most amazing girl in London?

Jenny looked good even now, wearing just one of his grey athletic 'Z'-shirts and nothing else. She lay on the bed with him, arms outstretched and legs curled up, her long hair splayed over the pillow. He tried to avoid the obvious distraction as he thumbed through the morning post looking for the one envelope that he was expecting, the one with the distinctive Steens crest in the top left-hand corner.

'What will we do today, Tony? Browsing in Camden? Down to Little Venice for a canal barge trip? Shopping in Regent Street? Just stay here in this bed and get totally wasted? Any option will do me as long as we're together.'

Anthony found the envelope among all the junk mail and opened it.

'I think the latter, because unfortunately I haven't got much time for anything else today.'

'Why, what could you be possibly doing that's better than being with me?'

Anthony pulled out the flight ticket that his temp secretary had mailed to him yesterday. 'I'm off to Hong Kong in four hours' time.'

'Oh. What an exciting life you lead, Tony. Can I even dare to ask what you're doing out there? Is your trip connected to the recent deaths in Steens by any chance?'

She never stopped working, even between bouts of energetic sex.

'I can't say. I don't even know myself yet, to be honest. I'll talk to you when I get back.'

'Don't wait that long. Give me a call when you get there. Let me know you arrived safely.'

He would. Jenny evidently cared. She scribbled an 0171 home telephone number on the back of his flight ticket, then etched a small heart beside it in red pen. Nice rounded handwriting too. Always a good sign in Anthony's opinion. Jenny couldn't compete with one of the most exciting cities in the world. But only just.

CHAPTER SIXTEEN

5.00 P.M.: SATURDAY 13 APRIL: HEATHROW TO HONG KONG

Virgin Atlantic simply exuded sex appeal, right from the moment when the gleaming courtesy Range Rover set Anthony down outside Terminal 3 and he was personally escorted to the red-carpeted check-in of Upper Class. Then on to the Clubhouse Lounge, where the staff in crisp white blouses and crimson pencil skirts leaned nonchalantly to place a G&T on the motif coaster as he idly paged through the international corporate news in *Fortune* magazine. Then the opulent interior of the Airbus 320 Upper Class cabin tantalised the senses and heightened the expectation of what was to come. Reclining in seat 2A on Virgin was the only way to spend thirteen hours in an aeroplanc.

This particular Saturday-evening flight was no different. Anthony didn't fully recline his seat just yet. The cabin staff were awesome. Anthony already knew who was his favourite. The brightly polished engraved gold namebadge of the sallow Asian girl said Tasha. She handed him an amenities bag and pillow. He wondered if the flight crew ever made furtive comparisons of the passengers in the galley? Would any of them talk about the guy sitting in 2A? Strange. Watching Tasha in action only made him think about Jenny.

Three hours ago, on the doorstep, they had parted company. He boarded the Range Rover and Jenny walked back towards Regent's Canal. It had been a great twenty-four hours, one with an ominous beginning in a graveyard in Suffolk but with a glorious climax in a W9 king-size. The mere memories of her aroused him in the fifty-two-inch pitch seats, so much so that he had to clandestinely adjust his seating position to regain some semblance of comfort and dignity. He was already beginning to miss Jenny after just a few hours apart.

Anthony couldn't physically read the entire Saturday *Times* newspaper. There was simply too much. Even if he were setting out on a twenty-four-hour trip to Steens in Sydney or Auckland with a Bangkok or KL stopover, he could never read all the news, the sports supplement, the personal finance tips, the style section, the exotic travel supplement, the glossy photogenic magazine, the prospective TV guide and the collectors' car supplement. As a compromise, he paged through the magazine with news of the London social whirl, pictures of moneyed middle-aged men with gelled-back greying hair and thin-stemmed English roses on their arms, reports of polo matches with royalty in attendance and breaks in exclusive Caribbean island retreats which made Virgin's Neckar Island seem mediocre. Anthony had such a distance to go to attain that type of lifestyle. Only the directors, those still alive that is, could truly aspire to that. And a board appointment was a long way off for Anthony, if ever.

Reading the business section reminded Anthony of work. There would be time enough in Hong Kong to follow his instincts and learn more about this wonderful Asian pricing account. He had a minimum of perhaps two or three days, a week at maximum, until Alvin Leung returned from his London meetings with the other directors. Time enough for Anthony to complete the puzzle, perhaps.

He dined on a mixed-leaf salad with artichokes and basil vinaigrette, Cantonese spiced beef fillet with saffron rice and spinach leaves and a redcurrant mousse with berry coulis, all complemented by an oaky French red. In truth, the menu sounded better than the food actually tasted at thirty-five thousand feet. Anthony blamed the recently developed art form called menu-writing. Mere food was no longer enough for the veteran Upper Class palates. Instead, every *petit morceau* needed an adjective: pan-roasted, marinated, char-grilled, peppered, sautéed, stir-fried, corn-fed, tossed.

Thirteen glorious hours later, Anthony felt the plane bank sharply to the right as he looked out at the grey South China Sea. They were approaching the new airport at Chek Lap Kok but were still going to enjoy the skyscrapers of Hong Kong island. The view in the distance from 2A was a feast for the eyes: the harbour alive with tugs, naval patrol boats, white millionaire-style cruisers, floating cranes, laden barges, company and fishing junks and the familiar green and white Star ferries plying their ceaseless passage between Kowloon and Central. It was one of the great views that anyone would see in their lifetime. It was an intense city that you could literally plug into and feel energised and revitalised, Anthony felt the rush already.

The Bank of China's angular silver tower was the tallest building in downtown Central. The

Hongkong Bank's award-winning masterpiece by Norman Foster dominated the gardens of Chater Square, surely one of the most valuable unused acres in the world. The ex-governor's palatial mansion could be seen just behind. Every inch of space of this phenomenal city was developed, with gleaming symbols of money and wealth crammed into a few square miles. Anthony saw the Steens building near the waterfront which they shared with a few other big US and European investment banks. Every time Anthony returned here he saw more fifty-storey towers under construction up in the residential midlevels. Six million people living in four hundred square miles.

The new airport was less fun than the old facility at Kai Tak, less of a challenge for the enthused pilots. Anthony recalled the popular traffic roundabout in Mongkok at the end of the old runway where tourists and locals congregated in the late afternoon as the European- and US-originated jumbos touched down after their intercontinental marathon.

Anthony once experienced the sensation here as a fully laden screaming 747, wheels down, wings back, flew two hundred feet over his head. No one at Steens knew that Anthony was a closet plane-spotter. It didn't fit with the expectations of his peers. Anthony had been fortunate to be a guest of the Royal Hong Kong Aeronautical Club, whose clubhouse was positioned on the right side of the perimeter fence, where one could enjoy the same views and noise pollution in comfort on the balcony with a few expats, a comfy seat and a cold Heineken in hand. Touchdown. He missed Kai Tak.

He bustled through the glitzy arrivals lounge with his flight bag slung over his shoulder and got into the Virgin courtesy limo. He felt surprisingly good despite the long flight in the dry cabin air. Flying east was always worse than flying west, but over time Anthony had learned how to beat the great enemy of investment bankers, jet lag. Many's the deal that had been ruined by seriously fatigued investment bankers sitting at the same conference table as fully acclimatised locals on a Monday morning. Wearing casual clothes, leaving one's shoes off on the flight and travelling light was always taken as read for an experienced traveller. Gary's cure for jet lag was to get hammered in London the night before the flight, get hammered on the plane and then get well and truly hammered upon arrival. With the incredible hangover he had the next day, jet lag was the least of his worries.

Anthony's cure was different. Get flights at the right time of the day. Drink lots of water on the plane and stay off most of the alcohol. When you arrive, stay in the natural light and fresh air outside for as long as you can if you want to stay awake. Then get a good night's sleep. And, most important, never ever think about what the time is back home. Or what someone like Jenny would be doing in London. Shit. He was doing that right now.

The limo driver had worked for Virgin for three years. He had once driven the famous Richard. And he sometimes drove the crew. He knew their regular hotel. Interesting.

*   *   *

292

Stepping out on the first morning in Hong Kong was always a shock to the system. Even in April at 8.30 a.m. the heat was tangible, humidity in the high eighties, and the typhoon season was only months away. Anthony took an air-conditioned taxi to Steens' office in Des Voeux Road in Central, where so many banks had their offices. It was the locals' answer to the City of London, their own little Square Mile. In the wood-panelled reception on the twentieth floor he asked rather naively to see Alvin Leung. Much to his relief the receptionist confirmed that Leung was in London all week. Perfect.

Anthony then asked to see Peter Cheung, the head of operations of the Hong Kong office. He knew Peter from one of his prior visits. He had been good to deal with. Peter has left, he was told by the receptionist. Where to? Don't know. Sorry. Can't help. No option but to meet the new head of operations. Called Edwin Li, according to the receptionist. He was told to wait in reception. Li took his time arriving from behind secure doors in the lobby area.

Anthony was greeted coolly by a small Chinese man in his forties, wearing bifocal glasses and a short-sleeved shirt that was about two sizes too small for his protruding belly and stocky arms. The man didn't have the air of someone who could be in charge of a Steens' office. This might be easier than first imagined. Li gave Anthony a suspicious look. Perhaps not.

Anthony sat in Li's office looking at the operations staff working outside. Rows of Chinese youths and girls sitting at VDUs inputting equity and bond deal tickets into pro forma screens.

293

Crammed into tiny desks with little space in between, largely due to the cost of floor space in Central but also partly due to the practice in every investment bank of giving the best facilities to the dealers, sales staff, analysts and corporate financiers while leaving the worst for the operations staff, who generated no revenue whatsoever. Li asked Anthony for his business card, as if to verify where he had come from and his authenticity. Time to start the real work.

'I'm looking at operational matters in various offices of Steens, to make sure that they are as efficient and as cost-effective as possible. I am sure you can appreciate the need for that.' Li looked decidedly unimpressed by the explanation. 'Naturally, I've come to Hong Kong because the office here does so much of our Asian trade bookings. I would like to talk to some of your staff about which accounts are used and what they are used for. That's all. It shouldn't take more than a few days.'

Li frowned and spoke in his broken English. 'What do you propose to do exactly?'

Anthony had to dangle a few red herrings so as not to reveal his exact intentions. 'I would like a list of all the ledger accounts to which we book trades. Both the client accounts and all the house accounts of the firm itself. Then I might look at a few in detail and talk to staff here. Can I get a desk and a computer terminal outside here?'

Li leaned forward in his chair, those short arms propped on the edge of the desk. 'I will see what I can do for you. I can give you the account list, but please be warned that it is very long. It will take time to print it out and much longer to read it all.

We have thousands of accounts in the office. But I don't want you talking to the staff here. We are busy because trade volumes are high at the moment. The market is very active, and everyone is dealing. You can therefore talk to me about any accounts. There are no free desks outside, so I will get you an office on your own. And you can't have access to a computer terminal. You know that we cannot allow just anyone to have access to systems here.'

It wasn't the desired outcome. Anthony was seated in a windowless room that was too small to have ever been an office for a normal human being, more like a prison cell. He had a bare table and telephone and nothing else. He sat for a while thinking about what he was doing. Was he mad? Had he come out to one of Steens' most important offices without the knowledge of any of the directors on a wild-goose chase that was going to cost Steens thousands of pounds in travel expenses, about which he had never told Derek in advance, and where the results might be far worse than Anthony had contemplated?

Li's glass office was directly outside. When Anthony left to use the washroom, Li eyed him as he walked by, no greeting, but just acknowledging that he knew Anthony had gone walkabout in his domain. And he didn't like it one little bit. Then visible relief as Anthony returned to his office and closed the door. There wasn't much to uncover in a bare office. Anthony was beginning to wish he had stayed in London when a spotty youth came in to the room, sullenly dropped an enormous computer listing on the table and left without uttering a single word. The staff did nothing to make

Anthony feel welcome. Li had not even suggested lunch, which was the common practice for overseas visitors to Steens' offices. Sometimes much more could be achieved over a sociable meal than over an office desk.

Li probably thought that this long account list would faze Anthony. Not so. This time he knew exactly what he was looking for, the Asian pricing account. He hoped that the list was in alphabetical order and then the search would be easy. It was not. It was in numerical sequence of the account numbers. He ran a pen down the accounts, looking for what he wanted. As he turned page after page his hopes faded. It all seemed to be just clients' accounts. There were no accounts in Steens' name at all. Had Li given him a list that wasn't complete? Did he know what he was looking for? Had he been warned? Anthony knew that it was a waste of time as he turned the last few pages of the printout. He was a beaten man.

Then salvation. The very last two pages had a list of accounts prefixed by the numbers 99. These were accounts with Steens' own name. They were not client accounts. They were error accounts. Suspense accounts. New issues accounts. Underwriting accounts. Syndication accounts. Even among all these it would have been difficult to pick out the one account that Anthony wanted to see. And then suddenly there it was on the list. Account 99656, called the Asian pricing account. It actually existed on the books in Hong Kong. The trail was getting warmer. Anthony scribbled a few of the house account numbers on a yellow post-it note, including his 99656 account. He returned to Li's office.

These are the accounts I wish to review.'

'What do you want?' Li enquired as he suspiciously eyed the list of 99 prefix numbers.

'I'd like a printout of all account activity on these for the past few months.'

'That will take time. I'll have it for you after lunch. Have you got lunch organised?'

No.'

'Then maybe you can go and get a sandwich now?'

No chance of a free lunch. Anthony could try it on Li instead.

'How about going out for some lunch? On me.'

Li didn't bother to raise his eyes from some papers on his desk. 'No. I'm too busy.'

*   *   *

Anthony used the overhead walkways between Hong Kong offices to get to a small European-style sandwich bar where the shocking price of a single roast beef salad sandwich was only compensated for by a genuine greeting from the Thai girl behind the counter. But it paid to shop well. On his last visit the Central sandwich bar that Anthony had frequented was suddenly closed by local health authorities after a hepatitis scare. Best to be safe. Within twenty minutes Anthony was back in his cell, waiting for Li's staff to produce the goods yet again. After another hour he was about to storm into Li's office when the same sullen youth delivered a handful of computer listings. Anthony made straight for account 99656.

Disaster. It was blank. The page simply contained the account header with the number and name and columns with debit, credit and balance headers. Anthony couldn't believe it. The account had to be active. God knows, it had been paying out money to Walker just months ago. He was frustrated. He had to confront Li.

'This account 99656 seems to be inactive. I thought it would have some trades in it.'

'No, it doesn't.'

'What's the account used for?'

'Just what it says, I guess. Asian trades.'

'Can I check on screen to see what activity is going through the account?'

'We are busy. Many staff are working late tonight. Maybe tomorrow we can look?'

It was only four o'clock, but Li was signalling that it was time for Anthony to finish up for the day. They had reached a stalemate, and Anthony decided that tomorrow might have to be handled by him in a different way. More aggressively if necessary. Time to turn up the heat. He tried one last option.

'Last time I was here I met Peter Cheung. Do you know where he's working now?'

'He retired from the business.'

Cheung was too young to retire. Anthony desperately needed to meet Peter again.

'Where 'Where would I find him?'

'Try the telephone directory.'

Anthony acquiesced, picked up his briefcase and took a taxi back to the hotel feeling deflated and in need of a shower to refresh his flagging spirits after a fruitless day in Central. Thanks solely to Edwin Li.

*   *   *

Anthony did as suggested and paged through the telephone directory in his hotel room. He found the Cheungs easily enough, but was aghast at the number of Peter Cheungs listed. Hundreds of them. It was like looking up John Smith in the London directory. Impossible. He could ring each name one by one, but it would take all night. Li must have known this when he suggested looking up the directory. The guy was having a private joke at Anthony's expense. Peter Cheung was uncontactable.

Anthony's job took him to the most exciting cities in the world, and now he had a whole evening ahead of him. There were a myriad of choices in this Asian hot spot. He could amble around the Causeway Bay shops and malls to stock up on the best CDs, designer gear, sportswear, electronics and gold at half the price of the West End. Maybe get something for Jenny. He could be a tourist for a day, take the historical Peak Tram funicular rail service to the top of Victoria Peak and view the night panorama of the harbour in all its splendour from eighteen hundred feet. He could take a bus to the far side of Hong Kong island and visit Stanley market and the sandy beaches of Repulse Bay. He could go to the bars and nightclubs of the hilly underworld of Lan Kwai Fong, where the beautiful people drank designer European beer from the bottle as they debated who earned the most.

But there was something that Anthony always did on the first night in Hong Kong. He would visit Harry Wu over on the Kowloon side to see about another hand-made suit that he knew would be ready to pack into his flight bag by the end of the week.

Anthony took the MTR train from Causeway Bay, changed at Central, went under Victoria harbour in minutes and reappeared at ground level in Tsim Sha Tsui station. The train carriages were air-conditioned, spotlessly clean, regular and safe. Late commuters sat with him as they also travelled to the action in Kowloon. Outside, on Nathan Road, the Golden Mile, the night sky was lit up by neon signs advertising electronics goods, bars, restaurants, massage parlours, karaoke clubs. Many were in Chinese script and were indecipherable to Anthony. The streets were jammed with locals and tourists fulfilling the urgent desire to consume and spend as much as they could in as short a time as possible.

Harry Wu's shop was located down a narrow side alley that no tourist would ever accidentally stumble on. That was the way Harry liked it. He catered to the serious customers who shelled out for a good suit and didn't haggle over a few dollars like a tourist. Harry greeted Anthony like an old friend. He knew who his best customers were. Harry was simply Harry, an ageless Chinese man in his fifties with a thriving solo business. He was personable and friendly, keen to help every customer without the hard-sell pressure that so many other nearby tailors inflicted on their clientele.

Harry took business cards from all his customers and sent them personal Christmas cards wherever they were in the world. It was rumoured that Harry had the largest collection of Steens' business cards, which wasn't surprising since so many of Steens' investment bankers, dealers and salesmen visited

300

him on the personal recommendation of their colleagues. That was how Anthony had got his first suit from Harry years ago.

'Mr Carlton, it's good to see you. Welcome back to Hong Kong.'

Harry always offered his customers a cold Carlsberg from the fridge. There was no rush to do business. Harry knew that he had a sale the minute Anthony entered his shop. They discussed the handover experience and life afterwards, Hong Kong nightlife and restaurants. Anthony chose a rich navy wool material. He must be addicted to blue suits. Harry used a tape measure for the vital measurements.

'You have put on an extra inch around the waist since last time, Mr Carlton. Bad sign.'

Blame it on too many long-haul flights and rich food and too little time for playing tennis. Anthony moved round to face Harry, but his attention was caught by his reflection in the shop window. Or was it his reflection? A man's outline was silhouetted in the glass. A face that wasn't his stared back into the shop. He made eye contact with dark, sunken eyes and then the outline stepped back into the darkness of the alley and was gone. Someone had been watching him. A Chinese man in a dark jacket.

'Did you see him, Harry? That man?'

Harry had seen nothing but obliged by stepping towards the open door. 'There's no one there. Maybe it was just someone admiring my excellent window display?'

The Carlsbergs were finished. Harry would telephone the office to set up the first fitting. Anthony didn't know if he could find enough work to do if Li continued with his obstructive attitude, but he was determined to stick it out so that at least he could collect that suit. Thoughts of the office again made him think about people in Steens whom Harry must know.

'You know lots of Steens' staff from your work over the years. Do you know Edwin Li?'

'No, but I have heard of his name. He's not very popular there, I think.'

No surprise. Anthony thought of Li's predecessor whom he couldn't contact.

'Do you know Peter Cheung?'

'Yes. Peter was a good customer of mine. He bought many office shirts with his initials monogrammed on the breast pocket. That was his favourite item. You want a few shirts too?'

'No, thanks. Seen Peter at all recently?'

Harry shrugged his shoulders in disappointment.

'Not for a while. He has left Steens. He probably doesn't need good shirts because he doesn't work any more. He doesn't live in Hong Kong now. That's probably why he doesn't come here any longer. Still, he is not far away. He will drop in again.'

'Do you know where Peter is?'

Harry rummaged in a box of business cards behind the glass counter which contained cufflinks, ties, cummerbunds, waistcoats and cravats. The box looked totally disorganised, but Harry found what he was looking for instantly. He held out Peter Cheung's business card with Steens' blue and gold logo in the corner. It didn't seem much use. It told Anthony nothing new. Harry saw his disappointment. He smiled again as he turned the business card over to display a hand-written address and telephone number.

'Peter told me he was going to live in Macau. This is his new address.'

Anthony tried to take the card but Harry refused to let him.

'I will write it down for you. Otherwise I can't send Peter his Christmas card in December.'

Anthony left the shop. He had met an old friend, had a couple of perfectly chilled beers, ordered a fine suit for collection and obtained the contact details of the one man who might just tell him exactly what the hell was going on in Steens' Hong Kong office. Things were looking better. He had also encountered someone he felt was watching from afar, someone who was interested in what he was doing in Hong Kong.

*　　　*　　　*

Anthony took the MTR back to Causeway Bay and his hotel. He sat in the train carriage and engaged in his favourite pastime of people-watching. Just like the tube in London. Shoppers returning laden with packages and bags, youths with hissing walkmans and earphones nodding to the rhythmic beat of the music in their empty heads, anaemic tourists with video cameras, bulging wallets, Cokes and creased street maps. There was no chance of seeing anyone he knew in a train carriage in Hong Kong.

He glanced further down the half-empty snaking carriage. A Chinese man sat alone, staring blankly ahead. He looked familiar. A dark jacket, lightweight, but still excessive for the cool of the evening. That face. A Chinese face. Anthony recognised it. The same face from Harry's shop window. Or was it? It couldn't be. There were millions of Chinese faces here, for God's sake, and they all looked alike to a Westerner. Cop on to yourself Anthony. Get a grip on reality. That face. Was it or wasn't it? One sure way to find out.

Next stop Causeway Bay station. Anthony alighted and followed the crowd up the escalators, through the ticket barriers and the overattentive staff and into the station concourse. Lots of people about. He stood by an exit map on the wall as if to examine which was the best of the twelve different exits by which to reach his hotel. He knew the best already. It was a ploy. Then a casual about turn and a visual search. The Chinese guy was there. He stood across the concourse, a newspaper in his hand, looking at his watch. The oldest trick in the book. Jesus. Someone was following Anthony around Hong Kong. Anthony was only doing his job. What was going on?

Panic set in. This was getting serious, too serious for a middle-management banker from London. Got to lose this guy, but how? Impossible in a city where Anthony was a stranger and the guy had local knowledge. His imagination was running riot. Jeremy Walker with a Hermès tie knotted around his neck. Johan Verhoeven falling from an eighth-floor balcony. Who was next?

There was always safety in numbers. Anthony had an idea. Get with the crowd. Don't be on your own in a hostile city, ever. Don't be sitting in a hotel room waiting for a knock on the door from room service or whoever. Especially not in a room on the twenty-ninth floor of a Hong Kong skyscraper with a big welcoming balcony outside.

304

Anthony looked again at the street map on the wall, this time for a genuine reason. He knew well that his hotel was situated out of exit five. Instead, he took exit eight and walked briskly towards the Regal Hotel.

Through the sumptuous hotel lobby and into the busy bar. The lighting was muted as Anthony looked around for his saviour. No sign. He sat by the bar that allowed him a good view of the main entrance. It was just after eight o'clock. Perfect timing. He ordered a San Miguel which came in a tall, chilled glass. He surveyed the bar, but nobody was paying excessive attention to him. Relax, Anthony. Now the wait to see if he was right.

By twenty minutes past eight he'd had two San Miguels and was wondering if he should order a third. Two European girls who came in and sat at a low table nearby caught his eye. One was a brunette, the other a blonde. He didn't recognise them, but they looked like the Virgin stewardess type. Hopefully. In the next ten minutes four more girls and two guys joined the two early arrivees. It was amazing how every group of people who ever stayed in a hotel anywhere in the world, before heading out on the town for an evening, always arranged to meet in the hotel bar for a drink at eight or half-past eight or nine. True to form, the Virgin crew from Anthony's flight hadn't disappointed him yet.

A dark-haired sallow Asian girl entered the bar. She wore a simple crisp white shirt, the sleeves fashionably rolled up to her tanned elbows, and a pair of figure-hugging, perfectly faded blue 501 jeans rounded off by a worn brown leather belt. This time her long black hair was falling loose

305

around her shoulders and her perfect oval face. Her jet-black eyes were sparkling, confirming her vivacious personality. It wasn't always the case, but she looked even better than when Anthony had seen her in her red Virgin uniform. Tasha had made a great first impression with Anthony. The group was ready to leave. It was now or never. He needed them so badly, for the protection they would offer. The crew walked close by him as they went towards the exit of the bar, and Anthony swivelled on his bar stool.

'Tasha. I didn't think that I would get to see you again so soon.'

A look of recognition appeared on her face. He persevered. 'I'm Tony. I saw you on the flight over here. Can I buy you a drink?'

'Well, Mr 2A. I didn't think that I'd see you again, except possibly on the return flight.'

She had remembered his seat number. God was good.

'I'd love to stay, but we are going to the Imperial for some food and then on to JJ's club.' She saw his look of disappointment. No. Despair. 'If you want you can come along too.'

Salvation personified. No sign of anyone hanging around the lobby. He left the hotel in the safe company of the crew. No one would dare touch him in the mêlée of a crowded restaurant. They went to JJ's in the Hyatt, where Anthony swayed to the Euro-pop from Ibiza and Tasha got real close when the slow numbers came on. Too close. Her white shirt shone in the fluorescent spotlights as she eased her body towards him, arms swirling round in the heady, smoky atmosphere. Temptation on the dancefloor. Then memories of

Jenny. Time to leave. Alone. Tasha wasn't happy. Sorry.

Back in the safety of his hotel room, Anthony made one call as requested to that beautifully written 0171 number in West London to confirm that he had arrived safely and simultaneously to erase the guilt of almost being unfaithful to Jenny. Unfaithful? This was getting serious.

And then one call to a private residence in Macau to confirm his travel plans for tomorrow.

CHAPTER SEVENTEEN

9.30 A.M.: TUESDAY 16 APRIL: HONG KONG TO MACAU

Anthony telephoned Edwin Li to report a dose of food poisoning from last night's alleged seafood meal at the floating restaurants of Aberdeen Harbour. Edwin Li advised him to take time to recover and not to rush back into the office. Anthony honestly believed his sentiments.

Anthony had never been to the old Portuguese colony of Macau, Somewhere new to discover. The high-speed jetfoil surged from the Macau Ferry Terminal in the Shun Tak Centre in Central. Once they left Hong Kong territorial waters the surly Chinese crew sold Macau instant lottery tickets to the Chinese passengers to sate their addiction to gambling. This was their only other opportunity for a legal gamble apart from horse racing at Happy Valley and Shatin in the New Territories. The serious passengers were heading for the casinos in

Macau. Anthony was already doing enough gambling with his career.

The twin Boeing jet engines ensured that they covered the forty nautical miles in just under an hour. They arrived at the decrepit harbour silted up by the deposits of the Pearl River delta. Macau had been prised from the Chinese centuries ago by the Portuguese, and at first sight it looked as if nothing had changed since that time, as if a part of Iberia had been transplanted to this distant part of the world.

The sleepy disembarkation area was a welcome change from the frenetic pace of Hong Kong. Anthony took in the pastel-coloured buildings, winding streets up potted hills, historical cathedral spires and an old fort with rusty cannons protruding from overgrown castle walls. He did his best to ignore the ugly modern side to the island, characterised by anonymous high-rise apartments, office blocks and industrial factories with belching chimneys.

The taxi driver who read Harry Wu's scribbled note immediately recognised the address. He took off at a speed reminiscent of the annual Macau Grand Prix held every October on the island. They pulled up at a secluded bungalow set back from the road, with a panoramic sea view. Anthony didn't need to knock on the door. A small, neatly dressed and immaculately groomed man in a patterned casual shirt, flannel trousers and open-toe sandals was standing in the well-kept garden toying with a hoe. Although they had last met years ago in Steens' office when Peter was in a suit and tie, Anthony recognised his former colleague immediately. But Peter was different now, somewhat gaunt, stiff, even jaundiced. Peter might not be enjoying his somewhat premature retirement as much as he deserved

'Welcome to Macau, Anthony. We have met before, once, I recall. Thanks for the telephone call last night. We don't often get visitors from Steens out here. Come on in.'

Peter was genuinely welcoming, and they sat together on a patio at the back of the house looking at the wonderful view of the harbour and the regularly departing sea craft. The full heat of the midday sun approached. Only for mad dogs and Englishmen. True to form, Anthony hung his jacket on a nearby chair and sat directly facing the sun, never one to miss an opportunity to top up his suntan. Orientals don't care much for the sun. Peter sat under a canopy and somehow felt the need to explain his choice of retirement residence.

'Macau is a great place. It's so peaceful here, and yet only a short commute to Hong Kong. And a nice commute by ferry, not by gridlocked car or crowded MTR. Very agreeable.'

A Chinese lady came out of the house carrying a tray with cold drinks. Peter's wife. She, too, greeted Anthony warmly. Doris Cheung joined them for a polite five minutes while they exchanged pleasantries about Macau and its amenities and lifestyle. Then she sensed the two wanted to talk shop so she returned to the welcome coolness of their air-conditioned home. She was right. Anthony got down to business.

'Thanks for inviting me over here.'

'No problem. Steens were good to me for many years. I guess that it must be something important for you to come out here and speak to a retired gentleman like me.'

'Well, that surprises me for starters. You've retired at a very young age.'

'Steens made me an offer I couldn't refuse. It was attractive financially, if you get my drift.'

'I want to ask you about your time as head of operations here. In particular I want to talk about some of the trade bookings that were made in a certain pricing account.'

Immediately Peter looked at Anthony with real surprise. 'You've found it, haven't you?'

'Found what?'

'The Asian pricing account?'

'Yes, I guess I have.'

Anthony knew he had found something, but he didn't know exactly what it was. He took a sip of the cold drink to make it clear that he would not interrupt. He would let Peter go on. Tell me more. Peter obliged.

'That account is the reason for my early departure from Steens. My retirement, as Alvin Leung and Edwin Li called it. At the tender age of forty-eight. That pricing account has been in use for years. I was never happy about it. At the start it made small bucks and I didn't really worry about it. But then the market volumes grew and the money it generated became enormous. I wanted something to be done, but no one else was interested. It isn't right. It must cease.'

'And that's why you retired?'

'In a word, yes. We are not supposed to talk about the account openly. But I began to make waves about it. Alvin Leung didn't like what I was doing. He told me to shut up talking to other Steens' staff about the account. He threatened to fire me, saying that he would ensure that I would never find another job in Hong Kong. Then he offered me a deal to leave Steens, and he made it worth my while. I couldn't turn it down. So I just got out.'

Anthony bluffed from what he knew about the moneys that Walker had received. 'It amazes me that the pricing account generates so much cash.'

'It's not a coincidence that there's so much cash. It's a sure thing. A one-way bet.'

A pause. Difficult silence. The two men evaluated each other. The searing sun and Peter's inquisitive eyes bearing down on this English visitor to a distant colonial outpost. Lost in every sense. Geographically and professionally.

'You don't actually know what's happening, do you, Anthony?'

'No, Peter, I don't. That's why I came here to talk to you today.'

'Well, I can't tell you. It's too dangerous to speak about something like that. Alvin Leung has threatened me in the past, so I have to be careful.'

'I must know. Otherwise it might ruin Steens and be our downfall. You don't want that?'

Peter deliberated, considering the choice open to him. The silence was punctuated by the horns of sea craft manoeuvring in the harbour below. 'I gave Steens the best years of my life, and then they just let me go. That was bad enough. Retired with a six-figure bribe. But do you know what? All that money is no use to me now. When I retired I went for a medical with my life assurance company and the doctor got real worried. I've got the big C. Cancer. Still can't believe it. Who's going to look after Doris? Who will provide for her?' Peter held

311

his head in his hands. 'I'm going to die. Much sooner than I ever thought.'

The jaundiced look had been explained. Anthony felt embarrassed to raise the matter of a mere securities account when life was ebbing away from the man sitting in the patio chair before him. Anthony couldn't find words to ease Peter's pain, but Peter had come to a decision.

'Jesus. What does all this matter? It's only Steens, it's only one company in a world of sleaze. It's about time people knew the facts about this Asian pricing account. It's so simple that it's unbelievable, yet it generates millions of dollars every year for absolutely no risk. Except the risk of actually getting caught, that is. And that's been zero until now.'

Anthony took out a notebook and pen. It was more for effect than real purpose. Peter objected. 'No notes or anything like that. That's too dangerous. Just listen. This is off the record between two Steens' people.'

Anthony put the notebook away and indicated his agreement.

'I worked at Steens for twenty-four years under various people. It all changed when Jeremy Walker took charge out here some years ago. He wasn't a director then, but he was under a lot of pressure to develop the office because the Asian business was slow to grow. Walker would do anything to bring in any revenue so it would make him look good in the eyes of Sir James and the directors back in London and improve his chances of getting a seat on the board in due course. I guess that at least worked out for him, although he didn't get to enjoy his directorship for very long. I heard about his death in London a few weeks ago. It was a great shock.'

Anthony noticed that Peter didn't express any regret at the loss.

'Steens' business is very simple here. We don't punt in the market or speculate for the short term. We just execute client orders in the local market and make a good commission from that. And some of the commissions are large, so we do well. All the orders are passed from our office to our floor traders on the Hong Kong Stock Exchange and executed with other local brokers. But Walker saw that our traders and staff on the floor of the Stock Exchange were good at their job. Excellent, in fact. They read the market very well and often get the highest prices for shares that clients wished to sell and also manage to get the lowest prices for shares being bought. They knew the right time of the day to buy and sell, and our clients got great price executions.'

Jesus. No. Not now. Doris returned with a top-up of iced lemonade. The conversation stopped. She took away an empty decanter and left the two alone again. She had disturbed the flow. Anthony dared.

'What do you mean by great price executions?'

'It depends on the price of the share in the market. Say you want to buy a share here, say Hong Kong Telecom. Say it closes at HKD 15.00 on the prior day and on the day you want to buy it trades in the range of HKD 14.95 to HKD 15.25. And it closes at HKD 15.25, that's up by more than one per cent, which is not unusual in these types of volatile markets in Asia. Just read the papers every day. With me so far?'

Anthony was indeed.

'Steens might have an institutional client who wants to buy. Our floor staff are good, and they buy his shares at various times of the day, and say the average price works out at HKD 15.05 because they bought most of the shares before the price edged up later in the day. So if you were a client and Steens told you that the share closed at HKD 15.25 and that you had bought at HKD 15.05, how would you feel?'

'I'd be delighted.'

'Exactly. But how about if Steens told you that you had bought at HKD 15.10 instead?'

'I don't think I'd notice the difference, to be honest. It's still a good price, below the end-of-day close and still around the mid-range price for the day. Yes, I would be happy.'

'Exactly again. The difference is that HKD 15.05 is a great execution price and HKD 15.10 is just a good execution price. That's all. It's only a five-cent difference.'

'So what's the catch?'

'Walker realised exactly what you've just realised. Clients don't mind if they get a slightly worse execution price than the price they actually get on the floor of the exchange. He ordered me as head of operations to open the Asian pricing account at our office and told me that he would be booking intra-day trades through it. In and out on the same day. In fact, Walker arranged to book trades in and out at different execution prices, in at the price done in the local market and out at whatever price he thought that the client would accept.'

This didn't really make any economic sense to Anthony. Was he missing something?

'But that's hardly worth the effort, just for five cents per share?'

'Walker didn't put all the orders through the account. He was selective. Remember the types of orders that we get here in Hong Kong. We don't get crappy little orders to buy a few hundred shares or so. We get big orders passed to us from Steens' offices all over the world, from institutional clients, pension funds, life assurance companies, mutual funds and other banks. We regularly get single orders here for a million US dollars' worth of shares or more. Five cents on a HKD 15 share is a third of one per cent of a price adjustment, or thirty-three basis points, as we say in the trade. Thirty-three basis points on a million bucks is three thousand three hundred bucks. Do twenty-five of them a day and you are clearing eighty grand net a day. That's four hundred grand a week or twenty million Hong Kong dollars a year. Nearly two million sterling. Not bad at all.'

Anthony was impressed. Peter was either highly numerate or else knew these types of numbers very well from his years at Steens. Anthony was still evaluating the practicalities.

'But wouldn't the clients realise that they weren't getting the best price in the market?'

'Remember what I said earlier. Walker just arranged to make great execution prices into good execution prices. He never even let a good execution price become an average execution price. He was very careful about the trades that he adjusted. Walker told me once after work over a beer in the early days that he had never received even one complaint about an execution price from the clients. He was so careful. We had all the market technology here, like Bloomberg and Reuters screens. Walker would look at all the price data and weighted averages to make sure he got his price just right.'

He smiled knowingly, recalling something that made an impression.

'Walker was good. Do you know what he did sometimes? When we got a bad execution on the exchange because our floor staff screwed up an order or read the market wrongly, Walker got the execution price adjusted in the client's favour and Steens took the hit. The client never even knew. He was so careful about keeping the big clients happy. That's one of the reasons why Steens out here ranks so highly in the independent surveys of broker satisfaction by Greenwich Associates and Extel. That's why you will see some loss-making trades going through the Asian pricing account.'

Peter was like a man in a confessional, cleansing the sins of a past life.

'Walker was careful about the type of client he messed around with. He never adjusted an execution price for the really sophisticated clients, those global funds that have twenty-four-hour-a-day trading staff who monitor real time share prices. These clients might phone a Steens office somewhere in the world in the middle of their night to ask us how a big order is going. They were much more likely to notice something amiss, so Walker left their orders alone. And Walker never touched small trades because the price adjustment in terms of dollars wasn't worth the risk. You must also ask yourself why it happened here in Hong Kong and not in, say, our London or New York offices?'

Anthony didn't have the answer for this either.

Peter obliged.

'It's all due to the time difference. You can't adjust prices if the client is in the same time zone as you are because then you have no idea of what the intra-day price range and end-of-day closing prices are when you confirm the execution price back to the client. But the price adjustments can work perfectly in Asia. If Steens get an order in London or New York or Frankfurt for Hong Kong shares then pass it over here to us at the end of their trading day, the clients go home for a good night's sleep and leave the execution to us. We can wait here until the end of the day to confirm the exact execution price to the client, who then gets a fax or a voicemail message at our close of day, which is still well before when they come into work the next day. The timing is perfect. It gave Walker lots of time to fix the execution price to his optimal advantage.'

Anthony was beginning to see that there might be more to Walker's death than he and Palmer thought.

'As time went on, Walker got greedy. He realised that the basic principle works in any Far East market, as long as that time difference exists. He knew that he had to get control over the bookings of as many Far East trades as possible so that he could manipulate the execution prices. So he came up with an inventive solution that actually had some commercial advantages also. He proposed that we move all the Asian trade contracting to Hong Kong because we had a better computer system and because operations staff are cheap here. This worked fine for markets like Malaysia, Singapore, Korea, Taiwan, Indonesia, but he had big difficulty getting the Tokyo office to agree. But that was the one that he wanted. In the late 1980s the Tokyo stock market soared, and Walker needed the volumes to boost his take. He finally got board approval, and the Tokyo office objections were overruled. All the Asian bookings came to Hong Kong. Jesus, that's when the money really started pouring in. The Japanese equity trades alone more than doubled the volume of trades going through the Asian pricing account. It was enormous. I had to hire lots more operations staff to process the trades each day. Walker didn't mind at all. He could have let me hire a hundred new staff, and we would still have covered our costs tenfold.'

This was getting worse. Beads of sweat ran down Anthony's face. He didn't know if it was due to the overhead rays bearing down or the information he was receiving.

'And why did all the staff go along with Walker? Didn't anyone object?'

'They went along with his plan for the same reason that everyone does in this business. Money. It was all about greed. He identified the opportunity, and they executed it. The exchange floor staff got some more money in bonuses. It was easy at the start because none of them had any idea just how much money was being made collectively in the account. They thought they got a lot, but they didn't. Then it just became a culture here. Everyone who joined us entered into the same activity. No one rocked the boat or they would lose their job. Walker tried to justify what he was doing. He called it by different names, rather than mere price adjustments. He dreamed up bizarre titles for it, like riskless trading activity, marking up the

318

price, and value added pricing. People really got into it. When a big price adjustment was done on a trade of several million dollars, the floor staff would cheer and holler as if we had just made a killing trading in the bond market or the futures market'

'So what happened when Walker left Hong Kong a few years ago to return to London? Didn't the whole process unwind then?'

Peter was truly hesitant for the first time.

'I can't say much. Alvin Leung had previously been the head floor trader on the exchange, and he was the biggest proponent of the price adjustments. I reckon that his enthusiasm for it was one of the reasons why Walker personally recommended Leung to replace him in Steens' top job in Asia. He appointed that weasel Edwin Li to run operations once I had left.'

Anthony was thinking about his fruitless work so far in Hong Kong.

'A sceptic might say that you're a disgruntled ex-employee of Steens. How do I know that all this is true? Are there any records kept of the price adjustments?'

'You must be joking. All the trade tickets and confirmation faxes were shredded as soon as possible. You would never be able to find much paperwork. The only thing you can be sure of is that every trade had to be booked on the computer system in the bank. I can guarantee that because it was the only way we could contract and settle the trades. The Asian pricing account is definitely an accurate record. I suggest that you follow the trail of the money.'

'All this money is in the pricing account?'

'Yes, it was easy. Just book one side of the trade to the local broker at the correct price, and then book the other side of the trade at the adjusted price to the client. The net difference of a few thousand dollars on each trade just built up in the account on the credit side, showing a very profitable trading account. The corresponding debit side just accumulated in our company bank accounts that we use for settlements.'

'Wasn't the extra money in Steens' bank account ever noticed?'

'If you want to hide money, where is the best place to put it? With other money, of course. Our main bank accounts here have billions flowing through them every day, and the balances can swing from a few hundred million bucks in the black to a few hundred million overdrawn just by a client paying us one day late for some big trades. No one would ever notice extra money from the price adjustments in the bank account'

'So how much money did this account generate annually?'

'It varied from year to year, depending on the volume in the Asian markets. In a bad year it generated, say, four million pounds. In a good year it was more than double that.'

'So who got the money?'

'Listen, Mr Carlton. I can tell you what happened in the account, but I am not going to incriminate anyone else involved in this. You and I know that Walker was involved, but I don't mind telling you that because he is dead and can come to no further harm. Alvin Leung runs Steens in Asia and Edwin Li is his operations guru. That's all I will say. No other names. As I said, follow the money.'

'OK. I'll do that, but give me a clue where to start.'

Peter had come so far that there was no going back now. 'When I was at Steens, I heard that Alvin Leung kept a file of special payments that were made from the main settlements bank account. If you got hold of that file you would be on to something.'

Peter stood up from under the canopy and stretched. Their conversation was almost over.

'What are you going to do next about what I told you?'

'I'm going to get to the bottom of this. Tell Sir James and the directors back in London.'

Peter smiled a knowing smile. He still knew more than he had divulged to his visitor. Time, gentlemen. Anthony rose and carefully took his jacket off the nearby chair.

'Be careful. Just before I left Steens, things were getting nasty. Leung is a player here and has some heavy friends, big shots in property, bars, gambling, importing, the underworld. Some of these want a share in the spoils. Leung's old colleagues who work on the floor of the Stock Exchange are nasty enough too. I wouldn't want to cross them. Remember that there are millions of dollars of easy money involved here. Corruption isn't just a crime in Hong Kong: it's a way of life.'

Anthony's mind raced over the implications of what Peter had told him. What would the other directors in London make of all this? They would be impressed at Anthony's diligence. As he sat in the back of the taxi on the way to the ferry terminal, he took the Dictaphone out of the inside pocket of his jacket and switched it off. The one-hour tape had been sufficient to record every word of the conversation.

*　　　*　　　*

Anthony reached Hong Kong as the sun set over the bustling harbour. There was something else he planned to do. No one had asked him to, but Anthony felt that it had to be done. He was curious. He looked up his hotel room telephone directory and immediately found the surname that he was looking for, the one Karen had given him last week from Steens' personnel department files. It was much easier than his abortive search for Peter Cheung because there was only one person of that name listed. He dialled the residential number and a polished female English accent answered. 'Sylvia Travers.'

Jeremy Walker's ex-wife was at home today under her original maiden name. This wasn't going to be an easy conversation. Anthony had thus rehearsed his words. 'My name is Anthony Carlton. I work in London for Steen Odenberg.'

'I see . . .

'I'm in Hong Kong and I wondered if we could meet?'

The voice grew distant. Less interested.

'Why?'

'I wanted to express my condolences to you on the death of your former husband.'

'That's not necessary.'

Sylvia had overcome her grief in a remarkably short period of time.

'And I'd also like to talk to you about Jeremy.'

322

There was a pause on the line. Sylvia was evaluating his request. He thought that he'd been polite enough. He had.

'All right, then. But tonight isn't good. I'm going out shortly.' She paused again, and then had second thoughts. 'Do you enjoy horse racing?

Anthony hadn't been to a meet since Steens' last corporate bash at Royal Ascot. Him and the Queen Mum. But this might be his only opportunity to meet Sylvia. 'Very much so.'

'I'm meeting some friends in Happy Valley this evening. We have a table booked for dinner in the Hong Kong Jockey Club at seven, but one of my party just cancelled. Just tell the doorman at the club entrance that you are in my party.'

Anthony hardly needed directions to get to Happy Valley racecourse. As he exited his hotel he mingled with the massed race-goers heading in the one direction with one purpose. To win some Honkie dollars and clean out the jockey Club Tote. He entered via the private gate of the jockey Club. Inside the busy dining-room he was directed by an obsequious Chinese maître d' to a table at which five middle-aged and pickled ladies sat. Well preserved, actually. Coiffured greying hair, designer labels, conspicuous jewellery, all-year tans and bulging purses were their common denominator. They were enjoying the good life.

There was one empty chair. One lady stood to greet him. Sylvia indeed. The others smiled at each other, perhaps impressed by Sylvia's new mystery friend, half her age. Very impressed. She sat next to him as they started on the ample buffet. For the duration of the meal they made small talk about living in London versus Hong Kong, long-haul flying, horses as Anthony bluffed as best he could, local shopping excesses, the price of getting staff at home and property prices. Anthony didn't think it was appropriate to talk about Steens or Walker just yet. Then Sylvia changed the conversation voluntarily.

'What brings you to Hong Kong? It's a long way to come to offer condolences to someone you don't even know.'

'Work brings me here.'

'How are things at Steens these days?'

'Everything's going very well at the bank.' Not.

Anthony took her easy manner as a cue. 'I didn't see you at Jeremy's funeral last week in Farningham.'

'No. It wasn't worth the trip just for that. Jeremy and I haven't spoken since the divorce.'

Someone shouted from the balcony that the first race was off, and they went outside to look down on the brilliantly floodlit racecourse and teeming crowds gathered below. A raked dirt track encircled immaculately groomed lawns. Giant video pixel screens showed the latest prices and close-ups of the horses in the paddock area. Millions being bet. Anthony hadn't yet laid a bet on any horse, but evidently Sylvia had. Her horse won, and she was delighted, even though she apparently didn't need the incremental money. They were alone on the balcony as the other racegoers returned to grab iced lychees and decaff.

'That divorce was a messy business. We both had damned expensive lawyers who fought long and hard for our interests. But in the end I got lots of Jeremy's assets.'

She looked happy. Did she know? That banker's

324

box in Anthony's hallway revealed that Walker had had at least ten million pounds of assets when he died.

'Did you get half of Walker's many millions?'

'What do you mean? I had lawyers crawl all over his bank accounts and investments and pay cheques. We got as much as we could, and then a bit more. But there weren't millions. Do you know otherwise?'

There was no harm in telling her the truth.

'Jeremy was very wealthy. Did you know about the accounts he had in Jersey and the Isle of Man, the mutual funds in the US, the gold deposits in Switzerland, the Wall Street shares?'

She grew pale and leaned against the balcony. Anthony feared she might topple. Not another one, surely?

'No. I didn't know that. How much in all?'

'He was worth a minimum of ten million sterling. It all goes to his parents in Suffolk.'

'No way. I would have found out about that. Where did it all come from?'

'I don't know. Can you think of a legal way by which he could have got so much money?'

'I honestly can't, but if he had more than he was letting on, then I'll go after him again. Even if he is dead.'

Hate knew no bounds. Maybe there was more to this? Anthony followed his instincts. 'Can I ask you why you divorced Jeremy?'

'We didn't get on over time.' She looked at him directly, cast her eyes out over the racecourse below and returned to face Anthony. 'You've told me something important I didn't know this evening. So I'll reciprocate. You want to know the exact reason why I divorced Jeremy? The one thing I couldn't live with? No one else knows this, but now that Jeremy is dead it can't do any harm to anyone. The reason I divorced Jeremy is that one day I came home to our apartment and found him in bed with someone else.'

This wasn't particularly earth-shattering. So Walker had succumbed to the temptations that many wealthy bankers faced and had been caught in the act. God knows Verhoeven had been at the same thing with his Vanessa, as was Leung in the fleshpots of south-east Asia. Sylvia could see his unimpressed reaction.

'You don't understand, do you? I found Jeremy in bed with one of our hired house servants from the Phillippines. A nineteen-year-old who came from Manila only weeks beforehand.'

She wasn't impressed by Anthony's reaction.

'You still don't get it, do you? You're thinking of an innocent virginal girl in a white maid's uniform with a willing smile to match her desire to please? Aren't you? Let me spell it out for you then. Think instead of a nineteen-year-old naked boy lying face down on the pillows of our own double bed, muffling his screams as he is buggered by an overweight, overpaid sweaty investment banker. Now do you get the picture? My husband was the other way inclined. And I never knew until it was too late.'

The bitterness showed. She wiped a tear from the corner of her eye.

'I never knew. I lived with him for seventeen years, and I never really knew him. Now I know why he never wanted to have children. Our sex life was non-existent, and I assumed that he was seeing

326

some young thing at work. I never guessed. We agreed to keep it quiet from our family and friends. It would have disgraced us. Jeremy might even have had to leave Steens and his job and that lifestyle. We fudged the whole issue and cited the usual irreconcilable differences in out divorce papers. People asked fewer questions. It worked.'

Jesus. Immediate thoughts ran through Anthony's mind about Walker's death. Walker had a secret life outside of Steens. Homosexuality didn't stop just because you left the tropics of Hong Kong to live in respectable London. Walker couldn't just switch his desires off. If he had brought an Asian youth into his own bedroom in Hong Kong, then he could have done it time and time again since. In Wapping?

Palmer had said that Walker had probably been killed by someone he knew. A meal for two beforehand. No sign of a struggle. Walker had died with a tie knotted around his neck. If he was into homosexual activities, was he also into bizarre practices? Was he playing a sex game that went fatally wrong? Who was the Chinese youth in the baseball cap who had featured so prominently on the *Crimewatch* programme last week. Had Walker developed a particular taste for oriental youths? Anthony was beginning to see how Walker might have died. And it might have nothing to do with the complaints from Amsterdam, with NedCorp, EPIC or the bounteous munificence of thc Asian pricing account. What had Anthony inadvertently stumbled across?

*   *   *

327

Anthony left Happy Valley racecourse not so happy, with a few hundred dollars less from unsuccessful betting and more questions than answers. He melted into the thousands of people emerging from the racecourse and walking towards the neon glare of Causeway Bay and Wanchai. The crowds flowed over from the narrow pavements as the punters fought for their own personal space with aggressive drivers in taxis, cars and trucks.

Maybe his mind was wandering, not paying attention to the bustle all around him. People jostled him, the crowd of brisk walkers stalled, then started again. He was swept along in the tide. If he wanted to turn left or right, he couldn't. Sheer weight of numbers alongside prevented this. He brushed by cars, grazing paintwork and knocking back wing mirrors, to the annoyance of the drivers. Horns honked in frustration as man fought machine in one of the most densely populated cities in the world.

A rumbling commercial truck with illegible Chinese characters daubed on the side was beside him. People all around pushing and shoving each other. Anthony was unbalanced, leaning against others for support. No way to stop the constant motion. Pushing from behind. Then a sharp push from the side. Intentional or not? His legs were caught with others, then gave way. He fell on to the unforgiving tarmac among the torn betting slips, the discarded rice take-aways, squashed chips, dismembered burgers and flattened Coke cans.

Bruised and stunned. Eyes closed in the pain of the fall. Eyes wide open to see wheels. A set of large black tyres a foot or two away. A pumping exhaust and revolving camshaft above him. The underside of the truck. His burial chamber. The chatter of the crowd was replaced by a revving engine as the driver saw his chance to break free from the masses. A woman with a good view screamed in the crowd at the death that was about to pass.

Instinct played a part. Anthony rolled to the left in the dust. The engine roared overhead, not stopping to save a life. He rolled in time. The wheels passed inches to his right. He lay in comparative safety among the people, feeling the feet and shoes kicking against him. Still preferable to the grinding wheels that never stopped. The truck melted away. The woman shouted again. He could see the sky and stars above. He got to his feet with difficulty. No locals paused to help the poor foreigner.

Faces in the crowd staring back at Anthony. All Chinese, all the same to him. Then a youth's face. No one he had seen before but did he recognise that baseball cap on his head? Dark with a wide peak and some red logo. It could be any logo, but it was familiar. The last time Anthony had seen it was while watching BBC1's *Crimewatch*, and before that when Palmer passed him a CCTV still from Wapping underground station on the night Jeremy Walker met his untimely death. Traffic accident or not? No time to debate now.

Anthony ran in the opposite direction. He shouted at the crowds. Some people moved out of his way; others objected as he barged past. A glance around to see if he were being pursued. That face again with the baseball cap. Twenty feet behind, following in his wake. Got to get away. He pushed onwards and found an immediate obstacle in his path. A Toyota Crown taxi, stationary at red traffic lights. No way past. People on either side. A Chinese couple gazed at his angst-ridden face from the security of the back seat, wondering who the foreigner was pushed up against the door. The youth behind was ten feet away.

The traffic lights changed from red to green. Now or never. Anthony opened the back door of the taxi and dived inside, pushing the couple along the back seat. He hammered down the lock on the door with a clenched fist. The stubbled driver turned to Anthony in annoyance. This taxi was taken. Get out. Then he saw the fear on Anthony's face. He was momentarily undecided about what to do. The bus driver behind honked impatiently. The taxi had to move. A face pressed up against the glass by Anthony. That face with the cap. A vicious scowl. The taxi revved and moved off at speed. The face disappeared into the sea of other faces. Safe at last. What the hell was going on in Hong Kong?

*　　　*　　　*

Anthony threw off his torn shirt and dusty chinos in his hotel room and spent ten minutes under the steamy shower in an effort to wipe the nightmare of Happy Valley from his mind. What had really happened just an hour ago? This was getting out of control.

He thought about Sylvia Travers and the revelation of Walker's sexual preference, then toyed with the idea of ringing Palmer. But it was late in London, and Palmer would have left work. The news could wait until he got back. Then Anthony would enlighten Palmer and perhaps help

330

him solve the murder of Jeremy Walker.

Instead, Anthony called Jenny in Little Venice to get real personal. They spoke for forty minutes. The call would cost a fortune on the hotel bill, but Steens were paying. The conversation was effortless. He didn't mention the incident at Happy Valley. He didn't want to worry Jenny. Anthony wished that he was back in Maida Vale right now. Not just to be with Jenny. It was more important than that. It was a lot safer at home than being alone on the deadly streets of this Asian hot spot.

CHAPTER EIGHTEEN

9.05 A.M.: WEDNESDAY 17 APRIL: HONG KONG

Another wasted morning in the office. Edwin Li enquired if Anthony was well again. Anthony nearly forgot that he had allegedly been ill. No one else knew that it had almost been fatal. He wondered how much Edwin Li knew about last night. The new printouts on his desk confirmed that there had been no activity in the Asian pricing account since the start of April. Perhaps practices had changed since the death of Walker in the past few weeks. He confronted Edwin Li.

'I need to see some more months activity in the Asian pricing account.'

'Not possible.'

'Why not?'

'We have only this month's data on the trade system. All data from prior months is stored on backup tapes, which we would have to reload into the trade system. That takes time.'

'Then let's do that.'

'It's not so easy. The tapes are stored offsite. We have to request them back and that might take a few days if we are lucky. It's best to use the report you have.'

The report was useless. They both knew it, but Anthony wasn't going to admit it to Li. Stalemate. Then Anthony remembered Peter Cheung's words. Follow the money. Get that file of payments that Alvin Leung was supposed to possess. Leung was still in the UK with the other directors. The only obstacle between Anthony and that file was Leung's personal secretary. Anthony hadn't met her before, but he knew from the internal office telephone list that she was a Chinese girl called Lilly Pang.

Now was the time, too, to try the unkindest cut of all. If one thing scared a diminutive Chinese girl, it was a loud aggressive visitor from the London head office. If she didn't oblige, then Anthony might have to resort to his *alter ego*. No sign of Li. He took one photocopied page from his briefcase and went towards the executive offices near the front of the building. All the best offices looked out over the harbour panorama. It was lunchtime in Hong Kong, five a.m. in London, where Leung would be fast asleep in his Tower City Hotel suite. She wouldn't dare wake him. Surely.

Lilly Pang was sitting outside Leung's office. There was no one else nearby. Anthony's hopes rose. She was young and timid-looking, wearing a white cardigan, glasses and no warpaint whatsoever. This might be easier than he'd thought

332

He produced his business card as she smiled blandly at the stranger. Time for a dangerous bluff. 'I'm from the London head office and I'm reviewing some of the bank's accounts. Mr Leung left the payments file for me to look at if required. Can you get it for me?'

'I am sorry. I don't know anything about a payments file.'

She was good. That was to be expected from a senior secretary. Leung had picked the best.

'It's a file of payments made from the Asian pricing account Number 99656.'

A note of recognition at the mention of the account number. But that was all. Anthony played his trump card. He produced the one page of paper and put it on her desk.

'I have this bank statement which shows that we paid Jeremy Walker five hundred thousand dollars a few months ago, but the money arrived late into his Jersey account. I need to see when the money was paid from this end.'

The copy of Walker's bank statement visibly impressed her. She didn't know it had been copied last week from an original in a corner shop in Maida Vale. She knew Anthony was aware of the account, but it still wasn't enough to convince her. Time to up the ante.

'I haven't got time to sit around asking for this file all afternoon. I have to examine this payment. I want the file now. If you have a problem, then we'll just ring up Alvin in London right now and ask him to confirm that I am to get this file. And he won't appreciate that.'

She knew that. She didn't like the developing confrontation. She spoke in poor English. 'All right.

I'll get the file.'

She took a key from a drawer, went into Leung's office, removed a lever-arch file from a locked cabinet and brought it out. Anthony walked off with it without another word. He wasn't going to give her time to ask for it back.

Still no sign of Li. Anthony opened the bulky file in his office. There were payment instructions on the file. Each one was just a simple bank transfer form with standard fields for the payee name, destination bank account, narrative, currency and amount. The file had some alphabetical tabs on card dividers. Might be surnames of people? Instinctively, Anthony went straight for the W tab to see if what he suspected was true.

He saw a bundle of payment instructions stapled together. The first was in Walker's name, and the instruction was to send two hundred thousand US dollars to his account in Jersey. And so was the next. There were lots of them. The details were exactly the same as the entries that Anthony had on the photocopied bank statements. Anthony now knew for sure that Walker's cash had come from the Asian pricing account. Each payment instruction had details of the Steens account to be debited, and they were all from account number 99656.

He paged backwards through the file to the next alphabetical tab. It was V. Before Anthony even opened the pages he knew that these payment instructions would relate to Johan Verhoeven. There were fewer payments, but the money amounts were still sizeable. Payments went to an account in the Netherlands Antilles. It was another offshore tax haven, but at least Verhoeven had stayed loyal to his Dutch connections. The last payment was dated in early April, just days before Verhoeven's untimely death. There were no payments on the file to him since then. Jesus. Verhoeven was another recipient.

The M tab was even more worrying. M for Masterson? Surely Anthony's own boss couldn't be involved in this too? Anthony saw the typed name on the payment instruction, there in black and white. Payments were made to an account in Derek's name in Bermuda. Maybe that explained why on occasions Derek was known to take that weekend stopover in Hamilton on his way home from business in New York. That American Airlines flight. Now Anthony knew that his boss was going there to visit his private banker and make sure that the next Hong Kong payment had arrived safely.

The L tab was next. Easy by now. The payment instruction form stated that two hundred and fifty thousand US dollars went to a bank account in Liechtenstein in the name of Alvin Leung. No surprise. If Leung were going to run this illicit activity in his own office, then he would surely ensure that he, too, benefited personally. Four directors so far. This was getting worse. Sir James would be appalled at what Anthony had uncovered in this overseas office.

The F tab. This was going to be Bill Fitzpatrick. He didn't have any involvement in Steens' activities in this part of the world, yet he was on the Hong Kong payment list. His money went to a bank in the Cayman Islands, still protected by the United States. He had also picked some connected offshore tax haven to deposit his ill-gotten gains, as if it gave him some comfort as to its security.

Then the H tab. Was there a director with that initial? Of course there was. The lesser seen Lord Herne, Tory do-gooder and well-connected man about town. Their one token non-executive director. A sop for the public investors. He had only one cash payment, to a private bank in Gibraltar. A cool round-sum million sterling, dated a year ago. The bottom of the payment instruction had a hand-written note pencilled in. It said Lloyd's insurance settlement per Sir James. Lloyd's of London. That disastrous insurance underwriting business where all the privileged Names had so recently taken a bath after years of effortless earnings. Lord Herne had indeed been caught in a poor underwriting syndicate and had lost a fortune. Only Steens had bailed him out. And Sir James even knew about it.

Anthony was near the end of the file. The last tab was D. No? Sir James Devonshire? Anthony couldn't believe it. Payments to Sir James's account in Jersey. Sir James banked at the same bank as Walker. That was more than a mere coincidence. Sir James had received hundreds of thousands of dollars too. No one was immune from the Asian pricing account.

There was a knock at the door. Jesus. Edwin Li was back, and he knew that Anthony had the payments file. No. Edwin wouldn't bother knocking. He would just barge in and be his natural objectionable self. Anthony closed the file and opened the door. Lilly stood there. Did she want the file back? Apparently not. She had a bundle of papers in her hand. 'I am so sorry. The file is not up to date. These payments have to go on the file too.'

Efficiency personified. She was terrified of the loud Englishman from London. Sorry, Lilly. Anthony took the proffered papers, payment instructions dated just last week, but he didn't recognise the payees' names. They were not directors of Steens. They were unpronounceable Chinese names. Five of them. All living in China but all with accounts here in Hong Kong. The payments were for two hundred thousand dollars each. A million in total. That number was familiar. That conversation with Dave in the tennis club? The South China Iron and Steel issue? That alleged bribe to the officials? It must be the same. Here was the proof that Dave's market sources had been correct. The Chinese had got their dollars, paid to their newly opened accounts in Bermuda. Every last piece of this financial jigsaw was fitting into place, and Anthony did not like the completed picture.

The entire board of directors of the world's leading investment bank was in this together. The chairman was involved. This went all the way to the top. Anthony was shaking, his hands were clammy as he held the pages. This payments file was dynamite. It was the evidence that any regulator would love to have. His standard work practices told him to take a copy of these payment instructions because no one would ever believe him otherwise, but did he dare do that?

What if someone saw him copying the pages? Or if a page got stuck in the copier and he couldn't retrieve it? Photocopiers were always crashing at the wrong moment, just when you needed them most. What if Lilly Pang walked back into the room right now and asked for the file back immediately?

His opportunity would be gone for ever. He might never again have this file in his possession, in Hong Kong at a time when Alvin Leung was out of the country and Lilly Pang had swallowed his oppressive lies.

He removed one payment instruction for each of the seven directors, five still alive and two recently deceased. He folded the pages carefully and left the office, making directly for the lift. He felt as if hundreds of pairs of eyes were looking at him, but no one stopped him. In the lobby of the building he entered the office supply and stationery shop in the shopping arcade beside the Espresso Café bar. The photocopier was at the back of the shop, and Anthony quickly made a copy of each page and paid the cashier. As he exited the shop he almost collided with Edwin Li, who was coming out of the coffee shop with two large plastic mugs of pungent roasted coffee. Li noticed the bundle of papers in Anthony's hand 'What's the paperwork?'

'Just some notes,' said Anthony, tightly holding the pages facing his shirt.

They rode the lift. Back in his office, Anthony replaced the pages in the file and returned it immediately to Lilly Pang.

'Is everything there?' she asked

'Yes. I've seen it all.' And he had.

'Oh, there was a message for you.'

Jesus. Who knew he was out here? No one from London hopefully? Like Alvin Leung?

'A Harry Wu in Kowloon called. Your suit is ready.'

*   *   *

338

The new navy suit fitted perfectly. As ever. A few thousand Hong Kong dollars changed hands, and Harry wrapped the suit in a complimentary carrier bag. Anthony glanced at the shop window on a few occasions, recalling what he had seen the last time. A touch of *déjà vu*. No one there this time. Safe at last. He left the shop and surprised a man outside. That same youth who was at Happy Valley last night.

This was no coincidence. They knew where he was going. Lilly Pang had taken the telephone call. She had told Edwin Li. They knew his every move. Back into the shop on the pretence of leaving something behind. Harry was puzzled, but he did have a rear exit in the shop. Anthony took it, didn't know where he was going for five minutes and then saw the welcoming signs of the MTR station.

Back into TST station and down to the platform for Victoria Island Rush hour. Thousands of people entering the station by twenty different entrances, all intent on getting back to their tiny high-rise apartments as quickly as possible. Thousands of others hoping to alight from the train at this major interchange in an equally short space of time. Two irresistible forces destined to meet. They all knew it.

Before the train even came into the station the crowd on the platform bunched together. Little old ladies, students and clerks moved forwards a few spaces to stand on the marked platform area where they knew the train doors would open. No way were they waiting until the next train tonight. Anthony found himself near the front with Harry Wu's bulky suit carrier receiving angry glances from those who brushed against it. The train screamed somewhere in the distance in the tunnels. Minutes to go.

The dazzling lights of the front carriage appeared. This was the signal. Bodies from behind moved forwards. Limited space ahead, just a few safe feet before a concrete lip with yellow trim, a five-foot drop, a set of gleaming rails and ten thousand volts. Anthony stood his ground as best he could. Then he felt it. A firm hand, perhaps an open palm, right in the small of his back. Decisive and strong. He lost his balance and fell forward, seeing the yellow hazard paint of the edge of the platform. He was going over.

A hand in his way. His jacket grabbed from the side. His body hit the ground, legs and torso on the platform, head and arms over that edge of death He was pulled again. He lost his grip on the suit carrier bag as it slipped into the void. He was dragged backwards away from the edge. He looked down at Harry Wu's logo as the bag lay directly over the near rail track. The noise was intense, the sound of an engine right beside him. Then screaming wheels as brakes were applied too late. The wheels came and went, splicing the suit bag in half Harry Wu's two-piece suit had just become a four-piece.

A friendly guy in faded jeans and a polo shirt knelt beside him, asking if he was all right. Anthony got to his knees and took the proffered open hand of assistance. Mere words of appreciation were not enough to acknowledge this Good Samaritan on platform five of TST station. A life-saver indeed. Anthony slumped alone on to a platform bench, inhaling and exhaling repeatedly to recover his composure. He was all right, so he told the Good

Samaritan. The train carriage filled with the onlookers, moved off and the station was totally deserted. No one else around. Or was there?

A shadow moved further along the platform. A youth emerged from behind a concrete pillar, also alone, just thirty feet away. He stood menacingly, looked around and then walked decisively towards Anthony. That youth with the baseball cap. He was coming for his prey. His right hand moved inside his imitation leather jacket and produced a blade: The polished silver glinted in the harsh fluorescent light. It was serrated along one side and about nine inches in length. Lethal. The two men faced each other.

Anthony looked behind him. There was no other exit to the platform. He was trapped. Ten thousand volts to the left and a tiled wall to the right. A platform ten feet wide. Jesus. This was it. His life had all come down to this moment. His life, his education, his career, his investigation, Amsterdam, EPIC, SCISCO, Frankfurt, Macau, Asian pricing account trades, directors' payoffs. Did any of it matter at all? Not now. Anthony would have gladly exchanged everything he knew for the chance to walk out of this station alive. To return to Jenny in London. Would she miss him?

He could smell the youth now. Spices? Curry? He was that close. Anthony froze on the spot. They made eye contact and then the youth looked past Anthony, as if distracted. A look of annoyance on his pockmarked face. A moment's hesitation. He said something in Chinese. Anthony didn't understand but knew it was a swearword. The knife went back into his jacket, he turned sharply and ran up the escalator to anonymity.

What had happened? Anthony turned around again. What had frightened his would-be killer? No one there. And then Anthony saw it. A single closed-circuit television camera hanging directly overhead, pointing at the spot where they had both stood. A red flashing light indicated that the camera was active. The youth had almost stepped into the range of the camera. Perfect evidence for the prosecution if required. It had been enough of a deterrent.

Anthony took the next train. He ran into his hotel shattered, suit-less but alive. There was no doubt in his mind that he was out of his depth. He was getting out of Hong Kong fast.

*   *   *

The travel desk was located in the public safety of the hotel lobby. He took out his passport and flight ticket from his wallet, noticing Jenny's home telephone number scribbled on the back, and handed the documents over to the bow-tied girl from the travel agency. Must fly.

'I'm booked on Virgin on Friday night. I want to go tonight. Can you change this ticket?'

She hit a few keys and perused a glowing monitor on her desk with apparent success. 'I can get you on the Virgin flight tonight to Heathrow.'

Perhaps a chance to meet Tasha again? Would she be on the return flight? Second thoughts. Virgin was too obvious. Take an unnecessary detour to Europe for safety. 'No. How about a Lufthansa or an Air France flight?'

'To London, sir?'

'To anywhere but London. To Frankfurt or

342

Paris, and then a connecting flight to Stansted.'

Got to avoid the regular airlines and airports. Keep them guessing. Whoever they were.

Anthony left his Causeway Bay hotel for the last time at eight o'clock. Torrential rain poured down and a long line of people waited in vain for taxis. Whenever it rained in Hong Kong the taxis mysteriously disappeared. Some in the queue looked particularly anxious as they stood guard over battered suitcases and wondered if they would ever get to the airport in time for their European-bound homeward flight.

The complimentary Lufthansa limo pulled up outside the hotel entrance and the driver greeted Anthony with an open umbrella: He sank into the plush leather seat of the air-conditioned black Mercedes and watched those in the queue through the rain-speckled windows. If you are going to travel half-way around the world on a regular basis, then you had to do it in Steens' style. Alternative measures were required this time, though. Anthony told the driver to reverse up to the queue where a middle-aged couple were first, a collection of suitcases arrayed beside them.

'Wanna lift to the airport, folks?'

They were delighted at his generous offer. This young investment banker was so kind. Really. Anthony just felt safer. No one would try anything on the way to the airport. Not with four of them in the car.

CHAPTER NINETEEN

11.46 A.M.: FRIDAY 19 APRIL: MAIDA VALE, LONDON W9

The taxi fare from Stansted to W9 cost thirty-five pounds, but it was a small price to pay for personal safety. Anthony was back in the UK, back in his home patch. Safe. The unusual flight connection via Frankfurt Airport had cost him several extra hours in transit time, so it was almost midday when the black cab pulled up by his parked Audi, unused for the past week, covered in pigeon droppings.

Despite thirteen hours in German business-class luxury, a fully reclining seat with complimentary pillow and years of accumulated jet-lag experience, Anthony managed absolutely zero sleep during the night flight. How could anyone sleep knowing what he knew about one of the greatest investment banks in the world? He had been on the go for thirty-six hours non-stop and he was physically exhausted. His first thoughts were of sleep in the king-size.

When he opened the hall door he knew that the apartment felt different. Something wasn't right. The first clue was a week's supply of junk mail. He should have heard it rustle along the carpet as he pushed open the door, but the mail was already lying away from the door by the wall. Someone had opened this door in his absence. Had he been burgled, always a hazard for the frequent flyer away from home too often? A search of his living-room revealed that all the typical valuables much loved by the criminal fraternity—stereo, VCR, TV—were still there. The apartment didn't feel right.

His thoughts turned to Mrs Harris, his cleaning lady. She came every second week, but she had been in the week before he left. The apartment wasn't that clean, and there was no overpowering odour of a domestic cocktail of Pledge, Jif and Harpic. She hadn't been. Then he thought of Vanessa, who still had a door key. She must have come back to collect her things from the apartment. Still looking for that Gucci scarf? He went into the bedroom to check the wardrobe and threw his flight bag on the bed. The bed looked disturbed, a slight dent in the middle, bedclothes moved. He didn't need to check the wardrobe.

His one and only silk Hermès tie lay on the bed. He hadn't left it there, he was sure of that. The gold material lay carefully in the definite shape of a noose, with a gap just big enough for a man's neck. Whose neck? His neck? A not-so-subtle reminder of what had happened to Jeremy Walker in his E1 bedroom. It wasn't going to happen to Anthony. Self-preservation was of the essence.

Anthony could try to crash out on this bed right now, but there was no way he could sleep in peace, not with the thoughts of that abused tie. This apartment wasn't safe any more. He had to get somewhere else. He thought about going into work at Steens, but that was the last place he wanted to be seen at right now. To face Derek and Sir James? To answer their questions and bluff it out. He needed a bolt hole.

In the old glory days he could have telephoned Vanessa, but not now. He could try Gary, but he

345

would be at work in Steens, not at home. Likewise with Dave. He needed someone with no connection to Steens at all. These people who knotted ties so expertly would know all his colleagues from Steens. That was the first place they would look. Then the solution came to him. Anthony needed Jenny. More so now than ever before.

Jenny worked crazy, unsociable hours at the Standard, lots of flexitime with a demanding boss, up at the crack of dawn to write for the first edition at eleven am. She had been up early in Wapping on the morning after Walker's death She might be back at home by now? He knew her home number verbatim, what with four days of consecutive telephone calls from his Hong Kong hotel room. The number rang and rang and then her answering machine connected. What sort of a message could he leave her? Hi. I'm going to be murdered next. Help. Did he even want to leave her a message? She picked up the call.

'Jenny speaking.'

'Hi. Tony here. I'm back.'

'Great. Glad you made it, and a day early too. When will I see you?'

Anthony couldn't tell her what was happening. Time for a little white lie. Sorry, Jenny.

'Sooner than you think. I'm locked out. Can't find my apartment keys and I am absolutely shattered. Can I drop round to your place for a while?'

'Sure. Are you all right?'

'Yeh. Why do you say that?'

'You sound different.' She gave him her home address. Very near.

Anthony lugged his flight bag back up the road towards Jenny's apartment. He had to make this lie look realistic and at the same time guard the evidence on his person. The photocopies of those cash payments to the directors. The tape with Peter Cheung in Macau. Unfortunately, Jenny lived on the third floor of a period mansion block so the six flights of stairs were a killer. He could have done with prior altitude training. When they met in her hall doorway, they kissed briefly and then he literally fell into her arms, exhausted by lack of sleep and the stress of recent events.

'Where's your bed, Jenny?'

Jenny never thought that Anthony was so keen. She was genuinely disappointed when he collapsed on to the middle of the mattress and dozed off immediately. She returned to typing her copy on some mundane piece on the PC in her living-room.

*   *   *

Anthony felt as if he had slept for days, but it was only just getting dark when he awoke. Maybe five p.m.? He had no idea where he was until the earlier events came back to him. Jenny's bed. Comfy. He could easily get used to this. He had to get up. Things to do. Mysteries to solve. A life to keep. Jenny recognised the familiar creak of her bedroom door as it opened.

'I'm in here.' She was unwinding on a large sofa in an impeccably decorated living-room. Beautiful relaxing pastel wall colours, two matching three-seater sofas with enormous patterned cushions, stripped-pine floors and linen curtains hanging from gilded curtain rails over the windows. Plants in terracotta vases on the windowsill framed the view of trees outside. Impeccable taste all round. Anthony couldn't have done a better job himself. A wall-to-wall CD and paperback collection, but Anthony didn't have time to examine her taste right now.

'Nice place.'

'It's not mine. I'm just the poor lodger who pays the rent each month. Just about.'

She patted the space beside her, encouraging him to climb on board the ample sofa and rest beside her. He needed no invitation. The denim of her faded jeans felt warm to his touch, her loose shirt was tantalising in what it didn't reveal, her bare feet with toes curled like a comfortable cat by the hearth, her ballpoint pen juggled effortlessly between delicate fingers, the natural fragrance of her body fresh from the shower. God. He had missed her more than he thought. Up close he saw the only imperfection. Bitten fingernails. She was real indeed.

'That must have been a nightmare trip to Hong Kong?'

'Why? What have you heard?'

'Relax. I just mean the flight You must have been delayed to get in here at midday because most of the Far East flights land at Heathrow at six or seven a.m. And to be so jet lagged too. And then to lose your apartment keys. By the way, where did you call me from?'

Another white lie was necessary. He couldn't have been in his apartment. Sorry, Jenny.

'From my mobile.'

'Funny. Didn't sound like a mobile. It was a good line.'

Jenny was intuitive, perhaps using her journalistic instincts. She sensed something was amiss. Anthony wanted to tell her how much he had missed her, how much he was enjoying her company right now, the closeness and comfort of lying beside her, but he couldn't bring himself to say the words. Too much at stake. His whole world, his career with Steens, his company shares, his monthly paycheque and annual cash bonus, his entire livelihood in the City, even his life was in danger. But Jenny was good, real good. A born journalist. 'What's wrong, Tony?'

'Nothing.'

'C'mon. I've never seen you like this. Is there another side to you that I don't yet know about? A dark, moody side? Show me the Anthony of a week ago. Something's wrong. What happened in Hong Kong?'

'I can't say. You know that. It's all confidential.'

Jenny looked over at the flickering PC screen and then seemed to recall something of note. 'Speaking of Hong Kong, do you know a Peter Cheung out there?'

How the hell did Jenny know Peter Cheung?

'Know him? I know Peter well. I met him last Tuesday in Macau. Nice guy.'

'Then you don't know about Cheung? He died yesterday.'

She had to be joking. Anthony had met him only days ago. Sure, Peter had cancer, but he couldn't have gone downhill so fast? He seemed fine on Tuesday. Such a shame. 'Cancer, wasn't it?'

'What was?'

'How Peter died?'

'No. He died on the ferry from Macau to Hong

Kong. Fell overboard and drowned.'

Jesus. No. Not another alleged accident. Not someone else in Steens who knew too much and talked. Jenny saw his reaction, his disbelief and got up from the sofa.

'Look, I'll show you what I read. I only found out a few hours ago on the Web.'

She sat by her desk, cluttered with press cuttings, magazines, post-it notes, printouts, photocopies. The computer was barely visible among the work in progress. She clicked on the Internet Explorer icon, opening up a world of instant information. She chose her favourite search engine, typed in the key word of Steen Odenberg and hit the search key with the mouse. Yahoo! The engine instantaneously trawled a million or more Web sites looking for any recent articles, stories and press cuttings about one of the world's greatest investment banks. She explained the background.

'Ever since I started on the Amsterdam story I keep an eye on what's happening newswise with Steens. The Web is the easiest way. It's brilliant. I'll do myself out of a job one of these days. My old boss might be right, after all. Who needs journalists? Who wants to read the *Standard* when it's all on *www.standard.co.uk* every day? All the Reuters agency stories about Steens are here.'

If only she knew the full story. The Web search was complete. The relevant sites and key headlines were listed in reverse chronological order. To the bottom were stories like CITY BANKER DIES IN LONDON MURDER, DUTCHMAN KILLED IN HOTEL FALL. Gripping stuff, usually, but still old news now. Then more mundane genuine business stories, such as STEEN ODENBERG RAISE THREE

350

HUNDRED MILLION DOLLARS FOR INDIAN POWER DAM PROJECT and STEEN ODENBERG WIN FRENCH PRIVATISATION MANDATE FROM GOVERNMENT. It was the top story from Reuters' Web service that caught Anthony's attention. MAN DIES IN MACAU FERRY ACCIDENT. An accident? Really? Jenny printed a hard copy on the laser printer and handed it over.

'HONG KONG NEWS BUREAU—18 April. A passenger drowned yesterday after falling from the ferry service which runs between Macau and Hong Kong. The body was later washed up on a beach on Lantau Island. Peter Cheung, 49, was a retired banker who lived in Macau and was formerly employed by Steen Odenberg Asia Limited. Other passengers or crew did not notice the accident at the time. Police said that he had fallen overboard while the ferry approached Hong Kong Harbour in rough seas, and they are not treating the death as suspicious. © Reuters Asia Ltd. ENDS.'

'That's a pile of crap. Reuters have it all wrong. That was no bloody accident.' Anthony had said too much. Too decisively. They both knew it.

'Tony. How can you say that? You've gone pale. What's wrong? What do you know?

Too much for his own good. He needed to talk. His life was in danger. No going back now. 'Jenny, you must promise me that you won't divulge this to anyone else. It's top-secret. If one word of this appears in the *Standard* tomorrow evening, then I am dead. Literally.'

'OK. I understand.'

'I'm serious. This isn't like that first time we met in the Flute when you went off and wrote an exclusive tell-all column for the *Standard* before my glass of wine was even empty.'

'Trust me, Tony. That was a mistake, and I've apologised to you. I wouldn't do it again.'

He had to tell her. Share the burden. He talked. About what really happened in Amsterdam. About the private clients and the special deals for NedCorp. About his Vanessa and Verhoeven in the Tower City Hotel. About Frankfurt and the closing of the EPIC fund and the wasted millions on dud property and the personal payments to Walker and Verhoeven. Then Hong Kong and the Asian pricing account and the payments to all the directors. The payoff to Lord Herne. Those bribes to Chinese party officials. The meeting with Cheung in Macau and the illicitly taped conversation. The incident under the wheels of the truck at Happy Valley and the push on the MTR train platform and the youth with the blade. The early flight back home to evade the pursuers only to find a noose on his bed just hours ago. He felt all the better for talking. She was the one who was pale now.

'Christ, Tony. You're in real danger. Walker's dead. Verhoeven too. Now Cheung. Someone's had a go at you twice. You must protect yourself. You'd better do what anyone else would do in the circumstances.'

'What's that?'

'Call the police.'

Call the police? Like call D-S Palmer and ask for his help? No, thanks.

'I can't call them. Steens' reputation will be ruined. I'll be an outcast for ever.'

'Tony, there are more important things in life than Steens and the City. Firstly, there's the difference between what's right and what's wrong. You've gotta do the right thing. If you know all this and do nothing, then you're worse than the directors. You are an accomplice. You could go down with the rest of them. You've known about most of this for weeks and you've told Palmer absolutely nothing. Secondly, there's the matter of personal survival. Nothing is more important than your life. Right now you are in mortal danger, and I don't want to see you harmed. I like you just the way you are. I need you.'

Wise words from someone so young. Anthony had no choice. If he didn't get help, he might not even be alive to go to work on Monday morning. And what sort of work would it be? How could he carry on working in a bank that was rotten to the core? Where the corruption led all the way to the entire board of directors?

He thought about the past, about a parallel in the little village of Northwold where fraud and embezzlement in a branch office had once wreaked such havoc on the impressionable lives of a young boy and his family. The pain of that experience still lingered. He had to make that call. He used Jenny's cordless telephone. She clutched his left hand as he dialled with one hand, offering tangible support.

'Bishopsgate Police Station.'

A pause for the switchboard connection.

'D-S Palmer, please.'

Another pause.

'Palmer speaking.'

'Tony Carlton here. We need to talk.'

'We do indeed.'

Did we? 'Can you come around urgently to Maida Vale to meet me?'

'Can't you come down to the station?'

'No. It's not safe for me to be out and about.'

'Not safe? Why?'

'What I've got involved in is dangerous. I'll tell you when you get here.'

'I'm busy here, I don't know if . . .'

'I'm desperate. I've helped you out in the past few weeks. Now it's your turn.'

'If this is to do with Walker's death, then don't worry. We've solved the murder.'

Had he really? Anthony doubted it. Palmer didn't know the half of it. Anthony needed to tempt the reluctant policeman. 'It's to do with City scandal, fraud, corruption, bribery, theft, manipulation, threats, murder. All that. Is that enough? Interested?'

'I'll see what I can do. Gimme an hour or so.'

Anthony gave Palmer the address of Jenny's flat. 'Come in an unmarked car. I can do without the attention.'

Salvation was on the way, and it was coming in the form of a middle-aged shiny-suited policeman from the City. Jenny pulled him closer, wrapping her arms around him. She eased a warm hand towards his lower regions. Not now, Jenny, please. He felt her hand too close to his waist. He was becoming aroused. She delved into his pocket.

'What's this, Tony? A set of keys? Looks like your apartment keys. You really were scared, weren't you?'

'I'm sorry I lied. Palmer is coming, and I've got to get the evidence for the prosecution.'

*   *   *

354

As soon as he stepped out into the Maida Vale fresh air, Anthony didn't feel as safe as he used to here. Knowing that people were watching him, not just in Hong Kong but also in London. No sign of anyone loitering on the road so he walked onwards.

Paddington Sports Club was filling up with locals who needed three sets of hard tennis after a harder week's work. Anthony made straight for the locker-room, prematurely fingering the key to his personal locker in his pocket. The room was almost deserted. He half-expected everything to be gone, taken by those same people who had invaded his home.

Not so. It was all there. The Amsterdam report with all the damning facts, taken from Verhoeven's hotel room and never shredded despite Derek's explicit instructions. The photocopies of those cash payments to Walker and Verhoeven from the EPIC fund. Perfect to go with the more recently accumulated evidence from the Far East

'Tony. Long time, no see. Welcome back.'

He knew that voice. A tennis partner. Dave. The last person he wanted to see now. Dave noticed the bundle of papers. 'What's all that, then? Working from the tennis club now? Take a break, Tony.'

'I will.' Then a glimmer of hope. Dave was back from work. Could Anthony talk to Dave? Was Dave on his side or was he in on this whole scam? How close was he to the directors, to his boss Sir James?

'Tony, I called early in the week and your temp secretary said you were in Hong Kong.' He had told her to tell no one. Typical. Useless. 'What were you doing over there?'

'Just work, as usual.' Time to test out Dave.

Check his loyalty. Anthony motioned for them to move to a discreet corner of the locker-room. No one about.

'Dave, you remember we spoke here a few weeks ago about that SCISCO issue, the deal you were uncomfortable about, where we paid a million bucks to some Chinese government officials?' Dave nodded in agreement but did not look enthused at the mention of the topic. 'Whatever happened on that? Did you find out any more, Dave?'

'Yeah, I did. I was wrong. I made a mistake. It's a red herring. You should forget about it entirely.'

Surprising. Especially when Anthony had seen definite evidence of the five payments to the Chinese guys in Leung's file.

'Who says it's a mistake?'

'I got it from the best source. Sir James told me. It was a mistake by Walker. No money ever moved per Sir James. So forget about it. End of story.'

Dave had just failed the loyalty test with a decisive no grade. What had once been a valid concern for him had become a non-issue in the space of a few weeks. Someone had bought Dave's loyalty. What was the price? Perhaps it was just a few hundred thousand pounds, the size of his bonus to come in less than a week?

*   *   *

Palmer was true to his word and turned up within the hour wearing a very dapper suit and silk tie. The ensemble looked brand new. Palmer was getting into City life. He was enjoying the exposure to the City. Anthony introduced Palmer to Jenny, who left them.

356

'Nice apartment, Tony.'

'It's not mine. I live down the road. It's my girlfriend's.'

There it was. It just slipped out like that. It was official. They were an item at last.

'Nice girlfriend, Tony.'

They sat in the living-room as Jenny distributed mugs of freshly ground coffee. Even her coffee mugs were tasteful. Anthony had assembled the documents in a pile on the coffee table. As Palmer placed his steaming mug between the papers and Jenny's back catalogue of dog-eared *Cosmopolitan* and *Hello* magazines, he couldn't ignore the evidence. Anthony felt that the mere sight of the documents would underline the urgency of his case and the reality of his cry for help. Palmer had other, more pressing matters to attend to. He unbuttoned his jacket and sank further into the sofa.

'We are not investigating Verhoeven's death any further. We deem it to be an accident. The post-mortem showed us that Verhoeven was not restrained in any manner before he died and his blood alcohol level was sky high. He was drunk. He also had all the tell-tale signs of frequent soft drug use. The exact time of death was actually in the early hours of the morning, so it means that Vanessa had long gone when Verhoeven went over the edge of the balcony. Accidents do happen. Guess all that he took pushed him over the edge. Literally. That's one death neatly resolved.'

One down, one to go. Palmer knew that too.

'Let me tell you some good news about Walker's murder.'

Anthony hadn't heard any good news for at least

a month. Worth listening to?'

'We have Jeremy Walker's killer. We arrested and charged him earlier today.'

'Really? Who is it? It's not someone from Steens, is it?'

'Sure ain't. It's the young guy in that photograph, who only knew Walker briefly. All the time we were investigating Walker's death there was one piece of vital information about his private life which we were missing. Have a guess, Tony?'

It wasn't the most difficult question in the world. Anthony signalled immediate recognition. 'Walker was gay, wasn't he?'

'How do you know that? Have you known all along? Was it common knowledge in Steens?'

'I only found out last week in Hong Kong. I met up with Sylvia, Walker's ex. She told me it was the sole reason for their divorce. She caught him in bed with a Filipino youth.'

'Jesus, what a way to find out. Why didn't she tell us that?'

'No one asked her. Don't forget she's been in the Far East for the past two years. Out of sight, out of mind.'

Palmer felt the need to expound on his recent success.

'The action started on the day after that *Crimewatch* TV programme. We got some good phone calls but the first calls were all about Jeremy Walker himself. Lots of anonymous men rang in and said that they knew Walker from some of the pubs around the West End, King's Cross area, Soho, Victoria and the like. Shit. His photograph had been in all the papers on the day of the murder, but it takes a television programme to jog people's minds. Typical.' Palmer shook his head in annoyance. 'Walker led a double life. During the day he was a highly respected director of Steens and a divorced man without any children. But by night he was cruising bars looking for young men to take home. Several callers said that they had visited his apartment in Wapping. He must have been mad, taking home men whom he knew absolutely nothing about'

'So who's the guy you've charged?'

'A youth called Billy Jackson. Aged just nineteen. Son of an immigrant Chinese girl and an English wife-beater. She's gone back to Hong Kong, and he died in a pub fight in Camden years ago. Jackson is mixed race, as we thought originally. Spent most of his young life in care and then with foster-parents who didn't care. Came down from Birmingham to London and lived rough in a squat in Leytonstone. Needed some easy money so turned to the game about a year ago. One caller saw Walker with Jackson in Brewer Street on the night Walker died. He gave us Jackson's address. When we first called round yesterday he was out overnight, but he turned up this morning. He hadn't seen the *Crimewatch* programme because he's working nights, and he doesn't have a TV in any case. He can't read either, so hadn't even followed Walker's death in the newspapers. Couldn't even read a *Sun* headline, he's that illiterate!'

Anthony wasn't yet convinced. This death had to be connected to the Hong Kong scam.

'But why do you think Jackson killed Walker? What's his motive?'

'Jackson says that Walker was into the more

bizarre stuff. Liked to be tied up and restrained, including being gagged. Claims that it heightened his pleasure, of sorts. Auto-asphyxiation, the experts call it I'm told. Some of the other telephone callers who met Walker and went home with him confirm this preference. On the night of the murder, Jackson says that Walker asked him to tie him up with his ties and put one around his neck. Walker kept asking for it to be tighter and tighter. Jackson says that Walker suddenly went quiet Jackson couldn't release the tie quick enough because the knot was tight When he did partially loosen it, Walker lay sprawled on the carpet and didn't come round. Jackson just panicked and left Walker by his flash suit and tie ready for the next day. Jackson left the apartment at half-eleven and got the last tube home to the East End. He has given us a full confession.'

Anthony thought about his experiences in Hong Kong. 'What about the baseball cap he wore? With the red logo on it? Does it mean anything?'

'Yeh, it does all right according to Jackson. It's a star shape, the logo of some gang in Hong Kong that grew out of the Triads. Now it's just a bunch of local criminals who muscle in on local business, vice, drugs, blackmail. Some of them are pretty lethal, by what I've heard. Jackson won't say much more about them. No names at all. He's terrified of them. I guess they can still get to his mother and the rest of the family over there, if they want to.'

Palmer rubbed his nicotine-stained hands together in obvious satisfaction.

'We have a watertight case against Jackson. He's going down for a long stretch at Her Majesty's pleasure. When we spoke first I thought that

Walker's death might have something to do with Steens' business or those letters of complaint that he'd received. But that came to nothing. I can safely say that we have closed our investigation into Walker's death.'

'I don't think you can. There's more to it than just a simple sex crime.'

'No way. Case closed.'

Time for some lateral thinking. Anthony could see the angles, even if Palmer couldn't.

'There is a connection to Hong Kong, and that baseball cap proves it. I saw someone with the same cap in Hong Kong last week, following me around. Did you find any money on this Jackson guy?'

'How did you know that?'

'How much?'

'Five grand in cash at his flat. On the mantelpiece in a biscuit tin.'

So Walker was only worth a mere five grand? A man with millions in the bank.

'That's the real evidence, D-S. Jackson was paid by someone to kill Walker. How else do you explain the cash?'

'Jackson earned it on the game.'

'If he did, he must be totally exhausted by now. Do any of the notes have sequential numbers?'

Palmer frowned, obviously displeased at the doubts that Anthony was sowing in his mind.

'Yes. Quite a few.'

'Then that's conclusive. The cash came from the same source.'

Palmer was wondering if Jackson was the fall guy. His nicely resolved crime was rapidly falling apart.

'But who else would want to kill Walker?'

Anthony got up and went to the window, taking over the conversation as Palmer and Jenny waited for the key explanation of recent events. One person knew it all and he was standing before them.

'There's a bigger story here. Something is going on at Steens. An underworld gang in Hong Kong is involved. Millions of pounds have gone missing, and whoever was about to rock the boat was killed. Three deaths are too much of a coincidence.'

Palmer was immediately thrown.

'Who's the third?'

'A manager who used to work for us in Hong Kong fell off a ferry and drowned yesterday. I think that I am next.'

Anthony showed Palmer the hard-copy print from the Web. Palmer was thinking.

'You could be right. There could be a connection to you. When we arrested Jackson he had two tube tickets on him. I didn't put two and two together until now. One ticket was bought in Leytonstone at ten-fifteen p.m. when he left home last night. The second ticket was bought in Maida Vale station at just after ten o'clock this morning. That's your local station, isn't it? Jackson was in Maida Vale for most of this morning. I just thought at first that perhaps he had been visiting a punter around here.'

Jesus. It made sense, all right. To Anthony at least, as he paced the living-room.

'I know where Jackson was all night. He was in my flat. The gang in Hong Kong knew that I'd escaped on the evening flight and that I would be arriving home at six or seven a.m. this morning. Jackson had been given another contract, and this time it was me.'

Palmer didn't agree. 'No. You're just speculating. There's no evidence of that.'

'Yes, there is. The post was moved back from the hall door. One of my ties was left on the bed knotted in the shape of a noose. Just think about it. Jackson lying on my bed all night playing with the one Hermès tie, waiting for a jet-lagged traveller to arrive home before he tried the tie on his victim for size. Another easy five grand. I guess once you've killed, it's easier the second time around. Only I was late and he didn't hang around long enough for me.'

Anthony felt weak. He sat down. He had come close. Thank God for the long Lufthansa flight. They had saved a life and they never knew it. The doorbell rang. Who was it? Someone looking for Anthony? No one knew he was here. Except Palmer.

'Jenny, are you expecting someone?'

'No, I'm not.'

They had found him. At least he had police protection. Did Palmer carry a piece to work? Unlikely. Palmer stood up, not to reveal a silver magnum 45, but to go to the hall door. *I'm* expecting someone, Tony. A colleague whom you will definitely wish to meet.'

Palmer returned in the easy company of a solidly built man in his late forties, probably the same age as Palmer but less weather-beaten and aged over time. They seemed to know each other well. Palmer obliged.

'This is D-S Michael Hunt. We were at police training college together many years ago.'

Why the hell was Palmer bringing his old chums

along to a crisis meeting such as this? Hunt sat down beside Jenny, looking comfortable and relaxed. He undid the button in his dark double-breasted suit, revealing fashionable braces, as he arched back his broad shoulders. His assured manner gave Anthony some additional sense of security. Was he really a policeman? He looked the look, walked the walk, he could have got a job in any City bank if he wanted one. Did he talk the talk? Palmer explained.

'D-S Hunt is in a different line of work from me. Mike does the important stuff. Mike has an honours degree and a postgraduate masters in finance and business. Mike now works for the SFO, the Serious Fraud Office to the rest of us. Hence the good suit. I thought he'd be a better person for you to talk to, Anthony.'

Perfect. Palmer had delivered the goods. Someone with whom Anthony could indeed talk the talk. Someone who would know a call from a put, an equity from a bond, a hedge from a speculative punt. And all that flash stuff. Time to delve into the papers on the coffee table at last.

Hunt spoke with a South London accent. 'I run one of the investigation teams in the SFO, based in the West End. We investigate instances of wrongdoing, fraud, embezzlement, deception, misappropriation of funds, breaches of company law. Have you come across any of these in your bank?'

All of them, if the truth be told Anthony pointed at the coffee table. 'This is the evidence I have. I'll talk you through it. Then we can decide what to do.'

Anthony went through the items on the table.

Amsterdam. EPIC. Frankfurt. Verhoeven. SCISCO. Hong Kong. The Asian pricing account. Cash payments. Offshore accounts. Bank statements. Photocopies. Tapes of conversations. Hunt grew more interested and picked up the Amsterdam report. After all, it was the logical place to start. Hunt paged through Verhoeven's copy of the report.

'Who wrote all these notes?'

'What notes?'

Anthony grabbed the report. He had never opened the cover before. He just assumed that it was the same as his report. The notes on the pages grabbed his attention. He stopped on the summary at the front. Certain lines and sentences were underlined in black ink. Other words were circled. There were some comments in the margin. Anthony recognised Verhoeven's handwriting. He never knew that Verhoeven had read the report in such detail before his death. There were annotations by the name of the clients who had complained and by the mention of the EPIC deal. As Anthony thumbed through the back pages, a piece of paper fell out on the floor. They all looked at it as it lay on the rug under the table. It was headed notepaper from the Tower City Hotel. There was untidy handwriting scribbled on it.

Palmer picked it up and read it aloud. 'Karla, I am sorry for what I am about to do but there is no way out . . .'

That was all it said. It was dated on the day of Verhoeven's death. It was unsigned, but it was in the same handwriting as the annotations in Verhoeven's report, and in the same fine black-ink pen. It was the nearest thing to a suicide note that

Anthony had seen. Addressed to his wife? Palmer would have found it had he read the report in the hotel room. He could have saved them all a lot of time. Verhoeven's death was a suicide. Hunt's attention turned to the tape of the conversation with Peter Cheung.

'Let's play it.'

Anthony left the tape machine on the table as they listened to Peter Cheung's last confession. A man telling all so that good will triumph over evil, a man who had entrusted Anthony with the secrets of the past, who had handed the baton to Anthony, who was now running towards the finishing line. Peter had paid for this disclosure with his life. The last words of the conversation were the most poignant for Anthony.

'What are you going to do next about what I told you?'

'I'm going to get to the bottom of this. Tell Sir James and the directors back in London.'

Anthony would. He owed it to Peter now. Hunt gathered the documents and tape.

'What we have here is enough for a major case against the board of directors of one of the biggest names in the City. This could be the case of the decade. Bigger than Blue Arrow, Guinness and Maxwell; all the others put together. But we need more evidence. We need a confession from the directors if possible. Anthony, all this has given me an idea, and I'm going to need your help.'

CHAPTER TWENTY

6.12 A.M.: MONDAY 22 APRIL: CITY OF LONDON EC2

Anthony survived a weekend of living on the edge, waiting for the next person to call at Jenny's or the next telephone call on the mobile. He didn't dare step outside and didn't want the offer of police protection, as suggested by Palmer and Hunt. That would draw too much attention to Jenny's safe apartment.

Instead he hibernated in deepest April, watching any old rubbish on television, reading every newspaper from cover to cover, exploring Jenny's compact disc and paperback collection, surfing everything on the Web, from aardvark to zebra dot com, and enjoying Jenny's spicy stir-frys. The highlights of the weekend were *Blind Date*, the *Sun*, *Soul to Soul Volume One* and *Netscape*. And, of course, Jenny's enthusiastic company in that comfy double bed.

When he awoke at six a.m. he caught the early tube to work. Five weeks had passed since he went in to discover that Jeremy Walker had died. For the first time since then he could see a way out of his plight. There was no sign of Gary, Derek or his temp secretary until just after nine o'clock. Gary was first in.

'I had no idea where you were until last Friday when Derek told me. You never said you were going to Hong Kong, Tony.'

A lot had happened since Friday. Everyone must

know that Anthony had been out east?

'Gary, you should have asked that temp who replaced Vanessa. She booked the flights.'

'That temp you refer to, incredibly alluring as she might have been, lasted just one week. Derek couldn't stand her so he hired someone else. Someone who knows exactly what to do, with years of experience. And here she is now.'

Vanessa breezed past them both and sat at her desk as if nothing had happened. Business as usual. The worst possible outcome. Derek had re-hired her and Anthony could see why. Vanessa knew what Verhoeven had done to those private clients in Amsterdam. She had put two and two together and got a very profitable securities account in the process. The thought of her working at another investment bank, passing derogatory comments about Steens, making libellous small talk by the coffee machine, would be too much for Derek to bear. A salary increase and the promise of a big bonus were a small price to buy her silence.

'Morning, Anthony. How are things?'

She was gloating. The secretary from hell had arrived, someone Anthony couldn't stand being near to, let alone have her preening herself outside his office for eight hours a day. She knew she was safe. Derek was in charge. Anthony ignored Vanessa. He didn't need her any more. She was excess baggage, the sort you hoped to lose on a long haul flight. He had Jenny. Gary made some inappropriate banter.

'I was expecting you to be wearing another new suit from Harry Wu. No shopping this time?' Gary knew Anthony too well. That suit was lying in pieces under the wheels of a Hong Kong MTR train. 'What were you working on out there?'

D-S Hunt had told Anthony what to do. Best to be vague. Anthony's mission didn't involve Gary. The less he knew the better. For his own safety.

'I fancied a week's paid holiday on Steens in a five-star hotel, Gary.'

'Well, you've picked a good week to come back.'

What did Gary know? What had Anthony missed on his week away? He looked vague.

'Cop on, Anthony. This Friday is the last Friday in April. Bonus day. We'll all be rich.'

Anthony had forgotten about bonus day. Money didn't seem to matter to him any more. There were important motivators in his life now.

*   *   *

There was no sign of Derek yet. Gary toyed with his PC. Vanessa sat at her desk displaying open hostility towards Anthony. Anthony would need to summon a UN peacekeeping force soon. She did nothing at all, but Anthony could hardly reprimand her. She stirred only to get coffee for them but ignored Anthony's request for a decaff without sugar and a Twix bar on the side. He couldn't work here for long with her odious presence. One of them would have to go.

Anthony played with his Dictaphone tape machine in his left hand, running it backwards and forwards incessantly in an aimless manner. Practising. No real work to do at all. One lazy eye on the scrolling Reuters screen. Steens shares up twelve pence on the LSE. The news ticker said good annual results were expected soon. Watching the wall clock and counting the minutes. Preparing.

369

It was the lull before the storm that was about to break in Broadgate today. Then it suddenly broke.

'What the hell were you doing in Hong Kong last week?'

Anthony had never seen Derek so animated. Bulging eyes, ruddy cheeks, veins visibly pumping on overtime. Perhaps the pressure of the past few weeks was getting to him? Derek slammed the door behind him and waited for an explanation.

'I was doing some work on our operations there.'

'Who authorised your trip?'

'I was going to ask you at Walker's funeral only you made me leave early.'

Derek paced the room, over to the window and then back again. At speed.

'With that fucking journalist. Where were you last Friday? You weren't in the Hong Kong office and you didn't come in here to work either.'

They had been looking for him last Friday. Derek had him cornered. Lies required again.

'I came back a day early but I was ill with a stomach bug from a seafood restaurant in Aberdeen.'

Then second thoughts. Did Derek know he had already used that excuse with Edwin Li for his Macau day trip? People would begin to think that he had a very weak constitution.

'The directors have decided that we should review your role to see if it should continue.'

P45, here we come. Anthony was going to have to call that head-hunter. Maybe he could ring up his ex-colleague Steve and ask him if rivals Mitchell Leonberg had a job for him?

'You will meet Sir James at eleven o'clock today in the boardroom. Don't be late.'

Perfect. Everything was going according to plan.

*   *   *

Anthony took his jacket from the hanger on the back of the door. The jacket was vital. Essential dress code for the seventh floor. The floor of the gods, those directors he had sought to emulate for so long. Now the dream was shattered.

The overseas directors had stayed on in the UK after Walker's country funeral. He sat across the narrow table from Sir James, Derek, Alvin Leung and Bill Fitzpatrick. Anthony left his jacket on the back of the adjacent chair for maximum effect.

Only feet separated the opposing parties. Four solemn-faced City players facing down one solo investigator who knew that he had overstepped the mark. Four multimillionaires versus one salaried employee with a mortgage. Four individually tailored cotton shirts and gold cufflinks versus one off-the-peg shirt. Four men sitting confidently in plush leather seats versus one leaning forward nervously, waiting for the inquisition to commence.

'Mr Canton.' A pause for dramatic effect as Sir James growled. It was Mr Carlton. Not Anthony. 'What was the purpose of your visit to the Hong Kong office last week?'

The conversation was starting off in the right direction. Might as well go for it.

'I reviewed some of the house accounts there.'

Leung cut in, leaned forward, visibly fuming, sweaty fists clenched in anger on the table. He contorted his narrow face. So much so that Anthony thought he saw that infamous wig rise an inch or two and then return to its owner's dome.

371

'Mr Carlton, I telephoned my secretary Lilly last Friday. She said that you showed her Jeremy Walker's personal Jersey bank statement? Where did you get that statement?'

'Walker kept personal papers in our storage centre in the East End. Walker's secretary decided that they should be given to his parents. She reclaimed them and gave them to personnel. Karen knows me, and she asked me to deliver them to his parents at the funeral.'

'Fucking personnel department,' fumed Bill Fitzpatrick. 'And I checked Walker's office before the police arrived too. What a waste of time that was in hindsight.'

Sir James visibly disapproved. Fitzpatrick had said too much too early. So an executive cover-up had started in Walker's office right from day one, even before Walker's body had turned cold, to cover the tracks of deception before D-S Palmer stumbled across them. It was turning into a full and frank discussion. Just what Anthony needed. Leung leaned nearer Anthony. He was just a foot away. His aftershave stank.

'So which house account did you review?'

This was the moment when the directors learned if perhaps their secret was safe. It wasn't.

'I reviewed the Asian pricing account. Number 99656.'

Leung sat upright Sir James shifted. Derek swore. Fitzpatrick frowned. Anthony knew everything. They all knew. This was a charade, a show trial for the accused before a summary public execution.

'And what did you learn about that account?'

'It's for money taken from large institutional

372

client trades all over Asia. The cash is paid to offshore bank accounts of the directors. Walker had the cash on his bank statement. That's how I saw it. And there was a million paid to Lord Herne to cover his Lloyd's syndicate losses and a million to bribe the Chinese party officials to give Steens the SCISCO mandate.'

There. He had said it. The deed was done. Leung almost composed himself and flogged a dead horse. 'Do you have any proof of this at all?'

'I have photocopies of the cash payments. They are somewhere safe.'

Leung unnerved him as he smiled in utter resignation at Anthony. One-nil to Anthony so far. Sir James resumed control of the meeting.

'You have stumbled on something that we know is wrong, but let me put it in context for you. The account was the brainchild of Jeremy Walker many years ago. None of the directors sitting here today played any part in its origination. The money involved on any one trade is only a few thousand bucks. No one suffers.'

The same reasoning exhibited by Verhoeven in Amsterdam. Equally hollow. Thoughts of Amsterdam. Anthony risked another loaded question.

'There's more to this than Hong Kong. What about Amsterdam? All those private clients?'

Sir James was almost apologetic. Perhaps he doth protest too much?

'When we read your Amsterdam report we were genuinely surprised at the content. Can't you see that Derek would never have let you go near that office had we known what was going on there. I let Johan run Continental Europe alone. In hindsight it was a mistake.'

373

'What about the cash payments made by EPIC to Walker and Verhoeven?'

'That, too, was a surprise for us. You were too good at your job and found too much in these offices. We all agree that the fewer people who know about events in Amsterdam, Frankfurt and Hong Kong, the better for all concerned. Do you understand what I mean?'

Shades of another cover-up. This one would involve Anthony. Not if he could help it.

'But we can't let this continue. It's wrong.'

Sir James was adamant. True colours shone through. 'There are a number of things that are wrong in this world. Try another reason.'

'You could end up in court or in prison. Steens would be disgraced.'

Sir James looked reassuringly at his co-directors.

'That's highly unlikely. You only found this because you did such a thorough job investigating a series of connected events that will never happen again in this bank. We are not going to lose two directors in as many months again. There is a solution. We will settle the complaints from the private clients by offering them some serious cash compensation. We will ensure that they sign confidentiality letters to keep this out of the public domain. Problem solved. Then we will repay the original investment moneys back to the EPIC investors and simply unwind the fund. We will say publicly that the property market in Eastern Europe has not taken off and that as a reputable investment bank we will make good their losses. That will cost us many millions of dollars, but we can fund that from the Asian pricing account. It may also rather perversely be viewed in a favourable light among the investment community. Good for our reputation.'

Then Sir James delivered the *coup de grâce*. The next piece of the final solution.

'We intend to appoint a new managing director for Europe to coordinate these corrective actions. Your friend David Chilcott-Tomkinson has accepted our offer of a directorship.'

They knew Anthony's friends. Sir James paused to let the name sink in. Dave had been bought off on the SCISCO deal. An offer of a Steens directorship. Lucky guy. Sir James handed down the final judgement. Dave's lies in the tennis dub now made sense.

'Forget what you have uncovered in the past few months. Destroy the reports and files that you possess. Wipe the word processing documents. Shred the photocopies. The past few months never happened. Carry on with your other work, like that long overdue Singapore report. Relax. Let's get on with being the best investment bank in the world.'

The directors nodded in agreement. The status quo was the preferred solution. They wanted an immediate answer. Anthony needed to aggravate them further.

'It sounds like a cover-up.'

Sir James gave Anthony a withering look.

'We want you on board. You might think that you have a choice, but in reality you don't. If you wish to continue to work for Steens you must do what we are asking. It's what we expect of every employee. Otherwise there is always the revolving door in the main lobby for your personal use.'

Toe the line or find a job somewhere else. Anthony thought about the implications of leaving

Steens, something he had rarely thought about before the events of the past few weeks. Sir James was a step ahead.

'Remember, Anthony, we can't just let you leave Steens knowing what you do about this bank's operation. There is much too much at stake. Steens is worth billions of pounds, and no one will stand in our way. If you were to leave Steens, life could get extremely difficult for you in the City.'

Anthony bluffed out a token response, but he knew it was somewhat optimistic. 'Head-hunters call me regularly. I'd have no problem getting something in the City.'

Sir James joined his hands together in an arch, elbows on the mahogany, fingers extended. Eyes cold and hostile. Grim expression.

'Don't imagine you would be allowed to resign. We would fire you. We wouldn't officially give a reason for firing you. Prospective employers would make up their own minds about that. Then we put the word about in the City. Perhaps mention that you were guilty of misconduct or theft or fraud. All informal, of course, but it would be enough. Then we would refuse to give a reference for you to any prospective City employer. After that I doubt whether you'd be able to get a job even as a junior post-room clerk. You could try to bad-mouth Steens, but we would deny everything. Whom do you think people will believe? An unemployed ex-banker or the collective wisdom of the directors of the most prestigious investment bank in the City? Think about it, Mr Carlton.'

'So I stay at Steens and forget about the past few weeks, or I am ostracised in the City?'

'Correct. We understand that it's a difficult

376

choice so we'll give you time to think about it. A few hours. Wait outside. We will call you when we are ready to see you.'

Anthony left the boardroom. He made sure to take his suit jacket with him.

*   *   *

Anthony sat alone on a Regency chair outside the boardroom like an errant schoolboy by the headmaster's study waiting to learn his awful fate. Secretaries passed him in the corridor and gave him a knowing look. Yes, he had been bold. Yes, he was going to get well and truly caned. There was no choice to be made. He had to stay at Steens until some external forces moved into play, courtesy of D-S Hunt. He didn't know how long the directors would make him wait. It was past twelve o'clock and he was growing hungry.

At precisely one o'clock a waitress from the executive restaurant pushed a laden trolley past Anthony and on into the boardroom after a polite knock. A platter of freshly made sandwiches, rolls of smoked salmon nestling with sliced lemon, jumbo prawns on cocktail sticks, cuts of rare beef and honey-roast ham, Stilton and Brie cheese, wafer biscuits and crackers, bananas and plums. Complemented by bottles of Evian and orange juice. Anthony was starving but could not leave his post. He waited while they dined.

By two o'clock he would have killed for one of those sandwiches. He wanted to leave but dared not. This had to go according to plan. The boardroom door opened and Derek motioned for him to return to his seat of inquisition. Sir James looked at the other directors, who signalled their implicit agreement. Sir James smiled to reveal glossy white teeth. Unnerving. Was there some new development or had it just been an exceedingly fine lunch? Anthony could see the remnants on the sideboard. Curling sandwiches, broken biscuits, banana skins, half-empty glasses and rolled napkins. Tempting, all the same.

'Anthony, you have a difficult choice, so here's something to help you in your deliberations. How would you like a directorship at Steens?'

Anthony had misheard Sir James. He thought he had said a directorship. He had.

'What do you mean?'

Sir James was fawning. This must be the softly softly approach.

'Steens has been without a director of compliance since Jeremy's death. We need someone to fill that vacancy immediately, someone who knows all of Steens' operations, who has visited our overseas offices, who knows about investment-banking controls, who can impress the Bank of England and the SFA and the regulatory people. Does that remind you of anyone?'

Anthony knew that he met all of Sir James's job criteria. Maybe he was even overqualified?

'We also need someone who empathises with the directors, who won't rock the boat and make things difficult for the board, who will stall any enquiries if they ever again lead to anywhere remotely near Hong Kong, if you understand what I mean?'

Anthony did. He was being offered the biggest bribe of all. Just like Dave. He could have only dreamed of a directorship a few months ago. And now, when it was within his grasp, it was in the strangest of circumstances. It was an offer to help run an investment bank whose reputation and market share were built on lies, abuses, fraud, deceit and even murder. Sir James read his mind. Indecision.

'Think about the prestige, Anthony, about why we all really work in the City. You will be earning a serious amount of money as a director of Steens. How about moving from your Maida Vale apartment to one of those period houses overlooking Little Venice and Regent's Canal and that excellent Thai restaurant? A four-storeyed white-stucco residence with a garage, a garden and conservatory? Sure, they're a million quid each, and celebrities own them all, but you would be an equal among them. I'm not talking about walking into your local Abbey National branch in Kilburn cap in hand to ask for a million-pound mortgage. You will be a cash buyer after just a few years as a director.'

Sir James was pushing the right buttons. He had done his homework on Anthony, even down to identifying his favourite eating locations in West London. The hard sell continued unabated.

'You'd have enough money to satisfy your every whim. To fly on Concorde for a weekend's shopping in Manhattan with your girlfriend. To buy a pool-side villa with a tennis court in the Caribbean. To have a Mercedes coupé, a Range Rover and a Morgan. To be able to retire early in your forties. Not to have to work another day in your life. Just spend. Join the club.'

More evidence of homework done on Anthony. Tennis courts. Flash sports cars. Someone had researched his material preferences before this offer had been made. Maybe Dave had helped the directors over a lunchtime conference call down to the second floor?

'We need an answer, Anthony. We can't have this hanging over us any longer. Uncertainty is always bad for the markets, and it's even worse for Steens. We need to know now.'

Anthony was out of his depth. These were men who had ascended ahead of their peers to their positions of power and were not going to relinquish the material benefits of their directorships under any circumstances. They had limitless financial resources and too much to lose. Walker and Verhoeven had died. Cheung too. Would anyone notice another dead Steens' employee? Would there be another accident? Was their offer of a bank directorship really genuine or was it a ruse to set him at his ease before they decided on an alternative and more lethal course of action? Time to play the innocent.

'I'm worried about becoming a director. There have been too many deaths.'

Alvin Leung seized the opportunity to assuage his fears. He was unnervingly friendly, animated in his body language and hand movements. What a change a few hours and a good lunch makes. They needed him. Perhaps more than he needed them.

'That's all behind us. I saw it all happen out in Hong Kong when Walker got in with some vicious local people. He had a bad gambling habit. Went to Happy Valley every night when a meet was on there. Lost major money. Borrowed more. Got involved with underworld gambling syndicates and failed to make repayments on big loans. That's when he began taking cash out of Steens' client

380

trades. He had to cut these locals in on the lucrative scam. But he couldn't handle the sudden wealth. Spent too much money and developed a taste for fine oriental art. Went to auctions and spent millions on oils, vases, artwork, ivory. Walker got careless, greedy. It's all about cash at the end of the day. He wanted to exclude the underworld from his scam. They were livid at the mere suggestion. A month later he was lying in his Wapping apartment with a tie around his neck He won't make the same mistake twice with those gangs. Hong Kong people play by different rules, remember that, Anthony. It's a sobering thought. You don't want one of that gang after you again. But you already know that, don't you? Edwin Li made sure of that last week.'

They knew that he had been followed last week, harassed, pushed, almost killed. This was hardball. Leung could make the Second World War look like a minor domestic dispute.

'Walker's death is good news for us. It's perfect. There's no connection to us. D-S Palmer told us last Friday morning that Walker picked up a rent boy in the West End and died in some sex game. The gangs knew that Walker liked sex with oriental youths, the younger the better, so they paid one to meet him in his favourite pub in Soho. The youth the police arrested, Billy Jackson, is so scared of the gang that he won't say a word about being paid to kill Walker. He knows that if he talks then his family back in Hong Kong will meet with a nasty accident.'

Leung gave a wry grin and let his sick imagination run riot.

'There are many apartment fires in Hong Kong,

all those people living so close together and so high up. There are few survivors. Which is it to be, being burned alive or a ten-storey jump to your death? Jackson knows that well enough. There is no trail back to Steens. We don't need Walker. Edwin Li knows how to operate the Asian pricing account for us. It's business as usual, although we did close the account for a few weeks in April after the murder just to be safe. There are two fewer directors now. All the more for the rest of us. You included?'

Anthony had seen Verhoeven's suicide note. The directors hadn't Time to test them. 'Do you think Verhoeven was murdered too?'

Sir James was vague in his response. 'What do you think?'

'It was a definite suicide.'

The directors leaned forward. Anthony knew more than they did. He let them wait. Like he had waited in vain for a few scraps of lunch. Build the tension. Tell them when he felt like it. If he'd smoked, it would have been the time to light up a cigarette. Just for dramatic effect.

'I found a half-finished suicide note in Verhoeven's copy of the Amsterdam report.'

Derek was aghast. Real surprise from him. The tide was turning.

'Be bloody careful about that. If the police know there was a note in Verhoeven's copy, they'll want to see the entire report. I don't want them to know what went on in Amsterdam under Verhoeven's tenure. Imagine, Verhoeven gets jilted in love and does a stupid thing like that. All for Vanessa, who was engaging in a bit of gold-digging. I had to re-hire her to buy her silence too.'

382

There was a time when a comment like that about Vanessa would have angered Anthony. Not any more. He nearly even enjoyed it.

'What about Peter Cheung's death last week on the ferry?'

Alvin Leung had evidently already researched the death.

'Walker's murderers are dedicated to keeping the Asian scam a secret, and anyone who talks is in danger. You were followed to Macau. Cheung just said too much and paid the price. Remember that.'

So it all came down to a simple choice. Good or evil. Truth or lies. Honesty or complicity. A directorship or job insecurity. Unbelievable wealth or mundane poverty. The sort of choice that everyone hopes to make at least once in his or her life. Anthony had thought about nothing else for the past forty-eight hours. He knew there was only one choice that the directors would accept right now. Four on one was an unfair match in any event. 'I'll take the directorship.'

Sir James smiled across the table, as if this were the decision that Anthony was always going to take. He thought he knew Anthony's primary motives. Money and power. Anthony had to make this look as realistic as possible. More conspicuous greed was required on his part.

'On one condition. I want a hundred thousand more in my basic salary immediately.'

If you were going to damn yourself for all eternity, then you might as well do it in style. Sir James evaluated Anthony's monetary demands.

'You young guys think you're the hottest things in the City. That shows a serious amount of balls. I like that. A 100K is pin money to us. I wouldn't get out of bed for less, and I wouldn't be happy if any director of Steens earned less than a quarter of a million a year. You've got the 100K. Anthony, congratulations on becoming a director of Steens.'

'Is it really just as easy as this?'

'We will nominate you as a director at the next Annual General Meeting. That will be in May when we announce the full year's results. It will be a mere formality because the institutional investors use their block votes to support everything that the board proposes. You'll look very good on paper to them, the right credentials. We'll put an announcement in the *FT* appointments page this Friday so that the entire City and our staff will know. Please refrain from telling anyone until Friday morning.'

Sir James's mention of the annual results was a trigger. Anthony played the part royally. 'What will our full-year results be like, and what will my own bonus be on Friday?'

'If I were to divulge non-public price-sensitive information to you before the results are announced then we could be in trouble with the regulatory authorities. And we don't want that, do we?' Deep irony from a chairman who had presided over flagrant abuses of every regulation in the City. 'Let's just say that the bonus will be generous, about twenty per cent higher than last year.'

Anthony did a few quick mental calculations. Last year he got twenty thousand. Sir James was a step ahead of him.

'Don't worry about your own bonus. This year we have decided to reward your untiring work with a special payment. This Friday we will pay you a bonus of one hundred thousand pounds. A nice round sum.'

Time to trade up from the Audi soft top. Just in time for a hot summer in London. If only.

'Anthony, can I ask about your colleague in the Control Group, Gary Benson. Is he good?'

'He's a good worker but needs a bit of direction and motivation sometimes.'

Sir James didn't mind the qualified response. Quite the contrary, in fact.

'Excellent. Then he is the ideal person to take over the running of the Control Group. We don't want an expert doing the job, or he might uncover something untoward out East. You and I don't want that happening ever again in Steens.'

Sir James rose. The others followed. They stood by Anthony. They were all in this together now. Anthony was as bad as the rest of them. Handshakes exchanged in congratulations. Grease the palms. Sir James patted Anthony on the back in a tangible display of comradeship and pointed to the laden sideboard.

'Would you care for a sandwich or anything else? There's lots left.'

They were about to break bread together. Symbolic or what? Anthony tensed at the proximity of his boss. Sir James had come close to discovering something else when he touched Anthony's jacket. Food was now the last thing on Anthony's mind. The plan had worked.

*   *   *

The offer of the directorship hadn't been part of their game plan. D-S Hunt and Anthony had never rehearsed it in Jenny's apartment. Anthony had played the scene unscripted as it unfolded in the boardroom. All that power, prestige and money were within his grasp. The offer was there. If he wanted it. Decision time.

Anthony could do a Dave. Just roll over and say nothing. Go with the flow. Take the cash. Tell D-S Hunt that nothing went to plan. Destroy the new evidence that he had collected in that crucial meeting on the seventh floor. Do more shredding in his office. Get severe memory loss. Don't rock any boats.

But this wasn't about material benefits. It was about people. No one mattered now more than Jenny. Would she be happy living with a lie personified, someone who earned hundreds of thousands every year but ran the daily risk of being picked up by the police as their chief suspect in an international banking scandal? People like Palmer and Hunt mattered too. Palmer, who had rescued him from the fear in Maida Vale, and Hunt, who had suggested the way out of the dilemma.

And it was all about trust. Could Anthony ever trust Sir James and his colleagues? The lies, the cover-up, the deaths that they glossed over, the fear, the threats, the exploitation of innocent investors, the breaches of an unwritten City code of ethics carved out over the past centuries. Had he seen the real directors in the hostile morning meeting or in the amicable afternoon meeting? Hard to tell. They were such damned good liars. Practise makes perfect.

Anthony cast his mind back to life as a twelve-year-old in his Northwold primary. The Monday morning when young Mark Thomas didn't come to school. The maths teacher who explained that Mr Thomas had died over the weekend, that Mark had lost a father. The drizzly graveside a few days later as Mark shared his tears and huddled close to his mother in mutual protection. So much grief wrought upon innocents. All due to the lure of easy cash embezzled from a benign employer. A lesson in truth well learned.

* * *

Anthony left Steens early that evening. His mission was still unfinished. He was surprised to find Karen from personnel leaving at the same time. Normally she worked longer hours. More surprised to find that up close her mascara was ruined around her eyes. Tears flowed.

'Karen. What's the matter? What happened?'

'I've been fired. Sir James called me in this afternoon and said that he's reorganising the structure of the personnel department and that I'm surplus to requirements. That's all. Seven years of my life I gave to that bank and that man. Now I feel I never knew him at all.'

No one knew Sir James. On the exterior he was a charismatic, flamboyant businessman, but Anthony knew him as the best-dressed, best-spoken criminal in the City of London. It was too much of a coincidence for Sir James to fire Karen on the day that Anthony had told him that he had received that box of Walker's private papers so naively from personnel. That had been the vital clue in his search for truth, and Sir James knew it. Revenge was sweet for the man in charge. Karen would never have the chance to make the same mistake again.

Anthony couldn't find words to console Karen. It was his fault that she was going home jobless, but he could say nothing. How many more colleagues might lose their jobs? He hoped for few, just the culprits. They parted company by Liverpool Street tube station.

'Tony, are you going on the Central Line?'

'No I'm taking a cab to the West End.'

A black cab was Anthony's preferred method of transport for his subterfuge trip. The cab delivered him to a narrow street in WI, and he entered an anonymous building with a small brass nameplate outside. He was shown immediately into a windowless meeting room; the adjoining door opened shortly afterwards.

'Did it go OK? Did you get it?' asked D-S Hunt.

Anthony put his right hand into the inside pocket of an old Kowloon jacket and took out his much-used Dictaphone machine. There was no need to answer Hunt's question. He placed the machine on the Formica tabletop and hit the play button.

Perfect sound quality emanated, just as they had confirmed back in Maida Vale last Friday. Sir James's voice was crystal clear. So was Leung's. A damning recording of two meetings where the board of directors of the City's leading investment bank said too much and made a young man an offer that he simply couldn't refuse.

CHAPTER TWENTY-ONE

5.20 P.M.: THURSDAY 25 APRIL: CITY OF LONDON EC2

The waiting was the worst part. Anthony had handed D-S Hunt the damning evidence on a plate, and the next move was up to Hunt. But Anthony didn't know when that next move would be. Hunt would be sifting through the facts, perusing the photocopies, playing those tapes over and over, talking to in-house legal advisers at the SFO, debating his timing, consulting his regulatory peers in Amsterdam or Hong Kong and advising the top brass in the SFO and the City of London Police. Time marched on.

It could all take weeks, even months, of typical civil service bureaucracy. When was Anthony going to see Palmer or Hunt walk past Bill into Steens' reception and arrest the directors in the middle of the working day in full view of their staff? Anthony wanted a scene like in the movies where the mackintosh-clad Federal agents and slicked SEC men appear on the dealing floor to take away guilty dealers in handcuffs, to make a public example of them. Anthony was trapped in Steens until then, counting the few remaining twenty-four hours to a directorship and a hundred thousand pounds that he definitely didn't want tomorrow.

He toyed with a first draft of that long-overdue Singapore report for Derek, but it didn't matter to him any more. The contents were trivial in comparison with recent events. He had done enough investigating in the past few weeks to last a lifetime, and he honestly didn't want to uncover any more of Steens' ills. Management of the Control Group would be Gary's responsibility from tomorrow onwards, providing nothing terminal happened to Steens in the next twenty-four hours. Wishful thinking.

The atmosphere in the office was like death warmed up. Vanessa was even more hostile to Anthony, refusing to answer his telephone, take any messages, type his memoranda or acknowledge his presence. She could behave however she wanted to, thanks to Derek. Anthony wondered if he could sack her again on Friday when he became a director, when he would be at the same level of management as Derek. Sacking her the second time round could be even better than the first. Anthony dreamed about his office on the seventh floor. Would they give him Walker's old office and that tearful secretary?

He killed time by browsing the Reuters screen for market information. The Footsie was depressed too, down forty-three points in nervous early-morning trading. Steens' shares had bucked the trend, up by another ten pence on persistent rumours of good results and possible consolidation in the banking sector. If only those investors who were bidding up Steens' share price knew what they were buying into. The shares would be almost worthless if Steens' directors were arrested by the SFO. No. Not if. When.

Derek walked into Anthony's office and held up a single Dictaphone tape in his hand. Jesus. He knew about the illicit tapes that Anthony had made. Or did he?

'Anthony, this is what we should say in the staff announcement tomorrow about your and Dave's appointment as directors. Listen to this. If it's factually correct, then get Vanessa to type it up and leave it back on my desk. Tell her it's embargoed until tomorrow morning under pain of death.'

Relief. Derek didn't know. The content was fine. Anthony never knew that his curriculum vitae could ever sound so good. He left the tape with Vanessa with minimalist instructions.

'Type this. Top secret.'

'I can't help you, Anthony. I'm too busy.'

'It's for Derek. Just do it.'

*   *   *

It was traditional for Steens' staff to decamp en masse to the Flute early on the eve of bonus day. Anthony had to go, just to be seen. His absence would have been noted. He loathed this place now, the superficial atmosphere, the loud dealers, the flash suits, the absence of normal non-City folk, the overpriced drinks and food and the pretentious staff. But he did like one personal memory that the Flute now held for him, that of meeting Jenny for the first time.

The wine bar was packed tonight with familiar faces from the sales and dealing desks. Many were still nameless to Anthony. However, tomorrow they would all know his name, as he became the youngest director in the history of Steens. Sir James was right. The word was out. Everyone knew that the bonuses would be generous.

There was no excess like the bacchanalian excess of a dealer at annual bonus time. It was a disgusting spectacle to behold. Obnoxious dealers with sweaty armpits, unbuttoned shirt collars and gelled-back hair held dripping flutes of champagne in one hand and the waists of their lithe desk assistants in the others. Giggling girls in black micro-skirts and high heels gazed back in admiration, looking forward to receiving their meagre five thousand pounds from the desk's bonus pool tomorrow morning. Not knowing that their selfish desk heads were getting hundreds of thousands each from the same bonus pool. Less for the desk assistants meant more for them. Such inequality among people who all sat at the same desk and worked the same hours from seven a.m. to five p.m. All because the fortunate had gone to the best public schools, and the others had gone to any old comprehensive around the corner.

The heads of Steens' departments threw their Amex corporate cards behind the bar counter and outdid each other to order Bollinger, Moët & Chandon, Veuve Clicquot and anything else that fizzed. Some fashionable types inhaled enormous Cuban cigars, specially hoarded for this celebratory evening. If only they knew what Anthony knew, that the demise of the directors of Steens was imminent. Just weeks, perhaps days away. Whenever Palmer and Hunt got their asses in gear. In the meantime these players had more important matters on their mind. So little time, so many different brands of champagne to get through. Mr Loud Obnoxious Dealer spoke. No. Yelled.

'What's the most fucking expensive bottle of poo you've got?'

The girl behind the bar held up a bottle and shouted that they were seventy-five pounds each.

'Then gimme all you have and keep it coming. Go down to the cellar and get every crate of it up here. No, better still, call the fucking vineyard and get them to send some more right now. Here, use my mobile. Steens are celebrating like never before in the history of this life-saving drinking establishment.'

Dave held court among a group of his vocal syndicate desk staff fulfilling his managerial obligation to buy alcohol for them all evening. Debs, his lovely desk assistant, hovered. Vanessa was there, apparently preferring Dave's company to that of Anthony or Gary. She didn't know too many others in Steens, just a few of Anthony's friends like Dave. Or former friends. Serves her right. Dave was talking to her in hushed tones. That knowing look on her face and then a glance straight over towards Anthony. Something about tomorrow's directorship announcements perhaps? She had already played Derek's tape. She knew.

In just a matter of hours the directors' appointment would be published in the *FT* and on the office noticeboards and then Anthony was part of the problem, not the solution. He wished he could have said no to Sir James's unscripted offer that day, but if he had, he'd be history by now. This was all going horribly wrong. He didn't need the publicity in the *FT* appointments section. Dave raised a glass in Anthony's direction.

'Congrats, Tony.'

'On what?'

'On a great year, and the best is yet to come for both of us.' Dave drew closer and lowered his voice. 'Who'd have believed it a few months ago? Walker's and Verhoeven's deaths are the best news we ever had. You and I will both be directors of Steens before we're even in our early thirties.'

So Dave now knew of Anthony's appointment. Word had spread among the board.

'This is where the gravy train starts, Tony. I'm moving out to Amsterdam in a few months time to run the European offices from over there. Sir James gave me a mega expatriate package. Free housing, free car, flights back to the UK. I won't have to spend a damned guilder while I'm there. A personal fiefdom too. Lots of staff reporting to me. And a new secretary. I met her last week, a girl called Anne van Halle. A good-looker too.'

What had Anthony's loyal friend in Amsterdam done to deserve Dave as a boss?

'You and I are going to make so much money out of this bank in the next few years that it's scary. Once we pay off these shitty private clients in Amsterdam and the EPIC investors, it's all going to be plain sailing for us.'

Anthony wasn't convinced and had the courage to say so. 'Doesn't that client stuff bother you? It's all illegal, isn't it?'

Dave took another gulp and came up grinning.

'You guys in the Control Group worry too much. Stop worrying. Everyone in the City is making a few extra bucks on the side on some little scam. No one ever gets caught. When was the last time anyone in authority brought a successful prosecution against a player in the City? I can't think of one decent example. The Bank of England is full of old buffers in suits having lunches with other old buffers in suits. They wouldn't know a complex derivative from a buttered bread roll. The Serious Fraud Office hasn't got a clue either. If they can't make a case stick against Deadly Ernest or the Maxwell brothers, they'll never make one stick against an institution like Steens. Relax. I'd only be worried if this involved overseas regulatory authorities. Look at the evidence. You get five years in a stifling Singaporean jail if you mess with SIMEX futures, or you get ten years in the New York State Pen if you're caught falsifying US Treasury Bond holdings at a Jap bank. And don't mess with the Chinese in Hong Kong or they'll get a new tie already knotted for you. Yes, indeed, the City of London is the best place to be for a decent scam.'

Where was the same naive Dave who had been on that graduate induction programme in Steens all those years ago with Anthony? What would his parents back in middle England think of their son now? Why had Dave succumbed to the lure of easy money from Sir James? Where were his principles, or had he sold them for cash, like everything else he sold at the syndicate desk on the second floor? There were no answers. Money does that to a person. Dave had changed irrevocably. For the worse.

'See you later when we go for our annual curry fest, Tony.'

Anthony was distracted. Something wasn't right about this evening. Usually one or two directors turned up at bonus time in the Flute, when they exhorted their frontline troops to do even better next year and at least stay with Steens rather than join a competitor like Mitchell Leonberg. There were no directors in the Flute this evening. No Sir James or Derek. Bill Fitzpatrick and Alvin Leung must have flown home. Walker and Verhoeven had imbibed their last celebratory bonus drink in the Flute exactly twelve months ago. No sign of Karen either. Evidently her dismissal was with immediate effect. She was going to miss out on the largesse of wealth that was to be distributed to staff tomorrow. Sir James had ensured that. Ironic, since she had spent weeks agreeing the bonuses with department management and providing the final numbers to payroll. Gary recognised the exterior signs of anxiety.

'Tony, you're looking like the market tonight. Very bearish. Be happy.'

Anthony debated what he could say. He had his orders from Sir James. Drop a hint instead.

'I am. Very happy. Just make sure you read tomorrow's *FT*. There's going to be some news about Steens. You won't believe it when you see it, but it's true.'

An old face appeared. Another Steens' tradition: those who had left during the year often returned to share a drink with ex-colleagues and tell tales of their new employer. Steve Massey had made it to the Flute, still the baby-face of the Control Group of a few weeks ago but hardly recognisable.

Mitchells had cloned Steve into one of their crack troops. He had that American high-school haircut, short back and sides and a sharp parting. And a button-down white shirt. A white shirt. Anthony never thought he would see the day. Steve's eyes looked tired, the visible signs of longer hours at his desk at their hated rival bank. The sharkish characteristics of Steve shone through. The size of his wallet was almost too much to carry.

'Shit, Tony, it's such a drag earning all that money at Mitchells down the road!'

Never ever move for the money. They all knew that Mitchells was a tougher place to work at. A US Wall Street culture, more aggressive, pressurised, longer hours, hassle, firings. They often joked that in Steens a colleague might stab you in the back. In Mitchells he'd do it facing you with a smile.

'Steve, you won't catch me working in Mitchells ever. Not even for a million bucks a year.'

'Who told you about the standard salary package? Anyhow, you mightn't have much of a choice in that regard soon.'

'Why?'

'The word in our place is that Mitchells are running the slide rule over a few European investment banks. We need to expand out of the US. Some of our top executives are in Europe right now. Who knows? Maybe we'll be launching a hostile takeover in just a matter of weeks.'

'Get lost. You could never buy Steens. You've been listening too much to the company song. Go and buy a leaking Jap securities house instead and watch your money disappear.'

Steve broke off to reminisce with Gary. Vanessa saw her opportunity and gravitated towards Anthony. What's with this change of heart?

'Can we talk, Tony?'

'There's nothing to talk about.'

'I'm sorry about what happened with me and Johan Verhoeven.'

Too late for an apology. Vanessa persevered, moving too close to Anthony.

'You know I always liked you, Tony. I've missed you too.'

Always liked him? This was too obvious. She knew about the forthcoming directorship and sensed the amount of serious money that was about to come Anthony's way. Another opportunity for more gold-digging perhaps, to get back into the Broadgate shopping arcade with a vengeance, preferably with someone else's gold credit card. She did, after all, have a noticeable weakness for Steens' directors. Perhaps she was working her way through the entire board?

'Vanessa. There's no point. I'm seeing someone else now. Don't bother.'

They left the Flute after eight o'clock for another of Steens' eve-of-bonus tradition, the hottest curry they could find in nearby Brick Lane. Anthony had to tag along. Again, his absence would have been too obvious. There was another rule on this annual occasion. No girls allowed.

Thirty loud and drunk investment-banking types invade an unsuspecting Indian, eat the owner out of house and home, trash the entire restaurant, throw poppadoms at other diners until they leave, sing lewd rugby songs, manhandle the sublime waitresses, finish the last few kegs of Elephant draught beer and give the staff a two-hundred-quid tip for the service and the damage they caused. And then they try unsuccessfully to book the same table for the same day in twelve months' time. Always refused for some unknown reason by the proprietor.

Anthony was looking forward to another night with Jenny, so much so that he left before the others. As time passed he felt safer in London, each passing day reducing the likelihood of meeting some Chinese immigrant paid to corner him with a blade on his way to the tube. Jackson was behind bars. Palmer told him that there were

398

no other suspects or known associates.

Nevertheless, Anthony always preferred the anonymous security of a black cab. Drizzle spattered down on the half-open windows. It was cold for April, and he had no coat. The traffic was backed up all the way along the Embankment, and every short cut the driver tried proved even worse. The evening just about summed up Anthony's mood. Overcast. The cabbie swore at a driver who cut him up on the inside. Pedestrians gesticulated at the cab near a flashing pedestrian crossing. The joys of living in friendly London.

London. Who needs it, anyway? The nine-to-five routine, the hours of commuting in packed rush-hour tubes, the gridlocked traffic among a sea of plastic cones and endless roadworks, the delays and anonymity of Heathrow, the search for a car-parking space without being clamped for a hundred quid, the car stereos stolen by louts from Luton, the Beamer Cabriolet roofs ripped by Stanley blades, the stares from hostile Londoners, the absence of eye contact or a voluntary smile, the awkward silence while ascending in a lift, the communal anxiety at Sainsburys on a Saturday morning, the lemming-like rush to the West End for Christmas shopping, the nightmare of IKEA, Brent Cross or the A23 on a bank-holiday Monday, the lead oxide pumped into the atmosphere, the eight million people incessantly grinding down London's arteries, the weight of all that concrete bearing down on a landmass weakened by underground train tunnels and effluent-laden sewers.

Anthony was trapped in a world that he no longer enjoyed. Perhaps it was time for a change of scenery? Working in the City would never again have the same appeal. But what else could he do? The ways of the City were all he knew. He had no other talents and no other visible means of support.

He stared at the neon reflections in the rain-soaked streets near Piccadilly Circus. The statue of Eros gazed back at him. Time to think. Jenny mattered most now, more so than Steens, the City, money, bonuses, power or a new Cabriolet. A job lasts only so long, friends like Dave can turn, girlfriends like Vanessa can betray his trust, but a love like Jenny's could endure for ever. Tomorrow he would move back into his apartment, but tonight would not be his last in Jenny's place. He was sure of that.

*   *   *

'Bad news, Jenny. Nothing happened today. Again. It's business as usual in Steens. You're looking at the next director of Steens. It'll be announced in the *FT* appointments section tomorrow.'

She offered him words of encouragement in the hallway. Nothing helped. Harry Wu's suit stank of alcohol, sweat, cigarette and cigar smoke and mixed Indian spices. Fear too. He threw it on the floor and stepped into Jenny's shower. Pity she didn't feel like joining him tonight. He was wiping away the accumulated layers of grime when Jenny barged into the bathroom. Correction. Maybe she would join him? No. She was fully clothed.

'Steens have collapsed.'

Anthony didn't fully understand what Jenny said. He killed the shower. Did she say collapsed? He should never have mixed so much fine champagne and cheap beer over the past few hours. He may have already consumed a significant portion of tomorrow's unwanted bonus in the form of liquid nourishment.

'What do you mean, collapsed? The Broadgate building has collapsed?'

'No. The entire bank has collapsed. It's been closed down. Hunt acted quicker than you thought.'

Jesus. It had happened. So soon.

'Who closed us down?'

'The Bank of England. They can do that, can't they?'

They damn well could. He threw on a bathrobe and dripped his way into that living-room surrounded by those pastel shades. The colour portable was tuned to Sky news. Jenny pointed at the television like a guilty suspect in a courtroom.

'I had it on in the background while I was working on the PC. The business news said that a leading investment bank in the City had been closed down by the Bank of England. Then they mentioned Steens. They cut to some sports news and said nothing more about it. I had to find out more. I just rang a friend on another paper, and she confirmed it. They're already working on the front-page stories for tomorrows broadsheets. It's going to be a mega story. I guess I'll be writing the front page for the *Standard* tomorrow evening. That's one in the eye for my boss. Wanna do some ghostwriting for me, Tony?'

'Not particularly. We need more information about this.'

Anthony looked at the timer on the video recorder below the television. Nine fifty-three. The

News at Ten would be on soon.

'Put on ITV.'

Jenny switched channels with the remote control. Anthony's mind raced over what had happened at Steens in the last few months. He watched the dying minutes of some inane low-budget situation comedy wondering if he had a job to go to tomorrow. He held Jenny's hand instinctively. The closing credits rolled, and then some trailer for another programme appeared. Then bloody advertisements. It seemed an interminable wait.

Anthony's heart was pumping, droplets of water still running from his hair down the small of his back. Sweat or shower water? The sofa would be ruined. The familiar drum music for the news rolled, the picture of Big Ben appeared and then the news desk hove into view. Trevor sat behind it in one of his hallmark red-patterned silk ties and a white shirt. Behind him was the unmistakable crest of Steens, those intertwined letters in gold and blue. Before Trevor spoke, Anthony knew the story was true.

'Steen Odenberg, one of the City of London's largest and longest-established investment banks, has been closed down on the instructions of the Bank of England. In the last hour a spokesman for the regulatory authorities confirmed that the action was taken after serious regulatory breaches were discovered in its international offices. Administrators have been appointed by the High Court to manage the bank, and the Serious Fraud Office is to investigate Steens' banking activities and practices.'

The newsreader continued with irrelevant

headlines about the Middle East and domestic politics. Anthony was still mesmerised by the blue and gold crest. The news returned to shots of Steens' Broadgate offices. He recognised Bill the security guard, who looked hassled, just like he had on the morning after Walker's death. Steens were now an all-too-frequent reporting location for these media people.

'We now go over live to the City to a spokesman for the Serious Fraud Office.'

Cameras and microphones and strong floodlight surrounded a strong-featured face in an impeccable dark suit. He stood in the drizzle ignoring the drops falling on his serious demeanour. The caption gave his full name as D-S Michael Hunt of the Serious Fraud Office. Hunt read from a prepared text.

'Today the SFO has advised the Bank of England in its capacity as lead regulator in the City to close down Steen Odenberg & Co. This action was taken when the SFO became aware of a serious breakdown in internal controls within the bank's operations, specifically regarding the Amsterdam office, the syndication and management of an Eastern European property investment company, the illegal price adjustments of agency securities transactions in Asian stock markets, bribes to Chinese government officials and the payment of illegal cash amounts to the directors of the bank.' Hunt spoke clearly and eloquently as he enjoyed his Warholian moment of fame. 'The SFO regrets the decision which has been taken, but believes it to be in the best interests of maintaining the high reputation of the City of London.'

The reputation of the City took precedence over the reputation of Steens. Steens had been sacrificed. The greatest investment bank in the City had shut its doors. It had actually happened. Trevor doesn't lie. Palmer and Hunt had delivered in one week.

This wasn't what Anthony had planned. He just wanted the rotten apples removed from the scene, the Sir Jameses, Dereks, Leungs and Fitzpatricks of this world. The entire bank wasn't supposed to crash. The staff needed their jobs. So did Gary and Dave and Anne. They had mouths to feed, mortgages and car loans to repay, tennis club subscriptions to fund, holidays to take, social lives to lead. Hunt had never prepared Anthony for a collapse. Or the unemployment that was sure to follow.

The full impact on the last Thursday of April hit Anthony, one day before the most awaited day in the year of every Steens' employee. The bonuses were due tomorrow. They would hit their bank accounts with a same-day credit transfer. But if Steens closed tonight, would the bonuses be paid tomorrow? Possibly not. Sir James and Derek wouldn't get their few hundred thousand Dave wouldn't get his two hundred thousand. Gary wouldn't get his twenty thousand. Vanessa and Debs wouldn't get their five thousand. Some of the innocents would suffer along with the guilty. Anthony would get nothing at all. Suddenly he was poor.

'Jesus,' exclaimed Anthony to Jenny. 'The shit is going to hit the fan tomorrow.'

CHAPTER TWENTY-TWO

6.50 A.M.: FRIDAY 26 APRIL:
MAIDA VALE, LONDON W9

In theory it should have been a great day to go to work in the City, the day that Anthony's directorship at Steens was announced to the entire world, the day that Anthony got his hundred-thousand-pound cash bonus. But instead it was the first day after the closure of the bank. Anthony managed only a few hours' sleep beside Jenny during the night. She wanted more contact. More climactic union. He hadn't the energy.

Now he was wide awake, yet simultaneously felt exhausted and deflated. He went through his early-morning routine on autopilot but without the same conviction that he normally exercised. The power-shower had no beneficial effect whatsoever. The blunt blade prevented a good shave. He skipped breakfast. It didn't matter what Kowloon suit or West End poplin shirt or designer silk tie he wore today. There were more important considerations, like whether there was a job for him in Steens.

He used his mobile telephone as he strode towards Maida Vale tube station to call his twenty-four-hour personal banking service. An anonymous girl in a chattering warehouse in Leeds working crazy unsociable hours asked him the usual inane security questions before he could request confirmation of today's balance in his current account. A mere twelve hundred and thirty pounds. Was there not a big lodgment today? No sir, there was not. No bonus. It had been a telephone call in vain, and at peak rate too.

The old Scotsman on the steps to the tube station made eye contact with Anthony and sensed that today for the first time since he had started selling newspapers to these West Londoners, Anthony might just spend some cash. To hell with all that black ink on Anthony's hands and the likelihood of the *FT* waiting in his office. The newspapers on the stand proclaimed almost identical banner headlines: STEENS CLOSED BY BANK OF ENGLAND AND SFO; REGULATORS CLOSE LEADING INVESTMENT BANK; CITY SHOCKED BY COLLAPSE OF STEEN ODENBERG.

Anthony opened the inside pages of the FTinside the lurching tube carriage. No surprises. He read the fine print on the front page wondering if his name would appear anywhere. Relief. It didn't. Nowhere did it say that an insider in Steens had talked to the SFO. Hunt had kept his promise to keep him out of the news for as long as he could. There was a photograph of people outside Steens' offices last night and one of Hunt on the steps in Broadgate. He had even made it in person to the pages of the *FT*. DOCUMENTS SEIZED FROM HEAD OFFICE. DIRECTORS LIKELY TO FACE CRIMINAL CHARGES. That word criminal hurt. Were they all criminals? Was Anthony himself, as a director, a fellow criminal?

Time to look up the appointments section for an immediate answer. Had the notice of his directorship appeared, as promised by Sir James? A directorship at Steens would be a news-making appointment any day, and these notices were placed in a subtle order of importance. He scanned the first appointment notices in the immediate knowledge that he was safe. The first few notices concerned irrelevant manufacturing-sector appointments at some widget-making firms in the North of England and Wales. The notice had been pulled from the paper. He would not be a director.

The stock-market report on the back page had another relevant headline. Steens' shares had been suspended from the London Stock Exchange at the request of the authorities in order to avoid dealing in a false market. In truth it had been a false market for years. No one could deal in the shares until they were relisted, and that could be months away, if ever. Pity about the thousands of Steens' shares and those options over more shares which Anthony had accumulated effortlessly over the years. Now his whole investment could be worthless. Anthony was even poorer than he first thought. Church mouse time.

The passenger beside him was reading the Steens story over his shoulder. That annoyed Anthony. Other commuters sat opposite staring directly back. Anthony folded the newspaper out of their view. The man beside was frustrated, perhaps even enough to get off early at Baker Street. Unfortunately, the act of self-denial did nothing to deter the middle-aged man opposite, who leaned forward.

'Bit of a disaster at that City bank? Wouldn't fancy working there much. Eh?'

Joe Bloggs had just broken the golden rule of tube travel. He had spoken to a complete stranger. Did he know where Anthony worked? Was the angst that obvious? Did Anthony want to discuss Steens? No way. Anthony avoided future eye contact and sank back into his seat. One-nil to the unknown commuter.

He inhaled. What was that awful smell? That odour of stale cigarette smoke and cheap beer and curry? God. He was wearing the same suit as last night and all the smells of the celebratory evening had returned to haunt him. Harry Wu would kill him if he knew. No wonder the seat beside him in the tube carriage was now empty.

He glanced at his reflection by the Underground logo in the window. Not a pretty sight. Shirt cuffs protruded loosely below the jacket, he had forgotten to insert his matching set of humorous silver cufflinks. Not feeling so humorous this morning. The tie was knotted awkwardly and the back portion hung down further than the front portion. Disaster. He wasn't convinced that the tie matched the pink finely striped shirt. His shoes had survived unpolished this week. Too busy.

He noticed a droplet of blood on his finger. He had nicked himself when shaving. He was a mess, but did it matter today? His career was fading faster than his skiing tan. If there were a competition for the best-dressed man on the Bakerloo Line this morning, Anthony would probably come second last, just ahead of the Rasta train driver in the first carriage.

He tried to pass the time on the tube in the usual manner and eyed up passengers. They were the usual types, but Anthony was envious. These civil servants, teachers, sales assistants, cleaners were going to a job that they knew existed. Anthony was travelling in the hope that his job existed. He raced up the left-hand side of the escalator in Liverpool Street Station. He hadn't ran up an escalator since being late on that morning after Walker's death.

*   *   *

The first tangible difference in Broadgate Circle was the policeman who stood in front of Steens' main entrance. His uniform and the gleaming City of London crest on his helmet exuded authority. His presence served to remind all that the authorities were in charge of Steens, and not Sir James and his fellow directors. He didn't have to do anything specific because there surely wouldn't be a disturbance outside Steens. This was the City, after all.

Anthony recognised him as the police car driver from Bishopsgate Police Station. Palmer's chauffeur. Anthony nodded in recognition, but his gesture was not reciprocated. This was serious, no longer a cosy chat in a police station or a Wapping apartment or a Tower City Hotel room. The officer remained focused on his task, standing with his hands clasped behind his back, keeping a watchful eye on the crowd in the plaza.

There was an ugly media gang, reporters, camera crews and other vultures coming to pick at the remains of a once-great bank. That good-looking Asian girl was here again doing a piece to camera on live breakfast television. Eager production assistants tried in vain to persuade Steens' staff to talk into microphones thrust at them. Either they didn't want to talk or they were just too gutted to utter any words.

The other onlookers were City staff going to work in nearby banks, and brokers who passed by with a mixture of curiosity and relief. Curiosity at what was happening in the media scrum, relief that it was Steens who were in the news today and not their own bank. A month ago most of them would have joined a queue to work at Steens. Now they were happy to work at a less prestigious investment house that at least was still in business.

A few elderly people congregated together. What were they doing here at this early hour? One fragile lady wrapped up against the cold approached Anthony.

'Do you know what's going on here, dear?' Dear? Of course he knew. She was close to tears behind thin spectacles and shivered in the cold. 'It's all so terrible. Steens managed my private investments account. I think I've lost my life savings. Tens of thousands of pounds all gone. Just like the Queen's investments too. Such a pity.'

She was overreacting. No client assets would be lost, including the royal funds under management. They would be protected by the authorities. He gave her the assurance she required and tried to direct her away from the crowd. Best to get her home. She refused, as if her physical presence here would somehow make her long-lost cash appear in a pile in the middle of Broadgate Circle.

Anthony recognised the sombre Steens' faces, disillusioned and standing in small self-comforting groups of four or five with hands buried in regulation dark wool coats and backs facing the early spring breeze that blew across the exposed plaza. Broadgate didn't feel so good today. The faces told the story: no laughter, no smiles, no jokes. It was a sea change from the exuberance and optimism of last night's celebrations in the Flute.

Some unknown faces entered Steens. Intense,

sad-looking people with briefcases and banker's boxes who showed shiny new ID passes to Bill on security duty in order to gain entry.

The accountants sent in by the SFO to administer the affairs of the bank, mousy men with glasses, receding hair and even less personality, with a predominant fondness for grey. Large women in brown worsted suits with thick ankles. Yes, they must be the accountants.

Anthony went towards Bill, but the scene was confusing. Members of Steens' staff were trying to get in, but most were being turned back. Anthony would try. Then he saw Gary.

'Tony, I can't believe this has happened. We are ruined. You must have known this was going to happen and you never told me?'

'What do you mean?'

'Last night in the Flute? I remember what you said, what your exact words were. You said that you had some news about Steens, that it would break today in the paper and that I would be amazed. Well, you're damned right on every single count.'

'I didn't mean that. I meant something else.'

'What else could it have been?'

Anthony couldn't tell Gary about the abortive directorship. It was too embarrassing and too self-incriminating. Focus back on work instead.

'Gary, can we get inside the office today?'

'Well, I can't. I tried, but Bill has instructions from the SFO administrators to let in only essential staff this morning. He allowed in traders who have to unload some of the bank's positions in some sort of an orderly fashion in the market. He let in some operations staff so that they can settle yesterday's trades. But no salesmen or syndicate desk staff

411

have been let in as far as I can gather. I guess that there are no sales and no new issues today, and there won't be for a long while. Very few people from the support departments like finance, credit, tax, legal and compliance got inside either.'

'Well, hopefully I can get in. I am management.'

Anthony went to the revolving doors as if going into the bank on any normal day. Bill stood before him blocking his way. 'Sorry, sir. Restricted admission today.'

'It's all right, Bill. I think you can let me in.'

Bill looked at Anthony hard, lost for a moment. Memory powers temporarily deserted him. 'And your name is, sir . . . ?'

Unbelievable. Bill didn't know who he was. Anthony knew why. In five years at Steens Anthony had never had more than a one-liner conversation with Bill before this moment. Bill had always been there to let him in with his magnetic security pass, to politely open the door for clients, run errands for them and watch over the courier deliveries. But Anthony had never thanked him for the unseen work he did, and now he was paying the very high price.

'I'm Anthony Carlton. Manager of the Control Group.'

Bill looked at a list of names on his desk. Anthony could see some dealers' names listed.

'Sorry, sir, but you're not on the list of essential personnel. I can't let you in.'

'There must be some mistake. Surely my name is there?'

Then second thoughts.

'Your name *is* here, sir, but you're on the other list,' said Bill, pointing to a page overleaf. 'This is a

412

list of people I have been instructed specifically by the administrators not to let in today.'

He was on a blacklist. Worrying. Bill motioned for him to leave, and he had no choice. Bill could get inside. Anthony could not. Bill had a job today. Anthony had none. Then bigger problems. Dave had left a crowd of second-floor staff and rushed over to him in a rage.

'Tony, what the fuck's going on here? One day we are trading away and the next day our very own fucking security guard tells us that we can't go in to work, and the bank's being run by a bunch of accountants and policemen. You must know more about all this. It's about whatever happened out in Amsterdam, the EPIC issue and this Asian pricing account. You've been on to me for weeks about EPIC. You've been out to Amsterdam several times in the past few months. And you've just come back from Hong Kong. If anyone knows what's really happened here, then you do, Tony.'

Words failed Anthony. This was getting ugly. Dave stood even closer, almost shouting.

'I'm not messing about here. My directorship is gone for good now. Did you tell someone about this?'

A beery, overweight colleague interrupted Dave's flow.

'Yeah, it was him all right And I know how too. It's all come back to me. This guy is shagging some journalist from the *Standard*. Jenny somebody. I've seen her picture in the paper. You were at Walker's funeral in Suffolk. He brought her along. And I saw the two of them together in the Flute a few weeks before that having a friendly chat. She was all over him at the time. If he knew anything then,

413

he's gone and told that bitch about it. Carlton is the mole in Steens.'

Wrong explanation but correct end result. That was all Dave needed to hear.

'You told a journalist? We're fucked, then. We've all lost hundreds of thousands of quid in bonuses today.' Dave pointed at the assembled syndicate desk staff. 'At least if this had happened next week, we'd all be richer people today. It's bloody awful timing.'

Before Anthony could see it coming, Dave leaned back and delivered a straight blow to Anthony's jawbone. He definitely wasn't expecting it from a colleague and friend. He lost his footing. The crash on the concrete hurt more than the pain of the blow, but it was politic to stay on the ground and avoid further damage. The policeman on guard looked over but failed to intervene. Good enough for those City types. Dave's thug colleague was impressed.

'Serves the fucker right.'

'Leave this poor man alone. Go away.' Dave backed up. Who was his saviour? That elderly lady hove into view, bending over Anthony. 'Now, now dear, are you hurt?'

Dear? Again? He was hurt indeed but only on the inside. Nothing she could do to help. Anthony stumbled to the sanctuary of a marble seat by the edge of the plaza. As he revived himself he took in the view, knowing that it was the end of an era.

Steens' staff stood around feeling utterly useless. The Flute was not yet open. No one felt like going there anyway. It was too early for a sandwich for lunch. They discussed all they could with each other. As word spread among the mutinous rabble, they progressively excluded Anthony from their conversations and looked at him sitting alone from afar. Dark glances were thrown in his direction. They knew.

More conversations with the likes of Gary and Dave were now impossible. There was a massive gulf between former colleagues. People reluctantly started drifting away one by one towards the tube station, from where they had come a short time earlier. They were going home from the City at ten o'clock in the morning. It felt strange. Bad.

The return journey took forever. Anthony had never travelled before in such an empty tube carriage on a weekday in his working life in London. There was no one to watch. As he exited Maida Vale tube station, the newspaper vendor was packing up his newsstand until the later rush for the *Evening Standard.* Jenny was probably writing the front page right now. He gave Anthony a strange look, as if he knew that Anthony was in a good suit in the wrong part of London at the wrong time of the day. Anthony already knew that.

*　　　*　　　*

Anthony was not prepared for a day of inactivity such as this as he nursed the bruising pain along his jaw. If he took off Harry Wu's finest jacket at this early hour of the day, it would be an admission of failure. What does one do if you are sitting at home on a Friday morning in your apartment? Do you just go back to bed? He slouched uncomfortably in his own living-room with an empty coffee mug in hand. It was worse being back in his own apartment, rather than Jenny's. He was truly alone.

415

He still harboured hopes of a telephone call summoning him back to work at Steens. In the meantime he had time to kill, and the choices were unappealing. He didn't want to watch Steens on television, nor listen to news on the hour on Kiss 100 FM, nor read any more in the press. He heard a rattle of keys, then a key placed in his door lock. It turned smoothly and the door opened. Maybe it was Jenny? He had left her a set of keys in the hope that she would visit.

'Oh, Mr Carlton. You gave me such a shock. I wasn't expecting you to be here.'

It was that second Friday morning. Mrs Harris from the Harrow Road had turned up to clean his apartment and do those work shirts as usual. He didn't think he had seen her for a year or more. He just left her twenty quid on the mantelpiece once a fortnight. She had aged but still looked alive enough to do for him. She started rabbiting on immediately.

'Not feeling too well, Mr Carlton? Come home early from work?'

'Not exactly. Trouble at work. My bank has closed.'

'Has it really? And which bank is that, then?'

'It doesn't matter.' She would never have heard of Steens.

'Don't worry. Maybe it will be open on Monday.'

Ignorance is bliss. She disappeared down the hallway. In two minutes she started the Hoover and was thundering up and down the apartment in search of those phantom specks of dust that had mysteriously materialised since last Friday week. The noise was unbearable.

'It's OK. Leave that till next time.'

416

She wasn't giving up that easily. She was a woman with a definite mission.

'I'll do the laundry, then. I'll iron your shirts for next week.'

'I don't think I'll need any shirts next week. Here's a twenty. Thanks.'

'Will I see you in two weeks' time, then?'

Depends if I can afford you? That was the easiest twenty she had ever earned. A solitary peace returned until the communal doorbell of the apartment block rang. Someone looking for him downstairs. Anthony's hopes rose. Maybe he was essential personnel at Steens? Then second thoughts. They would telephone him, not call around. Who goes around Maida Vale ringing on doorbells mid-morning? None of Anthony's friends would expect him to be at home on a Friday morning. More likely to be London Electricity or British Gas reading a meter or some pushy salesman flogging aluminium windows or life assurance or burglar alarms. He ignored the doorbell. Fuck them. If they were keen, they would ring again.

They *were* keen. The doorbell rang persistently. Anthony furtively pressed his head against the window to view the main porch door below. He saw the top of a head, a man with carefully parted, well-groomed hair in a dark suit. And another, stockier man beside him. He knew them from previous meetings. He saw the car across the road, illegally parked in a Westminster residents-only bay. It was a Rover saloon with a luminous red circle and black numbers on the roof, that same car that Anthony had twice travelled in to Bishopsgate Police Station. Palmer and Hunt were at his front door.

Anthony had a sudden panic attack. He feared the worst. Steens had collapsed and the directors were going to face criminal charges. Had the directors somehow implicated him? Were they going to bring down as many Steens' staff with them as they could and apportion blame to others? Had they lied to effect another cover-up? Anthony had known so much so long ago. He had already seen the inside of Bishopsgate Police Station twice and had no wish to view the inside of some dark basement cell from the wrong side of the metal door. Panic.

Anthony let the visitors into the apartment. Palmer appeared in minutes and immediately looked anxious, perhaps guilty about what he was about to do. He noticed the bruising around Anthony's jawline. Years of practice.

'Bit of trouble today?'

'Trouble with an ex-colleague,' Anthony said, stroking his jaw. 'They're all ex-colleagues now.'

'Nasty business, all this. Good news and bad news today.'

Anthony let Palmer continue for the simple reason that Anthony didn't want to say anything until he had a legal adviser present. Less incriminating. Hunt explained.

'Everything went smoothly. My boss at the SFO arranged a short-notice meeting with your directors. We descended yesterday evening at five o'clock when the office was empty because people were out for celebratory drinks on the eve of bonus day. Few saw us arrive.'

'Me included. I was one of those celebrating in the Flute.'

That was why there had been no directors at the Flute. They had a more pressing engagement with the regulatory authorities. As the others drank to excess, the directors tried to save Steens.

'We met for three hours with Sir James and Derek Masterson. Leung and Fitzpatrick were overseas. They accepted the events in the Amsterdam office, but they blamed Verhoeven. They accepted the abuses in EPIC and blamed Walker and Verhoeven. It's always easy to blame dead men. They offered to compensate investors. It was a confrontational meeting, but we played it cool. It was touch and go until I played your tape to Sir James.'

Jesus. Anthony didn't dare to think about the reaction of the directors to that tape.

'The tape was convincing. Their faces gave them away. After that it was easy. We just discussed closing down Steens in an orderly fashion.'

'And where are the directors now?'

Palmer cut in. 'Sir James and Masterson spent last night at our station in the cells. We charged them with counts of corporate fraud, embezzlement and personal tax evasion. They could have been bailed last night, but D-S Hunt wanted them to sweat it out for a night in the basement. Some of those flash suits they wear don't look too good when they have no tie, belt or shoelaces. They'll be bailed today to appear before Bow Street magistrates in a few weeks time. I guess they're avoiding the press and taking legal advice now. God knows they can afford the best, but they'll need it. The SFO are really going after them big time.'

Hunt had a wry smile, recounting other recent

successes.

'Leung was back in Hong Kong when we closed Steens. He immediately caught an overnight flight to Malaysia, where he thought the chances of discovery and subsequent extradition would be lessened. I guess he was worried about how the Chinese authorities would deal with their first major financial criminal, and he didn't find the prospect of a stay in a mainland Chinese labour camp too appealing. We got a break this morning. A financial journalist from the *South China Morning Post* with good local Malaysian contacts heard Leung was in the Genting Highlands resort in the hills north of Kuala Lumpur. Leung had conspicuously drawn attention to himself by gambling in the hotel casinos and offering financial inducements to the more attractive croupiers to engage in what I can only call after-hours activities involving the exchange of body fluids. The local police arrested him at the request of officials of Bank Negara, the Malaysian Central Bank, who we got the Bank of England to lean on. Leung is booked on a flight from KL to London this weekend. He won't be in the first-class cabin, he won't be able to use his airmiles for a long time afterwards and he'll be sitting between two colleagues of D-S Palmer who will likely detest the slippery oriental in their charge.'

'What about Bill Fitzpatrick?'

'We got him too. Much easier. New York State Police picked him up at home for us in Westchester County. We're sending the necessary papers over so we can get him back here immediately. We've got them all. We even got that guy Wilhelm Gausselmann in Frankfurt and Edwin Li in Hong

Kong.'

So that was the good news. Anthony felt pity for Gausselmann, a man who had been in at the deep end and couldn't swim at all. He felt no pity for Li. Hunt was providing a comprehensive briefing.

'I can give you the news breaking this morning. Since the SFO raided the London head office, there has been similar action by other regulators around the world. The German police have raided the Frankfurt office to seize the files of EPIC, and the Dutch authorities are interested in that too. The Amsterdam Stock Exchange has suspended EPIC shares and has also suspended Steens as a member of the exchange. The Dutch Central Bank is investigating the Amsterdam office. The Securities and Futures Commission in Hong Kong raided the Hong Kong office late last night and seized transaction records for Asian securities going back over several years. Even the Americans got in on the act, though there's no real evidence of wrongdoing in the US operations. The Securities & Exchange Commission visited your Wall Street office an hour ago at the crack of dawn as Fitzpatrick was arrested.'

It was all going to plan. So what was the bad news? Anthony risked a question. 'When I saw you here this morning I feared the worst. Am I going to be all right in this?'

Palmer was edgy; that guilty look returned He fingered his knotted silk tie nervously. Nice tie, observed Anthony. Nice animal pattern. Looks like a good make too. New?

'D-S Hunt has a proposition for you.'

Anthony was wondering whether it was an offer he couldn't refuse. Hunt stood before him.

'I want you to testify against the directors as a witness for the Crown prosecution. In a big case like this we'll need someone on the inside. It will make our job much easier. We have bigger fish to fry than you.'

The thought of giving courtroom evidence, the publicity, the hostility, was distinctly unappealing.

'And what happens if I don't want to do that? I'm innocent in all this.'

'You're not quite as innocent as you think. When did you first learn about the events in Amsterdam and the payments from the EPIC fund?

'Weeks ago.'

'Precisely. And when did you tell us?'

'Last Friday?'

'That won't impress a jury if you end up in the dock with the accused. I guess it was only the fear of imminent death that made you seek our help. In some people's books that's almost complicity.'

It was an offer that Anthony couldn't refuse. He mentally debated the lesser of two evils. Hunt gave him some additional encouragement.

'You don't get time to think about this. Either you agree to my offer or else you come back with D-S Palmer to the station and we charge you as an accomplice. It's that simple.'

It was too much of a transition to move from a West London apartment to live in a twelve-by-six cell in some middle-of-nowhere prison, to cease eating prawn and avocado sandwiches in favour of lukewarm sloppy shepherd's pie from caked metal trays, to cease wearing Thomas Pink tailored shirts in favour of rough denim prison overalls and donkey jackets emblazoned with HMP, to exchange the mobile phone for a greasy communal wall phone which took twenty-pence pieces. No choice, really.

'Do I get total immunity from prosecution?'

'I guarantee that.'

Hunt had just bought himself a witness for the prosecution.

'I'll do it.' There were still unanswered questions in Anthony's mind. 'How come all this happened on today of all days? You know the significance of the last day in April in the bank? How come you close us down on the evening before the bonuses are paid?'

Hunt had an answer for everything this morning.

'It's no coincidence. We knew today is bonus day, and that's why we acted when we did. Otherwise Steens would have paid out a hundred million pounds in bonuses to staff. We wanted to keep that money within Steens, so we pulled the bank transfers at midnight from the central clearing system.'

Hunt knew the total amount of the bonuses for the year. Anthony did some quick arithmetic. A hundred million quid. Three thousand staff. Thirty-three thousand each. The authorities had ensured that no one would benefit from the activities of Steens. That was it. The end of their visit. Palmer rose. Nice suit too. Gone was the shiny suit. Sad in a way. Times had changed. Hunt made for the door with a swagger.

'See you in court, Anthony.'

CHAPTER TWENTY-THREE

SIX MONTHS LATER SOUTHWARK, LONDON SE1

STEEN ODENBERG FRAUD TRIAL OPENS: PROSECUTION STAR WITNESS FORMER EMPLOYEE OF STEENS

One of the most significant court cases in recent years opened this morning when four directors of the disgraced City investment bank Steen Odenberg & Co. appeared at Southwark Crown Court. Sir James Devonshire, Derek Masterson, Alvin Leung and Bill Fitzpatrick are charged with multiple counts of fraud, embezzlement, breaches of company law and personal tax evasion. Given recent press revelations about the alleged practices within the bank, there was audible laughter in the public gallery as each director pleaded not guilty to the charges when read.

The *Evening Standard* has learned exclusively that the prosecution will largely rely on the evidence of Anthony Carlton, formerly manager of the Control Group at Steens' head office. Mr Carlton, 31, is credited with uncovering the alleged irregularities and advising the City authorities last April. The Serious Fraud Office are thus confident about the outcome of this landmark case, having suffered previous reversals in similar high-profile cases, such as the

Guinness affair and the Maxwell pensions scandal.

A spokesman for the SFO, D-S Michael Hunt, said that records and letters recovered from Steers' international offices will prove that the directors were negligent in failing adequately to supervise the activities of two deceased directors, Jeremy Walker, formerly director of compliance at Steers, who was murdered in his Wapping apartment earlier this year, and Johan Verhoeven, their former director for Europe, who committed suicide in a City hotel before the bank's collapse. The SFO also claim to have proof of illegal payments made from a listed property fund and from Steens' Hong Kong office to the director's personal offshore bank accounts. The SFO have since frozen these bank accounts pending the outcome of the trial.

A spokesman for one of the most expensive defence teams ever assembled confirmed that they dispute the allegations put forward by the SFO, and claim that wrongdoing, if any were indeed committed, is attributable solely to the actions of the late Messrs. Verhoeven and Walker.

The start of the case was delayed for several days while a suitable jury was selected. The Right Hon. Justice Williams, renowned for his somewhat controversial rulings in prior cases, advised jury members that the evidence before them was complex and demanding, and that they would all be financial experts at the conclusion of the case in approximately two months time. The trial continues tomorrow, when the Crown prosecution begins the presentation of its evidence.

Jennifer Sharpe
Evening Standard
13 October

PROSECUTION PRESENTS CASE AGAINST LEADING CITY BANKERS: DIRECTORS RECEIVED TWENTY-FIVE MILLION POUNDS IN FAR EAST SCAM

The Crown prosecution opened its case against the former directors of Steen Odenberg today with damning evidence against the four accused bankers. Counsel presented documents to support claims that the accused and two deceased directors together received a total of approximately twenty-five million pounds over a period of six years from accounts in Steens' Hong Kong office. The directors sat expressionless in the dock as police-officers and regulatory authorities gave evidence of the payments.

D-S Bob Palmer of the City of London Police described how he investigated the murder of director Jeremy Walker, when the first evidence of allegations about Steens' practices came to his attention. Clients' letters complaining about Steens' Amsterdam office and the EPIC property fund were later discovered in Walker's City office. D-S Palmer was subsequently advised by a member of staff that illegal payments had been made to directors.

426

In cross-examination D-S Palmer confirmed that Anthony Carlton is the relevant Steens' employee. He is expected to give evidence next week. D-S Palmer passed the evidence to the Serious Fraud Office and assisted in the arrest of Sir James Devonshire and Derek Masterson at Steens' Broadgate Circle offices last April.

D-S Michael Hunt of the SFO presented photocopies of bank payment orders and bank statements from Jersey, Bermuda and Isle of Man accounts that proved the funds were received by the directors. D-S Hunt outlined the process by which amounts were taken out of Asian equity trades and kept in an account known as the Asian pricing account. Some jury members were noted to have puzzled looks on their faces at this time as details of agency securities executions were outlined.

Jennifer Sharpe
Evening Standard
17 October

**FORMER STEENS' EMPLOYEE TESTIFIES AGAINST DIRECTORS:
DAMNING TAPED EVIDENCE PLAYED IN COURT, FORMER BANK SECRETARY SLEPT WITH DUTCH DIRECTOR**

Anthony Carlton, formerly manager of the Control Group at City bank Steen Odenberg, was the main witness for the prosecution today, where he delivered crucial evidence.

Carlton spoke of trips to Amsterdam,

mismanaged client accounts, a meeting with deceased director Johan Verhoeven in the Tower City Hotel, his former secretary's affair with Verhoeven, a bribe to Chinese government officials, a trip to Frankfurt and the investigation of the EPIC fund and a trip to Hong Kong to review the Asian pricing account. Justice Williams, presiding, commented in an aside to the jury that Carlton must have been a busy man in the weeks prior to Steens' collapse.

Carlton also spoke of a day trip to Macau to meet Peter Cheung, formerly of Steers Hong Kong. Mr Cheung drowned when he fell from the Macau ferry, a case that Hong Kong police have reopened in light of the revelations about Steers' alleged activities in the Far East.

The major new evidence of the day came in two tape recordings that were played several times to the hushed courtroom at the request of certain older jurors, believed to be hard of hearing. The first tape was a conversation between Carlton and Cheung in his Macau home outlining the operation of the now-infamous Asian pricing account, just days before Cheung died. When asked by the prosecution if he thought Cheung had been murdered, Carlton replied that he believed murder was the most likely cause of death.

The second tape was of two one-hour meetings that Carlton had with the four directors in the week before Steens collapsed. The accused directors appeared visibly agitated as the jury heard their collective admission of the Far East payments and other offences. This tape confirmed that Carlton accepted a directorship of Steens, although on examination from the prosecution counsel he stated that this acceptance was not genuine. The tape revealed that another senior employee of Steens, David Chilcott-Tomkinson, formerly head of Steens' syndicate desk, was also offered a directorship and accepted. Mr Chilcott-Tomkinson was uncontactable last night at his Chelsea home.

Mr Carlton, wearing a hand-tailored dark suit and tie, remained calm under hostile questioning from the defence. He refused to speak to waiting press after the court adjourned, left the Crown Court by a side exit and was believed to be at a secret address in West London to escape media attention.

Jennifer Sharpe
Evening Standard
20 October

YOUTH SENTENCED FOR MANSLAUGHTER OF CITY BANKER

A Chinese youth was found guilty at the Old Bailey today of the manslaughter of a leading City of London investment banker. William Lee Jackson, 19, of no fixed abode, was convicted when the jury returned a unanimous guilty verdict after just two hours of deliberations. They had previously refused to consider a murder conviction on the grounds of insufficient evidence.

The dead banker was Jeremy Walker, formerly a director of the now disgraced bank Steen Odenberg & Co. The jury heard that Jackson met Walker in a bar in the West End on the evening of 17 March last and the two men returned in Walker's Mercedes to his luxury penthouse apartment in Wapping. Jackson was placed near the scene of the crime in a CCTV still from a nearby Underground station, and his fingerprints were later matched to those found on a set of chopsticks in Walker's home. The case also featured on BBC's *Crimewatch* programme.

The prosecution argued that Jackson tied up Walker with his own silk ties and then strangled him in a bizarre sex game. Defence counsel brought forward witnesses to testify that Walker had on previous occasions asked other youths to tie him up before having sex. They argued therefore that there was no intention to kill and pleaded for the jury to consider a manslaughter verdict. Persistent rumours circulated during the court case that Walker's death was intricately linked to the Steens' fraud trial running simultaneously in Southwark Crown Court. Informed sources suggested that Jackson was paid five thousand pounds to kill Walker when unknown underworld gangs in Hong Kong grew dissatisfied with Walker's desire for more money from the Asian pricing account, frequently referred to in the Steens case.

Jackson was probed about this allegation in court by defence counsel but refused to answer any questions on the topic. It is believed that threats have been made by a Far East Triad gang against his family and relatives who still live in Hong Kong.

Jackson, with a crew-cut hairstyle and wearing faded denims and a tracksuit top, showed no reaction when sentence was passed. Every day during the case he wore a baseball cap with a distinctive red star logo which sources say is linked to the Hong Kong Triad gang. Jackson left court under armed guard to begin his ten year sentence in Wandsworth Prison.

Jennifer Sharpe
Evening Standard
4 November

WIFE OF LATE STEENS' BANKER REOPENS DIVORCE CASE

The wife of the murdered Steen Odenberg investment banker Jeremy Walker commenced a civil court case today in London to retrospectively amend the terms of her divorce settlement with her former husband. Sylvia Travers, 51, arrived from Hong Kong last week to brief her legal team.

Ms Travers alleges that she was seriously misled regarding her husband's net worth at the time of their acrimonious divorce two years ago. She received approximately one million pounds as a settlement, half of Mr Walker's estimated wealth. However, Ms Travers now claims that her husband's net wealth was closer to ten million pounds at the time.

Ms Travers is proceeding with her court case despite independent legal advice that her action is likely to fail. Her former husband's accounts and assets have been frozen since last April, when Steens collapsed in a blaze of publicity. Most of her husband's wealth is believed to have been obtained illegally, and funds are unlikely to be paid out to any third party pending the resolution of the current criminal case against the directors of Steens.

The executors of Jeremy Walker's estate are his elderly parents, Arthur and Jane Walker, presently living in Suffolk. On hearing of this court case Mrs Walker commented, 'if that dreadful little woman gets one more penny from Jeremy, it will be the last nail in the coffin of British justice.'

Jennifer Sharpe
Evening Standard
7 November

JUDGE HALTS STEEN ODENBERG TRIAL IN SURPRISE RULING: DEFENDANTS FREED IN CITY TRIAL FIASCO

The criminal case against the directors of Steen Odenberg collapsed in bizarre circumstances at Southwark Crown Court this morning when Justice Williams made an unexpected ruling on the evidence presented to the jury to date. Pandemonium broke out in the courtroom as the judge threw out the case. The prosecution immediately filed an appeal to the High Court.

The sudden twist came as prosecution witness Anthony Carlton was being cross-examined by defence counsel on the tape-recorded meeting that he held with the directors on Monday 22 April just prior to the collapse of the bank. Mr Carlton admitted that the idea for the taped meeting had come from D-S Michael Hunt of the SFO and that he had been extensively coached over the prior weekend on the particular questions to ask so that the directors would sufficiently incriminate themselves. Mr Carlton also admitted copying confidential bank documents and providing them to the authorities before the arrest of the defendants on 25 April last.

In his ruling given just before lunchtime, Justice Williams determined that these circumstances amounted to police entrapment of the four defendants and therefore ruled that the taped evidence and related material were inadmissible and should not be considered by the jury. Consequently, he dismissed the case.

Outside the court, Chairman Sir James Devonshire said that the reputations of all the defendants had been vindicated, and he looked forward to a similarly successful outcome in the appeal case. The SFO were unavailable for comment. A representative of the Steen Odenberg Shareholders' Action Group said the outcome was a farce and they would pursue the directors through every possible civil means.

Jennifer Sharpe
Evening Standard
17 November

HONG KONG POLICE SWOOP ON CHINESE TRIAD GANG MEMBERS

Police in Hong Kong yesterday arrested seven individuals who are believed to control one of the most feared local criminal gangs. A police spokesman said they had acted on information received from their British counterparts following revelations in the recent Steen Odenberg court case.

The seven individuals are being held in the main Lantau Island jail. They include a leading residential property developer, a Causeway Bay hotel manager, a Wanchai nightclub owner and a taxi firm operator. All are believed to have benefited personally from Steens' Asian pricing account that was allegedly used to make illegal payments to directors and others connected to the scam.

The seven are charged with various counts of racketeering, extortion, fraud and tax evasion. If convicted, they will face punitive sentences in the harsh prison regime of the former British colony. Lawyers acting for the seven accused say they will vehemently deny all charges.

Hong Kong has long suffered at the hands of Triad gangs who use Mafia-like influence and threats to control business communities. This particular gang was known as the Red Star Triad, and gang members sported fashionable peaked baseball caps displaying a distinctive star logo.

Among those arrested was Lin Hwa Poon, 24, a part-time barman with an address in Kowloon. Poon was additionally charged with two counts of attempted murder. He is believed to be the previously unidentified Chinese youth referred to by Anthony Carlton in the Steens case. Mr Carlton survived two attempts on his life while undertaking investigations in Hong Kong earlier this year, including a traffic-related incident at Happy Valley racecourse and an attempted stabbing on a platform of the local Mass Transit rail system.

Poon is also being quizzed about the death of retired Steens' Hong Kong banker Peter Cheung. Mr Cheung died when he fell from the Macau ferry last April in what was believed originally to be an accident. It is understood that Poon took a day off from the bar where he worked on the day of Cheung's death and his movements on that day are unaccounted for at present.

Jennifer Sharpe
Evening Standard
22 November

MITCHELL LEONBERG INC. COMPLETES ACQUISITION OF DISGRACED BANK

The giant US investment bank Mitchell Leonberg Inc. today completed its surprise acquisition of Steen Odenberg, the disgraced City investment bank at the centre of the recent failed court case. An overwhelming eighty-nine per cent of Steens' shareholders accepted the terms of Mitchell's takeover offer. Market observers said that Steens had been 'in play' since the very day it collapsed, and that its extensive dealing, sales and asset management presence in the world's major financial capitals would prove attractive to many global financial companies.

The president of Mitchells, Norman 'Stormin' Newman, said in Wall Street after the announcement that 'Mitchell need a bigger foothold in Europe and Asia and Steens fit our global expansion plans perfectly. Our offer of six pounds fifty pence per share values Steens at a fair price of three billion pounds, and the positive response today of the shareholders confirm this. We are going to ensure that the Steens business gets back to where it was before the regrettable events earlier this year.'

A hostile battle for Steens has raged for months as two opposing camps courted the large institutional shareholders. Pitted against Mitchell Leonberg was a counter-offer from Kapital Bank AG of Frankfurt, a German commercial bank keen to expand its investment-banking business and invited to be a white knight by Steens' directors. Kapital Bank almost matched Mitchell's cash offer with their own part-share and part-cash offer worth six pounds twenty pence at current market prices. Sources close to the deal made it clear that Steens' directors loathed the domineering and insular attitude of Mitchell and did their utmost to save Steens, albeit unsuccessfully.

A corporate financier in the City who wished to remain nameless said, 'The real voting power in takeover battles such as this lies not with the man in the street who owns a few hundred shares but with the institutional investors who own millions. The bulk of these are the same investors who we now know were screwed royally by Steens over the years in their Far East equity trading. It's poetic justice of the best kind when these investors can now screw the directors in turn, particularly when our judicial system appears to have failed the City of London on this occasion.'

Mitchell Leonberg confirmed that the historic name of Steen Odenberg would disappear shortly when the bank is integrated into Mitchell's existing London operations. The impressive Broadgate Circle office has already been sublet to a Japanese securities house. The majority of sales, dealing and operations staff will relocate to Mitchell's existing office near the Embankment. The remainder of Steens' employees are expected to lose their jobs in the acquisition, although Mitchell will make severance payments to the affected staff.

Jennifer Sharpe
Evening Standard
7 December

FURTHER TWIST IN COLLAPSED STEENS FRAUD CASE

The bizarre decision of Justice Williams to dismiss the Steens fraud trial in Southwark Crown Court last month took a dramatic turn following revelations in this week's edition of *Private Eye.*

The magazine's infamous 'Justice Cocklecarrot' column disclosed that Justice Williams was a member of several London gentlemen's clubs where Steens' chairman, Sir James Devonshire, was also a member, and he attended the same college at Cambridge with Sir James in the 1960s. He was also known to hunt frequently with Sir James, and has been an investor in several new issues and funds launched by Steen Odenberg in the recent past.

Following these previously unknown connections, Justice Williams has been suspended from the judicial bench by the Lord Chancellor pending an internal investigation by his office. A spokesman for the SFO said that they would now press for a new trial under a wholly impartial judge.

Jennifer Sharpe
Evening Standard
12 December

BANK DIRECTORS LOSE APPEAL CASE: ALL DEFENDANTS FINALLY CONVICTED IN HIGH COURT CASE

The prolonged legal battle over the collapse of Steen Odenberg finally came to an end this morning in the High Court when an appeal jury found all four defendants guilty of fraud, embezzlement, breaches of company law and personal tax evasion. A year has now passed since the demise of the bank in a blaze of publicity. Sentence was passed immediately.

Sir James Devonshire received an eight-year prison sentence for his part in coordinating the illegal activities within Steens over a period of six years. The other three directors received terms ranging from three to five years. In addition, sizeable monetary fines were imposed on all the defendants, and their illegal funds located in offshore accounts are to be returned to the court to cover the costs of the court administration of Steens by a leading City accountancy firm.

Outside the court, D-S Hunt of the SFO said that the Steens case should be a warning sign to all in the City, and the full vigour of the law would now be brought to bear on any future offenders.

The four defendants were taken to Ford Open Prison after the sentence, a prison predominantly occupied by white collar criminals and known to have a relaxed regime.

A spokesman for the Steen Odenberg Shareholders' Action Group said this was further proof that 'there was one law for the rich and one for the poor'.

Jennifer Sharpe
Evening Standard
25 April

EPILOGUE

THREE MONTHS LATER:
REGENT'S CANAL, LONDON W9

'This has all gone wrong. It was never supposed to end like this.'

Anthony and Jenny sat at their regular corner table digesting two green Thai curries with steaming rice and Singha beers. The evening sunshine reflected off the canal as idle barges disturbed the calm water. Twelve months had passed since Anthony's world had begun to implode. Jenny was treating Anthony. Anthony was complaining too much.

'I'm the good guy? How come I uncover everything that's illegal, help the authorities as much as possible, get my name splashed across the papers for months and then lose my job when Mitchell Leonberg say I have too many links to the dark past in Steens?'

He was desperate. He had spent months looking for another job in the City but could find nothing. Not even a pen-pushing position or a data-entry job in an operations department of some second-rate Japanese bank. When he was an employee of Steens the head-hunters and recruitment consultants had been queuing up to get him a job. Now they wouldn't deign to meet him or return his increasingly desperate telephone calls. The mere mention of Steens on his CV was a stigma. He thought about changing the wasted five years to a stretch in the psychiatric wing of Broadmoor. It would be less damaging in the eyes of prospective employers. Face the facts. He wasn't just unemployed. He was unemployable.

'This is getting serious. I can't live without a job and some income. My savings are down to nothing. I sold my Steens shares in the Mitchell takeover and even that money has gone. I spent the severance money in Sainsbury's. I'm getting letters from my bank manager. He never even knew me before all this. My tennis club subscription is overdue. The Audi went back, and now I'm on public transport all the time. It's getting to the point where I can't even pay my mortgage. I need that apartment.'

There are those who have and those who have not. Anthony now found himself by default in the latter category. Without a career in the City, London began to look less appealing.

'The others have done all right. Gary got that finance job in that clearing bank. Anne in Amsterdam and Gausselmann in Frankfurt kept their jobs with Mitchells. Karen got a personnel job in the West End, and I still can't believe she's going to marry that bastard Dave. She was dating him before the collapse. Even Dave got a job with Mitchells just because he was a revenue generator of such size and he sells those profitable new issues. Mitchells liked that and they brought him into their integrated London operations as co-head of Global Equity Capital Markets. He had the gall to tell me in the tennis club locker-room that they gave him a senior vice president title and doubled his annual salary and bonus. He took most of his syndicate desk staff with him, too, even that Debbie from Essex. She has a job. He says working at

Mitchells is even better than Steens, the deals are bigger, the clients hungrier and there are significantly more salesmen to swear at. Says he's bumped into Steve a few times on the dealing floor. Apart from that he wouldn't give me the time of day at the club. He'll never forgive me for what I did to Steens.'

Another large portion of green curry went down with some difficulty. Damned hot.

'Sir James and the others in Ford Open can't be that badly off. Palmer and Hunt say that the directors will be out in less than a year. Early-release programmes, community service, good behaviour, overcrowded prisons and all that. It won't be long before they assimilate themselves back into society, get a few plum non-executive jobs, some easy consultancy fees under the table, City lunches in private dining-rooms with their old pals from Cambridge, grease a few palms, meet the royals at a charity bash, a spot of hunting with their pal Justice Williams and his like in their country estates, spend a bit more of that wealth. Palmer says that Sir James is suffering from a mild form of senile dementia and wants an even earlier release on medical grounds. Only that's been tried before, so this time round the authorities will be wise to that ploy.'

He quashed the tremendous heat of the curry with an iced Perrier. The hotter the better.

'Palmer and Hunt both got promotion to D-I for their part in the case. Hunt's been on every TV show from *The Money Programme* to *Panorama*. He's a bigger media star than most of the professionals. He took to the limelight like an investment banker takes to Moët.'

Jenny let him carry on. Talking was a way to ease the pain.

'Look at what happened to Vanessa. I thought my revelations in court about her and Verhoeven would ruin her. I didn't want to talk about her, but that prosecution lawyer just dragged the words out of me. And what happens to her? She walks out of the courtroom and into the arms of an agent for the *News of the World*. Two articles on consecutive Sundays. Centre-page spreads about her and Verhoeven. MY DUTCH SEX ROMP WITH DRUGGED DEAD CITY BANK BOSS. All those tales of debauchery, rolling joints and having sex in the bank's lifts can't be true. But does it bother her? Not at all. Not at seventy-five grand for the kiss and tell. She was true to form. Go for the money. I bet she's spent most of it already.'

More curry. More heat. More water. More pain.

'I guess there are losers, too, like me. Like Edwin Li, who the Chinese made an example of with a fifteen-year hard-labour stretch in Lantau. I bet he wishes he was a British passport holder like Alvin Leung and then he would have been extradited here. And Sylvia Travers wasted a pile of Walker's old money on that pointless civil case. Sometimes I think I made the wrong choice with those tapes I had. I could have been a director. It's all gone belly up.'

Jenny placed a fork down on the plate and gave him the reassurance he needed. 'No, it hasn't, Anthony. You chose the side of truth and honesty. You'll find something to do. Remember, the good guy always gets the girl in the end.'

'I can't survive on love alone. I'm going to have to leave London, lie on my CV and just get any old

444

job. I can't afford to live here any more, and I can't ask my parents for any more cash. They haven't got much left, and they've been too good already. Maybe I'll go back to Surrey.'

'I've got a proposition for you.' Jenny swirled around at the table to catch a passing eye. 'Waiter, two Irish whiskies please, to finish off.' In a Thai restaurant? Anthony had never seen Jenny drink an Irish whiskey before. 'I'm leaving London next week for three months.'

'What? You can't do that. I need you. You pay my restaurant bills. Where are you going?'

The whiskies arrived just in time. Jenny handed one to him across the table.

'Take a hint? Have a drink. I'm renting a bleak cottage in the west of Ireland, near Clifden on the Atlantic coast. Miles from the nearest shop or house. I want somewhere away from all the hassle of the past year. And I need space to think and to create.'

'Are you mad? What about your journalistic career?'

'It's all part of the deal. My editor has given me time off—a sabbatical, as he calls it.'

'So what's the proposition?'

She leaned forward and ran her finger around the edge of the half-finished glass of Irish.

'Do you want a job working for a crazy woman who's also a tough boss? Long hours, lousy pay. Bed and breakfast included. I need an assistant. An expert. Someone like you. No, it has to be you. Interested?'

*　　　*　　　*

Anthony gave up on the City. Harry Wu need never make him another fine suit. The Flute lost one of its oldest customers, as did Thomas Pink in Jermyn Street and Hermès in Heathrow duty free. Anthony rented out his apartment to a young couple from the City who could easily afford the twelve-hundred-pound monthly rental. They had jobs. The girl from Chesterton's property agents told Anthony that his rental was higher than others in the area. She added on a notoriety value since a celebrated Steens' ex-employee owned it. Mrs Harris on the Harrow Road got a new biweekly customer.

Jenny was right on the first occasion that Anthony had met her. Steens was her story. It was fate. Right from her first early-morning trip to Walker's Wapping apartment, their Broadgate eye contact on that first Monday, the Amsterdam office exclusive which happened accidentally over a bottle of Pouilly-Fumé and some outrageous flirting in the Flute, and the collapse on bonus day. Jenny had followed it all up real close. Real personal too.

During the court case, her articles in the *Evening Standard* were essential reading for every dealer or salesman over their corn-fed roast chicken sandwich in Broadgate Plaza while simultaneously watching the effervescent players in the city. She won promotion to senior reporter. The *FT* approached her to join them as the newspaper followed the long-established City practice of head-hunting the best talent. Jenny stayed loyal to the *Standard.*

Like many who have been closely involved in a major financial scandal, they both took the optimal course of action. The cottage near Clivden was

446

ideal. In three months the task was complete. Jenny had the journalistic talent. Anthony knew what had happened within Steens. They wrote the bestseller. All of Steens' failings became public knowledge. Full circle in the Square Mile.

The author welcomes feedback and may be contacted by email at paulkilduff@tinet.ie

6/2.